# PAN

I watch him come, stepping with elven grace, hooves entering and leaving the stream without so much as a splash.

Slanting sunlight through the branches gleams his flanks, polishes his high cheekbones, is swallowed in the darkness of his eyes. When he moves his head, light ricochets off his horns. I do not move or speak.

His cloven hooves cut deep into the moss, scoring the rich earth below the green carpet. It is no longer the friend of my childhood who stands there, but the forest god, the hooved and horned one beholding an intruder in his domain.

# CLOVEN HOOVES

## Megan Lindholm

BANTAM BOOKS
NEW YORK · TORONTO · LONDON · SYDNEY · AUCKLAND

CLOVEN HOOVES
*A Bantam Spectra Book / December 1991*

SPECTRA *and the portrayal of a boxed "s" are trademarks of*
*Bantam Books, a division of Bantam Doubleday Dell Publishing*
*Group, Inc.*

ISBN 0-553-29327-3

*Published simultaneously in the United States and Canada*

*Bantam Books are published by Bantam Books, a division of Bantam*
*Doubleday Dell Publishing Group, Inc. Its trademark, consisting of*
*the words "Bantam Books" and the portrayal of a rooster, is*
*Registered in U.S. Patent and Trademark Office and in other*
*countries. Marca Registrada. Bantam Books, 666 Fifth Avenue, New*
*York, New York 10103.*

PRINTED IN THE UNITED STATES OF AMERICA

RAD    0 9 8 7 6 5 4 3 2 1

# CLOVEN HOOVES

# One

*In Flight March 11, 1976*

I turn away from staring out the window, lean over to check my child in the seat beside me. There's nothing to see out there, anyway. Outside the oval airplane window, a night sky jets soundlessly by. Overcast covers all but a few stars. Nothing to keep my mind from chewing on itself. Inside is the sound of the engines, of the tiny seat fans whirring as they stir the stale air. Rows of red upholstered seat backs, backs of heads. Most of the overhead seat lights are off. Tiny airline blankets are tucked around the shoulders of some dozing passengers. Others read newspapers and magazines, smoke, or talk softly to seatmates. A few drink industriously. Nothing in here to keep my mind busy, either.

Teddy is asleep. He had asked for the window seat, and of course we had given it to him, even though we knew there would be little to see on this night flight from Fairbanks, Alaska, to the Sea-Tac Airport in Washington. Still, he got to watch the tower and runway lights vanish away beneath us, caught a brief glimpse of the lights of some little town down there a while later. Then he used the airplane's bathroom twice, giggled over finding the barf bag in the seat pocket, got a coloring book and crayons and plastic pilot wings from a stewardess, colored for a while, and got bored and wiggled for a while. And now, finally, he is asleep. I carefully move his copy

1

of Sendak's *Where the Wild Things Are* because the corner of it is digging into his cheek. I give a sigh of relief that is partially anxiety. With Teddy dozing, there is nothing to distract me from my worrying. Except Tom. I turn my attention away from my five-year-old son and to my husband.

Who is also asleep in his seat on the other side of me.

Light hair is falling over his forehead. He breathes softly, evenly, at peace with the world and himself. I know I should let him rest. This is the horrible leave-Fairbanks-in-the-middle-of-the-night,-arrive-in-Seattle-too-early-to-be-awake flight. I should let him sleep, so he will be fresh and alert when his parents come to meet us at the airport. I shouldn't wake him just to talk to me and reassure me. I really should let him sleep.

But I touch his hair lightly back into place. He smiles, and without opening his eyes, his hand comes up to hold mine. For a time we are silent, shooting through the night. Strangers occupy other seats around us, and doze or smoke or read papers or sip drinks. But Tom and I are alone among them. It is something we have always been able to do, make a quiet, private space around ourselves, no matter what the circumstances.

"Still worrying?" he asks me softly. His eyes remain closed.

"A little," I admit.

"Silly." His hand squeezes mine briefly, then relaxes again. He sighs, shifts in his seat to face me. He leans his face against the seat back while he talks to me, as if we were in our bed at home, lying face-to-face, heads on pillows, talking. It makes me wish we were, that I could snug my body up against his and hold him while he talks. He speaks softly, his deep voice soothing as a bedtime story. "We're going to have a good time. Well, you will, anyway. I've got to fill in on the farm and in the shop until Bix's shoulder heals. Fields to plow, tractors to fix. But you and Teddy will have a great time. Teddy's going to have the farm to run around on. Eggs to gather, chicks, ducklings, pigs, all that stuff. And my mom and sisters are going to love having you. Ever since

I married you, Mom and Steffie have been dying to get their hands on you. Go shopping, introduce you around. Steffie had so many plans when I talked to her on the phone, I don't know how you'll keep up with her." He smiles at the thought of his younger sister.

I edge closer in my seat, lean my head close to his. "That's just it. I don't know how I'll keep up with her, either." I think of Steffie as I last saw her, on a brief Christmas visit two years ago. She had been just out of high school that year. She'd come home from some party, into the living room of the farmhouse, dressed in a dark green velvet sheath and high black heels, begemmed at ear and throat and wrist. Like a magazine cover come to life, but rushing to hug us, to say she was so glad we'd been able to fly down for Christmas. The memory reawakens in me the same twinge I'd felt then: awe at her beauty, and a shiver of fear.

Why?

Because she was so beautiful, so perfect. The ugly little jealousy that beautiful women always awoke in me had stirred. That she was Tom's own sister hadn't mattered. It wasn't a sexual kind of jealousy. It was the knowledge that I could never compete with women like that, that I'd never learned to be elegant and feminine and charming and stunning and all those other adjectives that Steffie and Mother Maurie embodied so easily. Yet these were the type of women that Tom had around him when he was growing up. How could he have settled for a mouse like me? What if he woke up one day and realized he'd been cheated?

I tune in suddenly that Tom is still talking. "Steffie and Ellie love you. Mom and Dad think you're great. Of course, I think a lot of that is that they were amazed that any woman at all would have me. Probably secretly grateful you married me and whisked me off to Alaska and out of their hair."

He is teasing, of course. No one could ever wish to be rid of him. Tom is as perfect a product as Steffie is, tall and handsome and muscled, charming and kind and intelligent. Tom could have had his pick of women. I am still mystified that he chose me. But he did. And six years of marriage have taught me that I can believe in that miracle. So I can say to him, honestly, "I'm just afraid I'll do something wrong. Put my foot in my mouth, spill soup in my lap. We've never stayed a month with them before, Tom. That's a long time to live in someone else's house, see them every day. I don't know how I'll handle it."

He refuses to share my worry. "You'll handle it just fine. They'll love you just like I do. Besides, we'll be in the little guest house. You'll have time to yourself. I know you aren't into socializing all the time. They'll understand when you need to be alone."

He believes it. There's no mistaking the calm assumption in his voice. I wish I could.

He senses my doubt. "Look, Evelyn, it'll be easy. Just let them make a fuss over you. They'll love that. Go shopping. Get your hair done, buy some earrings, do, oh, I don't know, whatever it is that women do together. You'll have a great time."

I look down at my sedate black skirt that matches my sedate black jacket that covers my simple white blouse. I think of the jeans and sweatshirts and sneakers in my luggage. I try to imagine shopping with Steffie. Green velvet. Sparkling earrings. The images don't fit. "I'll try," I say doubtfully.

"I know. You'll do fine." He squeezes my hand again, leans back in his seat.

"What about your dad?" I say softly.

Tom grins suddenly. "That old fart still got you buffaloed? Look, Evelyn, it's a big front. Just stand up to him and give him the same shit right back. He'll only push you as far as you let him. I found that out a long time ago."

"That's easier said than done," I mutter disconsolately, remembering his father's piercing black eyes and square jaw. "Kinda skinny, ain't she?" he'd remarked loudly to Tom the first time we were introduced. I'd stood still, too stunned to speak, until Mother Maurie shook my hand merrily and said, "Oh, don't mind him, he's just teasing." But I hadn't seen any laughter in his eyes. Only evaluation, like I was a heifer Tom had brought home for breeding stock. "He scares me," I confess.

Tom laughs softly. "Only because you let him. Hey, he's had to be that way to get where he is. If he hadn't been direct and assertive, and pushed people for all he could get out of them, he'd still be plowing the back forty and trying to pay off the mortgages. He pushes. I know that. But it's not like it's just you. He's like that to everyone, just to see how far they'll push. Draw a line." He sees the doubt in my face, offers an alternative. "But there are other ways to get around him. Hell, look at Steffie's way. Be Daddy's little girl when he's looking, and do what you please later." He chuckles fondly at how well Steffie gets around their dad.

It is all so simple for him. Tom is like that. People are easy for him. He meets them, he sizes them up, he knows just how to handle them. And they always like him. Instantly, the first time they meet him. And they go on liking him, always. When we were in college, all the girls had crushes on him and all the guys thought he was a helluva friend. The freaks and the bikers, the druggies and the straights, the profs and the frat guys: they'd all liked him. He shifts gears effortlessly, is never out of place. I have always envied him that talent; he is able to be anything that anyone needs, as required.

And to me, he is everything. Husband, lover, best friend. There are very few people in my life, but I have never felt alone since Tom came to me, he fills all the niches for me. I look at him and a wave of tenderness breaks over me. After all he has done for me, surely I can do this simple thing for him. Live near his family for a month, make them like me, be pleasant to them. It won't be hard. Make Tom proud of me. In a way, it is a thing I owe them. And whenever things get hard, I'll just remind myself that these people are Tom's family, that without them, he wouldn't exist.

For a moment, I flash back to the fact that without Tom, I wouldn't exist. Not as I am now. He had taken a horribly introverted, socially hostile girl and made her over into a competent woman who was satisfied with her life. I think of our little cabin and ten acres of woods, of my job at Annie's Organic Foods and Teas. I have friends now, real friends, something I'd never had when I was growing up. Annie and our regular customers, and Pete and Beth down the road, and Caleb our mail carrier and all the others that Tom had so effortlessly befriended for me. I'd ridden into those friendships on his coattails, learned to socialize by watching him. I should be past all these stupid doubts, should set them aside with the old scalding memories of grade school and high school and all the failed efforts of those times.

But still I hear myself say, "It's just that the way they live and do things is so different from, well, from the way I was brought up and the way we do things. I mean, Mother Maurie's house looks like something out of a magazine, and Steffie always looks like she's going out to tea with Queen Elizabeth."

Tom snorts a chuckle. "Yeah, well. I know what you mean. Sometimes it gets to me, too. But it wasn't always like that. When Steffie and Ellie and I were kids, the money was a lot tighter. I remember plenty of hand-me-down clothes from the cousins, and lots of secondhand furniture. I remember when Mom's end tables were wire spools with cloths over them. But in the last ten years, since the equipment dealership took off, Dad's been able to do better for the family. And he likes that. He likes giving Mom and the girls nice things, likes living good with new furniture, and indulging Steffie and stuff. Hell, I know he can remember enough hard times for us. He's worked damn hard to get the family where it is; don't look down on him for liking to flash around that money isn't so tight for them anymore. It's a point of pride for him. But it doesn't mean he's going to look down on us for being broke, and having to keep things simple and cheap. He knows where that is, too." Tom sounds a little hurt that I would find his family's prosperity daunting.

"I know, but . . ." This time even I can hear the whine in my voice, and I stop a fraction of a second before Tom says, "Hush. Stop it, now. You're just working yourself up over nothing. Relax. They're going to love you. All you have to do is just relax and be yourself."

"Okay," I concede. I can hear his unspoken hope that I'll stop chewing on my worries, and let him doze again. So I lean back in my own seat and close my eyes. I pretend to sleep.

# Two

*Fairbanks, Alaska, 1963*

Eleven. Betwixt and between. Two pigtails, the color of dirty straw. Fuzzy pigtails, down past my shoulders, the hair pulling free of the braid like strands breaking loose in old hemp rope. They have not been taken down, brushed, and rebraided in days, perhaps weeks. It doesn't matter; no one scolds. My mother has six children, and her two older daughters are at a much more dangerous age than I am. They are the ones who demand all her watching. What is it to her if my hair has not been brushed and combed, the stubborn snarls jerked from my tender scalp, the long hair rebound so tightly it strains at my temples? It is summer, school is out, and we live in an aggressively rural area. There is no one to see her youngest daughter running wild as a meadow colt.

And I do. Both knees are out of my jeans, and my shirt has belonged to two older siblings before me. Boy's shirt, girl's shirt, only the buttons know. It lies flat down the front of my androgynous chest. There are holes in my sneakers, too, and my socks puddle around my ankles. Yes, that is me, eyes the color of copper ore, hard and green, a scatter of freckles across my nose. Unkempt, neglected child? Hardly. Free child, unwatched, unhindered, unaware of being free, as it is the only thing I have ever known. Free child in the deep heat of July, the forest baking around me in the seventy-some degrees of the Fairbanks summer sun.

I am where I should not be, but I do not even know it, nor would I care if I did. I am between the FAA tower on Davis Road and what will eventually be the Fairbanks International Airport. It is supposed to be a restricted area, but no one really cares about that. Not at this moment in time. If I want, I can follow the surveyor cuts through the forest until I'd come out to the small plane tie-downs. A bit farther, and I'd come to wide pavements of the airport, where the airplanes let people down right on the asphalt of the runways. There would be people and noise and traffic. All the things I hate. Where I am is much better. I am sitting on the bank of the slough and thinking it is the most beautiful place in the world.

The slough varies with the seasons, like a snowshoe hare varying its coat, but it is always beautiful to me. During winter it is a wide white expanse of snow, broken only by the protruding heads of the tallest grasses. The snow humps strangely over the mounds and hummocks of coarse grasses. Owls hunt over it, watching for tiny scurrying shrews and mice to break to the surface and brave the flat whiteness. If I walk cautiously, I can move across the frozen crust without breaking it, standing tall above the earth, my feet supported by millions of tiny ice crystals. Treacherous trickling sunlight sometimes softens my floor, and then I break through it and wallow up to my hips in snow that infallibly finds every opening in my clothing. That is the winter.

Then comes spring and breakup, when the slough fills with water that reflects the sky and the tangled branches of the trees on its banks and the tiny leaves budding on them. The white snow sinks down to isolated hummocks cowering in the narrow tree shadows, bleeds to death as seeping water that fills the slough. The slough flows with a perceptible current then, carrying off the melted snow to the Chena River, and birds cry above it, ravens black against the transparent blue sky. The wind of breakup reddens my cheeks, and my old socks wad down inside my battered boots. During the spring thaw, the slough is deep, how deep I do not know, for it is much too cold to think of wading in it. I jump from niggerhead to hummock to clump of grass to cross it, and at its highest flow I cannot cross it at all. I go home wet, my hands red-cracked claws of hands, my nose dripping, my eyes green with spring.

But that is not now. It is summer now. The early greenness has passed. There are tall yellow grasses, higher than my head, with waving tasseled heads of wild grains. The water has hidden itself beneath the living earth, only appearing in secret pools of shallow water banked with green mosses and ferns and squirming with mosquito larvae. Low-bush cranberries, tender little plants with tiny round leaves, no taller than my hand-span, coat the bank where I sit. Behind me, closer to the edge of the true forest, are twiggy blueberry bushes, bereft now of their tiny bell-like flowers, and not yet heavy with round blue fruit. Today I have seen a red fox with a spruce hen clamped in its jaws, and a litter of tiny rabbits just ventured from their burrow. I have seen the green bones of a winter-kill moose acrawl with beetly things, and pushed the bones aside to see the white grubs squirming beneath them. Myriad small creatures besides myself live and hunt here. The faun is one of them.

He is beside me, likewise lounging on the bank. He is stretched out to the lingering touch of the sun on his belly. He is totally unremarkable and completely marvelous. I love him as I love the sound of wolves at night, and stories of wild horses in thundering herds on the plains. I love him as I love my hands and my hair and my ice-green eyes. He closes the circle of who I am, and makes me complete. In loving him, I love myself. In my mind I call him Pan, but aloud I have never spoken a word to him, nor him to me. We are the closest of friends.

He has a boy's face and arms, a boy's curly thatch of hair atop his head, interrupted only by the nubbins of his horns, stubby things shorter than my thumbs, shiny brown like acorns. He has a boy's chest, tanned and ribby, flat nipples like brown thumbprints. From the hips down he is neatly and unoffensively goat. His hooves are pale and cloven, slightly yellower than my toenails but much thicker. The hair on his legs is like that on any goat, smoothly brown, growing so closely it hides any trace of skin. His penis is gloved as neatly as a dog's, held close to his lower belly in its coarsely haired sheath. The most I have ever seen of it is the pointed pink tip, moist like a puppy's. To my eleven-year-old mind it is a superior arrangement, much better than my younger brothers' dangling, wrinkled genitalia. More private in a way that is not prissy.

He rolls to face me, yawning, and then smiling. His teeth are white as only the teeth of young carnivores are white, and his eyes are a color that has no name. His eyes are the color of sunlight that has sifted through green birch leaves and fallen onto a carpet of last year's leaves. Earth eyes, not brown nor green nor yellow. The color of a forest when you stand back from it.

He rises and looks at me askance, and I shrug and rise to follow him. My dog falls in at our heels. He pants delicately in the heat of the summer, making hardly a noise at all. Not for him some doggy lolling of a long pink tongue. He is more than half a wolf, my Rinky, with his sleek black coat and his pale cheeks and eyebrows. In the woods with me, he is all a wolf, and I am his cub as surely as Mowgli belonged to Akela. He has taught me everything, this dog, that a young creature must know to stay alive in the forest. From him I have learned to be still and to be silent, and to move with the forest instead of through or against it. I have watched him and seen how well he fills the niche that nature has allotted to him. I, too, will be as he is, perfect in my place.

We follow Pan, Rinky and I, and he leads us down the slough. We walk in the flat troughs that meander between the tufty niggerheads. Short weeks ago, water flowed where our feet walk now. We flow as it did, silent and seeking our level. Pan has neither hips nor buttocks, but only the sleek flanks of an animal and the restless tail of the deer kind. His cloven hooves leave more of a mark than Rinky's wolf feet, and my sneakers leave the least discernible track of all. Insects chirr around us, and the air is heavy with pollen and sleep. I can believe that, save for us, nothing larger than a shrew is stirring in the forest at this hour.

Then the duck explodes in front of me, right before my feet, her brown pinions slashing my face as she rises on her battering wings. Her nerve has been shattered; she withstood the passing of Pan and Rinky so close to her nest, but I, a human, am too totally foreign to her experience. I fall back with an incoherent cry, my hands rising to protect my face, but she is already gone. My eyes tear from the slapping they have taken, but that is the sole extent of their damage. When I lower my hands and blink my eyes clear of tears, they are laughing at me.

Rinky's pink tongue does loll now, mockingly, dangling over his picket fence of white teeth and his smooth black doggy lips. Pan is worse. He clutches his belly, bends over it, brown curls falling into his eyes as he shakes with silent hilarity. His teeth are very white, his mouth is wide with mirth. Miffed, I ignore both of them, and crouch to examine the nest.

The nest is a late one, probably the duck's second effort this year. To the casual eye, it is empty. But with thumb and forefinger I lift the soft blanket of down that covers the fourteen pale turquoise eggs. The eggs are not much larger than grade-AA chicken eggs from the store, but they are much more real. Eggs from the store are cold and bony white, their surfaces dry and chalky, trapped in cardboardy trays. These eggs are warm, and smooth, almost waxy to the touch. I take two and Pan takes one, and we carry them off with us, leaving the duck free to return to her brooding.

We go back to the sunny bank of the dried-up slough and sit on the moss and eat our eggs. Pan and I bite the ends off ours and spit the crumpled bits of shell aside before we suck out the warm white and the sudden glop of the yolk. Rinky puts his between his front paws and delicately breaks it with his teeth so that he can lap up the egg and eat the shell that held it.

And that is all that there is to this day, but it needs nothing more. It is complete, like the scene trapped inside a glass paperweight, a whole sufficient to itself. I am eleven and lying there between a dog and a faun. We three make a circle, from human to beast and back again. I love them as I love my hands or my hair, unthinking, totally accepting. They are the two most important creatures in my life and always will be. When we grow up, I will be Pan's mate and we will live and hunt in these woods and Rinky will always run beside us. I know these things as well as I know that the summer sky is blue and permafrost is cold.

# Three

*Tacoma May 1976*

I hate to shop for clothing. I hate to try things on. I hate the cramped dressing rooms with curtains that gape at the sides, with their floors littered with straight pins and tags. I hate pulling stiff, unfamiliar clothes on over my head, clothing ensorcelled with hidden pins and buttoned buttons that snare me inside their unyielding depths. I hate standing nine inches from a full-length mirror trying to see what I look like in this foreign garment, my hair mussed and my makeup smeared by my struggle to get into it. It makes me sweat.

Stupid. Stupid is how I look. The bosom gapes hungrily for my nonexistent cleavage. My socks-and-sneakered feet stick out the bottom where sheer-stockinged calves and slender ankles and chic white sandals should be. I smooth the dappled-leaf muteness of the fabric, loving it, wishing I could look as if I belonged in it. But I cannot. I look like a homely carnival Kewpie doll stuffed into Barbie's prom dress. Ken would be horrified. I claw and fumble the buttons open, begin an attempt to slither out the bottom of the dress. It jams on my too-wide shoulders.

A saleslady whisks the curtain open. My olivine eyes peer at her from the dress bodice, my pale thighs goosebump in the sudden draft. "Oh, dear," she says, and I am sure her sympathy is for the dress, not me.

"You didn't like it. Can I bring you a different size, perhaps? Would you like to try it in another color?"

Another body, I think. Another face. Bring me those, and I'll try the dress again. "No, thank you," I say aloud, and her eyes narrow with disapproval. She must be on commission. Mother Maurie and Steffie trip merrily past my compartment. They are having a wonderful time. Both my mother-in-law and my sister-in-law love the gay whirl of shopping, adore endlessly trying on clothes, just for the fun of seeing what they will look like. I, exposed still, shiver as they pass. Another saleslady trails them, her arms heavy with bright garments. "Evelyn," Steffie calls without pausing. "We are absolutely starved! We're going to that restaurant, you know, the one down near Fredericks? Okay?"

"Okay," I mutter. I don't know the restaurant, having never been there. I am not even absolutely sure where Fredericks is. It doesn't matter. I'll cope. The dress has a half nelson on me. My saleslady sighs and whisks herself off to another dressing compartment. She peeks into that one, exclaims delightedly, "Not everyone can wear that look, but, oh, on you!" She clasps her hands delightedly.

I free a hand and arm somehow, and tug the curtain back so that it gapes no more than three inches on each side. I inch painstakingly out of the dress, making a sincere effort not to tear the shoulder seams. I shiver in my underwear as I wrestle it back onto its hanger and suspend it from the hook in the dressing room. Once on its hanger, it resumes its original gentle lines, looks beckoningly lovely as it never will on my frame. I snarl at it as I stoop for my jeans and shirt, catch the snarl reflected in the mirror. For a brief instant I am eye to eye, fang to fang, with myself. It is not a pleasant experience.

Someone who once said he loved me compared me to a stag. An odd compliment, and not one that reassures one's femininity. But a compliment, nonetheless, to be collected and clung to. I straighten and look at myself in the mirror, trying to find the stag he saw. I see only pieces of myself, I cannot perceive myself as a whole.

Sensible cotton panties that magically guard me from
yeast infections. Legs that remind me of the dark, footed
legs of my great-grandmother's piano bench. I can see
the lines of my ribs. There are muscles in my belly,
good, that is good. I think. Maybe it isn't. Maybe it isn't
feminine. How do you get rid of muscles on your belly?
I wonder idly. My stubborn breasts have refused to
follow me into womanhood. They are a seventh-grader's
breasts, their disgrace hidden inside smooth cups of
foam-lined nylon that bring them almost to woman size.
My collarbones stand out, my shoulders are wide, my
neck is long and graceful. Is this the stag he saw? I roll
my shoulders, watch the smooth muscles move under
the skin. My face. I cannot see my face. I see the lines in
my forehead, I see my wide cheeks, I should have
plucked my eyebrows, the lipstick looks silly on me, not
a clown's mouth, no, more like I have eaten something
unwholesome and it has stained my mouth this wretched
color.

"Can I show you anything else?" It is the saleslady,
peering in at me. She can show me nothing that I have
not already seen. I clutch my jeans and shirt to myself.

"No," I mutter. "Thank you, no, not today. Thank
you."

She leaves again. I wonder if someone is waiting for
this dressing room. A tall, elegant woman, garments
draped gracefully over her arm, folded money inside her
pocketbook. Her high cheeks smooth as polished wood,
salesladies never wrench her curtains open. Things like
that are reserved only for those like myself.

Stop making yourself miserable, I scold myself.
Why stop, I respond, when I do it so well? Everyone
should be good at something. I pull on my jeans.
Wranglers, size nine, as familiar as my own skin and
more becoming. My shirt. A plain and simple button-
up-the-front blue shirt, tuck it in, zip my fly and button
it, buckle the leather belt. Better than armor and
buckler is a pair of jeans that fit well, a leather belt that
buckles snugly, a blue work shirt that doesn't pretend to
be anything else. I button my cuffs, and grin at myself in
the mirror. Better. I take a worn tissue from my jeans

pocket, smear the lipstick from my mouth. Better and better. I feel more like myself.

There are bright plastic sacks laden with trove collapsed in the corner of the dressing room. I gather them. Sears, The Bon, the 3-5-7 Shoppe. Mother Maurie's and Steffie's bags, full of dresses and shoes and . . . No. Gay little frocks, and bright sling-back pumps and sun togs and beach cover-ups. Maurie and Steffie would never buy anything so mundane as dresses and shoes. I smile at the thought. Their bags hang on my arms, cut into my wrists as I hurry down the wide avenue of the mall, looking for them.

I am not good at malls, either. Steffie has tried to make me feel at home in them, but it does not work. They are too foreign to my experience. She swims through them as easily as a tropical fish glides through its pebbled and planted tank. But I am constantly distracted, bombarded by their infinite variety. There are too many possibilities, too many things to buy. Usually, I buy nothing simply because I cannot decide what to choose. Steffie selects effortlessly from the racks, tries a dozen garments, and buys two, never worrying that perhaps in the next store there will be a dress even more fetching, slacks even more flattering to her derriere. I envy her that certainty. I know I will never achieve it.

I slow, or try to. The stream of moving people pushes me on, so I continue down the mall. Perhaps I mistrust places where the sun never shines, where time stands still and the weather never changes save for the window displays. I lose all sense of direction, all ability to make decisions. Streams of people move both with me and past me. Sometimes I feel giddy and wonder if I am standing still while they pass. But here I am, at the end of the mall, and it is the wrong end, Fredericks is at the other end of the mall. I about-face and begin the trek back.

I wonder if Mother Maurie and Steffie will be impatiently waiting for my arrival. Or will they order without me, and begin their meal with no more thought than they give to a cockapoo waiting outside in the car? I have been a member of their family for six years. What is wrong with me that I cannot feel toward them as I should, cannot be free and easy as if I were really part of their family? It's not them. It cannot be their fault. They are always correct, always calm and composed, always kind. Steffie is so polished, so incredibly perfect in all her roles. Today she is the fashion-conscious woman of the world. And Mother Maurie is, as always, perfect in the supporting role of "Steffie's Mother." I know I am jealous of them and the easy way they fit into this place. I know they do not intend to make me feel awkward and homely and provincial. But they do.

I am halfway up the mall when it happens. From out of nowhere, a man's arm around my waist, closing tight, pulling me from the stream of shoppers as easily as a bear hooks out a salmon from a spawning run. He is a rapist, a ritual killer, a mugger, and I am too startled to even speak, and then a voice by my ear says, "Evelyn."

I have never heard his voice before, so how do I know it? Is it the way he says it or the timbre of his throat that slackens my muscles, leaves me standing in the circle of his arms like a doe poised in oncoming head-lights, my smile as blank as the mannequin's watching us from the display window?

He grins at my expression, his brown curls falling into his eyes, his teeth very white, his mouth wide with mirth. He holds me in the backwater of his arms, safe from the current of mindless shoppers that brush past us. He is taller than I remember, and his eyes a more honest shade of brown. We stand without speaking, and I have the eerie sense of a circle completed.

He leans forward then, his mouth by my ear. His breath is warm. He smells like the summer forest, like wild raspberries and leaf mold, like tamarack trees and high-bush cranberry blossoms. Like Alaska. "I was afraid you had forgotten me," he says, his voice like the wind through branches. "But you haven't. Not any more than I've forgotten you. I'm still here. If you need me. If you want me."

"I . . ." It is all I can manage. The mall is suddenly a cardboard set for a pretentious play. It cannot contain me. I need not act the part that has been assigned me. I could knock over the stucco wall, step out into daylight and wind and forest. Step back into being whole and belonging to myself.

"Come with me," he urges me. His fingers track down my spine. "Now. Come back."

I want to. In that instant, I really want to. But a jaw trap holds me fast. Boundaries spring up around me. The mound of laundry left unfolded on the table at the guest house. The refrigerator needs defrosting. Things I should do, things I meant to do, things I must do before I can call my time my own. Commitments. Duties. Things that make me real. Oh, and people. Belatedly, I remember people. I have a small son, a husband. They depend on me. They love me. What would they think of me if I just ran away like this, abandoned my responsibilities? Who would respect me if they didn't need me? Who would I be, shorn of them? And I, don't I love them, aren't they my whole life? How could I even think of leaving them, even be momentarily tempted? The thought shocks me. I'll tell him all this, tell him I am happy where I am, that there isn't room for him in my life anymore. That I don't need him anymore.

"I . . ." I repeat, choking on the word.

"Come soon, then," he invites me, sure of my assent. His forefinger touches my jaw, a fleeting farewell.

Then he releases me, and he is gone, blending in with the flow of people. I stare after him. He wears only a denim vest over his bare chest, and cutoff jeans do little to mask his strangeness. His hooves clack clearly on the smooth linoleum of the mall floor, but no one notices him, no heads turn to watch him pass. Only I stare after him as he is borne away by the current of shoppers. I hear his hooves long after I lose him in the rippling tapestry of people.

I close my eyes, try to still the quivering that besets me. Glass cold against my sweating hands, smooth against my back. I realize that I am backed against a display window, leaning against the cool pane. I straighten guiltily. My palms leave their imprints outlined in mist of the smooth glass. The bags of garments have fainted, have crumpled about my feet. Absently I pick them up, smoothing their sides. All my many minds are chattering at once. Someone is hoping that Maurie and Steffie will not notice how crumpled the bags are. Someone else is shouting that he spoke to me, that he uttered my name, that I have finally heard his voice. But the one in charge hushes all of them, tells them to be still. Firmly I tell myself that I have been daydreaming again, silly escapist fantasies to make myself feel important, and that if I don't hurry up and get down to the restaurant . . . I am not sure just what will happen if I don't get down to the restaurant soon, but I have an oppressive feeing that it will be dreadful. The chance for something to be wonderful has come and gone in a heartbeat, and I have missed it. Only the dreadful is left. So I go, sacks swinging with my stride, moving purposefully now, cutting in and out of the crowd like a freeway driver weaving among the slower cars. I try not to think I am disheveled, guilty, musky with secrets. I forbid my eyes to watch for him.

The restaurant is a dark cave that opens up suddenly in the wall of storefronts on the mall. There are no doors, there is only the open space with the rack of menus, the cash register, and a hostess standing guard. Beyond, all is dimness and muted music. The tables are shrouded with deep red cloths, the menus are gilt and scarlet, the place is cushioned with a red carpet. One wall is mirrored, but it takes some moments for me to realize this, to see that I have been scanning the mirrored tables for a glimpse of Mother Maurie and Steffie. The hostess does not approve of me, and makes no attempt to greet or seat me. I am used to such as her. "I'm meeting someone," I say, and breeze past her, trying in vain to keep my bags from brushing the backs of chairs and catching on the corners of tables.

Just when I am sure they are not here, that there must be another restaurant near another Fredericks, I see them. They are sitting in a booth at the very back, looking cool and chic in their summer city dresses, an advertisement for champagne or lip gloss. I stack the bags against the end of the booth and slide in beside

Steffie. I realize I am breathing as if I have run a footrace. I push the hair back from my face and feel the sweat wet on my palm. I don't believe Steffie has ever sweated in her life, and she stares with frank amusement as I wipe my palm over my forehead and then slide my hand down the leg of my jeans.

"Did you get lost?" Steffie asks kindly.

"A bit," I admit. "I always get turned around in malls."

"Oh, me, too," she lies companionably. She is perfect, as Steffie is always perfect. She wears a perky little outfit that reminds me of tennis whites, made dressy by her earrings and the slender bracelet on her graceful wrist. She dresses to go shopping with more care than I dressed for my wedding. Her skin is golden tan; her huge eyes are brown; if I were a man I would kneel at her feet.

In the silence that follows, Steffie takes a long sip of her drink. I cannot help but feel it is a thing she has been taught to do, that at some point in her adolescence Mother Maurie sat her down at the kitchen table and taught her just the way to sip discreetly from a tall glass of iced tea. She does it too well for it to be an accident of nature. I watch her as the naked brown savages must have watched Magellan claim their lands. The same awe and incomprehension. She glances at Mother Maurie and then back to me. Then she clears her throat, having selected a suitable topic for conversation with me. What, I wonder, were they discussing before I arrived? And why are they so painstakingly kind to me, when I obviously do not belong to their world?

"Did you decide to buy that green dress you were trying on? We didn't mean to hurry you, but I was simply dying of thirst. I hope you don't mind."

"No, not at all," I lie, half a lie. What I would have minded even more was if they had waited for me outside the dressing room, chirping helpful comments. Sometimes they do that. I suspect they believe that if they had enough time and money, they could fix me. Like detailing a used car for resale. Cut my long unruly mane into something cute and perky, dress me in cunning outfits

that disguise my unshapely legs and flat chest. Trans-
form me into a wife worthy of Tom Potter. The idea
terrifies me. It makes me talk too much, too fast. "I
didn't get the dress. At the last minute, I decided it was
just too young for me. And I always feel naked somehow
in a sleeveless dress."

"You make yourself sound like an old lady," Mother
Maurie chides smilingly. Her smile seems a bit stiff.
Suddenly I realize that my remarks have not been
exactly tactful. The dress I have rejected is cut very
similarly to the one Mother Maurie is now wearing. But
on her its youthfulness looks appropriate. Mother Maurie is a tiny, delicate woman, a ceramic doll with large
blue eyes, and Steffie is a long-legged golden blonde, a
beach-party Barbie. It strikes me that they are the two
ends of the spectrum for American femininity, and that I
do not fall anywhere between them. Off the bell curve,
that's me.

"What are you having, Mother?" It is Steffie, con-
sidering a red-and-gilt menu. "Shall we have just a bite,
or dinner?"

"Let's go ahead and eat dinner. The boys will be
ravenous when they get here, and it will save us the
trouble of cooking and dishes at home."

I smile and nod, pushing my tangle of brown hair
back a little from my eyes. The boys, I think as I peruse
the menu, the boys. And we are the girls, at least Maurie
and Steffie are. The boys are her husband, my husband,
her brother, her son, and my son. And yet there are only
three of them. Eliza, Elizabeth, Betsy, and Bess, the old
nursery riddle-rhyme rushes unbidden into my mind.
Five names for three men. Or boys, I mean. All boys,
forever boys. And we are the girls forever. Even when
Steffie gets around to getting married and settling down,
she will still be a girl. And probably a virgin, as near as
I can make out. All the women in their family are
virgins, except when they are "in a family way." Then
Grandpa Potter's teasing is vigorous and crude beyond
my belief or endurance, as if they were children caught
in a dirty game.

I order and eat mindlessly, finishing while they are

still dividing sandwiches into dainty triangles, still nibbling small forkfuls of cottage cheese. I drink coffee to
pass the time, adding more sugar and creamer each time
the waitress refills my bottomless cup. I roll the empty
sugar packets and the foil-lined creamer packages into
tiny tubes, and make stars and hexagons and parallelo-
grams on the tabletop. Infinitely amusing. Only boring
people get bored, my mother used to tell me.

"... any other errands for you, Evelyn?"

I jump, and sit up straight in my chair. Both Steffie
and Mother Maurie are staring at me, polite inquiry in
their eyes. Sleeping in school again.

"I, uh, I want to stop at the music store and look at
the tapes." Suddenly it seems like a very juvenile
errand. As well to say I was stopping by the candy store,
to get red and green suckers and a handful of Double
Bubble. I am embarrassed, and they know it.

"You and your music!" Mother Maurie gives a
condescending snort of laughter. "All right, but you'll
have to do it while we're in the drugstore picking up
Tommy's prescription. Did you remember to bring it?"

She goes right on talking as I dig through my purse,
finally coming up with the small empty pill bottle for
Tom's allergy medication in my coat pocket. It is sticky,
Teddy must have played with it, and I surreptitiously
wipe it on my napkin before I hand it over. I try to find
the threads of the conversation again, only to realize no
one is talking, they are all waiting expectantly.

The men are here, and I don't know how or when
they've arrived. Grandpa Potter, stooped but daunting
still, rests his big hands on the edge of our table. His
eyes scan the table, feasting on his wife and perfect
daughter. He is given to saying things like "The Potter
men have always been proud to say that their women
dressed well, no matter how bad the harvest has been.
We take care of our women." His eyes skid over me, roll
briefly toward heaven. He is a strange old man, I think,
proud of his wife's and daughter's gentility and polish,
but equally proud of his own rough edges and crude
ways. He never minces words, never worries about
giving offense. Of all Tom's family, Grandpa is the one

who never bothers to hide that he does not understand
me, does not believe I will ever quite fit. He scares me,
and I wish I could hide that from him. Right now, I want
to sink under the table to escape that sharp stare. But
suddenly Tom pushes into the seat beside me, his thigh
warming against mine, and instantly all is well, no price
is too great to pay for possessing him. Tall and golden he
is, blond hair, brown eyes, big hands, and one big hand
surreptitiously strokes my thigh before coming to settle
demurely on the tabletop. He smells of Old Spice tinged
with diesel oil, the mechanic's smell that never quite
leaves his skin. The hostess has followed them to the
table, and I feel her eyes move from Tom to me and back
again. She does not understand it any more than I do,
why does this man who looks like a cigarette billboard
cowboy, this gorgeous perfect man, sit down beside a
woman like me? I move closer to him, and set my hand
atop his on the table. The hostess looks away, moves
away. I take a breath. I am safe now. My Tom is with me.

My Teddy is with him, clinging to his grandpa's
hand, his small head looking defenseless, his hair newly
shorn and slicked. I don't like it, and for a moment my
anger flares, who does that old man think he is, always
carrying out his compulsion to "keep those boys looking
like boys" upon my little son? No one asked me if he
needed a haircut. I love his dandelion tuft of fine hair, I
don't care if it covers the tops of his small pink ears. But
Teddy is looking at me, his brown eyes big and round.
He has been brave this time, not flinching when the
buzzing razor nibbled down the back of his unprotected
neck. I smile at him and try to put my approval in it, try
not to remember how, when we first arrived in Washington, Grandpa took him to the barber, without my
knowledge or consent, and brought him back, red-eyed
and disgraced. "Momma's little tit cried when the barber
tried to shave the back of his neck and over his ears.
Well, no grandson of mine is going to run around looking
like a goddamned hippie. You wanna be like that, you
stay with your mommy, baby boy. I'll tell you, no son of
mine ever behaved like that in public! Five years old,
and he acts like a goddamned baby."

And I had watched Teddy shrink with each contemptuous statement, and had foolishly made it worse by putting my arm around my little son, hoping to shield him from his grandfather's disgust. And Teddy, my Teddy, had flung my arm aside and pushed me away, run out of the little house and into the fields to cry, newly ashamed of being afraid of something unfamiliar, newly ashamed of letting his mother hold and comfort him. And that wicked old man had glared at me and said, "You coddle that boy too much. Gonna ruin him. Time he was with men more often, instead of hanging around your skirts like Momma's little tit."

And I, too cold with anger to speak, had stared him down, driven him from the little house with my frozen green eyes.

But that was in another time and another place, and I cannot afford to think about it now. Instead, I make my mouth smile, and reach past Tom to hold out a hand to my Teddy. But my little son only smiles, a smile that is at once secretive and begging. He slides into the other end of the circular booth, forcing everyone to scoot over and sending Steffie up against me on the other side. Grandpa has missed none of this. "He's Grandpa's big boy today, Mommy. He's gonna sit over here with me."

Grandpa's eyes are black, like little bits of anthracite coal set into his pale, soggy face. He was a big man once, had stood tall and had tanned, weathered skin. Maybe then the lines around his eyes had been laugh lines. Now he looks bleached, like something found under a pile of old trash, a soup label with the colors gone all wrong, the green beans turned blue, a farmer turned entrepreneur, a corned and blistered foot crammed into a pointed Florsheim shoe. I could have pitied him if he hadn't been so hateful. Our eyes don't meet, I don't let him have the victory. I squeeze Tom's hand and look into his eyes instead.

"Did you find the part?" Mother Maurie demands.

Tom nods. "Junkyard had it." He turns to me. "You eat already?"

"Yeah, but if you . . ."

"How much was it?" Mother Maurie cuts in irritably. This is business, and Tom has no sense, mixing it up with a conversation with his little wife. Mother Maurie has shifted gears, is no longer the chic shopper but is now the shrewd businesswoman, versed in every facet of the family's farm equipment dealership.

"Seventeen-fifty. New one is twenty-two, but if old man Cooper wants his tractor back in the fields by Tuesday, he's gonna have to be happy with secondhand parts." Tom goes back to scanning the menu hungrily, fielding Mother Maurie's agitated questions easily.

She is upset with the parts supplier and doesn't care who knows it. Wants everyone to know it, as a matter of fact. If they think they can get away with treating Potter's Equipment this way, they are in for a surprise, she'll go right to the factory for parts after this, just cut them out entirely, and let them eat that. Why, she must order two or three thousand dollars' worth of parts a year from them, and for them to let us down like this just isn't good business, as they'll soon find out. Her own ruthlessness is giving her great satisfaction. She speaks clearly and almost loudly, so that other people at other tables hear and know just how hard-nosed a little businesswoman she is. She is proud of her savvy, and so is Grandpa Potter, for he nods sagely as she carries on.

Tom's fingers close over mine and hold me fast. The others at the table are talking, and he is replying to them, but his fingers against mine are a different conversation, and a different man is speaking to me from the one who they know. I listen to him alone, letting the other voices fade into a background hum like summer bees. I know I do not belong in their world. What matters to me is that somehow, Tom's world and mine have intersected, and that in that brief crossing, we can be together.

# Four

*Fairbanks Winter 1963*

My family is a family of poachers. Very few people know this outside of the immediate family, and almost no one else would believe you if you told them, for we seem very ordinary people. My mother works making floral arrangements in a flower shop. It is a part-time job, and she is always home before we are. She believes children need a mother to come home to. My father works for Golden Valley Electric Association. He works in the coal-fed GVEA generator building that is right across the playground from my school. Sometimes, when I miss the bus, I walk across the street and sit amid the darkness and noise of the big generators until he is ready to take me home. I think of the electrical power plant as a great cave full of large machinery exuding a constant deafening level of sound. There are ladders, and gauges to check, and it is always warm there, in contrast to the immense cold outside.

People call my father the plant engineer. I find this tremendously confusing. For one thing, my mother works with plants, not my father. For another, although there is a train that goes right past the back of the GVEA plant and leaves mountains of coal there like gigantic mounds of droppings, to my knowledge my father never runs the train engine. But this is not the sort of thing I am adept at explaining to adults, so when they say he is the plant engineer, it is easier to let them persist in their ignorance.

The GVEA building is grey with black windows and tall black smokestacks that speckle the snow outside our school with black soot almost as soon as it falls. The snow outside the school never tastes good, and I never eat it, no matter how thirsty I get.

The name of my school is Immaculate Conception School, and I go there with my two younger brothers and my little sister. My two older sisters go to Monroe High School, which is joined to ICS by a lobby, like Siamese twins joined at the hip. Both schools feature Jesuit priests in black cassocks with the unnerving habit of sometimes turning up in plaid flannel shirts and black pants, looking almost like anybody else. There are also nuns in white wimples and long, whispering black skirts interrupted only by the chattering of the rosary beads that hang at their hips like holy six-guns. The nuns are more honest, and never dress as anything other than nuns.

That is me, out on the playground, and I am easy to spot because I wear a battered play parka of lined corduroy, and my legs are bare. It is twenty below zero, but it is still required that we spend the morning recess outside. Little girls are likewise required to wear dresses or skirts to school. No one but me seems to find a contradiction there. We are supposed to play games, I suppose, frolicking about in fifty-two degrees of freezing while remaining girlishly modest. The boys play games, running and falling on the snow, tackling one another, yelling with smoking breaths. I stand and watch them, unable to comprehend their pointless energy. The other girls stand in clusters and talk. Most of them wear nylon ski jackets in bright blues and reds, and their waterbird legs are encased in bright tights that match their pleated skirts. I hate tights. They are always puddling down into little circles of fabric around my ankles, and then I have to pull them up by grabbing the waistband through my dress and trying to heave them up. It is impossible to do this in a ladylike manner. It is easier to go bare-legged and endure the cold than to endure the superior looks of little girls whose tights never puddle around their ankles, the shocked scowls of the playground nun as I try to wrestle my tights back up into place. I'd rather have chilblains and frostbite.

Making me go to school in winter is one of the crueler things my parents do to me. Although all my brothers and sisters attend school also, I always take it as a personal torment my parents insist on inflicting on me. I do not complain much about it. I am even good at school, very good, if academics are what you consider important. I am academically vindictive, ruining class curves with my hundred percents, doing fifteen book reports instead of the required five, but it is never enough to counteract tights that go with your dress and match the ribbons in your hair. Vaguely I know that I do not know how to compete. I always put my energies into the wrong arenas.

But it is more than that. School is not my turf. I resent wasting the brief daylight of the winter days trapped in a classroom instead of running through the white and silver of a Fairbanks winter landscape. Yet even that isn't it. I believe there is something unnatural about school, something damaging. To take a young creature and force it into an enclosed space with thirty others like it, all of the same age . . . would you do this to a puppy or a young chimp? You know what happens when you do it with chickens or rats. The same thing happens when you do it with children, only the damage is less visible. If I were a chick, pecked until my entrails hung from my rectum, someone would have taken pity on me. But I am a child and children are expected to endure the tortures of the damned stoically. I believe, perhaps self-pityingly, that it is worse for me than it is for other children. The ones who play in playgrounds, who visit one another's houses, collect toys, and have sleep-over parties, never perceive how peculiar an institution school is. But I am a healthy young animal, taken from my hunting, from my running and growing, and thrust into an exhibit more inhumane than any concrete-and-steel zoo pen. From the moment I step onto the bus every morning, all power deserts me, and I am less than

ordinary. I am prey, and I know it. Within the walls of
the school, I know that fauns are Fantastic Animals,
imaginary creatures those benighted and bedamned
Romans and Greeks believed in, and that good little girls
put their faith in Jesus Christ alone. Playing with a faun
is probably a mortal sin, like calumny and detraction,
niggardliness and sloth. I think I am going to hell. I think
there is nothing I can do about it, anyway.

But release me from the bus in the evening, and the
world is mine. The misery of the classroom seems an
imaginary fairy-tale dungeon, nothing worth telling my
parents about. The bus drops us by our orange mailbox
on Davis Road. My brothers and sisters start the walk
down the lane, but I stand on the road, waiting until the
bus breaks down into orange and red taillights and then
disappears altogether. My siblings hurry through the
dark, eager to be out of the cold. I stand, clutching my
book bag, waiting. Around me is the silver darkness of an
Alaskan midwinter afternoon. The stars are out, and the
Big Dipper swings low. Silver birch and cottonwood
line the lane to our house. Our house is the only house
on the lane, and not even its lights can be seen from the
road. I do not know why we call our driveway the lane.
We just do. It is only one car wide, and in winter it
divides itself into two tire tracks with a hump of brushed
snow down the middle. My siblings are far down the
lane now. I walk alone between trees that lean in over
me with their burdens of snow like ermine capes upon
their bare arms. It is night, and yet it is easy to see. The
snow is white on the ground and on the branches, the
trees are ghostly grey, and in between there is darkness.
The dry snow of the lane crunches and squeaks under
my boots.

First the house is a few stripes of yellow light
through the trees. Then I come to where we have
cleared for our garden. The trees are cut away and the
once-furrowed soil is now covered with a wavering quilt
of snow. I see the house squatting darkly amid the snow,
long and low like a crouching animal. The snow-load is
heavy on the roof, but earlier snows have slid off the
peaked aluminum, to create a wall of snow around the

house that makes it look like my home has pushed up from under the earth and snow like a mushroom.

And then I am up on the wooden porch that rattles under my boots, and the door must be shouldered open because the frost always coats the bottom edge of it and tries to freeze it shut. I thud it open, breaking into my mother's territory. Our house is made of dark logs chinked with pink and yellow fiberglass, and the ceiling is low. Yet I remember it as being full of an amber light, rich as honey, breathing out the warmth-and-cookies smells of home. Moose stew, as inevitable as thrice weekly math assignments, is already bubbling over the blue flames of the gas stove. The radio is always on, and my mother is always doing something in a highly untidy and inefficient manner. When she does laundry, she does mammoth loads of it, heaping chairs full of warm laundry, weighting the table with stacks of folded underwear and towels, heaping a box to overflowing with mateless socks. If she bakes cookies, there are tall leaning stacks of sticky bowls, showers of flour on the counters, the floors, and the husky dogs that sprawl everywhere in their sleep, and scatters of cookies cooling on every horizontal surface in the kitchen. When she knits us hats and sweaters, one pattern is never enough to please her. She must combine patterns, change the colors, rework the instructions. She has knitted my father a parka with twenty-seven different colors in it that is a combination of fourteen different patterns. It is an epic work of needles and yarn. My mother is of mythic proportions in my mind. To say that I love her is like saying I love the earth. My love is a puny thing beside her, unnecessary to her continuance. She is the home, the house, the food, the warmth, the hearth-witch. She leaves me almost entirely to my own devices; this makes me love her even more.

Down into the basement, rattling down the steep old stairs. Down here it is like a den, beds here, walls there, more beds, more walls. A veritable maze of nesting places for children, stacked bunk beds, green metal army surplus bunks, a menagerie of dressers, every horizontal surface festooned with laundry both clean and dirty, with papers, books, and a scattering of toys. I change clothes, pulling on layer upon layer upon layer of worn-out jeans and corduroy pants and T-shirts and shirts and sweaters and a surplus U.S. Air Force parka. Put on my socks, my brothers' socks, and my father's socks and a pair of canvas military surplus mukluks. And up the stairs and out the door with Rinky at my heels. Disappear into the night of the forest. Run silently down the rabbit paths, bent almost double to keep from disturbing the snow that rests so delicately upon each twig and swooping branch. Rinky ranges ahead and beside and beyond and behind, but is always there whenever I pause and crouch down in the snow. He grabs the sleeve of my old parka, leaving teeth marks in the fabric. Sooner or later, all my clothes bear the mark of his teeth. I do not mind. He tugs at me until I rise, and then we range together, he and I, following the paths we have created and keep packed, looking to see what is different from the last time we passed this way. Here is the blood-speckled trampling of the snow that marks a fox's kill. Here something has gnawed the bark from a fallen branch, and there something large and heavy has crossed our path. This trail and its faint musk fills me with excitement. Moose. Moose in our woods. The time will be soon.

I never need to tell my mother when I have found signs of moose. She knows. Perhaps she is a witch, the way she knows. I will find the knives sharpened on the counter, I will see a new roll of butcher paper. Days ahead of time. Then, one evening, it will happen. All six of us will be clustered around her table, our heads bent over our books. One cannot move an elbow lest one obscure a sibling's math book, shuffle the pages of someone's report. Pencils scratch, the dogs snore beneath the table, someone mutters over a stubborn calculation. It is unnaturally quiet for a house inhabited by eight people. My sisters have their hair in curlers, there is the muted chink-chink of my father's pipe against the ashtray.

Then it happens.

"Evelyn. Turn off the lights."

My mother is standing close to the cold blackness of a window. I rise and turn off all the lights, flicking switches until the darkness outside flows in from the windows, oozes out from under the couch, and fills up the room. No one moves, save my father. As I stand by the light switch in the darkness, I hear his heavy tread as he crosses the room to stand beside my mother. They peer out the window and speak softly to each other.

If I am silent and unobtrusive, I can slip to a parallel window and likewise peer forth. They will be in the garden, pawing the snow away from what remains of the cabbage patch, churning to the surface a scatter of frozen leaves, a half-rotted head, a tough green stalk now frozen solid. They remind me of ships, tall sailing ships, I cannot say why. This time of year their racks have fallen, leaving their heads misshapen and knobby. Their noses are long and seem saggy, like stuffed animals without enough stuffing. Their huge Mickey Mouse ears swivel in the darkness like antennae, but they are not really alert. Their attention is all for the paltry leaves of cabbage, the frozen broccoli stalks, the forgotten head of cauliflower they have churned to the surface. They are unaware of the darkened house and the silent watchers marking one of them for death.

There are four this time. There is a game I play, predicting which one we will take down. I play it now. Not the cow. Never shoot the goose that lays the golden eggs. Leave the cow. Not the old bull. Why he is with them now, at this time of year, I will never understand. But there he is, and his meat is sure to be tough. That leaves two, the young calf, born this spring by the look of him, and the older calf from the spring before. It will be him, the older calf, I am sure. But of this I say nothing aloud. The chain of command does not appreciate such speculations.

"Let's get ready," says my father. And it is all he needs to say. My younger sister and my two little brothers are already gathering their books and heading for the basement. They are all still too small to be anything but a nuisance out there tonight. I hear them go down the darkened stairs, and in a moment a light clicks on in the basement. Yellow light wells up from the stairs, bleeds into the darkness around me, lending vague shapes to the hulking darkness of the furniture. Sissy and Candy, my two elder sisters, drift toward the basement and down the stairs to find suitable clothing. It will be hard for them. They own very little that can tolerate blood spatters and possible rips, very little that will keep out the deep cold as we crouch to our bloody work. I am already by the door, pulling on the garments I frequently leave heaped there, much to my sisters' disdain. By the time my father has pulled on his parka and chambered a round into the 30.06, I am ready.

He jerks the door open, letting cold spill into the warm room. The icy air condenses as it flows into the room, making great ghost fogs that venture a short way into the house before disintegrating. He shuts the door quickly behind him but not before I have slipped out. He does not notice me, or he ignores me; it doesn't matter which, it amounts to the same thing. I shadow him as he steps from the porch.

With night has come a greater cold. It is a cold that freezes the tiny hairs inside my nose, that makes my eyelashes stick together for a fraction of an instant when I blink my eyes. I push my muffler up over my nose and mouth to shelter my lungs from the icy air, and try to resist the temptation to lick my dry lips. All moisture has been frozen from the air, and the snow is a dry dust that creaks under my father's weight as he makes his way across the yard. We move slowly, drifting in the night like bodiless shadows, not stalking the moose, but moving easily and quietly in the darkness.

The old bull lifts his head. A frozen cabbage leaf dangles from his pendulous lips. He alone watches us, his ears cupping toward us like petitioning hands. He gives no sign of alarm, issues no warning snort. He only watches. I wonder if he knows what is to come.

My father stops and I halt behind him. We stand silently. He doesn't turn to look at me, but proffers the six-cell flashlight he has been carrying. "Put the spot right behind his ear," he says.

I nod as I take the flashlight, but he doesn't see me.

He doesn't need to turn and watch me nod to know I will obey. He is my father. He rules this night. He is the one who knows where to send the bullet to drop the moose. On other nights, he has stood in this yard and shown me the constellations. He has shown me Sputnik winking by, and told me that if I want it badly enough, I can go to the moon someday. He believes this of me, that I can do anything I want, if I want to do it badly enough. It is both terrifying and uplifting to have someone believe in you so. I point the flashlight at the young bull we have chosen. I watch my father lift his rifle to his shoulder. When he is ready, he makes a tiny move that is less than a nod. I push the button on the flashlight.

The light explodes, bursting the moose into reality. The shadowy shape leaps into detail, frosted whiskers drooping from his muzzle, shaggy hair on his neck, a great fringed ear, a single lambent eye capturing my light. In less than a breath, the rifle explodes beside me, and the moose falls, dropping from my circle of light into death and darkness.

It is done.

I click off the light. We stand in the darkness together, my father and I, looking at the thing we have done.

Animals are put together so neatly, almost as if they were intended to be taken apart. Interior organs packed together like a Chinese wood puzzle, awaiting the human hand, bared to winter but warm with fresh blood as it snakes in to lift the liver up, free it with a swipe of the knife. I put the liver in the bowl that is nestled in the snow, and surreptitiously take a lick from the knife. Electric. Fresh blood is electric on the tongue, like sparks snapping inside my mouth. It warms me, almost. An hour has passed since the shot, and I have not been inside. My toes are wooden inside my mukluks. I should have worn more socks.

My father's flashlight finds me. "Did you get the heart and liver?" he asks, and I nod briefly toward the heavy bowl. He tosses the tongue he has just freed, and

I catch it deftly in the bowl. I rise with it and start toward the house. "Take the knives," my father tells me. "They need sharpening again." They lie in a row on the packed snow beside the body, and I stoop awkwardly to gather them. Their metal blades are cold, and one sticks painfully to my bared fingers.

I am halfway to the house when Sissy reaches me. She comes from the warmth and light, and I can tell she still has her hair curlers in under the woolen knit cap she wears. "I'll take them," she tells me eagerly, and I let her. She would rather take the gut meat into the house, rather sit by the table with the oil and stone and put the edges back on the knives, than crouch in the darkness by the fallen moose, rendering it into meat. I do not understand her.

I think about it as my father and I work to break the moose up into smaller pieces. Some of it is hatchet and ax work, some of it is for the meat saw. Head off, front quarters, hindquarters, backstrap, neck. My sisters are sickened by this work. They flee the great darks and the heavy cold of the night, they shun the bright blood and the musky smell of just downed meat. Even my father does this work grudgingly, thinking of getting up at six tomorrow to go to work, wondering if we will be caught poaching, cursing when the heavy head refuses to come free of the neck section. None of them feel it the way I do.

They can no more understand what I feel than I can comprehend their feelings. I know what they think. They feel debased by this confrontation. Meat from the store in cardboard trays wrapped in plastic, meat with tidy price stickers and labels, that meat is food, is flank steak, chuck roast, ground round. None of it is labeled, "Cut from the shoulder of a large dead animal in a snowy field at night." There is nothing to remind them that the hide was pulled away from the flesh while it was still warm, and the steam rose into the night to the greedy waiting stars. They do not want to remember they are predators, carnivores. They'd rather eat the flabby muscles of an animal raised hock-deep in its own shit, castrated and injected and inspected, a smack in the head to fell it, a large white room to chill it, humming machines to cut it into neat slices. De-animalized meat. The thought disgusts me, as they are disgusted when they think of their sister putting her knife to the dead flesh of an animal, kneeling on it as she pushes the blade into the dead flesh. Once the guts are out of the way, the hindquarters are separated from the rest of the animal at the place where the ribs stop and only the spine connects. We hurry, hacking at it with knives and saw and hatchet, trying to ruin as little steak as possible. Then the hindquarters are spread, to reveal the inner side of the backbone, and we work down it with a hatchet, and then knives, cleaving it into the separate legs.

"You done?" my father asks, and when I nod he takes a grip on one hindquarter and heaves it up. I help, guiding more than lifting, and the leg is dumped onto a piece of polyethylene sheeting. I am obscurely shamed that I could not lift the moose quarter by myself, and so I am determined that I will at least ferry it to the garage on my own. There my father will tie a piece of yellow nylon rope to it, piercing through the leg between the bone and the long tendon, and hoist it up to the rafters and let it sullenly drip blood for four or five days. Bleeding the meat, this is called, and it is important, for otherwise the meat will be tough and taste gamey. But for now my father has turned back to his butchering, is using the hatchet to chop through the vertebrae. A tiny fragment of splintered bone flies up to sting my cheek. It reminds me of what I am supposed to be doing.

The piece of black polyethylene is the size of a bed sheet. I turn my back to it, grip two corners of it, and bring the corners up over my shoulders like a harness. The moose leg is heavy, but the polyethylene is slick against the snow. Once I have it moving, it glides along over the snow behind me. When we reach the packed snow of the driveway, it moves even more easily. I roll the leg off the sheeting onto clean snow by the garage, and run back for another load.

Before midnight, all the meat is hung. My father and I contemplate it. It swings slowly, eerily, with gentle creakings. The garage is unheated, but it leeches enough heat from the house that it stays just above freezing. The slow patterning of blood drips will continue to speckle the concrete floor. We nod in satisfaction, and my father slowly tamps tobacco into his pipe. He lights it, sucks it noisily to life, and then turns away from the moose. I pull the string that turns out the light. We step out of the garage into the night, and he reaches up to pull the heavy door down. We are in the blackness of night again.

My father's streamer of pipe smoke rises up, like the steam from the moose's exposed entrails. He has shoveled snow over the gut sack to hide it. By morning it will have frozen solid. The dogs will dig down to it, and spend weeks nibbling and licking at the frozen delight until it is gone. There remains only the head. We both know that.

"Get rid of the head," my father says simply, and turns toward the house. I watch him go. The windows of the house are warm and yellow. I know that by now my brothers and younger sisters are in bed, probably my older sisters as well. The skin of my face is so cold, it feels like a stiff cardboard mask. I can move my toes, pressing them down hard against my mukluk soles, and awaken them to pain. The moisture of my breath has frozen into a solid cake of frost on the muffler over my mouth. I want to go in.

But there is the head.

The door thuds behind my father and I am alone in the dark. I dare not even go in to fetch Rinky for company, for he would be too interested in the head and guts. He'd only make the task harder. I snatch up the black polyethylene sheeting and start off toward the garden.

A head is not as big as a hindquarter, but it is an awkward shape, and heavier than you might think. The best way to lift one is to grip it by the bases of both ears, keeping the hacked-off neck turned away. The nose is pressed to my chest, the empty jaws gape tonguelessly. Even in the frigid air, the smell of moose and blood is strong. I turn quickly, letting go of the ears so that the momentum of my turn flings the head neatly onto the

polyethylene sheet. I diaper the head up in the sheet,
leaving myself one corner to use as a handle.

The night is clear and cold. I turn my back to the
house with its warm yellow windows, and I pull. The
head rides along at my heels as I leave the yard and
the tire-packed snow of the driveway and enter the
woods. I have already decided where I am going.

I follow one of my favorite trails. The trees are
cottonwood and birch, alder and diamond willow. My
path winds among them. Smaller bushes claw briefly at
my burden, but don't manage to rip the plastic. I drag it
on, leaving a peculiar wrinkled trail, like the path of a
giant worm. The head pulls easily, the polyethylene
gliding over the snow. I am able to walk at a normal
pace, and fifteen minutes later I am where I wish to be.

Here there are spruce trees, sudden groves of them
in the deciduous forest. For some reason, they grow in
irregular huddles, in groups of ten and fourteen and
nine. But almost always in the center of each huddle is a
tiny clear space where no trees grow. I get down on my
knees and crawl beneath the outer swoop of branches,
past a trunk, and here the snow is shallower, for the
upper branches have caught most of it. Then out again,
through deeper snow, and I am suddenly inside the
grove. A moat of snow and a wall of needled branches
surround me. Looking straight up, I can see the black
sky and the Dipper hung on it. Unceremoniously, I
dump the head here and leave it. I wad the black plastic
up under my arm and crawl out again. The walk home
seems longer then the walk here. The woods seem
lonelier and darker, and I am shivering before the lights
of the house crack through the trees to beckon me on.

My father is in the bathtub, my mother is reading in
bed when I come in. No one calls out or questions me.
No one save Rinky greets me, and he greets me with a
wriggle of delight, his hackles rising excitedly at my
blood smell. I shed my outer clothing by the door, and
do not turn on the light as I go down the stairs. Everyone
down here is asleep, vague blanketed shapes like furniture in storage. I am still shivering when I strip in the
darkened basement and climb into bed. Rinky is snort-

ing and routing through my bloodied clothing as I fall asleep, my head cradled on arms and hands that still smell of sweet, sticky blood. I dream of bright white sunlight on the snow, and a faun gouging the frosted brown eyes from a moose skull and slipping them into his mouth. It is a good dream, and I smile in my sleep.

# Five

*Tacoma The Farm June 1976*

Ten or fifteen years ago, the farm was a dairy farm.
And the room that I stand in now was genteelly referred
to as the milking parlor. Now it is a living room, and is
part of what Mother Maurie calls "the little house" as
opposed to her own "big house." When she speaks of it
to company, she calls it "the guest cottage," but to her
own family she calls it "the little house." I find this an
interesting dichotomy. Lately I find interesting dichot-
omies in many things Mother Maurie says.

It is like a cancer, growing in me, a constant hidden
nastiness I can no longer control. A little secret anger,
like red eyes in the dark. When I first came down to
visit, and was shown the many ways in which the Potter
women were vastly superior to me, I was willing to
concede to them. It was the easiest path. It was also hard
to argue. I cannot shop, I do not color coordinate, I have
never ordered from the Avon Lady or hostessed a
Tupperware party. I was willing to be unschooled and
unsophisticated, the country mouse come down from
her little Alaskan cabin to be overawed by the style and
gaiety of the life in the Lower Forty-Eight. A week, a
month, or even two, I could sustain the proper humility.
But now it is all wearing thin. I am becoming defensive
about my inferiority, protective of it. I will be as I am. I
am also beginning to suspect their veneer may be only

41

contac paper. The Avon fragrances are beginning to
smell suspiciously like air freshener. My anger is a
simmering acid thing, eating me from the inside out,
whetting my tongue, putting cruel edges on my every
thought.

But that is my problem, not Mother Maurie's. And
this living room is also my problem. We have been
guests here since March. It is a bright and cheerful little
place, cuter than the cottage of the Seven Dwarfs.
There are big windows with wispy white curtains that let
the bright sun spill in onto the white tiled floors. The
furniture is white wicker and yellow cushions. There is a
little glass-topped table, too unbearably cute to be
useful, homey little rugs scattered everywhere, and two
kerosene lamps with colored water in them instead of
kerosene.

The kitchen is even better. There is a tiny white
range, with a little red ceramic kettle sitting on it. The
kettle is a masterpiece of Woolworth's engineering,
flawlessly useless, with a spout that dribbles and a body
that holds less than three cups of water. Next to it,
centered on the range, is a spoon holder shaped like a
yellow ducky. The tiny kitchen table has a red-checkered
oilcloth on it. There are plaques on the wall that say
things about the Number One Cook, and For This I
Went to College, and No Matter Where I Serve My
Guests, They Seem to Like My Kitchen Best. There is a
cookie jar shaped like a fat pink piggy. The dishes in the
cupboards are sturdy plastic with jolly red roosters on
every plate.

The bedroom is okay. The patchwork quilt came
from Sears, and the patches are only a pattern, but I can
forgive that. I can even forgive the lampshades with the
covered bridges painted on them, and the bases of the
lamps that are shaped like old-fashioned pumps.

What I cannot forgive is the bathroom. The theme
seems to be that defecating children are cute. On a
plaque over the toilet, a curly-haired cherub squats on a
potty. There is also an adorable little statuette of a small
boy with his bib coveralls around his ankles and a look of
concentration on his pink-cheeked face as he sits on his

little ceramic toilet. Even the toilet has theme clothing. The tank sweater and lid hat match, both depicting a little boy, his innocent bare butt toward us as he "waters mother's flowers." There is even an ashtray shaped like a toilet, with the motto "put your dead butts here" on it. The final touch is a tall book that hangs on a chain by the toilet. The cover proclaims it as *Poems for the John*. Few things are more excruciating than to be trying to make breakfast in a cutesy kitchen, and to have one's spouse holler from the john, "Hey, honey, listen to this one." Lately, Tom has begun to subject me to this.

It is a trap I have fallen into, all unawares. Even as we carried our suitcases in, Mother Maurie painstakingly pointed out to me that the furniture was "practically new, not a scratch on it." She walked me through the guest house, showing me all its marvels, and requiring me to chuckle appreciatively as she giggled over the "naughty but cute" bathroom things. Steffie did the decorating, she told me. Steffie may someday take some classes in interior decorating, she seems to have such a flair for it. Some of the ideas, she confided, Steffie got from magazines, but most of it came right out of her own head. And isn't that amazing?

And of course Mother Maurie knows she can trust me to keep it neat as a pin, and to make sure "that terrible Tom" takes his boots off before he comes in, and don't let "that rascal Teddy" roughhouse all over the furniture, it would just break Steffie's heart if anything happened to this place, all the work she put into it to make it just as cute as a doll's house. . . . And I nodded and blithely agreed, for such an agreement seems easy when you are only planning to stay a month and may not even unpack your suitcase all the way.

But that was March and it is June. Useless to whimper for my sturdy little house in the woods near Ace Lake on the Old Nenana Road. Foolish to think of a place with painted plywood floors, and a boot-scraper driven into the ground outside the door. I miss my sagging couch with its ratty afghan that all three of us can cuddle under while Teddy hears his good-night tale from *Just So Stories*. I miss the high bunk that Tom built for

Teddy, with all the shelves under it for toys and books. I miss my wood stove, and the sound of pinecones falling onto the corrugated tin roof at night. I want to go home.

But we can't. Not just yet, but soon, Tom tells me. As soon as Bix is better. Bix, Ellie's husband, is a very slow healer. Ellie is the eldest daughter in the Potter household, seldom spoken of, but there, nonetheless. And Bix is her sturdy hired-hand husband, as practical as a strike-anywhere kitchen match. A good son-in-law, none too bright, but handy around the place. Until he broke his collarbone. It's hard to run a tractor with a broken collarbone, and the fields have to be tilled and planted. The farm has to look prosperous and well run, for in front of the farm, less than an acre away, is the farm equipment dealership that fronts onto the highway. Tom's father owns it and runs it, with Mother Maurie and Steffie to do the bookwork and order parts and dust the shelves. Tom's older sister, Ellie, keeps the big house in order for them all. And Ellie's husband, as big and good-natured and farmy as she is, does his best to help out anywhere he can. But he's not the same as a real son, Tom has confided ingenuously to me, not to his dad. Dick Potter likes to know that the crucial work of the farm is in family hands. It's just like that fool Bix to have broken his collarbone in spring, the busiest time of the year. And so Tom must stay, just a little longer, to get the fields tilled and planted, to move the irrigation pipe that waters the tender young plants, to mechanic on the equipment that does the work, and to be Dick's son. It is his family. Family is important. I understand.

Sometimes.

Sometimes I am sweetly reasonable. Sometimes I understand all that Tom tells me, about how important his family is, and that they expect and need his loyalty. There is something all-American about the concept of the extended family and the old family farm, and pulling together to get through the hard times. Sometimes it is a thing I want Teddy to learn, and sometimes I want him to grow up remembering early mornings on the farm, feeding the chickens, riding the tractor behind Bix or

Tom, going to town in Grandpa's red truck, sitting by Grandma's feet and watching television in the evening.

And sometimes I want them back, all to myself, my Tom, my Teddy. I don't want to be Tom's wife. I want to be Evelyn, in the cabin Tom and I built, in a place more forest than farm. I want to go home to my own house, to my own furniture, to my books and garden and woods. I don't want to be careful of the rattan furniture and the bright cushions that show every smear of dirt. I want to flop down on my own couch and sigh heavily, and let all the tension out. I want to be home.

Lately, when Tom speaks of home, he means this farm. "Let's go home now," he said to me yesterday when I had stolen him away, to have him to myself for a few guilty moments on a spurious errand. I wanted to stop at a café, to have a cup of coffee and talk with him. But he was restless, his mind full of uncompleted chores. "I have to get home," he repeated, and my heart sank. Is my home now different from his? Sometimes I see it all as an elaborate con worked upon me, as when I was in grade school and there were cliques I could never belong to, no matter what I did, no matter how hard I tried. I am no different from Ellie's husband, I will never be as good as a real daughter, never part of the real family. And sometimes the Potter family farm reminds me more of a Japanese corporate structure than Old MacDonald's Farm. Sometimes I suspect them of shaving and shaping Tom, like a faulty cog that doesn't quite mesh, machining him to fit into the gear chain instead of causing it to jam. I think they will steal Teddy from me, will teach him that he is a real grandson of the real family, and therefore belongs with them, not with his mother who is only a married-on artificial part of the family.

If I think about these things, I can work myself up into a frothing rage. How dare they! I won't let them! Mine, all mine, Tom and Teddy are mine and they shall never have them!

Sick. Selfish. Sad. I know. But there is so little else for me to do. Tom goes off to work and Teddy trails off with him, or is "borrowed" by Grandpa to be shown off while he sits in Hank's Diner and has his morning coffee with the other good old boys. I stay here, in Snow White Steffie's enchanted cottage, and try to deal with an oil smudge on a yellow cushion, Teddy's sticky fingerprints on the glass-topped table, and the increasingly obvious sag of the rattan chair that was never intended for a man of Tom's size. I know Mother Maurie will quietly mention these signs of wear to other family members as evidence of my waywardness and inferiority to a real daughter. And I experience the amusing dichotomy of watching myself mutter that I never wanted to be treated as a real daughter even as I try to get peanut butter out of the weave of a rattan armrest.

When I run out of hopeless housework to occupy myself, I can fill my days with endless paperbacks. *Passion's Proud Fury* and *The Angry Heart* and *The Elegant Suitor* and *Flames of Desire*. Steffie has a wall of them in her room, and she has told me that I can borrow them whenever I like. They are all romances, in different series, and she keeps them arranged by number. She marks a little X inside the cover of each one she has read, so she doesn't accidentally start reading it again. It's easy to forget, she tells me, which ones she has read, and she used to get deep into one before she realized she had already read it once before. The X's, she tells me, keep her from wasting her time. The other books in the big house are technical manuals for tractors; Steffie is the family bookworm, all the Potters agree, and they are proud of her endless reading.

There is an alternative to rattan maintenance and *Passion's Proud Fury*. I can go visit the big house.

In the day I can go over and watch Ellie work. She is a big rawboned woman, Dick Potter's frame accidentally bestowed on a female child. Both seem ashamed of the error. Ellie mimimalizes it by hunching around the house, wearing her plaid housedresses as if they were a clever disguise, like a tablecloth thrown over a packing crate. Ellie does only one thing. She works. She mops tile floors and sweeps hardwood floors, she scrubs walls, she pounds yielding white dough into loaves, she chops vegetables and tumbles them into simmering pots, she polishes windows and dusts shelves. She never stops. If I arrive during the day, she assumes I have some purpose there and ignores me. She is not one to stop and have a cup of tea and chat. Conversation with Ellie is a difficult thing, a trailing net of words that follows her from room to room as she straightens and tidies, snagging on feather dusters and Pledge cans and sponges and Comet cleanser. How is she? I am fine, and excuse me, I have to mop where you're standing. And how is Bix? Bix is better, save for a crick in his back, serves him right for trying to work in his good boots while his shoulder is still banged up, and excuse me, I have to go get the Pine Sol.

What else can I do with myself? Once I got up early and fed all the chickens, ducks, and pigs. I gave the chickens too much, the ducks too much, and the pigs not enough, and the poultry food is expensive, almost seven cents a pound now, and the pigs will break out of their yard if they get hungry during the day, and of course Mother Maurie knew I was only trying to help, but it's not like farming's in my blood, like in Tom's, so I'm bound to make mistakes, but the wrong amount of feed can put the poultry off their laying, and of course that's critical this time of year, so maybe I should let Ellie do it like always, but thanks for trying to help, it was so cute of me.

Is it me?

Sometimes I think it's just me. I think there's something wrong inside me, something mean and selfish and small that puts the worst interpretation on anything that's said to me. When I try to tell Tom about what happened, he looks at me, puzzled. "Well, the wrong amount of feed can put the chickens off their laying," he says, as if that explains everything, and goes back to reading his tractor manual.

It is evening, night in the little house, but not at all peaceful. My nerves are trembling inside my body, I want to explode, to shriek and scream. And Tom, once so tuned to me he could answer my unspoken questions, does not even notice. So I will be good. I will be patient.

I will be a good wife, and contain this unreasoning anger. I will think of something worthwhile to do.

"I think I'll go get Teddy," I say. "It's getting late, and I think he's had enough television for one night. This time of evening, there's probably nothing on that will interest him, anyway."

Tom grunts, flips back to the index, turns more chunks of pages, traces his finger down an already grimed schematic. My hand is on the doorknob when he speaks.

"Oh, Teddy's sleeping at Mom's house. He fell asleep on the couch, so Mom just covered him up. No sense waking him."

"But," I say, and stop. But what? But I want my baby? I want to read him a story, tuck him into his madeup bed on the rattan sofa, look up from *Passion's Furious Pride* to watch is chest rising and falling under his blanket, his small mouth pursing in his sleep? Don't be silly, Evelyn. Let him sleep where he is, don't wake the child and drag him outside and across a damp yard just to put him back to bed again. Likely the boy will catch a chill from a foolish thing like that. You just leave my grandson be. I take my hand from the doorknob, return to my yellow cushion and white rattan seat. I try to immerse myself in Marlena's thwarted passion for Duke Aimsly, to believe in people who cordially hate each other for months and then fall into bed with each other, muttering about raven hair and bee-stung lower lips and throbbing towers of maleness and secret chasms of womanhood. I look up at Tom.

I met Tom in the winter of 1969. My parents had sent me "outside" to college, to the University of Washington, and we met during an anthropology class. It was one of those huge 101 classes that every freshman faces at least once. Every day a wave of students poured into an auditorium, flowing into the crowded seats with no set pattern, dragging up the tiny flop-out desktops that were never quite big enough to support a full-sized notebook. There was no personal interaction with the professor at all. He came, he lectured, he left. Attendance was taken by a paper passed for signatures. Tests were mostly multiple choice. It embodied all the worst elements of mass education.

But I had always been a dedicated student. I sat every day in the front row, center. I stared up at the professor. I strained to hear his words over the muttering and shifting of the restless student herd, and to make out the spidery notes he scratched on the portable blackboard. Tom sat beside me. After several weeks, we noticed each other. He was the handsomest boy who had ever looked at me and smiled. It is good to remember that on evenings like this.

Later, I am still thinking of him as I watch him undress. I am already in my nightgown, sitting on my corner of the bed, drawing a brush through my hair. My hair is the color of mahogany from the sun, and unruly as always. It is neither straight nor curly, but when it is damp it makes waves of itself, and wraps itself around the brush bristles and the handle. I draw the brush slowly down my hair as I watch Tom unbutton his shirt.

One of the nasty little intrusive thoughts is that watching him undress is not as intensely pleasurable as it once was. It is my attitude that has changed, not the man, for Tom takes pride in keeping himself in good condition. His body is fine, and more than fine, much better a body than my own deserves. Tom could pose for beefcake. I could pose naked, and folks would have to look twice to see if I was female. I try not to be grateful for his body, for his sharing himself with me, for a small part of me insists that ungraceful and curveless as my own is, it is still a sturdy and useful vessel, a fine little animal to live in. But I cannot help taking pride in Tom and basking in his reflected glory.

I watch him now as he bends over slightly to tug his T-shirt off over his head. He is tall and well muscled and he bends gracefully, the muscles off his back delineated along his spine. He straightens, and his soft blond hair falls back into place, almost brushing his shoulders. I love his hair. When we are making love, it falls forward and brushes my cheek. I like to reach up and grasp the nape of his neck, feeling the muscles beneath my hand and his hair soft against my fingers, like the mane of a stallion. Dick Potter hates his son's soft hair. Goddam Hippie Hairdo, he calls it, all in caps. But I feel a small victory in that Tom has not given in to his demands for a haircut.

He has been going shirtless for this last week or so, and the skin of his back is golden. When he straightens and looks at me, he is all tawny colors, golden skin, soft blond hair, and gentle brown eyes. Lion colors. He knows I have been watching him and he smiles, anticipating pleasure. He is so incredibly beautiful to me that an aching swells inside me. Not of desire, but of love thwarted. I love him so. And I am about to start a quarrel.

"Tom, honey, when are we going home?"

He stops in the act of lowering his pants and actually sits down on the bed in surprise. He turns to face me, his boyish face wrinkled with perplexity. He has been thinking of sex, not of neglected cabins and gardens going to weed. His fine lion hair is rumpled where he has drawn his T-shirt off over his head. His amber eyes, now the color of sunlight on beer bottles, go wide. "When are we what, Lyn?"

"When are we going home?" I repeat doggedly, patiently. "We were only going to spend a month here, remember? Just a pleasant spring interlude on the old family farm, camping out in the guest cottage, get Teddy out of Alaska for a while, let him see what a real spring planting time is like. Then somehow it became a month or so. Okay, May is fine, even though there's a lot of stuff I wanted to get done on our own place. Teddy's had a great time with the piglets and the chicks and the ducklings and all. But, honey, we're in to June now, and I was thinking we'd be headed home any day now. Then, at dinner tonight, all of a sudden your dad starts talking as if we're staying here the rest of the summer, and this winter, too." I hear the stridency in my voice, take a deep breath. I stop ripping the brush through my hair as I realize my scalp is sore. Carefully, I soften my voice. "Babe, can you tell me what's going on?"

Tom heaves the long-suffering sigh of the nagged husband. It is a new trick of his, one I don't particularly care for. "Lyn. Honey. Don't jump to conclusions. You've gotten so touchy lately. Yes, Dad did ask me if I would consider staying out the summer and part of the winter. You know Bix hurt his shoulder. Well, it's going to lay him up for longer than we thought. So that leaves Dad trying to run the place and the business. And this is the busy time of year. Not only the farm to tend, but this is the time of year when folks are buying equipment. Being a man short around here is no joke anytime, so Dad invited us to stay on. That's all. Just until Bix gets back on his feet. And between you and me, I don't think that's going to take as long as Dad thinks it will. Probably only another month or so. That's all. And I didn't give him a definite answer, because I wanted to talk to you about it first. But you know how my folks are. They think that if they just act like something is going to happen, it will."

And it usually does, where we're concerned, I think. No, I have said the foolish words aloud, I can tell by the sparks that light suddenly in Tom's eyes. He finishes undressing in silence, kicking his pants away into a heap on the floor. He pushes the covers aside and swings his long pale legs into bed. His posture tells me I won't be getting any tonight. He pulls up the covers before he speaks again.

His voice is a lie and a deception, reasonable and sweet. "If you want to take that attitude, then I suppose there's no point to our discussing it at all." You idiot, you spoiled brat, you cowering, narrow-minded little wretch, his attitude says to me. Refusing without even hearing me out. Heartless bitch. He hunches his shoulder under the white sheet and blue blanket. His soft hair fans out over the pillowcases. The pillowcases are white, but the cuffs feature Mother Maurie's cross-stitch embroidery. A gaudy rooster on Tom's, a plump little hen for me. The cross-stitched motto on Tom's proclaims that he's "all set to strut and crow," while my hen petulantly affirms that she'd rather "set awhile." They match a set we were given for a wedding gift. Steffie thinks they are adorable. They make me want to retch. Tom's voice draws me back to our argument. "I'll just tell them you didn't like the idea, and that will be that."

Oh, goody. You do that. I'd love to see their faces. I take a deep breath, put pettiness aside. "Tom. Don't snap at me. You know what I'm thinking about, or at least you should. There's our house. It's been sitting empty since March, and we're just asking for vandalism. God knows it's probably full of mice and red squirrels already."

"Pete and Beth said they'd keep an eye on it."

"Pete and Beth both work, honey. Driving into our place twice a week only means they can let us know after the windows get broken. We're not as isolated as we once were out there. Last summer I saw hikers and backpackers almost every day. And poor Bruno will be wondering what happened to us. I know they'll feed him, but he's only a pup. He'll be half wild when we get back there as it is. And there's Teddy's school. He starts kindergarten this fall. I don't want to have him start here, and then pull him out halfway through the year. Starting school is tough enough on a kid without doing that. And, last but not least, there's the small matter of my job."

In spite of my best effort, my voice was getting cold and rocky. Don't make this a fight, I beg myself. Make it a discussion. He has to see the logic of what you're saying, you don't have to be a bitch about it. Just tell him. Lay it all out for him. I pause a moment, hoping he'll say something. He doesn't. I take a breath and go on.

"It took a lot of nerve for me to ask for this much time off. If Annie weren't my friend as well as my boss, she'd never have said yes. But she can't keep running the store on her own. She's got some kid in there for the summer, but come winter the kid has to be back in school and she'll be on her own. She'll have to hire someone to take my place, and there won't be a job for me to go back to."

I pause and gather the reins of my self-control. Tom will see. He's a reasonable man, one who has always treated me as an equal, as a person to be considered. But the silence lengthens and it looks as if he is having to struggle to control himself before he speaks. Neither of us are good at this, at quarreling. We do it very seldom, most things are settled conversationally, or one or the other of us will demur to the other's area of expertise. I let Tom select the used truck we bought, he let me choose the insulation for the attic, we recognize there are areas where one of us is more knowledgeable than the other. But this is a different thing, an area of opinion based on emotions. And we are both experts on our own emotions.

"Jesus Christ, Lyn," he sighs at last. "You make it sound like I'm contemplating murder. All we're thinking about is spending a winter here with my folks and giving them a hand over a hard spot. I mean, hell, they paid for my college, they brought me up . . . I feel I owe them. And I have thought about all the stuff you mentioned. There's a good school for Teddy just down the road from here. The school bus stops right by the gate. And I bet Pete and Beth could rent our place out for us in only a couple of weeks, if we let them know the kind of tenants we want. Taking care of Bruno would be part of the deal. And, hey, Dad said that if we were staying the winter, he saw no reason why Teddy couldn't have that little pony that Red has up for sale. You know how he drools over that little pinto every time we drive past there. His eyes practically popped out when Dad mentioned it."

"You discussed that in front of him? Tom, that's not fair! You get his hopes all set up, and when Mommy wants to go home, that makes her the bad guy. And you still haven't mentioned anything about my job."

I am honestly angry now, paying no heed to the little sane voice inside telling me to be cool, be an adult, try to see both sides. Tom is frozen by his outrage, stiff as a corpse between the cold white sheets. The tendons stand out against his jaws when he speaks.

"You're making a big deal out of nothing. Teddy is big enough to understand that what he wants isn't always what he gets. I don't see why you always have to get so mad. Any idea I have, if I talk it over with Mom or Dad first, you automatically hate it. It's wrong, no matter what it is. And so what about your job? Clerking in some weird little shop, that's not a big deal. I mean, what are you going to become, manager of the fruit and nut section? The buyer for organic teas? It's not a big deal, Lyn! You can always get it back, or another piss-ant job just like it!

"It is a big deal! It's a big deal to me! And you're damn right I don't like it when you take your ideas and plans to your parents first! You're supposed to be my husband! Remember? Usually married people make their decisions with each other, not with their mommys and daddys. And I happen to like my crummy little unimportant job. It's hard to find a job you like, you should know that. You've walked out on enough of them. And my crummy little job was just fine with you last winter when it was the only damn thing that was feeding us!"

I stop suddenly. Carefully I fit my knuckles against my mouth and teeth, feeling where they would strike if I could hit myself, wishing I could. I wish I could. I've gone too far, way over the edge, past the unspoken boundaries we've set up for our quarrels. Never have I thrown things like that at Tom. He cannot hold a permanent job, that is something we both silently acknowledge, not as a fault but as a facet of his independent ways. Never have I thrown it at him like a dagger.

His eyes are wide open with vulnerability and hurt. I have struck true and deep, wounding him where the blood will puddle and congeal inside him. I have demanded my own way as something that is owed me, throwing his failures in his face to make it his duty to comply. He looks at me silently, his pain trickling through his guts, too badly injured to even fight back anymore.

"Tom, Tom, I'm sorry. I just got so mad, I started to say anything to hurt you back. I didn't mean it that way, you know I didn't mean it. I understood about those jobs. I didn't want you to stay with them. But I'm hurt, too. When you go to your folks all the time, for advice and make decisions with them, it makes me feel so small and unimportant. There's nothing for me here, and it makes me feel like nothing."

"Teddy and I are nothing." He says it acceptingly, dully.

"No. No, that's not what I meant. You and Teddy are everything. Don't listen to my words alone, you know what I mean behind the words. Please, Tom. I'm sorry for what I said."

I crawl across the bed to him, wrap my body around his stiff one, my belly to his warm back. I bury my face into his hair, so soft against my face, and rock his unyielding body on the bed. My anxious hands run over his body, kneading at the hard muscles, stroking, caressing the stiffness out of him, massaging away the anger and hurt that divides us. Eventually he relaxes in my embrace. He rolls in my arms, embraces me.

"It's okay, baby, it's okay," he mutters, his lips by my ear. "Let's just forget it." His voice is soothing. "We're both too tired to be discussing anything, much less fighting about it. We both said a lot of nasty things. If you want to go home at the end of the summer, well, that's all there is to it. I can understand how you might feel a little overwhelmed by my family. Mom and Dad have had to be aggressive, just to survive in this business, and they encouraged it in us kids as we grew up. Grab the buck, make the deal . . . you know how they are. So when I saw a chance for us to make rent off our place, and both of us pull in wages here, and Mom picking up the grocery bill, well, I thought it might really set us up, financially. Put us on our feet, give us a second swing at things. I didn't know you felt so strongly about going home, that's all. I'll just tell the folks tomorrow that summer is the end of the visit. They'll just have to understand." His eyes are opened wide as he says this, honesty and hurt gleaming in them as he gives it all up for me. Sacrifices it all.

And he has me. I capitulate instantly, telling him I hadn't thought of the financial angle, that certainly we can stay at least until the end of the summer, and we'll talk about winter when we're both rested, yes, it would be wonderful for Teddy to have a pony, and the job was, well, only a job. On, and on. Giving it all away. Making up for the hurt I had done. What did it matter, anyway? Tom and Teddy, they're what is important. What did I matter, anyway? Surrender to Tom, and it won't be scary anymore. I won't have to ask myself what would happen if just once I stuck to my guns, insisted on having my own way. I won't have to wonder if he'd dump me, or tell me to lump it or leave, wonder what would happen to me without him. Give in to Tom, and it isn't frightening, we aren't quarreling anymore.

Long after he tells me what an angel I am, and how much he loves me, and weren't we silly for arguing, and how much his folks will appreciate his help, yes, and long after he falls asleep, I lie awake and look at myself naked and helpless in my own mind.

I think of the little shop Annie runs. It's in the front half of an old house at Ester, not that far from the Malemute Saloon of Robert Service fame. Not that far for me to drive, even when the roads are white with packed snow-ice and my headlights cut through the black Alaska day. It is a warm place, a wood stove in the center of the room, and then all the bins full of nuts and seeds and organic grains and little cans full of spices and bright boxes of teas with wonderful names like Dragon's Mane and Orchard Spice, teas that Annie mixes herself in the tiny back rooms. It is an alchemist's shop for food, a place where the ordinary becomes gold. The walls are planks of honey-colored wood, and they are covered with shelves and hooks and alcoves full of merchandise, soft leather bags with porcupine quill embroidery on them, massage oils in precious bottles, ceramic teapots with whimsical faces, created by an old friend of Annie's, treasures and surprises, delightful things to sell. . . .

I won't be going back to that. I know it suddenly, with a sureness that trembles through me. My place there is gone, taken by another. If I go into that store again, it will be as a customer, as one who stands in the public area, not one who goes behind the Dutch doors and talks over the bottom half as she mixes a special tea. I won't be the one to indulge someone's child in a horehound drop or a stick of real licorice root.

I touch Tom, running my hands down his long flanks, wanting him to roll back and hold me. I imagine him running his hands over me the same way I am touching him, stroking my flesh, making it desirable by his touch. Make me special by wanting me. I want him to put his hands over my diminutive breasts and make them important by pinching the nipples between his fingers, by testing his teeth gently against them.

I have stirred myself to heat, and I need him, I need him to bury me in physical sensations so my mind will shut up. I don't want to think about where I have heard those arguing techniques before. I don't want to remember Mother Maurie applying them to Steffie all this spring, how she acts hurt by her daughter's refusals but politely accepts them, all the while pointing out how logic and reason and good manners are all on her side. Eroding Steffie's belief in herself until Steffie gives in, and then pampering Steffie to show her how smart she is to obey her mother. It works every time for her. Don't I know how well it works?

I clutch at Tom, slipping my hand over his hip and down, cupping his balls, and then gripping his penis firmly. I will it to swell in my hand, to become a sword that will subdue my doubts. But he only mutters, sleep's grip on him more sure and intimate than mine. He doesn't need me, not the way I need him. He can quarrel with me, make up, and then turn away, go to sleep, forget our temporary division. He is not frightened when we disagree. My nipples are hard, I press them into his back, feel the contact as agonizingly tantalizing. I rub against his passiveness, driving myself crazy. Turn to me, touch me, I beg him silently. Make me desirable, make me important, make me real.

"Lyn," he complains, wriggling out of my embrace, away from the thigh I have thrown over his hip. He'd only have to roll to face me, make himself hard for me, I'd do all the rest. "Honey," he rebukes me gently, "I've got to get up extra early tomorrow." He takes a deep breath, sighs it out. I lie in the warm place on the sheet that he has just vacated. His scent is on the pillows, and I breathe it in, savoring where his flesh has been like a dog sniffing after a bitch in heat. "Gonna show Teddy a deer," he mutters to his pillow. "Been watering at the duck pond. Saw his sign this morning. Don't know how he's been getting past the electric fence, but there're hoof marks all over down there. Gotta sleep, baby."

He goes away, off into sleep as surely as he will go off to work tomorrow, leaving me aching and alone. Unimportant. Of what value is a woman undesired, a woman who does no task, fulfills no function? The sheets chill around me, become wide plains of glacial whiteness, Tom a distant mountain range I will never scale. I'm alone.

Not alone.

His face fills my mind suddenly, and the musk I smell is not Tom's anymore. The lust that hits me now is sudden and unexpected as a hammer blow, a directed passion that makes my desire for Tom a mere itch, a passing fancy. I know him suddenly, more thoroughly than I have known any man. His tongue, I know, would be raspy like a cat's tongue, eager to seek out my secrets, and his cock would fill me and swell against me. To him I would be everything, companion, friend, lover. Merely by being me. I imagine the sleek fur of his flanks under my hands, how my fingers would find the rumpled nubs at the base of his horns as I directed his mouth on my flesh.

I move against the sheets, my nipples rasping against Mother Maurie's percale, and surrender to my fantasy. But my imagination is not enough to sate me, and I am still too proud to touch myself. Sleep is the only one who takes me this night, and my dreams touch me too softly to ease me.

# Six

*Fairbanks Spring 1964*

He is always there for me, in the woods. He is not a god to me, nor an animal. But in one sense he is like a spirit. He is the essence of the forest, of the moss and mushrooms and animals and trees and plants. When he is with me, then the forest is with me as well. And the forest is the only place where I feel whole. My world is divided into three parts: the school, the home, and the forest. Only the forest is peaceful, healing. Only the forest is mine.

With each passing year, school only gets worse. The pressure is on. Not for grades. I assume A's are my right, and I get them, without fail, despite teachers who dislike me and other students who harass me. I batter them out of Mrs. Haritsen, drowning her in extra-credit work I don't really need to do, always flapping my hand frantically with the correct answer, writing a five-page essay when a three-page is asked for, always using complete sentences, punctuating faultlessly, writing large and clearly on all my papers.

She hates me, of course. But she isn't allowed to show it. She's a lay teacher, a volunteer at the Catholic school. She's not a nun, and to my way of thinking she isn't a teacher at all. She is from the states and is young and is afraid of Alaska. I can tell. And that makes her hate me.

She can force me to do things. She will be giving the spelling test, strolling between the aisles of desks, giving a word, a sentence with the word, and the word again. "Pneumonia," she says. "The doctor says the sick child has pneumonia. Pneumonia. Oh, heavens!" The whole class looks up, startled, from their papers. She is standing over my desk. "Evelyn. Look at your hands! I am not going to correct any paper handed in by such a dirty girl. You go and wash them this instant!"

And I rise and go back to the big sink in the back of the classroom, to wash my clean but badly chapped hands. I use the coarse powered soap in the barely warm water, and dry them on rough paper towels. She continues the spelling test without me, as if I do not matter at all, and, of course, to her I do not. I store the spelling words in my head, "psychiatrist," "physician," "symphony," as I scrub at the backs of my hands where the constant chapping of cold water and wind has turned the abused skin dark, nearly black. I sand some of it off, leaving my hands raw and sore, and return quietly to my desk. I fill in the words quickly, ignoring the bird-black eyes she turns on me, hoping, hoping that I'll raise my hand and ask her to repeat them. I must never give her that chance to smash me. I know that tomorrow it will be something else.

One day I came to class after P.E., having changed too quickly, and all the boys laughed as I came in the door. I glanced down, chagrined, to find my shirt buttoned unevenly, the childish lace-necked little-girl T-shirt beneath it showing all my flat ribby chest and small green-raspberry nipples through its soft fabric. Any other teacher might have seen my scarlet face and called the class to order, pulled their attention away from me. Any of the nuns would have. But Mrs. Haritsen has none of the softness and kindness the nuns hide behind their flat black exteriors. All Mrs. Haritsen's softness is on the outside, in her curling soft hair and pastel dresses. Within she is colder than black flint. Mrs. Haritsen required me to stand at the board and write sentences. "A Catholic girl is a modest girl. A Catholic girl is a modest girl." Until the board was filled with my handwriting, and my arm ached with holding my hand up and my head ached with pounding blood. But I did it. And she must give me the A's I have earned.

I know what I am like to her. I am a wild and savage little animal. She perceives me as refusing the good civilization she offers me. Like a muddy feral kitten, rescued from a thunderstorm, spitting and sinking its impotent fangs into the hands that seek to smooth its rough fur, scorning the saucer of warmed milk offered it, choosing instead to huddle beneath the sofa and hope that someone will leave the door standing ajar, if only for an instant, so it can risk its draggled tail in a dash for the dark and storm outside. I am neither cute nor likable.

So she puts the pressure on me, and it is not for grades, nor for anything else I understand. I don't know what she wants me to give her. I only know that if I give it, I will no longer be me. Me is all I have, and I cling to me, instinctively, without even knowing how tightly I hold on to my selfness.

I am not like the other girls, who ask her questions about her clothes and her hair and her nails, who listen giggling in a circle around her desk at recess as Mrs. Haritsen tells them something cute her husband said, or something "wild and silly" she did in college. I don't like it when she talks about how much she misses Idaho, and how much we are all missing by growing up in "this wild place." She feels so sorry for the other little girls, and her pity makes them vaguely insecure, wondering what wonderful things they are missing that evokes so much condescension from her. I don't want her pity. If she doesn't like Alaska, she can leave. Does she really think the woods will turn into a city because she wants them to, that the roads will widen and be paved, that the winters will become less cold and dangerous because petite Mrs. Haritsen thinks they should? She's stupid. I force her to give me A's, and hope she will go back to the states soon. I pray that a nun will teach me next year.

Home is almost as bad. My sisters fight over boyfriends. Jeffrey met Sissy at a dance, but when he came to visit her at our house, he met Candy, and now he's asked her to the movies instead of Sissy. My mother is at a loss as to what to do about it. She tells my sisters that they must sort it out for themselves. She asks them, rhetorically, if either of them really wants to date a boy who could be that insensitive. Of course they do. He has a car. My mother folds her lips and irons a mountain of laundry, refusing to listen to any more squabbling. So Sissy cries and calls Candy "that bitch" when I am the only one around to hear it. And Candy primps endlessly in the bathroom mirror, ignoring the pleas of those with bursting bladders, when she isn't sulking because Sissy won't lend her blue eye shadow to her.

It makes my life miserable. First, Kimmy tells on me when, in agonized desperation, I go into the woods across the lane from the house and pee. Never mind that Candy was the one hogging the bathroom. I am "uncivilized" and my mother scolds me for it, not privately but in the kitchen where my little brothers hear and giggle endlessly about it. "What did you use for toilet paper," they demand, interrupting the scolding. "Leaves? Moss? Birch bark?" They giggle wildly, uncontrollably, even when my mother turns her scolding on them. They are unremorseful, and I am able to escape her, leaving her to tell them "It's not funny" as I tiptoe down the stairs.

But the room I share with Candy and Sissy is a sulfurous and brooding place. Candy is pulling her hair out of curlers, and Sissy is lying on her bed, reading, and not watching her. She is not watching her so intensely it is like the sharp edge of a knife blade pressed into the silence, and I am tempted to beg her to watch Candy, to stop ignoring her. One glance would be all it would take to ignite the storm, and then they could shriek and wail and slam hairbrushes down. The tension would be broken, and I could relax then, could read a book while they quarrel as imperturbably as I can sit out a storm under a spruce tree.

But Sissy won't look, and Candy is so miffed that she turns from the mirror and attacks me instead. "Did Mom tell you to stay in the basement when Jeffrey comes to pick me up?" she demands.

"No," I say, trying to make it withering, but not

succeeding. I am too surprised, and I am not able to hide it.

"Well, she said she was going to, so make sure you do." Candy turns back to the mirror.

This may be the opening Sissy has been waiting for. She slams her book and sits up ramrod straight, her face going rocky with righteous indignation. "She did not. She said you could ask Evvie nicely, and that sure wasn't nicely. I'm telling."

"Go ahead. Who cares? Not you, for sure. You don't care what people think of our family. Look at Evvie, for crying out loud. Look how she runs around. Susan Adams told me that Kerry Pierce asked her if Evvie was a girl or a boy. He couldn't tell by looking at her. No one could! Look at her! Last time Jeffrey was here, she was running around in that same shirt, and I swear the same dirt on it. He's going to think that's the only clothes she owns!"

"She's just a little kid!" Sissy jumps to my defense. "Leave her alone. She can't help how she looks!"

"Maybe not, but she could at least be clean. Look at her! Mud on her knees, God knows what on her chin, her hair full of twigs, probably from shitting in the bushes somewhere. Like a little animal."

"Whose fault is it that she couldn't use the bathroom?" Sissy demands.

I don't say a word. I am looking at myself in the mirror, over Candy's shoulder. It is a large dresser mirror, and I can see nearly my entire body. I stare at myself. I cannot remember the last time I studied myself in the mirror. I suddenly see what it is about, why Mrs. Haritsen hates me, why I eat my lunch alone. I suddenly see the raggedy dirty jeans and the shirt with the elbows out. I think of what I wore to school on Friday, the green pleated skirt with half the hem dragging out, the yellow blouse with the little flowers on it that has a coffee stain on the stomach. I wonder why I have never thought about it before, why I have seen everything else so keenly and never myself. I wonder why my mother lets me run around this way, and then I know. She doesn't have the time to worry about it. Squeaking wheels get oiled. If I don't demand new clothes, a trip downtown to get my hair cut and styled, money for hand lotion and nail polish and new socks, new shoelaces, jeans that aren't hand-me-downs, I will never get them. The money is already stretched as tight as it will go. Thank God for one child who doesn't nag and whine and beg. I think of Sissy's new nail polish, Candy's white mohair sweater, Kimmy's new Barbie doll camper, and I know that it should have been mine, my new dress, my new jeans. But what I don't demand I don't seem to need, and if I am content, no one will jar me from it.

I come back to the room and they are still fighting, my sisters, screaming at each other, ostensibly over me, but actually over Jeffrey. "You don't care about anyone's feelings, not Evvie's, not mine, no one's, as long as you get what you want!" Sissy is saying, and tears are running down her face.

"That's not true. You know that's not true. It's not my fault that Jeffrey liked me better, and it sure isn't my fault that Evvie looks like a pile of barfy rags!"

I snatch up Sissy's book from her bed and I let it fly. It's only a paperback, it shouldn't matter, but when it hits Candy in the face she screams, and even before the book is all the way to the floor, I can see the blood rushing out of her nose. She screams again, air bubbling past the blood from her nose, the blood that is falling on her white mohair sweater, and then I am gone, up the stairs, eeling past my mother as she comes down, making my escape before she knows I am the culprit. I grab a knife and a small bucket from the kitchen as I dash through it, trusting they will help me buy my way back into her good graces when I return. Rinky picks up on me as I race out the door and attaches himself to me like a sidecar. We careen down the lane and across Davis Road. And into my woods.

The path under my feet is hard, bare earth, beaten out by my own feet, and I fly along it, jumping fallen logs, veering around boggy spots. I could run this in the dark, I know it so well, and frequently do. It is fairly clear at first, as my path follows an old grown-over survey cut, but then it gets to the slough, still full of water this time of year, and I veer off, paralleling it, crouched over to run down an old rabbit trail, ignoring the branches that snatch at my hair and clothing, going to earth like an animal, fleeing into deeper forest. I run until I am sure I won't be able to hear them call me, even if they send one of the boys up to stand by the mailbox on Davis Road and yell for me. Then I stop and drop, panting, onto the deep moss. Rinky gives me one sniff, to be sure I am all right, pushing his cold black olive nose against my cheek and into my ear, and then goes off on his own business, whatever that is. I am alone with my images of Candy's blood bubbling over her mouth and onto her sweater. Dark red blood, clashing with her nearly auburn hair. I can't remember that she has ever had a bloody nose before, at least not one from getting hit with something. I know she will blubber for at least an hour, and Jeffrey is due to pick her up in only half an hour. I am betting the blood won't come out of the mohair sweater, even if they soak it in cold water and put meat tenderizer on it. Well, I reflect savagely, at least I won't be around to humiliate her when Jeffrey does come.

My small bucket is beside me on the moss, the short kitchen knife inside it. I pull my knees up, start to rest my chin atop them. Then I stop and look at them. Muddy, where I knelt down earlier today when I was roughhousing with Rinky. And torn, so that my knee, too, is dirty, and showing through the rent denim.

So? So.

I cannot forget the grubby, unkempt kid I saw in the mirror earlier. That is not how I've been imagining myself, all this time. I think of myself as me, as looking like me. I've been seeing myself in terms of what I can do rather than how I look. Runner. Stalker. Tree climber, ditch jumper, mushroom hunter, game spotter. I had no clear physical image of myself. I've only seen the view from my windows. I never thought to wonder how I really looked, to others.

It was bad.

And yet a stubborn part of me doesn't want to yield, refuses to rush home and wash up, brush my hair, put on clean clothes, and nag my mother for new clothes and new shoes. A part of me says, tough for them. Maybe I've only discovered this today, but I suspect they've known it all along. All along. They haven't done right by me, and even if I never knew it until now, they knew it all along. So let them live with it. If they're embarrassed by my looks, too bad. That's how I am. And if they've never cared enough to come to me kindly, to gently help me change, then screw them. I'll look this way. Always. Forever and ever and ever. And let them be ashamed. I won't ask for new clothes, for new shoes. And if they offer them, I won't want them. Not ever.

I close my eyes, imagining how horrible it would be if I went home and my mother and sisters had gone out and bought all new clothes for me, new shiny shoes, a coat with no teethmarks on the sleeve, jeans with knees in them. And if they gathered around me and brushed my hair and cut it and curled it. And then I went to school. And everyone would see the big change in me, and they'd gather around me and ask me questions. "Where'd ya get the new dress?" "Are those new shoes?" "I like your hair that way a lot better." "You really look nice." And I would have to smile and let them sniff me over. It would be admitting that I had been wrong, had been unkempt and shaggy. It would be admitting that they had been right to feel sorry for me all this time, to be disgusted by me all this time, to ostracize me all this time. It would be surrender. It's too late. It's gone too far, I can't even surrender now. Not if I want to survive as me.

My eyes are stinging like I'm going to cry, but this doesn't make sense. I'm angry, not sad. Angry. I take the knife from my bucket and stab it deep into the moss. Angry. I stab the moss again, and again.

Rinky comes back, snuffles my hair, snuffles at what I'm doing, nearly getting his black nose cut off by my knife in the process, finds it incomprehensible and hence uninteresting, and goes off again. Comes back a second later, licks my ear comfortingly, and leaves again.

The music begins, tentative and breathy. I lift my chin a fraction of an inch, and freeze, listening. There are only five or six notes to the simple melody, and it seems familiar, but I cannot put a name or words to it, nor say where I have heard it before. I turn my head slowly, listening. Sound travels strangely by water, and it takes me a minute before I am sure I have my direction. Across the slough. Damn.

I stand, catching up my bucket. There is a place to cross the slough, one where I will not get more than knee wet, and I head that way. As I go, I keep an eye out for wild mushrooms. My mother loves wild mushrooms, and has taught me twenty-seven different edible varieties, as well as those that I must not touch, and those that are merely useless or unsavory. I find several orange delicious, their caps actually a mottled green, but a secret orange ring hidden within their stems that makes identification easy. I draw the knife tip across the gills, watch the milky liquid rise to the cut. *Lactarius* family. Same as the pepper cap. I roll Latin names on my tongue as I scavenge mushrooms and walk.

The bottom of my bucket is covered with mushrooms by the time I get to the crossing place. I stand on the bank, picking my most likely path, and then set off, stepping from grass tuft to grass tuft, edging along an old log for part of the way, and then working my way again from tuft to tuft. Rinky comes, crashing and splashing to catch up with me, and nearly knocks me into the slough as he races past me. I have only two misses, and it is the same foot each time, so when I reach the other bank, I am only knee wet on one leg, and ankle-wet on both feet. Not bad.

The music has not ceased, but is smoothing out, as if the player is becoming more practiced. I know who it is, I do not need to catch the elusive tracery of his scent upon the air. I follow my nose and ears now, follow the sound and scent trickling between trees and brush, still pausing every now and then to add another mushroom or two to my bucket. Here is a hedgehog hydnum, a shingled cap with spiny little underpoints instead of gills, and a small orange boletus, its orange cap still tight to its white stem, hiding the soldierly rows of tubes that substitute for gills on it.

And here is a faun, goat legs akimbo, perched on an old log, cheeks red with puffing, eyes merry at my approach. He doesn't stop playing, but plays for me, deliberately, showing off how well he blows his pipes. For they are genuine panpipes, the little wooden tubes bound in a row with some vegetable twine. They look new, the wood unscuffed, unworn, new-made for spring. I sit next to him on the log, watching how it's done, how his mouth leaps from pipe to pipe. He is sweating, his curls are damp as they bob on his forehead, and I am struck again by his odor, sweeter than the warm breath of nursing puppies, pungent as crushed herbs, like tree resin and squashed raspberries and rich crumbly loam in the hand. Like all the sweetness of the earth embodied by a scent. It is a pleasure to sit beside him and smell him, and the music he plays has a similar unity to it. Breathless and soft it whispers like wind, like water over pebbles and rain dripping from branches, like birdcall and yet like the trumpetous sounding of an elk. He plays on and on and I listen.

When he stops, it is not the end of the song, but only the end of his breath. The song goes on around us, paler now, slurring its notes, but still there, breathing through the forest, and I understand what he has been doing. Not harmonizing with the forest, but amplifying it, anticipating its song, and playing beside it. He sees in my face my wonder and grins at me, unabashedly proud of himself. He wipes his pipes down one of his hairy thighs and offers them to me.

I take them cautiously, fearing for an instant that it is some kind of challenge from him, a dare for me to play as well as he has. If it is, I know I will not try. Something inside me is in full retreat from dares today. But in his eyes there is no challenge, only sharing. He watches me eagerly as I lift the pipes to my mouth, try my breath cautiously against one. It hoots softly, wistful as an owl, and my heart leaps in me with joy. Each pipe speaks to me with a voice I already know, and I forget the faun, forget everything but playing with the sounds I can utter now. It is like speaking a new language, no, like being mute all my life and then being granted speech, the speech of my dearest friends. I speak as the water, and then as the wind through branches, speaking as they do, not their thoughts but only their own being.

The faun's hand is on my knee, and I suddenly feel it, breathe the last of my breath down the pipe. I stop reluctantly, and wipe them on the cleanest part of my sleeve and then offer them back to him. He takes them with a smile that says, "Wait, wait now, just a minute." He holds them in his hands, and his rounded nails are the same color as his hooves, and two shades lighter than the tiny points that push up from amid his curls. His horns are growing this year, and I lean forward to touch one, knowing he will not flinch away nor resist my curiosity. Hard horn, smooth as polished wood yet knurled like diamond willow almost, the tip sharp against my palm. He angles his head away from my touch, gives me a glance that is through his lashes and over his cheekbones, then leans his head back, baring the browned swell of his throat, and lifts the pipes to his mouth. He closes his eyes.

He plays Pan.

He plays a glimpse of sunlight on a dappled flank in a birch grove, he plays brown eyes that light green with laughter, he plays the unwary clack of a cloven hoof against a glacier-worn stone, the deep breath drawn after a race through the woods, the grip of strong fingers on my wrist when he bids me be silent, the nudge of his shoulder against mine when our heads are close together over the first pale wood anemone, he plays the wind through brown curls and the trickle of rain over his shoulder blades. My throat closes up with how beautiful he is.

When I open my eyes, he has lowered the pipes, and I do not know how long I have been listening to the silence that is also a part of his song. He meets my shining eyes and his cheeks rose with more than the flush of his playing. He scratches his head, digging lovingly at the bases of his nubbly horns. With his free hand he offers the pipes to me again.

But this time I do not reach for them at all. I know what he wants to hear, and I do not wish to play it. I will

not play ragged jeans and dirty knees, runny nose and
scaly knuckles. I will not play my shame, and I try to
pretend I don't notice he is offering the pipes to me. So
he pokes me with them, and when I still don't respond,
he pokes me again, hard, prodding me in the short ribs
with their hardness.

I glare at him. He makes a face at me, sucking in his
cheeks and frogging out his eyes. I snatch the pipes from
his hand before he can jab me again. Immediately he
settles back on his log seat, attentive and polite. I want
to call him a bad name. He sits watching me, waiting for
me, and I don't understand why he is being this mean,
this nasty, to demand this of me. I know what I am, and
he can already see what I am. Why demand it be given
a tongue? But he is still watching me, waiting, his face
smooth, and I look long in his eyes, trying to find where
he has hidden the malice that makes him demand this.

But he is too deceptive for me, and at last, in anger,
I lift the pipes to my lips. I close my eyes, and squawk
out bony dirty knees and snarled hair. The pipes shriek
hilariously of a smudged face and hands rougher than a
dog's toepads, of ragged clothes that flutter in the wind
they croak, and then of thin arms and a bony chest.

The pipes smack against my front teeth, jarring me
to my very spine and cutting my upper lip and gum
before they fly past my face. I open my eyes, frightened,
and his hand is still lifted, palm toward me, as if his hand
will fly back again and this time strike my face. His eyes
are outraged and hurt. We stare at each other across the
torn place between us, and something is bleeding, I am
cut in a place that isn't even on my body and he shares
the wound, feels it just as I do. The hurt lasts a long
time, and I don't know how to make it stop.

I stoop slowly and pick up the pipes. They are
unhurt, save for a drop of my blood on the end of one. I
wipe it off on my shirt, cautiously offer them back to him.
He takes them as if they are encrusted with dog shit, by
two disdainful fingertips. He gives me a look I cannot
interpret and hops off the log and rubs the pipes over the
moss carefully, rips loose a handful of green willow
leaves and scrubs the pipes with them, staining them

green but ridding them of whatever uncleanliness he imagines on them. He is puffing when he sits back down. As he starts to lift the pipes to his mouth, I rise. I've had enough music for today, I decide. Especially I fear that he may play his own beauty again, a wicked counterpoint to my latest performance.

Walnut fingers grip my wrist, clenching tight. He has always been stronger than I am, but never before today has he used that, except in play. I refuse to struggle, knowing I cannot break free. Instead, I glare at him, then make my face cold and impassive as a bank of blown snow. I look past his shoulder into the moving shadows of the woods, for the wind has risen slightly and is stirring branches and grasses to dance. With the corner of my eye, I see his left hand lift the pipes to his mouth.

He plays, and I must listen, but I don't have to show I'm listening. I continue to stare past him as he plays a tiny green frog clinging to the underside of a leaf, a cluster of high-bush cranberries dangling beneath an umbrella of rosy leaves, tiny alder cones rattling down on new-fallen leaves, and spruce sap glinting in the sunlight. I watch the shadows sway.

He pauses, but not for breath. He shakes me, hard, by my wrist, and I try not to sway with his rattling. I look at him, making my eyes cold and hard. Something in his forest eyes keeps me from looking away from his gaze, even when he lifts his pipes and puts them to his mouth. He plays again, the same tune.

But this time I cannot deny the slender ankle wading past the frog, the strong brown fingers reaching for the cranberries, the laughter that echoes the rattle of the cones, the fan of hair the wind blows past the spruce tree that glints the same as the shining sap. He plays on, watching my face, and I hear warm breath stained with wild strawberries, the curved back of someone curled and sleeping in the deep grass, green eyes blinking with snowflakes on their lashes. What I hear is me, and not me, like a reflection in a pool is both me and the leaf-dappling light on the soft mud at the bottom.

He plays it twice again before he will let me go, his

eyes watching me as if commanding me to commit it to
memory. Evelyn Sylvia it is, Evelyn in the forest, the
Evelyn he knows, and the notes are my name as his
pipes say it, as the forest itself breathes it.

His fingers loosen around my wrist as he continues
to play. I draw my hand free of his, and gather my bucket
to go. Rinky comes to my tongue click, and splashes
beside me as we recross the slough. His black tail is
curled up tightly over his shining back, and I think of
going back and asking Pan to play Rinky for me. Another
time. Another time. His music follows me still, rising
and falling with the stirring wind, but as I get farther and
farther away, it blends with the forest's own singing, and
I cannot tell if I am hearing the forest itself or Pan's
rendition of it.

His music has driven the sense out of my head. I see
my mother's face as I shut the door behind me, and the
sound of the door shutting is like the clack of a jaw trap
on my ankle. Too late to run, and the mushrooms I offer
are not enough. I am required to sit at the table and peel
potatoes while I listen to a recital of my sins. She admits
that Candy said a lot of cruel things, but that doesn't
excuse my physical violence. Sissy and Candy come up
from the basement, both to listen and to chime in with
any crimes my mother may miss. Candy's nose has
stopped bleeding, but as I suspected, the mohair
sweater, though still soaking in cold water, is probably
ruined. I bite my tongue, refusing to say aloud that now
she will probably give it to me, hand down the stained,
worn-out stuff to Evelyn, she's too stupid to know the
difference.

Candy's eyes are both blacked, too, and this explains Sissy's sudden chumminess with her. Jeffrey
showed to take Candy out, but when he saw swollen
nose and puffing eyes, he backed out of the date, none
too graciously. Now they both agree that Jeffrey is an
asshole, but have no gratefulness to me for revealing that
to them. Candy is demanding I pay for her sweater,
which is a joke, as I never have any money except at my
birthday or Christmastime. I am judged and condemned
to clean up the room that we share. I don't say a word as

they rant at me, and I can feel how much angrier this makes my sisters. But it only seems to make my mother more thoughtful. As she swoops up the heap of potatoes I have peeled and splashes them into a bubbling stew and stirs it, she stares at the blank wall over the gas stove, and her grey-green eyes are distant, almost as if she were listening to music rather than to the nattering and bleating of my sisters.

The next morning I find that the hem of my pleated skirt has been resewn. The mohair sweater is dyed a uniform brown before it is folded into my drawer. I say nothing, and neither does anyone else.

# Seven

## *The Farm June 1976*

"Are we gonna stay so I can have a pony?" There is a ring of orange juice around Teddy's mouth, like a visible question mark at the end of his sentence. He phrases the words casually, but his eyes are vaguely accusing, as if he expects me to selfishly snatch all his hopes away. As if someone has warned him in advance of my cruelty.

I refuse to let their warning be fulfilled. "I guess so, honey. Daddy and I need to talk about it a little more. Do you want to stay here all winter?"

I reach across the table and rumple his hair, but it is too short to tousle now. He reaches up to smooth it, looks briefly puzzled at how short it is. But it will grow again. It is not permanent, none of this is. They can change the outside of him, but they cannot change what I have put within him. Child of my long days with you, full of stories read by me, of questions I have answered and questions I have asked, grown within my own body and then nourished by my mind. My own. My boy, I thought, mine. This one is all mine, Mother Maurie. You may be able to whistle up Tom, but not my Teddy. This one I'm keeping.

I cancel that thought as soon as it surfaces, disturbed by my own growing paranoia. I cannot understand what is happening to me. Sometimes, when I think about it, I am frightened.

Teddy considers my question gravely, and I await his answer solemnly. "Yes, Mom, I think I would like to stay. I could have a pony, and go to school in the very same school that Daddy attended when he was a boy my age. And when Bix gets better, he's gonna teach me to run the big tractor. And I'll be a man, not a little sissy."

His eyes light up as he finishes this speech. No doubt the thoughts please him, but it disturbs me a little to hear them couched in phrases fresh from Grandpa's mouth.

"Well, I suppose we'll probably stay then," I say lamely. A cruel temptation rises in me. It would be so easy to say, "Too bad your poor puppy will be all alone this summer. Too bad your Tonka trucks have to sit on their shelves and get dusty, too bad Eddie-down-the-road will have no one to swim with him in the gravel pit this summer. But I guess a pony is worth it. I hope our Bruno puppy doesn't run away because he's so lonely. I hope no one breaks into our cabin and steals all your toys. I hope mice don't chew up your stuffed animals." I could show them how it's really done, how you twist a kid's head until he doesn't know what he wants, how you scare him and torment him into wanting what you want him to want.

But you don't do that to children you love, and that is how I know they don't really love Teddy. By the way they use him to manipulate Tom and me. Perhaps tonight I will point that out to Tom, open his eyes to how we are being used. Or perhaps tonight I will step in front of a speeding locomotive and halt it with my upraised hand. Teddy finishes eating and carries his dishes unsteadily to the sink. He lifts his hand in silent farewell, the ultimate in cool, and I respond in kind. He grins suddenly and flashes past me and out the door, is gone faster than a red fox disappearing into tall grass. He will do whatever it is small boys do all day when their mothers are careful not to bother them. I will not spoil things by asking what it is he rushes off to do. Whatever it is, it belongs to him. A boy needs time on his own.

But what if he is not on his own? I begin to tot up the time he spends at home with me, as opposed to the time he spends at Grandma's big house. Well, they have the television. Add a lot of time on that score. And they have a full-stocked refrigerator, and a freezer that Auntie Steffie keeps full of Fudgsicle bars and Eskimo Pies. A major draw. And no one imposes discipline on him. If he becomes unbearable, they simply send him back to me. More and more, I slowly realize, I am becoming the punishment, the place you are sent when you're bad. I'm the "take a bath, pick up your toys, brush your teeth, go to bed" person. The candy givers live next door.

I realize my teeth are clenched so tightly that my jaw aches. I have been polishing the same spot of table for the last five minutes. I rock back on my heels and raise my cold hands to my sweaty forehead. Try to calm down, I tell myself reasonably. Every day you get further and further out. These are not wicked evil people. They are simply run-of-the-mill grandparents, enjoying their grandson during the first long visit they've had since he was born. All grandparents love to spoil their grandchildren, love to give them candy and privileges, toys and ponies. If Mother says no, ask Grandma, says the T-shirt. I smile ruefully to myself. Calm again. Real.

What is coming over you, I ask myself soothingly. What makes you think these wild things? What ignites your territorial fury, what sets you off so quickly these days? A shiver of cold fear touches me. What is happening to me? Lately I see only the worst in anyone's motives, including Tom, Tom who I love above all else, beyond all reason or safety. If I can doubt Tom, who is left for me to believe in? What has happened to the safety of our marriage? We never quarrel, we never nag each other, we laugh together, and he holds me warm at night. He is tall and handsome and strong and he loves me. I know this is so. But sometimes it seems that whenever his parents come into the picture, we are at each other's throats. What is becoming of my serenity, the inward peace I have so carefully cultivated? I feel pieced together, like a shattered china cup mended with the wrong glue, knowing that the next time they fill me, I will again shatter, scalding all within reach.

I make another little space in my self. There, I tell myself, you've seen the problem. Well, it's simply solved. Just start fresh, today, turn over a new leaf, be a better person, refuse to be prey to these feelings. Make a resolution, right now. No more nagging. No more emotional arguments. Decide all on logic. Show Tom a little more affection, make him love you again. Support your husband in this thing he needs to do. He perceives staying here as the payment of a debt, as evening out with his folks for all they have done for him. How can I begrudge him that? He needs to do this thing, to make peace with himself.

I make a hot cup of tea to calm myself. Tea bag in the cup. Water in the kettle. Kettle on the stove. Put the dishes away while the kettle heats. Pour the steaming water into the cup. Breathe in the comforting aroma of brewing tea. Remove the bag. Put in the sugar. Sit in the chair by the window. Concentrate for just a few moments on these very simple movements, let them be a ritual of serenity. Breathe deeply and unwind.

I sip my tea and shut my eyes for a moment. The old familiar images rise to my mind. Think of a black room, completely dark. A small shining white thread stretches across the floor of the room. That is my idea of sanity. If I can spend my whole life walking through that dark hall, balancing on the white thread, never breaking it, then I will remain normal. Be accepted. But it is such a temptation to just relax, to let go, to fall from the sharp and cutting edge of rationality into the deep warm blackness of my own world.

Pan comes from my blackness. I know that. Pan had to come from the blackness. When I had decided I wanted to be real, all those years ago, I had banished him to that blackness, to the hidden closet of my mind. Traded in a bizarre illusion for a real life, for Tom and later Teddy. I had left the old loneliness behind, and with it I had abandoned the dreams I had fabricated for dealing with it. Pan, my imaginary companion, had been a defense mechanism, a tool for dealing with isolation.

And now he is back. What does that mean?

Forget it. Just forget it for now. Turn to the matters at hand. Chores to do, a life to lead. I sip at my tea.

It's cold.

The rest of the day slips past me just as elusively. I do housework. That is all there is for me to do. There are no vehicles free for me to drive to town, and one does not drive to town frivolously, not when Mother Maurie is keeping track of the gasoline. The gardens outside the houses belong to Mother Maurie and are faithfully tended by Ellie. One must not walk through the planted fields lest one crush the new plants. There are the woods, of course, beyond the chicken yard. But there is nothing there for me, and no reason to go there.

So I do housework. Generic tasks. Sweeping the same floor I swept yesterday, dusting the same shelves, cleaning the same bathtub. I fix a careful lunch for myself at noon. Tuna-fish sandwiches, cut into triangles, a handful of potato chips, a pot of tea. Tom will not be home for lunch, he is discussing business at the big house. Teddy is with him. I eat my tuna in careful bites, wondering what would happen if I went over there, if I knocked on the door and walked in. Would they all look up from the big table in astonishment, wondering who had come to disturb them at their meal, who had come breaking into a family's time together? Ridiculous. They'd smile and greet me, make a place for me at the table. But there'd be the question, from Mother Maurie, most likely. "Why, Evvie, how nice! And what brings you over today?" And I would have no answer, would die before I said, "I'm lonely, I want to see my husband, I want to watch my baby eat." Those reasons are not good enough for practical people like the Potters. I have no real reason to go over there, nor desire to sit through a noon discussion of hydraulic hoses and whether the stock of gaskets is sufficient. It would be pointless to go over there, and silly.

After lunch, I have my lunch dishes to wash, and to dry, and to set carefully away. It is good to be busy. After the dishes, I read a romance. This one is about pirates. Their captain is actually a kidnapped nobleman who has won the respect of the pirates and becomes their captain by his skill with a sword. All he wants is to regain what is rightfully his, and he sets out to recapture one of his own ships, now carrying the loutish cousin who arranged to have him kidnapped so he could inherit the pirate captain's rightful place. Also aboard is his loutish cousin's beautiful and willful fiancée, Désirée. She has raven tresses and a bee-stung lower lip. She pouts beautifully, and doesn't wish to marry the loutish Alfred, but has been forced into it by her father, who thinks only of money. David, of course, captures the ship and takes her prisoner and holds her for ransom, thinking to make his loutish cousin Alfred very unhappy. Désirée hates David at first, thinking he is just a greedy pirate, interested only in money, much like her father. But even as she is hating him, she has to think constantly about his broad shoulders and white teeth, his roguish smile and dancing blue eyes, and the elegant way he put his own cloak around her to cover her after one of his less civilized pirates had ripped her bodice. . . .

"If we're staying here this winter," I say, being careful to always say, "if," not "since," "then I suppose I should look around for a job. What do you think?"

"Just a sec," Tom said, not even looking up. Evening has come, greying the windows and leaking shadows into the house. The table is an island awash with yellow light. The rest of the kitchen is a gloomy, huddling place. Tom's heavy tractor manual has a yellow cover, stained with diesel. Tom's notes and a schematic take up the rest of the tabletop. There is no room for me to share the table. "I'll talk to you in just a second, honey. I'm sure the problem is in this section of the hydraulics, and I think I can find it if I'm just left alone for ten minutes straight. Okay?"

I don't answer, but he doesn't notice. He is already submerged in valves and lines, filters and clamps. It doesn't bother me. There are other things for me to do. Teddy is ready for bed, has been tubbed and scrubbed, and now waits, red-cheeked, for a bedtime story. He is a little pinto himself now, my boy, his innocent butt white still, but the rest of him baked brown right down to the top of his sneaker lines. His fair hair has turned ashy white, his face tanned so dark that his blue eyes are a shock. I sit on the floor by the wicker sofa that has been spread up as a narrow bed.

"What shall we read?" I ask, but it is really a rhetorical question. *Where the Wild Things Are* is already set out by his bed. We have read it every night for the past three months, and he shows no sign of tiring of it. I do not mind, even though I can now recite it. There is something in this book for Teddy, and once he has digested it, he will be ready to go on.

"This one," he says, and presents me with a Little Golden Book about Scooby-Do. With some reluctance I accept it, leaf through its stiff newness.

"Auntie Steffie gave it to me. He's our favorite. When I go over Saturday mornings, we watch Scooby-Do together, with Pop-Tarts."

The ultimate cultural experience. We read the new book slowly, with Teddy taking great care to examine every picture. It is the same story that they use for all the cartoons, and Teddy seems pleased with its familiarity. When we are finished, I cannot resist saying, "Well, I think I like *Where the Wild Things Are* better."

"It's okay," Teddy concedes. "But it's not real."

"And a talking dog that hunts for ghosts is real?"

He frowns. "It's real in the story. Not a dream. Auntie Steffie says that Max falls asleep in his bed and just dreams the Wild Things. She says that he had a bad dream because he went to bed with no dinner, and that's what the story is really about."

"Oh," I say. I try to find the right words. "I don't think it's a dream in the story. It never says he falls asleep and then wakes up again."

"But then how did he get to where the Wild Things are?"

"In the boat. His bed turned into a boat."

"No. 'Cause that can't really happen. He just fell asleep and dreamed it. It's a dumb story, just about a dream someone had."

He stuffs the Scooby-Do book into the place of honor under his pillow. I pick up *Where the Wild Things*

*Are* as I stand and take it with me. I think it is my book now, a thing Teddy has outgrown and cast aside. Perhaps I am a thing Teddy has outgrown and cast aside. I feel gutted, hollow. Why did she have to take that away from him? I wonder. Did she even know what she was doing? Is it a malicious cruelty, or only ignorance? And why is it so important to me? Am I worrying about Teddy, really, or am I worrying about me and what she has taken from me, the thing Teddy and I shared? I feel Teddy's eyes on me and turn back to him.

"Can we get some new books next time we go to town? I had lots of books at our old house and here I don't have hardly any. Can we get some new ones?"

"What do you mean, our old house? Your books at home still belong to you, and they'll still be there when we go back. If we stay here much longer, maybe I'll send for some of them. But not too many, because we'd just have to pack them up again when we go home."

"Can't we just get new ones?"

"Maybe. A few. We'll see." I tug back the covers that are sliding off his feet, snug them around him. "Don't worry about it. Daddy and I are going to talk tonight and decide all about when we're going home. Then I'll tell you in the morning, and things won't seem so confusing. We can plan better."

"Auntie Steffie says she saw a Sylvester and Tweety book in the drugstore." His eyes are already closing. I don't reply but reach to turn off the lamp by his head. As I rise once more, he asks from behind closed eyes, "What if we never go back? What if we live here forever and ever? Then would we send for all my stuff?"

"Don't be silly," I tell him. "We'll be going home, and all your stuff will be there and just fine. Now go to sleep."

I leave his bedside like an actor leaving a darkened area of a stage, stepping into the yellow light of the kitchen and Tom's set. The light spills in a circle on the table from the pull-down fixture, illuminating Tom's manual. His hand moves, scratching pencil notes on a yellow tablet. He looks tired, older. His hands are graven dark with diesel and oil, the nails cracked, the downy hair on the backs of his wrists and forearms eaten away by harsh cleansers. The lines at the corners of his eyes and mouth, between his eyes and on his brow, are pale against his tan. He glances up from his manuals, gives me a smile, and goes back to tracing a diagram. As I walk behind his chair he reaches back with his free hand, hooks it around me for a moment, and pulls me up against his back. I hug him suddenly, impulsively, putting my face against his hair, smelling his true scent despite the diesel. He goes, "Mmmm," and is still for a second. Then he leans forward again, his fingers wander slowly across his diagram, his hand drops away from me. I stand clear of him.

I settle in another chair, across the table from him. I rest my pirate romance on the edge of the table, stealing a bit of light from him, hovering at the edge of his glow, and try to submerse myself in David and Désirée and Alfred. They are all idiots. Boring, stupid people, trapped in a trite plot, who will inevitably do what is expected of them. Alfred will be unmasked as the kidnapper and swindler he is. David will regain his wealth and marry Désirée. How can they be so blind to the other possibilities? And who could have put such an idea in Teddy's head? Live here forever and ever. The three of us in this cramped little house, forever under the sway of Mother Maurie. I can see me now, a junior wife in the Potter tribe. I smile at the idea and go back to my pirates. But after a while I find myself rubbing my jaw, where the knotted muscles ache.

"Tom? Tom?"

"Yeah, just a sec, Lyn. . . . Okay. What is it?"

He closes his manual on his pencil and looks up at me, sighing. I am seven years old and I've been talking during the spelling test. I grope for excuses. "I just wanted to talk to you for a second, honey. Have you given any more thought to staying here for the winter?"

"Sure." He stretches, rolling his shoulders under his T-shirt. "I told the folks today that it was all settled. Dad was really relieved." He pauses at the look on my face. "Isn't that what we agreed on?" He looks genuinely puzzled. Frantically I dig through my memories of the conversation. When had I agreed, when had I told him, sure, go ahead, we'll stay the winter?

"No, Tom, I don't think so. I thought we said we'd stay till the end of summer, and talk about the winter. I mean, we need to discuss it more. For one thing, I'd need to find a job, and I can't think what there is in town. And we'd have to have all our stuff shipped down, which means asking someone to pack it up for us. And we'd have to spend the whole winter here, in this tiny place, and try to find decent tenants for our place and hope they don't tear it to ribbons. . . ."

My voice runs down. The world tilts around me. Déjà vu. I know what comes next. Control becomes very shaky, things seem to have fuzzy edges. I cannot feel the book I hold. It's like being washed down a chute. First Tom will be puzzled at my resistance, then irritated. I will surrender rather than anger him. We will stay the whole winter in this wretched little place. Despair washes over me, almost a physical thing. No way to escape this, no way at all. The play is written, I must say my lines.

"Lyn, I can't go to Dad now, when he's counting on us, and say that . . . are you all right?"

I nod, swallowing the nauseous lump in my throat. A great wind of stillness is blowing past me, drowning Tom's voice. Talk to him, I urge myself, watching his mouth move, his head tilt as he coaxes me to be reasonable. I know what he must be saying, but my ears cannot seem to make out the words. Tell him you're afraid. Tell him they're going to take him and Teddy away from you, and you will be left alone in the darkness. Tell him. Tell him now.

But his words are flowing like a river, washing past me, barely touching my ears as they carry us inexorably on. ". . . that we were staying. It didn't seem fair to leave them wondering. Mom's got it all planned out. You can use her washer and dryer on Tuesdays, that fits in with everyone else's schedule. Steffie was really excited. She's really a sucker for her little nephew, and she gets so lonely around here in winter. She thought it was great that you and she would get some time together. She's just full of plans for canning and berry picking this fall, and sewing and cooking together this winter. She really wants to pull you into the family, make you feel like part of the gang. She thought maybe you'd want to go shopping, get some clothes more appropriate for this part of the country . . ."

The white noise comes up again, washing over me like a wave. I stare through it, trying to see Tom, my Tom. They would pull him into the family machine and absorb him. Then Teddy. Then me. First it would be helping out with the big family meals and sewing and washing in the big house. Maybe by next spring I'd be taking care of the chickens, helping plant the kitchen garden. By the year after it would be as if I'd never existed as a separate person at all. We would all live happily ever after. All I had to do was let go. Surrender. Admit they were right in feeling sorry for me. Admit I needed to be fixed. Stop being me and become Tom Potter's wife.

"Don't pull at your face like that, honey. You'll get wrinkles. So, what do you say?"

Fuck you, Tom Potter, you traitor, traitor, traitor. And fuck me, too, because I am saying, "Well, we'll have to work out the details as we go along, I guess. It's just for this winter, right?"

"Of course, honey. You don't think we're going to live here forever, do you?"

You bet your ass I do. Why do you smile so warmly and go right back to your manual? I look down at my own book, study the shapes of the words on the page. I read a few, they make no sense. So I try counting them. I used to be able to soothe myself by doing this, counting all the words on a page, but tonight it fails me.

"I'm going to bed," Tom announces, flopping the old manual shut. He stands and stretches, towering over me in the cramped room. "I want to hit the job early tomorrow, get this tractor back on line. So I'll get a late breakfast with Dad in town. If you want, I'll take Teddy with me, you can sleep in." He pauses. I count words, not looking up from the page. "You're coming to bed now," he asks, but it isn't really a question.

"Yeah, in a second. Yeah." I turn a page, count some more.

He stands over me a few seconds longer. I can feel his contentment, he has it all. He's come home to his family, to his old familiar world, his wife is tractable, his son is smart, he has it all. He waits for me a few seconds, then shrugs and trudges off down the hall. As soon as he is gone, I feel my shoulders drop. I can breathe, as if the air has flowed back into the space he occupied. I lean back in my chair, setting my book carelessly atop his scribbled notes, listening to the sounds of Tom going to bed. Water runs in the bathroom. Light switch clicks off in the bathroom, then on in the bedroom. Clump of falling shoes, a rustling of clothing. I hear his belt buckle ring against the floor. More rustling and the bed creaks. Silence. The silence grows longer, becomes indignant.

I know just how he is lying in there. His head is almost under the covers, he is curled on his side. He has left the light burning for me. His eyes are closed but he is far from sleeping. Duty calls me.

I arise and click off the kitchen light. Night flows into the room from the uncurtained windows. There was part of a moon, and stars peeping through the partial overcast. Rain tomorrow, maybe. Rain. Rain for the new crops rising in green rows. Good. Rain for the fields.

Rain. If you lived in the forest, what would you do when it rained? Take shelter at the base of some huge spruce tree, I imagine. Or, here in Washington, a cedar. Rain seldom penetrated through all their branches to fall near the trunk. It wouldn't be so bad. One could sit there, one's back against the trunk of the great old tree, smelling all the damp rich smells of the forest. Smells of wet moss and dripping flowers, of rich black silt and resin of evergreens. Maybe get a little sap in one's hair, but is that so terrible? Maybe get a little chilled, too, but nothing a sheepskin jacket wouldn't stave off. But the mosquitoes? I don't know. I drift away from the darkened window, seeking the lighted bedroom much as a moth seeks a candle flame. Good simile, I think to myself. Fly into the fire and destroy myself. But maybe I am dumber than a moth. A moth only does it once.

I flick off the light as I enter the bedroom. I shed my clothes in a heap on the floor. Brush my teeth? Too much hassle. I climb into the bed, stretch out on the cool sheets. Almost simultaneously, Tom reaches for me. He draws me close and smothers me in an embrace. I work my head free, turn it so I can breathe cooler, unused air. He kisses the side of my neck, strokes my body randomly.

"Do you mind, baby? I need you so bad." He mutters it into the side of my neck, punctuating it with soft, dry kisses.

Need, I think. That's the word, Tom. A word I could stand hearing from you more often. So you need me now, physically. Well, maybe it's the only need left that your parents and siblings can't satisfy for you. That's left for me. So maybe I should turn you down on that account, because it's not enough, it's not what I need. But I think not, Tom, my love. I think it's all the more reason to satisfy it for you.

Somewhere here in this bed, beneath this lithe golden body that is beginning to thicken at the waist, behind the face that is beginning to have lines, is the boy I loved so deeply once upon a time. And if he is still in this bed with me, although his form may be changed, how can I deny him? Never once, Tom, have you even mentioned the stretch marks that even now you are touching, never have you teased about the growing heaviness in my thighs and hips. Are you searching, Tom, as you knead that extra flesh, wondering where I went, how you can reach me? I'm here, Tom, I'm here and I need you, too. And need grows, a bridge between us, rising, building, ebbs for a moment, then returns stronger than ever. Builds again, and continues to build, until I teeter on the edge of a precipice. Then I feel him pulsing inside me and I slip and begin the long timeless fall into the warm darkness of release.

The sheets are damp with our sweat. I open my eyes to darkness that seems too bright. Hazily, I wonder why the windows are not fogged. We both shift, moving apart, seeking cooler spots on the humid sheets.

"I love you," he says, and for a moment all is simple

and true. And I can answer, without cynicism, without
anxiety, without thought, "I love you, too." This is how
it used to be, I think, this simple, this good. Just he and
I, together, and happy being together. In love. This is
how it was.

And I hate the thought, because it makes me know
that this is no longer the way it is.

He pulls me to him contentedly, snugs me up
against his chest like a beloved stuffed animal, his hand
flat on my belly, his wet penis soft against my buttocks.
He slips into sleep quickly. His breath is warm and moist
on my neck.

I slip carefully out from under his arm, pad down
the short hallway to the bathroom. My nightgown is
there, on a hook, and I drag it down and pull it over my
head. It is a diaphanous thing, a softly mottled pattern of
huge flowers in whites and pale greys. Tom bought it for
me, and I've always loved it. It is huge and lose and
moves easily around me, as if I have nothing at all on. I
remember a night in Alaska, a storm was coming up, and
Teddy had left Mr. Bojangles outside. I had gone outside
to find the stuffed raccoon. The wind was up and it blew
past me, streaming my hair back and my gown and
outlining my body against the blown fabric. I heard
Tom's truck engine and I waited for him to come up the
long drive, had stood still, my eyes averted from the
brightness of his headlights, the wind flowing through
my hair and nightgown. He cut the engine but not the
lights and sat there in the truck, staring at me, his face
white inside the darkness of the cab. Finally I moved to
the truck, the wind whipping my gown around me, and
when I moved he slapped off the lights, leaped from the
cab, and grasped at me with shaking hands. "It's you," he
breathed, and held me tight, clutching my body through
the silky fabric. He laughed and it sounded silly, his
shaky laugh. "I didn't know what you were at first, in the
dark. You looked like . . . a vision, a spirit, I don't
know what." He put his face against my hair and
muttered, "So beautiful."

And we had made love there, on the young lawn
that was more than half moss, in the dark of the rising

storm, the wind sweeping over us, and then the rain coming down, drenching us both, but failing to chill us.

I find I am standing outside the little house, on the prickly little lawn that surrounds it. My feet remember the cement slabs that make up the walkway, cool and rough against their soles. I look around me.

But there is no true night here. The big mercury lamps on their poles hum, and insects dance around them. The lights are still on upstairs in the big house. There is no darkness, only a greyness that wearies my eyes as twilight never does, a thirsty nondark that has drunk most of the stars away. The air is muggy and still, too warm for a real evening. The true night has been kidnapped, the moon itself is a mercury light, this stale air rushes up from blowers somewhere.

A few more steps and I am in the driveway, the toothy gravel pressing into my feet. I ignore it, walk lightly across it, my feet curling over the stones and taking no hurt from them, remembering lessons years old. Past the kitchen garden, to the edge of the pastures. I smell cow manure, and chicken-shit fertilizer and the dryness of the soil. We had better get rain soon. I stand, my hands resting lightly on the barbed wire, and my nightgown is limp around me. On the other side of this pasture is the chicken yard and a small pond. And the tracks of cloven hooves graven deep in the mud there.

I will not go. I will not.

I realize I am listening, not just with my ears, but with my skin, my nostrils are flared, all my senses are reaching, searching.

The hands I put over my ears are cold, and the gravel bites my bare feet as I run back to Tom's bed.

# Eight

*Fairbanks Summer 1965*

Blood. Blood on my cotton underwear, in the toilet, on the toilet paper in my hand. Red blood, my own red blood staining me. The bottom falls out of my stomach. I am caught, cornered.

This is supposed to thrill me? This is supposed to make me say proudly, "Now I am a woman! Ah, wonderful womanhood!" I feel sick and angry, not proud. This blood, leaking from me as uncontrollably as snot leaks from a runny nose. I wipe again at my furry little underbody, and the tissue comes away stained red, clots and strands of red. I'd feel prouder to look at my dog, gut shot. Are they crazy, all those stupid booklets about getting your period, your monthly, how neatly they put it, like it's a magazine you subscribe to, and the talk about the sweetness of knowing one is a woman? Anne Frank's diary, with that bit about "despite the smell, the mess and the bother, it is like I have a sweet secret." Or some bullshit like that. Damn and damn and damn. I know I will have to go to my mother.

And my mother, who has never failed me yet, does. She takes the news without surprise as I tell her, "Mom, I think my period's started."

"Oh, dear," she says, as if I had told her the dogs had pulled down the laundry line again, or that some idiot had shot up our mailbox. "Oh, dear." Third daughter, what do I expect, brass bands and banners? This is old hat to her. I don't want her to celebrate or announce it, but I want her to say something, to explain to me what has changed besides this annoying leakage of fluid from my body. Instead she says, "Well, you understand about what's happening, don't you?" and I say yes, because I do, I know all about the lining of my uterus peeling away, congealing and then uncongealing, sliding down my vagina like dirty dishwater down a drain. I understand all that, but that isn't what I need to understand. There must be something more, something that's been held back. I wait.

"Well, you'll need some things," she says, then, shocking me, she calls, "Sissy, Candy!" They come, rattling up the stairs from the basement, alert, responding to some note to my mother's voice, inaudible to me. When they reach the kitchen, she asks them in a lowered voice, "Do either of you have an extra sanitary napkin belt?" Exposing my vulnerability to them. I blush with anger, not shame or modesty. Fury like a fire bursting through me. I hate them all.

Candy does. She brings it to us in the bathroom where mother has taken me, holding it rolled and secret in her hand, lest any of the males in the household see it. I take it from her, feeling its unspeakableness and grubbiness despite its whiteness. It is a band of elastic that goes around my waist, with two teethed clips that hang down before and behind to grip the ends of the sanitary napkin. I have to adjust the elastic to my waist, and my mother insists on helping me, and on helping me fasten the sanitary napkin in place. For the first time in my life, I hate the touch of her hands on my body. I feel intensely, personally violated that anyone should witness this. The humiliation is too great for tears, only anger can suffice. I look up to find that Sissy and Candy are at the bathroom door, peeking in.

"Get the hell out of here," I snarl, but they stand there, unmoving, their eyes as open and stupid as cow moose when I startle them in my rambles. I take a breath to scream at them, but my mother makes a motion of her hand and they are gone.

"Now, you know," she says, as if she were speaking to a simpleminded idiot, "that you must change the pad when you use the bathroom. And dispose of it in the garbage, not the toilet. Wrap it so the dogs won't smell it and drag it out."

I am already pulling up my jeans, snapping and zipping them, so full of hatred and anger for what they have done to me that I cannot speak. Diapered like a baby, the hated white tissue snugged against me, rubbing against me with every step, I leave, going straight from the bathroom out the front door of the house. Heading for the woods. I whistle up my dogs. Minnie, my old bitch, is too hot and sleepy to want to go with me, but Rinky bounces up, always ready for a run. He stops suddenly, and then advances, his tail out straight, his ears up. He sniffs me rudely, shoving his snout into my crotch. I cuff him, hard, my cupped hand making a clopping sound as it connects with his muzzle. He backs away and gives his tail a desultory wag, as if to show he was only kidding, no insult intended, can't you take a joke?

No, I can't, not today, and I set off down the lane at a wolf trot, and he has to trot to keep up with me. At the end of the lane I cross Davis Road and enter the woods. The beaten earth of my path is firm beneath my sneakered feet, and I break into a run, needing the deep woods and exertion, needing to think while not thinking, while with every step the white pad chafes mockingly against my high inner thighs. I push myself, stretching my stride, feeling the heat of my exertion and the thin summer sun of Fairbanks warming my shoulders.

What it is, you see, is that I never really believed it was going to happen to me. Those stupid filmstrips with their sexless diagrams showing the uterus and vagina and ovaries in outlines of black and white have nothing to do with blood on one's underwear. The sappy hygiene talks, the nun's lectures about how it is the duty of girls to remain chaste and modest, lest they lead boys into temptation, the little booklets from Kotex passed out to take home and read, all that had nothing to do with me. That was something for girls who were wearing nylons and ratting their hair and sneaking cigarettes in the lavatory and passing notes about boys. Girls who wanted to be women, who dreamed of being feminine, whose barrettes matched their knee socks. Traders of lipsticks, stealers of their mothers' eye shadow. Ear piercers, boy kissers. They're the ones who deserved blood running down the insides of their thighs, not me. I never asked for any of this. I wanted nothing to do with any of it.

But it got me, anyway. Damn and damn and damn. Got me like a bullet in the neck on a cold winter night. Unavoidable and unchangeable. I am a female after all.

This is a major defeat for me. Up until now, I've been a human. I've been free to come and go as I please, with my mother giving no thought to it. This will change, I know, as soon as it occurs to her that I am not only capable of sex now, but of pregnancy. There will be limits on my running, questions about where I have been when I come home from the woods at ten o'clock on a summer night, my hair tangled with bits of moss and grass, the knees of my jeans damp and stained.

Up until now, I've been free to dream of anything. But now they will expect my dreams to be female dreams, of dates and dresses and husbands. Of perfume and jewelry and high heels. The substance of life replaced with trinkets. No hunts and kills and long cold runs in the grip of winter. No significance to anything, other than the catching of a good mate.

They will change me now. I know how it will start. Subtle, sneaky ways. When I am dragged into the stores in late August, to shop for school clothes, it will begin. Lacy, stretchy, flat little bands to go around where I'm supposed to have breasts but don't. Like a mocking reminder to my body that it is supposed to do something in this area, sprout out suddenly. Nylons, snaky things with absolutely no insulating value, replacing wooly knee socks. Tight, shiny boots that only allow one pair of socks under them instead of mukluks or Dingo boots. Ruffles on my blouses, lace, ribbons, anything to stick out on my chest and make it look like I've got something there. And at Christmas they will give me sweaters with bunnies on them, a new dress, a brush and mirror set. There will be no .22 ammo in my stocking, no wind-up toys, no bars of fat chocolate. There will be cute little bottles of cologne, and scarves, and costume jewelry. Good-bye reality, hello womanhood.

I remember once, when I was very small, my father took me out on the front lawn, and we gazed for long minutes up at the night sky until he suddenly said, "There it is, you see it, right there!" And it was Sputnik and he told me all about it, getting more and more excited as he spoke, explaining what it all meant that the Russians could get a satellite up into orbit, and that the moon was a satellite, too, and not so far away as people once thought it was. One day, he told me, if I studied hard, if I did well in my math and sciences, I could go to the moon. I suddenly know that when he told me that, he, too, was forgetting that I was a female and would someday be a woman.

It is a step backward, this becoming a woman. The diapering pad, the helpless dribbling of blood, the restrictions of activities—all moving backward toward an infancy of sorts. I am less today than I was yesterday, lessened by the leakage of blood from my body. And it isn't even my fault, but the punishment will go on the rest of my life.

I reach the wild meadow. I am winded, my throat is dry, and Rinky is panting. I stop running as suddenly as I began, and sink down to rest. The ground is damp, and the tall grass is over my head when I sit down. I am hidden, safe, invisible to all except the sun in the heavens and the occasional hawk. Rinky casts himself down beside me, flings his muzzle up onto my denimed knee. He pants, dribbling saliva over my leg with each exhalation. I scratch his ears absently and he closes his eyes in ecstasy.

Okay, I bargain with myself, not speaking aloud, for I never speak aloud in the woods. The human voice is too singular a thing, too jarring to be harmonious with the subtler speech of the forest and its beings. All right. It's bad, but let's look at just how bad it really is. Okay. This is going to last for three to five days, according to the booklets. Five days at the worst. Five days a month, twelve months a year. Oh, my God, that's sixty days a year, two months out of every year with this thing in my underwear. Trying to hide extra napkins when I go to school, damn, I bet that's why they carry purses. To hide these damn things in. Hoping your period doesn't start suddenly in the middle of the arithmetic test, or on a day when you don't have a sanitary napkin in your purse. Shit. Two months a year. But it doesn't go on forever, it stops sometime, when you are fifty or so, so that's, let's see, about thirty-seven years times two months, that's, oh, my God, that's seventy-four months, that's more than six years sentenced to this torment. Damn!

I fall back in the grasses onto my back, and stare up at the sky, sightless as a dead thing. The sky stretches away, blue and eternal and uncaring. Useless to ask it why I am cursed, useless to wonder if there is any way to circumvent my fate. I try to forget the cottony wad of paper jammed up against me and enjoy the day. The sunlight touches me, the grasses make thin shadows that dapple over me. Rinky, bored, rolls over onto his back also, bares his belly to the warmth of the sun, snorts, and then sighs in great contentment. Easy for him to do. He has a penis decorating his belly. Vaguely I wish I were a dog, enduring a heat and a flow of blood only twice a year. Much more sensible system. I doze, almost, content in my discontent.

I know he is near before I know it, the change in the air as subtle and slow as clouds moving across the sun. His scent is on the light wind, riding it, coming first in snatches of possibility, and then stronger, warmer, until it is a certainty that he is coming. I lie still, eyes half-closed, feigning indifference. It is a game we play sometimes, stalking each other. I am better at it than he is, once managing to startle him so badly that he leaped at my laughter and slipped into the slough. I know it rankles with him that I am better at stealth, but I do not let the slight smile inside me bow my lips. Let him think I am unaware of him right up until the moment that he leaps at me and I do not flinch. Drive him crazy.

Twice he circles me, and my ears track his movements. I hear the tasseled grass heads stroke his sleek flanks, hear the careful setting of his hooves as he moves in closer with each orbit. I smell his scent, shifting with the wind, changing with his changing emotions, as plain to me as speech. His excitement is rising as he thinks he has me unawares. I look up at the blue sky through my interlaced lashes, my face carefully impassive. His forest eyes will be shining, his cheeks flushed, his lips slightly parted as he breathes soundlessly through his mouth. I sense him beginning his third stalking circle, closing in tighter. He will be able to see me now, and I feel him pause, peer at me through the tall stalks of grass.

He halts. The wind is blowing from me to him now, and I cannot scent him, but I can feel his eyes on me, studying me to see if I am aware of him. Too much stillness will give me away as much as too much movement. I move slightly, feigning a stretch that rolls me just enough to see him through my shadowing lashes.

Yes, he is watching me. But he is frozen, a kind of awe or horror marring his face, and as I watch, his nostrils flare again, taking in my scent. Puzzlement ridges his brow. He lifts a hoof, starts to take a step forward, then replaces it. He rocks his weight, soundless in his indecision. Then he lifts the hoof again, places it, takes a soundless step.

Backward.

Away from me.

I open my eyes, heedless now of the stalking game. He meets my glance, and for an instant he pauses. He is looking at me as if I have betrayed him. I have changed, made a difference between us. I sit up, grass tangling in my hair. I do not speak. There have never been words between us. But I look at him, and I know he must be reading the same thing in my eyes. Betrayal. He has let the change in me make a difference between us. How could he, how can he draw away from me, be the first to scorn me because of my body's treachery?

I want to reach for him in some way, to lift my voice or a hand and beckon him, but I cannot. Instead I watch him as he takes another slow step backward. And another. And another. I rise, and the tall grasses between us become a waist-deep ocean rippling in waves of wind. It is a scene from a painting, the young girl and the faun, the blue sky, the yellowing grasses masking the brown of his flanks, his tanned skin, his hair the color of honey on polished mahogany. I can feel the sun touching me through my thin cotton shirt and his eyes also, puzzling out for the first time what must lie beneath the garments I have draped over my body. His forest eyes drop suddenly to my crotch. He takes another backward step.

It is all I can stand. The banked anger in my heart flares up into leaping tongues, and I launch myself at him, screaming something, to this day I don't know what, blasting him with my human voice, sending him stumbling to his knees, and then up he leaps, spry as a goat, and he is bounding away, leaping like a deer over the uneven ground as he flees me. Panicked.

Rinky leaps to his feet at the sound, bounds around me in a short circle, trying to see what has alarmed me. He spots the faun and bounds playfully after him, not interested in catching him so much as in seeing where he is running to. I scream again, after him, wordlessly, comforting myself with the pain of ripping my throat with the harsh sound. A scream like a stalking lynx's might sound, a cat cry of fury and threat. The faun reaches the edge of the meadow and the forest embraces him, many-armed mother reaching to comfort her child, to hide him in the safety of her bosom. Rinky takes a final bound, pauses on the edge of the woods, staring back at me with his round, brown wolf eyes. Aren't I coming? Don't I want to play today, to run on the rabbit trails with them, to hunt, and then to fling myself down and pant in the shade?

I stare at him, my heart hot and heavy, waiting to watch him vanish, for Rinky, too, to desert me. He stands still, puzzled, the sun striking glints off the sleek guard hairs interspersed through his black pelt. His small ears are pricked toward me, his jaw hung slightly ajar as he pants in cooling air. Go on, I mentally urge him, get lost, see if I care. Leave me. Go away. Who needs you, who needs anybody?

He shrugs. It is not a movement of his shoulders, but a wolf movement, a rippling of his scalp, a shake of his ears. And then he comes back, trotting back to me, the grasses parting before him and rippling in his wake. When he reaches me, he rears up on his hind legs, wrapping his front paws around my waist, playfully snapping at my face, catching the tip of my nose so sharply that I cry out and push him away, and then fall, and we are wrestling in the grass, his teeth closing on my thin wrist whenever I grab him, clamping down until I must release him, and then we are grabbing each other again, pinching and biting, snarling and yelping in our turns, until we are both tired and fall back, panting in the fading sun. I hug him tight, putting my face into the thick fur on the back of his neck, feeling his trueness, his loyalty like a closed circuit of warmth between us. He feels it, too, for he is still in my embrace, not struggling or trying to bite and start another tussle. Tears sting my eyes and I wipe my face against him, not in sadness but glad to know I have found one place to put my trust.

Fading sun. Yes, the day is going, not into night but into that cooler daylight that is the night hours of an Alaskan summer, a time when colors seem to have shadows of their own. This shadowed light is easy on my eyes, and it is easier to spot game, and not just because more game is moving this time of evening. This is the natural light of the hunter and the natural time for hunting. Both Rinky and I sense it, and as we head home, we move silently, moving with the woods, not against them, flowing easily between the trees, looping under low-swagged branches, moving purposefully, deadliness in our eyes and stride.

We spot the rabbit at the same time, but Rinky is the one who gives chase, springing forth soundlessly and stretching long and low as he races after it. I am unaccountably tired and my lower back aches. I continue toward home, knowing that soon Rinky will catch up with me, and his muzzle will be edged in red, and his front paws dappled with sweet blood.

Thoughts of blood bring me back to my dilemma. To be a woman and deny it, or be a woman and try to enjoy it. I can not think of the second alternative without disgust. But it is there, a possibility, and I force myself to turn it over. I think of Candy and Sissy, at home, doing whatever it is they do all day. How will they treat me, now that I am one of them? Are there secrets to share, a new camaraderie to be discovered? I imagine them teaching me, stroking bright reds onto my nails, outlining my green eyes in a darker green, and something very like anticipation shivers through me. Perhaps if I learn how to do it, it will not seem so bad; it may be a skill I can master and use as needed. Being a woman. Dabbing perfume onto pulse points. I imagine myself going back to school in September, a new sway in my walk, a new sureness in my eyes, my clothing bright and easy on my back, my hair soft around my face. Will it make me accepted, will it make anything easier? Then take what small good it will offer, and be it, since it is forced upon me.

I racket up the steps, and push open the unlatched door. I've missed dinner, again, who cares, peanut butter on half an apple later, that's plenty. For the first time that I can remember, I go seeking my sisters with no specific errand. They will turn to me and smile, and perhaps I will smile back, showing I share the secret.

I find them in the basement, their laughter leading me to them. I turn the corner from the stairs and freeze.

Kimmy is my youngest sister. Eight. Blond hair that curls at the ends of its own free will, perfect white teeth, dimples, everyone's favorite little girl. Cute. Little. Girl. Obviously destined to be a woman someday.

She stands between them, basking in their attention. Sissy is fixing curlers onto her flaxen hair, carefully rolling up the strands into fat bobbing sausages that cling to her skull. Candy is painting her toenails, a different shade of pink to each nail, Pearl Pink, Moon Pink, Opalescent Glow, Cotton Candy. Her eyelids are already striped with colors, her cheeks boast two red highlights, her lips are stained peppermint pink. She is smiling blissfully, and Candy and Sissy laugh aloud as they talk over her head about some boy at school.

"But," I say, wondering how they can make this mistake, forget that it is I who have started this miserable bleeding, I who deserve this measure of acceptance, this welcoming to womanhood.

Candy looks up. "Bet you think you got out of the dishes again, Evelyn. Well, you didn't. I left all the pots and pans for you, and Mom said it was okay, that you had to learn that skipping dinner is no way to get out of chores."

"Fuck you," I say in my coldest tone, and they gasp, and I flee up the stairs, fear balancing on a knife edge, knowing it will go hard with me if they tell my father I have said the F-word, but suspecting they are too scandalized to even be able to tattle about it.

It is as they have said, the pots and pans are sitting in the sink in cold, greasy water, and my mother looks at me knowingly as I come into the kitchen. I don't even bother to speak. I haul the pans out of the sink, refill it with pure hot water that scalds my hands as I scrub at the stubborn pans. "It's time you started doing your share of the chores around here, and I'm glad you finally seem to realize it," my mother observes as I take the last sudsy pan from the water and upend it in the drainer. I don't trust myself to speak as this first noose falls and settles around me. Tighter and tighter every day they will get, until I'm strangling in dainty femininity. I swallow, get two apples, and take a knife and the whole jar of peanut butter to the back porch. I eat in the dark, hunkered on the porch like a small animal, licking peanut butter from the edge of my thumbnail. Like myself.

Later that night I get cramps in my belly, deep aching cramps as my body gives up the semiclotted blood. I don't tell anyone, but I go to bed, calling Rinky up onto my bed and under the covers, curling my aching stomach around his warm back, putting my face into the fur on his neck so that my tears can remain secret in the shared bedroom.

And the damn booklets are wrong. Not three days, nor four, nor even five does this misery last, but seven fucking days of leaking blood. Seven fucking days. I say the forbidden word savagely to myself, feeling how appropriate it is.

# Nine

*The Farm June 1976*

"Tom, where's your dirty coveralls? Today is my wash day."

He doesn't answer. I pull my head out of the closet I am searching and turn around. He's gone. Probably in the kitchen, getting a cup of coffee. I trail him there, but he is already out the door and headed to the equipment shed. I venture out onto the splintery steps in my bare feet.

"Tom. Tom!"

He stops and turns an annoyed look on me. "What? I'm in a hurry!"

"Your dirty coveralls. Where did you put them?"

"Mom already got them. She threw them in with Dad's yesterday when she washed. See you later!"

He turns and swings off down the path again. I am left leaning out the door, staring after him. The day is already getting hot, and the sun bounces off his red baseball cap. There is a white patch on the front of it that says "Potter's Equipment." Truth in advertising. The anger inside me is like a clawed bug, growing by shredding the lining of my stomach. The screen door slams loudly behind me as I reenter the house. The kettle is boiling over on the stove, striving to whistle even as it pukes up gouts of boiling water through its spout. I turn off the flame and slam the kettle onto a cool burner.

Whoa.

Let's calm down now. You are angry, Evelyn. Would you mind telling me just why you are angry?

Because his mother washed Tom's coveralls, that's why. Just who the hell does she think she is?

His mother, that's who. Now calm down. Why is it so terrible that she washed his coveralls? Maybe she just had a load she wanted to fill up, conserve energy, save hot water, all that good stuff.

Maybe. But I doubt it. Usually it takes an Act of Congress to get Tom out of his coveralls. So what made her go after him, pry him out of them? She figures they were too dirty for him to work in, I bet. Bad image for Potter's Equipment for her poor baby to run around in dirty old work clothes, because his lousy wife doesn't look after him.

One. Two. Three. Four. Five. Six. Seven. All right. All right. Let's just look at this coolly. Make a cup of tea while you're thinking. That's right, get your hands busy, and see if we can't get your mind back to an adult stage. You, Evelyn, are offended because Mother Maurie washed Tom's coveralls. You feel this is a direct reflection on your skills as a wife, right?

Mostly.

Tsk, tsk, Evelyn. I thought you were beyond that. Weren't you telling Annie several months ago that you thought you had really made it to liberation when you could let the beds go unmade all day and not feel guilty? You and Tom both know he is a big boy now. If he feels his coveralls are too dirty to work in, he can tell you so. He can even wash them himself, or ask his mom to do it. Or do you enjoy washing coveralls, Evelyn? Do you get your kicks out of being Susie Homemaker?

No. No, it's not that at all, it's just that . . .

Enough said, Evelyn. You need a job. And I don't mean a job watching the jelly boil or canning peaches. You need an honest-to-God, eight-to-five job. You are beginning to get really weird, girl. It's time for a dose of reality.

Yeah. I guess so. And put Teddy in day care, with kids his own age, where he can play. All this bratty stuff lately is just from being the only kid around, from too much adult attention of the wrong kind. He needs to play. And I need to work. I need to find my own life again.

I drag myself out of the kitchen chair and return to the bedroom. The laundry basket is heaped. I fill a pillowcase with the overflow and head for Mother Maurie's big house. Go back, I forgot the detergent. Then out the door into the baking yard, squinting against the white light. The sun is beating down, the day is baked in hot ceramic colors, and smells of dust and growing plants. And something else.

I pause. I hold my breath, refusing to take that scent. But my arms are full, I cannot clap my hands over my ears, cannot block that faint sound.

It could be a car radio, playing down by the equipment shop. Playing faint and thin, left on in a car with the windows rolled up. But this is not country-western, "My Baby's Got the Hots for Someone Else" twang. This was the breathless panting of a hot summer day. Pipes. Panpipes. The sun is beating down on my bare head, making me dizzy, and sweat is running into my eyelashes, stinging my eyes. Another drop of perspiration slides like a sly finger down between my breasts. Reed pipes. Playing a green frog hiding on the underside of a cool green leaf by a stream, playing alder cones rattling on fallen leaves . . .

I am standing by the fence, leaning my laundry on the top strand of barbed wire. The woods are over there, beyond the chicken yard. Brush comes right down to the electric fence of the chicken yard. Behind the fence, the hills begin, almost abruptly. The hills are the source of the tiny trickling stream that feeds the pond in the chicken yard. There are small trees beyond the brush by the fence, and then larger ones on the hill itself. Tom has told me there is a larger main stream back in those hills that our little stream branches off from. A stream where one could catch small trout that flitted across the sandy bottom beneath the water. A long time ago, before we came to visit here, he told me that he and I and Teddy would go on a picnic lunch there someday, pack a big wicker basket with deviled eggs and cold pop and potato salad and cold turkey sandwiches with creamy mayonnaise and crunchy lettuce and go on out there. Tom would carry the rods over his shoulder, and Teddy would run ahead and then back to us, trying not to shout because he didn't want to scare the fish. I'd wear a white summer dress with no sleeves and my legs would be bare.

The piping seemed fainter. I cling to my images of Tom, how his white T-shirt would stick to his golden skin with perspiration, and how he would stand behind Teddy and cheer for him as he dragged the fish out of the water, but he'd be so careful not to touch the reel, not to take the triumph from him. Or so he might have been, three or four months ago. Now he'd be too busy to go fishing with his little son and wife, there were more important things to do, tractors to fix, parts to sell. The piping waxed stronger.

"Looking for Teddy, Lynnie? He went to town with Grandpa."

I jerk suddenly, dropping the pillowcase of laundry into the dust. The embroidered pillowcase with the lecherous rooster on it, I note guiltily as I hastily retrieve it. I spin to confront Steffie behind me. She is walking across the yard to me, talking from the big steps of the shaded and screened porch of the big house. After gazing at the sun-bright pond and hill, I can barely see her.

"Lynnie?" I say inanely. I am a dreamer awakened, and my dreams are sweaty, guilty ones. Am I blushing, or is it only the heat of the sun burning my cheeks?

"Sure. Lynnie. It fits in better, sounds more down home. Maurie and Steffie and Teddy and Ellie and Lynnie. Evelyn always sounded like a storybook name to me."

Steffie is trying to be friendly, I realize. She means this as a kindness, this altering of my name to fit her family. Like cutting off the stepsister's toes to stuff her foot in the glass slipper. I am still staring at her, I suddenly realize, for she feels compelled to add, "It's more countryish than Evelyn. Evelyn sounds like a city name."

"Wal, shure. Just pass me the freckles and the old straw hat and we'll both go milk cows somewhere."

We laugh, almost together. Steffie is pleased with herself, as if she has persuaded a shy child to take a cookie.

"Doing your laundry today?"

"No, just taking it for a walk." She laughs at my weak joke as if it's the line of the century.

As I cross the lawn toward her, she adds innocently, "You sure seem to like that view. What were you watching out there at night, a week or two ago?"

"I." The sun is too hot, the yard too bright. I feel I am falling into a whiteness, scalding myself. The brightness is her eyes watching me from the screened darkness of the porch, seeing through me, seeing everything. "Nothing."

"I thought maybe you were just too hot to sleep, but Mom said maybe you and Tommy had had a quarrel and I should leave you alone."

"Too hot," I repeat inanely. I imagine them as they must have been, all of them sitting on the wicker chairs on the screened porch, enjoying the cool of the evening, watching their crazy in-law wander around the yard in her nightgown, mooning out over the chicken yard. Shame washes through me, too deep for blushes, too sharp to cause pain as it cuts deeply in me. I find my tongue as I make my stumbling way up the steps. "Too hot to sleep that night," I lie feebly as the screen door wheezes closed behind me. "Probably going to be another hot night tonight."

Steffie nods wisely. "That's what I told Mom. I mean, I can't imagine you and Tommy fighting. Tommy's just too easygoing. I can't even imagine him having an argument. Even when we were little, he always gave in and gave me my own way rather than have a fight. My dad used to hate it if we kids had fights. Used to whip Tommy something fierce if he made Ellie or me cry." She muses back on this memory for a long minute, then shrugs. "Well, I gotta finish my own chores. See ya." She vanishes into the entrails of the house, leaving me to wonder if Tom and I actually have any privacy at all. How far would a conversation in the kitchen carry on a clear, warm night? From the bedroom? Do they sit out here nightly, the Potters, observing us? Am I becoming paranoid?

There is a second door into the house from the porch, and I pry it open and shoulder my way into the house. The kitchen stretches vast and white before me. There is room to slaughter an ox in there and butcher it on the table. It is that kind of a kitchen, built in the days when the kitchen was the heart of the home, a place for work and talk and growing up. The shining appliances on the back of the big counters look impotent and apologetic in this bastion of cooking from scratch. Forget Bisquick and Pillsbury here. This is a room for sacks of flour and china bowls of scrubbed white eggs, for floury hands and yeast rising. Only the cookie jar and the huge old ceramic canisters look comfortable and at home. This kitchen must have been laid out by a working woman, one who appreciated space and efficiency. I wish I could have known her, could have spent time with her here, watching the wizardry of her hands pulling loaves of bread from the oven, tucking berries into pies, rubbing butter and flour into pastry. I think we might have liked each other.

The steps in the kitchen go down to the basement laundry room. I shovel the first load into the waiting maw of the huge white washing machine. While it is comfortably sloshing and digesting, I wander back up to the kitchen.

The washing situation is an uncomfortable one for me. It is a weekly dilemma. Do I sit in the basement and watch the laundry slosh around? Do I sit in Mother Maurie's unprofaned kitchen and drink coffee while my laundry sloshes below? Or do I go back to the little house, to dust and tidy industriously, and run back every twenty minutes to check on the progress of the laundry? No matter what decision I make each week, it feels like the wrong one. Like it is not what they expect me to do, and they are having to adapt around my strange behavior. But then, what do they expect of a woman who runs around the yard at night in her nightgown, and stares longingly down at the chicken yard?

Today, I settle myself in the huge kitchen. I have a magazine from the bottom of my laundry basket, and I help myself to a cup of the strong black coffee from the shining stainless-steel dispenser that Mother Maurie keeps constantly perking. I prefer tea, but it takes a minor miracle to produce tea in that kitchen. I have only seen it done once, the first evening we arrived. When I was still a guest. Even so, the effort it took was prodigious, and Mother Maurie didn't bother to hide what a fuss it was. First, there was the hide-and-seek game of finding the few crumbly stale tea bags in the bottom of the half-crushed Lipton box in the back of the cupboard. "No one in the family drinks tea," Mother Maurie innocently explained. "So I just don't buy it. Why go to the extra expense, when it's only going to sit there for years?"

After the tea was found, then there was a search for a small saucepan to boil the water in. There is a large and gleaming copper teakettle on the big white stove, but it is for show, not for use. Its faultlessly gleaming sides have never felt the heat of the range. The tea Mother Maurie brewed for me was black and bitter, too hot to drink, and too bitter to tame with milk. But I drank it and thanked her for it.

I drink the coffee nowadays, black, because that's how they all drink it, there is no small pitcher of milk or cream in the fridge, no handy sugar bowl set out for those who differ in their tastes. There is only acid black coffee in sturdy white china mugs. Or Steffie's diet pop, Western Family Orange, the local store's cheapest brand. She drinks it in tall glasses with much ice. She offered me one once, but I said no thank you. Now I don't even think about sampling it. What if she counted her cans and found one missing? Would she ask who had drunk it? I don't want to even imagine such an encounter.

I sit at the big kitchen table with a mug of coffee and

a *Woman's Day* magazine, an old one from somewhere, a maverick issue that has wandered into the magazine rack in the little house. I sink into the magazine and the silence as if it were a hot bathtub. The big house is silent. If Ellie and Steffie are doing anything, it is in the mysterious upper reaches of the house, and silent. Teddy has gone off to town with Grandma and Grandpa. I have no idea where Tom is. I shut out the wondering, refuse to let it bother me. This afternoon belongs to me now. I can go home and scrub walls, or furtively read and laze about. I am soon deep into an article about what the ERA can mean to me. I hear the screen door slam and then the patter of small feet across the linoleum.

"Look at me! I'm a cowboy!"

I turn to take in this marvel. Sure enough, my Teddy is a cowboy, from boots to hat, complete with fringed tie-on chaps over his jeans and a fringe-sleeved brown shirt, a red-and-blue bandanna at his throat, and shining six-guns in plastic holsters. His face glows with joy and summer heat.

I take a deep breath, review all my resolutions about getting along. "You certainly are," I agree with false enthusiasm. "Except for those guns, of course. Real cowboys hardly ever needed guns. That's only on those phony television cowboys."

"Yeah, they did," he asserts, small hands aggressively fastening on the white plastic butts of his guns. "For shooting bad guys and snakes and stuff. Pow, pow!" He does a television quick draw and executes me on the spot.

My hands are quicker than my mouth. They grab his wrists and point the gun mouths at the ceiling. "Don't ever point a gun at Mommy, not even a toy one." I am making every effort to keep my voice level, but the words still come out like a brutal accusation. I try to soften it. "It's bad manners to point a gun at someone."

"Let go!" He wrests free of me, takes a step away, and once more levels his guns at me. "Pow! You're dead for that!"

"Teddy! That's enough. You're being silly. You know what Mommy and Daddy have said about guns. When you are big enough, you will have a real rifle, and learn to hunt. But not toy guns. Toy guns teach you bad shooting habits. Then, when you get a real gun, you have to unlearn all the bad habits before you can use it. Toy guns make you act like guns are toys. Why don't you take those silly things off?"

Teddy's jaw juts out stubbornly. "NO! They're mine. And Daddy doesn't care if I have them. He was there when Grandpa bought them for me."

I bite down firmly on my tongue. What is real here, what is important, what will we all remember years from now about this? I go searching for perspective and don't find it. A simpler thing. How can I take the toy guns from Teddy with as little hurt to Teddy as possible? Heavy footsteps coming up the porch and into the kitchen. The screen door wheezes shut, and Grandpa sets two bags of groceries down on the table.

"Looks like the shoot-out at the OK Corral in here!" It is Tom's dad, addressing me, sensing that something is wrong, why am I kneeling on the floor staring at Teddy, how is he going to shield his grandson from my temperamental foolishness? Tom is behind him. He sets down two more brown paper sacks of groceries and immediately pours himself a cup of coffee. I stare at him, but he shakes out the newspaper and settles himself at the table with his coffee, a neutral in this power struggle. Does he really think he can abstain? I will change his mind about that. I deliberately ignore his father.

"Tom, were you the one who gave Teddy toy guns? After we had agreed they were a bad idea?"

He looks up innocently, wearily, preoccupied. I am not fooled. "What? Oh, yeah, well, by the time I found out about them, Dad had already given them to Teddy. I didn't want to have him screaming his head off all the way home, and Dad didn't know we'd decided against toy guns. I guess just a couple won't hurt him. He'll grow out of them soon enough."

There. All explained. He tries to get back to his paper. But I am without mercy or restraint. So let it be public then, let his father listen and watch. Let him see what problems he makes when he assumes Teddy is his to do with as he pleases.

"Tom, we talked about this a lot. I'm surprised you can just let it go. Remember you . . ."

"Why can't the little guy have a couple of toy guns? He can't hurt anything with them." Tom's father to the rescue. Why are you nagging my son, you unreasonable wench? You should be smiling and pleased that I have seen fit to favor your child with gifts.

I take a deep breath, turn to this flank attack. "I know he can't hurt anything with those guns. But they teach him bad habits, give him wrong ideas about guns. That's how gun accidents happen, kids point real guns at each other, pull the trigger and say bang. And they're so surprised when someone really dies. Toy guns make a kid think he can point a gun at something and shoot it and nothing happens. It makes killing a game. When Teddy is old enough to have a real gun, he will have to unlearn a lot of bad habits about how to carry a gun and treat it and . . ."

"My kids always had toy guns. Never hurt them any. I mean, you ain't a secret murderer, are you, Tommy?"

Tom grins good-naturedly at this simple country jest as he reads his paper. He makes no comment. Let the old man straighten Evelyn out. He'll tell it like it is.

"I just don't want Teddy to think . . ."

"I don't think kids should have real guns anyway. Not until they're at least eighteen or so. They don't know how to handle them, and they might hurt someone." Steffie has materialized, to favor us with this gem of wisdom.

"They don't know how to handle guns because they haven't been around them, except for toy ones that don't do anything. I grew up around guns, Steffie. There was always a loaded one by the front door. I had my first gun, a twenty-two, when I was about ten. My dad taught me how to use it and how to care for it, and his job was a lot easier because I had never had any toy guns. I . . ."

"You mean you actually killed things with it?" Steffie is aghast. Her mental images flicker on the kitchen wall. There I am, at eleven, my arms red to the elbows with the gore of countless rabbits and dicky birds, slain for no more reason than to satisfy my lusts for carnage.

"Killing is what a gun is for, Steffie," I point out gently, easing her into that new idea. "I kept pests out of Mom's garden, and kept squirrels from stealing the insulation out of the attic. Later I used it to take biological specimens for a high-school project. I think . . ."

"I think that's sick!" Steffie is staring at me. "Imagine a little girl out killing animals for fun. At least toy guns . . ."

Grandpa Potter cuts in. "Well, Teddy is your child, Evelyn. If that's how you feel, that's it. I can't say I understand it. But you got your rights. You and Tom say no toy guns, then that's it. I'm not the kind to interfere. But you take those six-guns away from him, not me. I don't want to break the little guy's heart over something I can't even understand myself." His kindly voice is grieved over my heartlessness. "Poor kid," he adds.

There's the indictment, you rock, you stone, you heartless mother, you! I glance around for Teddy, but the object of this discussion has long since made a clean getaway. I am aware that they have all probably already noticed this and are secretly amused by it. Shall I pursue him, seize him and throw him to the ground, strip him of his cowboy guns in the dust of the front yard while hostile eyes stare at me covertly from the shelter of the kitchen windows? Shall I track him down with my killer instincts even as I once tracked small, defenseless rodents? They are watching me, waiting for me to do this awful thing to my son, so that he can run crying to them for comfort. No matter what I do, they will win.

I am saved. The washer buzzes that it is done. I beat a hasty retreat to the laundry room to shovel wet wash into the dryer, to heap more into the washer and start the sloshing, humming machines. I am deliberately slow, taking twice as long as needed to do this simple thing. When I surface, the kitchen is empty except for an abandoned newspaper, a cigarette sending up a futile smoke signal from an ashtray.

The anger inside me is alive, a separate growling

thing inside me. It is too strong a creature to be part of the weak thing I have become. I myself am a shadow, powerless as a dream to reshape the events that are forming around me. Only my anger has any strength, roaring its defiance from the poor citadel of my body, refusing to be conquered or placated. It would like to take Tom and shake him, shake him, shake him. Where was he when I needed support, needed reinforcement as a parent and an adult in this household? He was over at the kitchen table, being a child, a son, refusing to get involved in someone else's scolding. And I am angry at Steffie, and angry at Tom's father. But my anger also snarls at myself, menacing me, wishing it could destroy me and find a fitter vessel. I have become so impotent. Not once did I yell or insist. I am always so reasonable, so open to logic, so malleable, so humble. I sicken myself.

When Teddy came in, I should have simply and calmly removed the guns from him, and then explained. He is the child, I am the mother. And Tom is the father, but not today. No, today he is being Potter's boy Tommy. I have heard him called that, in the drugstore, the hardware store. When I hand them a check, they frown over it for a moment, and then say, "Oh, you must be married to Potter's boy Tommy." And I must bow my head and nod, even when I want to scream out that dammit, I didn't marry Potter's boy Tommy, didn't even know he existed for most of our marriage. And now that I do, I don't even like him.

I wonder what it would take to make Tom Potter come back to me, be a man to me again. I wonder what it would take to find my Teddy again, my little satellite who is now flung out free of my gravity and is finding others to orbit. I wonder what I have left, what holds me here. And the whole picture comes to me. We are a solar system blown apart and shattered. I no longer orbit Tom, Teddy no longers spins around my life. The desolation that engulfs me is suddenly, horribly familiar. I slam my mind shut on it.

Forget it. Forget all of it, don't think about it, it will probably straighten itself out. The sound of the machines is giving me a headache. Well, let them slosh and tumble on their own. They weren't going anywhere with my laundry. I stepped out of the cool cavern of the kitchen onto the big shaded porch. Gently I shut the screen door and the wooden door beside it, closing in the sounds of my work doing itself. I step out in the harsh brightness of the backyard. This part of the yard is all sunshine and dust, tire tracks and parked pickups ticking in the sunshine, sunlight glinting off blue paint. Around the front of the house is the lawn and flower beds and three big shade trees. But no one ever lazes there, lying on prickly grass or a saggy lawn chair and reading cheap novels. That part of the yard is for show, for the customers driving past on their way to the dealership and equipment yard. Stay away from there, lest you spoil the perfect picture.

I strike out across the dusty backyard, cutting through the heavy waves of heat like a little boat battling a storm. I walk through the dusky, musky interior of the barn and out into the cow pasture. Across the pasture, watching my feet and the languid cows for any possible hazards. They are Angus cows, black blocky things living placid lives that end in plastic wrap and roasting pans. They scarcely notice me at all. Across the wide pasture and through the barbed strands. I follow the fence of the chicken yard now with the electric wire along the top of it. It is snapping in several places, singeing grasses that have dared to grow too tall and breach its keep. The chickens are scratching in the sun or dust bathing, the ducks are playing on the pond, diving and flapping to get the cool water down through their feathers to their bodies. They look up, grow silent at the sight of a human outside their pen, on the wild side of their fence. But then they return to their play and I turn my back on them and look out across the useless lands.

The useless lands. The land too marshy for pasture or hay, land that would give foot rot, would drown seedlings, land with a wet layer of soil and bog plant and beneath it only gravelly, sandy soil. Useless land, left wild in the desert of orderliness that the valley is becoming. And beyond the useless land is no-man's-land, the land that belongs to no one and to everyone, the "govamint" land. Beyond the mushy stretch of useless land rises the rolling hills covered with birch and cottonwood, willow and alder, a scattering of madrona trees with their trunks of muted green and red. Down from those hills comes the stream, even across the useless lands I can hear the stream, and the wind blowing across the high tops of the trees like a lazy piper breathing across his pipes.

A path crosses the useless land. I knew there would be one. I follow it carefully, carefully giving no thought to who or what made it. Sometimes it dips beneath stretches of shallow water standing on top of mud and mush. There I parallel it, leaping from tuft to tuft of tall marsh grass, getting wet no higher than my ankles. Who cares if my sneakers are soggy? It cools my feet.

Gradually the path becomes drier, and I know the land is rising beneath me. At one moment I am walking on the useless land; the next I stand beneath the first shelter of the reaching trees, listening to the whispering stream and the call of pipes that are no longer to be denied.

I am not running away from anyone. Not from dirty dishes or laundry, not from an extended family or its extended quarrels. I am not running from anything at all. I am running to. I am running to the forest, to the place where loneliness has never been able to reach. I refuse to think of whether or not Pan is real, if there is a living creature blowing that music, if I am retreating from reality, if I am no longer even close to sane. The woods close behind me, and the pipes light the way.

The smell of warm earth rises around me, the years drop away. Here are plants more familiar to me than the changing faces of my parents. Here is dogwood and fireweed, wild rose and watercress, and dark violets twining through the grass. They welcome me, bowing before me and whispering in my wake. I part them with my hands and pass between them, and the friendly denizens of this place make a way for me. The tightness of my vigilance slips away. I am among friends, and my muscles move easily. I am lithe and spry and nimble as I move through the forest. I am a child again.

A young birch tugs timidly at my hair. I stop beside it, resting my palm on the smooth papery roundness of its trunk, taking its powdery whiteness onto my fingers. I can feel the life flowing through its sappy capillaries. We share a moment, quietly, two living beings who need to take nothing from each other. Then I gently disentangle myself and go on.

There is no hurry. I have lost my sense of time, left behind all clocks with their Veg-O-Matic approach to time. I would not let this day be diced and minced to flavorless, unidentifiable bits, to half an hour of walking, to three minutes of touching a tree. This time was a whole thing, to be savored as such.

There is no slap of branches against denim, no thump of shoe on leaf mold. I move as the hunting vixens do, warily following the sound and scent of my prey. Soon I feel the cooler flow of air on my face, see the tall reeds rise before me and walk the hard mud bank of the stream. I follow it upstream, moving toward its source, knowing soon I will come to a cleared bank, a place carpeted in deep moss, free of stones and slimy things, a place prepared for a meeting. I smell Pan's rich scent, breathing it in through my open mouth, tasting his flavor on the air. And I come to him.

# Ten

*Fairbanks The Late Sixties*

My childhood telescopes behind me. I think that was the last day of it, the day Pan left me bleeding in the grass and I picked myself up and went forward without him. I never saw him again in the woods. I tried to cut him out of my life, to tell myself that he had never existed. It was an angry denial, an effort to match him rejection for rejection. But despite my denials and his disappearance from my life, he wouldn't quite go away. He never left me alone, the goat-footed one. He was always there, just at the edges, hidden, almost completely hidden, but keeping everything from fitting together. Like a tiny piece of gravel caught under new linoleum, like a few forgotten flakes of breakfast cereal trapped under dinner's linen tablecloth and crystal wineglasses, like a single dead fly under the new wallpaper, keeping everything from lying flat and smooth. A little imperfection in my makeup, a little part that would never admit to reality. Like the invisible bits of something on your smooth percale sheets that bite into your flesh at night, that will not be brushed out of your bed, but only find a new spot to dig into you, under your hip, at the point of your shoulder. Pan was always there. He wouldn't let me grow up, and he wouldn't let me become totally real.

I had a suspicion, a secret fear.

He was keeping me for himself.

I was always afraid someone else would find out. How could I become a real adult, when my invisible playmate haunted me, taunted me, demanded, "Real or pretend? Real or pretend?" of every thought I had, of every accomplishment I achieved? He was the eye at the bottom left-hand corner of the night window, the shadow glimpsed behind me in a mirror, the single cloven hoofprint in the driveway the morning after the heavy rain, the tiny fragment of blue eggshell on the floor by my nightstand. Never enough to be real, but always too much to ignore.

That fall I entered high school. It was a whole new game. My sisters had preceded me through Monroe High School, setting a family standard I could not maintain. It wasn't the academics. I'd always succeeded there. Socially. They'd been their class presidents, the winners of elocution contests, editor of the school newspaper, the class sweetheart. It was an act I could not follow. All the teachers wondered what was wrong with me, why I wasn't like my sisters. They usually managed to pity and dislike me at the same time.

There were other things, too. Dances. Dating. Not for me, but for the other girls around me. Oh, I went to the dances, trailing after my sisters like a bewildered caboose. I stood against the wall and watched the people dance. If boys looked at me, they either smirked, or didn't see me. It didn't really hurt, because I didn't really expect anything else. But as time passed, and I went from freshman to sophomore, and the sneering grew more open, I knew I had to change if I was to survive. I had to find a way to belong, but I didn't know how to go about it. I expected there would be a price tag to the change, but I wasn't sure what it would be.

The price tag was to be my past.

First there came a flood, right at the end of summer. The Chena and the Tanana rivers rose, and their brown waters came flowing down the lane and spread and washed through my forest, drowning our garden, filling the basement full and barely sparing the house itself. My family sought out the high ground, spent days at the hill campus of the University of Alaska. Each day I could walk to the edge of the hill and look down at the flooded lands, watching it slowly, slowly drain away again. The flood left a coating of mud on the forest, a bathtub ring around the bases of the trees, a brown gritty residue on the low-growing plants. There was no autumn harvest of berries that year. I walked again through my forest, but it was a place dirtied and foreign, the moss hidden under a coating of mud, the low-growing bushes scummed and gritty. I promised myself the winter would purify the forest, that the melting snows of spring would bring its pristine green back.

But before that, fall came. And with it school, a new school. Public school, because the flood had left our family broke and Candy was already in college and Sissy was starting at the University of Alaska that year. For me, it was a reprieve in the form of Austin E. Lathrop High School. A place where no one knew me, or my sisters. A place where I could pretend to be someone else, where I could start fresh, as no one's younger sister.

I hardened my heart, and I did. I was tough. No girl in my family had ever been tough before, but I was. I had the clothes to fit the part, the worn jeans and boy's shirts, the battered jackets. I had the vocabulary. All it took was nerve, and somehow I found it. I kept my grades, the A's and B's that baffled my teachers, a secret from my new friends. I horrified the other girls. But boys began to look at me. I was the girl who couldn't be shocked, who knew more dirty jokes than they did, who wasn't afraid to take their dares. I was wild and tough and free.

I told myself that Pan never existed, never had been at all. I pretended him away, fiercely, excusing my betrayal on the grounds that he had left me first. I convinced myself that I believed he'd been pretend. But I dreaded the return of spring, when the forest would call me again.

But I was saved from that.

The tent caterpillars came, denuding the forest as fast as the new leaves came out. It became a bare place that the sunlight blared into unchecked by any softly flickering canopy of leaves. Worse, the insects left long dangling nets of their silken-sticky stuff ghosting from the trees, and as I walked my paths, it tangled in my hair, and the fat, wriggling caterpillars themselves fell onto my head and shoulders. It was a summer without green, and if I thought about it, I felt sick and stripped as the trees themselves. I was like an addict going through a forced withdrawal, deprived of my forest. Whenever I had to think about it, I insisted to myself that it would come back, that my woods would be as green and deep and cool as ever, that the slough would run silver and brown and the blue sky would once more be reflected in its waters.

But in the meantime, I filled my summer with motorcycles, and the dusty boys who came with them. Boys who liked a girl who wasn't afraid to get dirty riding the back trails, who didn't care if her hair tangled in the wind. My mother was so relieved to see me finally socializing that she gave me freer rein than ever my sisters had enjoyed. I took the bit in my teeth and ran. I ran fast and hard and wild, sampling beer, learning to drive a motorcycle, daring to kiss a boy.

And if, at night, in my bed, I looked back over my day and knew, somehow, that none of it had been as wonderful as I'd tried to pretend it was—if I knew the beer had tasted sour, the motorcycle been no more than a noisy, smelly machine, only as powerful as its engineering could make it, and the boy only a boy and no more than that—if I lay alone in my bed, and suspected that somehow I had traded my inheritance for a bowl of pottage, then I also knew in those long nights of Fairbanks's midnight sun shining in my window that no matter how fast or hard or wild I ran, I would never outrun the satyr. He'd drawn the circle that took me in, and he no longer needed to run to catch up with me. No direction I could take would ever lead me away from him. If on those nights I was hungry for more than peanut butter and apples and celery and raisins stolen from the night kitchen, if I was colder than the blankets and Rinky could warm away, if I felt more alone than the moon drowning in the night's blue sky, then I would promise myself that the tent caterpillars would be gone next summer. I promised myself the forest and the sky and the slough, and long days to enjoy them, days free of the complicated emotional negotiations that boys entailed, hours when I could be wild and free instead of striking the poses that others believed were true wildness, true freedom. Sometimes, on the edge of sleep, when I did not sit up in bed and look out the window for fear someone would be there, sometimes, hovering on the edge of consciousness, I promised myself the forest and the faun.

But it wasn't to be, not ever again.

The oil pipeline came and drained my Alaska away. The school became crowded, my Latin class was held on a stairway, yellow Alyeska pickup trucks appeared at every stoplight, the city tried to clear the winos and whores off Second Avenue. I didn't care about any of that. But then property values went up, and civilization came hunting me down, rolling over the woods and flattening them, sucking the sloughs dry. First came the surveyors, cutting perfectly straight lines through my forest, leaving behind a spoor of stakes and pink plastic ribbon. Then came the tractors, pushing over the trees into huge burn piles, scraping the topsoil carelessly aside to bare the sandy ice cream of permafrost beneath. The slough got filled with gravel. They cut the remaining scar up into small rectangles, and put up mobile homes, one on each. The trailer houses had snotty-nosed kids in brown corduroy pants who pedaled trikes in their front yards. They had scrawny yellow-patched lawns and parked snowmobiles in front of their Sears metal garden sheds. Many of the trailers sank and settled unevenly as the permafrost beneath them melted and gave way to their warmth. At first I took that as a positive sign. But the new people just jacked them up to level again, stuck a few more concrete blocks under them, and stayed. They never went away and the woods never came back. Everything that had been mine went away and never came back. The faun should have gone, too.

But he didn't. And I couldn't leave childhood with him still standing there.

I got older. Without the forest, I had no choice. I dated, I tried to be real. But it seemed to take me so much longer to grow up than it did for anyone else. As wild as I was, as tough as I was, I was still fifteen before I knew what thirteen-year-olds had known for years, I was seventeen before I felt like I was sixteen. But I tried. I went out with the boys and made out in back seats. But I never dared to go too far, never dared to let them touch the small naked breasts I shielded behind polyester foam padding and tricot-lined bras. Afraid that if they touched them, they'd see, they'd know that the faun wasn't letting me grow up and away from him. Afraid they'd know I wasn't real, not like they were, not truly growing into adulthood. Afraid my own breasts would betray me, would let those boys know that I already belonged to the faun.

My senior year. I only dated dumb boys. I was a four-point student, but I never went out with anyone who had better than a D average. I dated the bad boys, the ones who got picked up for shoplifting, for drunkenness, for breaking curfew, for vandalism. I learned how to hot-wire a car, how to slip a door latch, how to doctor an ID card. But I never got caught, I never got in trouble, I was never even suspected. I was invisible. I was always there, at the edges of their crowd, with their girls but not among them, because I intimidated their girls by not caring what they thought of me. I watched those bad boys go through their madnesses, their drunks, their dares, their sudden furies when they turned on one another, the punch-outs that ended in split lips and bloody noses and little more, that ended again with the bad boys soberly shaking hands, saying, "Hey, we were drunk, were angry, we didn't mean it, friends like us, ain't nothing going to come between us." I watched it all from the sidelines, not like a scientist watches a lab rat, but like a child peering down through the railings of a staircase to where the adults are drinking cocktails and conversing amiably. I watched from the borders, knowing that no matter how foolish it all seemed, they were all taking steps, growing up, going on a journey to adulthood. And I couldn't follow.

I rode on the backs of their motorcycles, hid from the cops in the cold shadows of the concrete supports under University Bridge. I went to the parties in the basements and garages, watched them drink and blow dope and neck and throw up in the snow, fight and cry. I watched what I could not do. I watched them growing up.

One night I climbed the FAA light tower at the end of Davis Road with David, him so drunk I thought he'd slip off the icy rungs and fall into the cold blackness that surrounded us. At the top he made a valiant effort to pee his initials into the pristine white snow so far below us, trying to make a D.P. bigger than any he'd ever peed before. But he was too drunk and his instrument wavered and the great experiment failed. In zipping up, he caught his foreskin in the icy teeth of his zipper, and I had to get it loose for him as he swore and yelped. It was twenty below in January and late at night and we were in a restricted area, one they took seriously, on top of the FAA marker tower with its flashing beacon, and that was the first time I'd ever touched a man's penis, and him too drunk and cold and sore to care. I was seventeen and he was sixteen, and that should be some kind of coming-of-age story, the beginning of my growing up.

But it wasn't.

See the pattern?

They grew up and passed me, and I stayed where I was. The tracks of cloven hooves still scored and crossed the paths of my long walks, the boys in my dreams had nubbins of horns and eyes the color of forests. If I left a book outside beneath a tree, the bookmark would be gone, and a fragrant white wood anemone would have taken its place. In mornings when I brought the family laundry in from the line where it had swung all night, my shirts would smell of more than clean night wind. A rich smell, one part forest to one part goat-footed one. I wore my shirts marked with his smell, branded as his territory.

And I didn't grow up. Not then, not later. Not when

my older siblings moved out, went on to college and dorms and marriages. Not when I graduated from high school and my parents gave me new luggage for a gift, not in fall when they packed me up and sent me off to Washington in September. Not when I sat through university classes, studying the botany and biology in their textbooks, getting A's again, but knowing that the books would never know the plants as I did. Not when I met Tom, not when we began dating. Not even when the telegram came to my dorm late one night, the floor monitor knocking on my suite door, handing me the ominous yellow envelope that told me both my parents had been killed in an auto accident just hours ago. "Come home stop" the telegram said.

I didn't go. Home wasn't there. Home was gone, was buried under tract houses and a new motel on Davis Road. The meat is not the moose, and I owed nothing to the bodies my parents had once lived in. I wasn't going to the moon for my father, and I wasn't being a botanist for my mother anymore. No center to hold, the merry-go-round gone crazy, pink horses and blue hippos flung out to the far corners of the earth. I went spinning off, free, homeless, heartless.

It flung me straight into Tom.

I had been seeing him, in a casual way, for nearly a year, off again, on again, no serious dates, no formal dances or dinners with wine. Only coffee between classes, a casual meeting in line for a movie, a shared ride into downtown Seattle. I did not phone him up and wail my loss to him. I still don't know how he came to hear of it. My suitemates knew, as they sooner or later knew, by osmosis or pheromones, almost all my private business. I suppose one of them could have called him. But the next afternoon he came to me, with a single yellow rose, and we cut all our classes and went to the zoo, walking silently among the animal displays, saying nothing, not even touching.

And that night we made love.

He had a sagging sofa bed in a tiny efficiency apartment. There was an empty milk carton on his kitchen table, and dishes in the sink. The braided rug by the bed was coming undone. The bathroom window had no curtain, only a towel thumbtacked over it. The pillowcase smelled like his aftershave. These are the things I would remember for years. It would take an effort for me to recall that peculiar newness, the stretched sensation of Tom inside me, opening that unused part of my body. An elusive memory, as difficult to remember as the scent of a particular flower. I would never remember how we got into doing it, only that I was grateful for his experience and patience. Grateful. And afterward, after he had held me and kissed me, and after we had gotten dressed, I washed his dishes for him.

From my father's house to Tom's. Hiding from myself as much as from the faun. Frantically clinging to the pretenses of normality.

This is how Tom was then. There was no need of words, we touched without touching. We drifted together painlessly, like two leaves caught in an eddy of a stream. I stayed on at the university, worked summers in the library, lived off my scholarship in winter. Tom came back in September, and he came back to me as much as he came back to school. He told me he loved me. It took a long time before I believed it, but even before I thought it was true, I was grateful for the words. Tom was beyond anything I had ever aspired to having; he was handsome, intelligent, and mannered. He got along well with everyone, drew friendships as a magnet draws pins. He became my new center.

We continued to sleep together, and it went better than I had ever expected it could. He made no disparaging comments on my underdeveloped body, but said he loved my small feet, my long hair, my green eyes. He was uninhibited in the use of our bodies, and soon I was, too. Tom was like coming home to a strange place, like every other cliché of rightness. I met his family briefly at one spring break, and Steffie confided to me that I was the first girl in years that he had brought home to meet his parents. They seemed relieved to meet me, and were very kind, if a little stiff.

At the end of his senior year, I dropped out of college. We got married. We moved to Alaska, and I don't remember whose idea that was. Only that it seemed right, and we were happy. We both worked and bought the lot with the little run-down cabin, and Teddy was born and I had everything, everything, the man, the baby, the dog, the truck, the land, everything. I refused to see cloven tracks by the pond, I refused to hear any more than the wind in the trees. My life was good, and I was content. How rare it is, to be happy and to know I am happy, at the very same moment.

We talked to his family on the phone, I sent them long detailed letters, baby pictures of Teddy, pictures of the cabin, the garden, Tom's first moose. They seemed happy for Tom's happiness, and although we could not accept their frequent invitations to visit, I would have sworn I had the ideal in-laws. Of my family, I heard little and saw even less. They were there, in Fairbanks, but the circles of their lives did not intersect with mine. I knew vaguely that they were well, and that was enough. I bore them no ill will, nor had any pressing desire to reconnect with any of them. They had their lives and I had mine, and mine was separate and different, as I had always been separate and different. I bore no one any malice.

There were too many good times to separate them. Dip-fishing for salmon at Chitna, where there are ghosts painted on the outsides of the buildings and the wind never stops blowing. Teaching Tom the pathways of my forest, the red fox that came boldly into the kitchen and stole the pound of bacon right off the table, Tom adjusting the truck's carburetor while I held the flashlight, walking together down our snowbound trail in the darkness, on our way down to the road to check for Christmas mail inside our big mailbox. I had it all.

I believed it was real, our life together, our baby, our home. But even as I believed, it was too good to be true. It was like the intermission in a long movie, like the break between SAT tests. My life with Tom was a thing outside my real life, a parenthetical comment in the sentence of my days. It could not join firmly to my childhood. It was a thing grafted on, a wish briefly granted.

I know that in the instant that I step into Pan's

clearing. As his eyes swing to meet mine, I draw breath again, and my interrupted life begins again. It is as if Tom and the baby had never been, as if college were a bad dream, as if my cabin were a fairy tale, too pretty to keep. This is not an excuse, nor even an explanation. It is only what happened.

# Eleven

*The Forest June 1976*

It is a little open place in the forest, and the stream runs through it like a bright string through an enameled bead. It is perfect, as such places never are, and always are. The bed of the stream is sandy, and it is edged with reeds. The trees stand back from the stream, so the sunlight wanders freely through their foliage, and its touch turns the stream to silver too brilliant to behold. The banks are wide and deeply mossed, greenery thicker than the finest carpet, and decorated with last year's leaves. A coolness rises from the stream to mingle with the heat of the relentless sun, mellowing and tuning it. Light cannot be harsh here, cannot burn and brown these plants. Summer does not lean on this place, but caresses it. And on the bank is the faun.

These are his colors: forest green and nut brown, and his skin all shades of polished wood. These are his scents: wisteria and musk, moss and berry, leaf and beast, and warmth rising like steam rises from the earthen floor of the forest when the morning sun warms it. I can feel him without touching him, his skin warm and smooth, the hair of his head fine and soft, the sleekness of his flanks, the smooth ridges of his hooves. He is goat and human, boy and man. His eyes are young, his cheeks ruddy above his close-cropped beard and mustache. There is a tracery of lines at the corners of his eyes, the wisdom of a man in his eyes, but it is balanced by the sweet curve of his lips, the agility of his dancing fingers. He is playing his pipes as he reclines by the stream, and the music is a tune I know well though I have never heard it before. It is Pan and Evelyn and the Forest, melded into a single melody. His eyes come up to touch mine, and the Panic I feel has nothing to do with fear.

I come to him like a doe comes to water, like a wolf to blood, like a raven to carrion. I am aware of his scent, and it is more than a scent, and I am more than aware of it. It is what I breathe instead of air, and it nourishes me, making strong what had grown weak, drowning civilization's touch upon me. I come to him, and as I do, he breathes more gently upon the pipes, passes the melody back to the stream and the gentle flutter of the leaves until they hold it and he lowers the pipes from his lips.

I stand, looking down on him. I don't want him to speak to me, and he doesn't. I don't want talk from him, I want only his healing presence, his reality that so quickly seals me off from the splintered stabbing world I've been living in. We are complete and a unity, we two. Our eyes have not lost their grip on each other, but to that look he adds a smile, a gentle baring of teeth. His teeth are whiter than a man's, and the canines are a shade longer and more pointed.

I seat myself on the bank beside him, and with the change in my position, I feel a sudden awkwardness. I shouldn't be here, something whispers to me, some harbinger of danger that I cannot pinpoint vibrates within me. My mouth goes suddenly dry, and I need to do something to distract myself. "Hello," I say, and curse myself as my human voice, so thin and sharp, seems to wither the ethereal life spirit of the glade.

"Hello," he replies, and the richness of his voice balances my utterance, brings it into harmony, makes me belong here. I suddenly want to split open like a ripe seed pod and scatter my thoughts before him, tell him all my griefs and fears, all the double-edged angers that cut me more deeply than anyone else. As I look at him, my throat closes and my eyes suddenly brim with tears,

making his image waver before me. I try to speak, but
only my tears spill out, running down my face, and I
can't get any air, I can't breathe, I am crying as very
small children do when seriously hurt and scared,
without sound, their faces screwed up so tightly that
only tears can escape them.

He sits beside me and lets me cry. He does not say,
"There, there, don't cry," nor does he say, "It's all right,
go ahead and cry, get it out of your system." Instead, he
lets me cry, watching me unabashedly as I weep, and
when my throat is sore and my head is pounding, he
goes to the stream and wets his hands and comes back
and wipes them over my hot face. The cool water soothes
my eyes, washes the stinging salt from my skin. Again,
he makes a trip to the stream and again returns, his
hands wet, and traces his fingers gently over the marks
of my sorrow, washing it away. Then he sits down beside
me again, his arm going around me as easily as my head
comes to rest on his sun-warmed shoulder. "I've got
you," he tells me, and those are the most comforting
words I have ever heard. His skin is warm against
my cheek and I close my eyes to feel it better. I am
suddenly as weary as if I have made a lifetime's journey
to finally reach this place and this moment. I go limp
against him as his fingers trace the musculature of my
back and neck. I feel him shift, turning to support my
weight. His beard tangles briefly against my hair, I feel
the press of his lips on the top of my head, a chaste and
comforting kiss. He answers the question that is a dozen
years old.

"I didn't know," he says softly, and I sense he has
waited as long to say these words as I have waited to hear
them. "I had not yet remembered female and male at
that time. The scent of you that day was like a trumpet
shouting to my senses. The realization that you were
female and I was male, that we were . . . could
be . . . the halves of a whole." He stops speaking, and
I can almost sense the swirling confusion he must have
felt on that summer day so long ago. "I panicked," he
says softly, and chuckles, holding me closer against him
as he does. "I ran away. And by the time my senses were

cleared, you were gone. And I did not know, then, how to draw you back. I had not remembered that yet. I watched you and I yearned, but I did not know how to bring you to me. And I do not think you wanted to come to me. Not then. You were no more ready than I was. I had to wait, to find patience as the knowing came slowly to me. How I struggled to remember. But when I did, I came seeking you. And found you had taken another."

He stops speaking, and in that pause I sense an abyss of despair. No words come to me. Instead, I have a suddenly skewed perception of my life with Tom. My years of happiness with him have been a stolen thing, a selfish indulgence on my part. I had always known my true place, but had willingly turned aside from it, denied it. How much pain had I brought the faun? How great had been the betrayal? But I had not known! The protest rises in me like a shout, is only stifled by his arm around me tightening slightly. I lift one of my hands to cover his, feel the knuckles, the tendons, the joints of his fingers, the reality of the hand that grips me. My fingers are cold against the warmth of his hand. I slip them inside the protection of his hand, his fingers wrap around mine in understanding.

"For a while," his voice comes huskily, "I tried to find another. I thought, if there is one like you, then there must be others. I would seek them out. So I looked. I waited and I wandered. I watched girls picnicking in meadows, watched young women picking wild berries, watched them gardening as I stood in the edges of the forest. But they were all wrong, and even those who were almost right, I could not make aware of me. They were not—attuned. They could not, or would not, perceive me.

"Eventually, I gave up. I began to follow you again. I knew you were the only one, then. If I could not have you right away, then the only thing I could do was— wait."

He puts a depth into that word that I have never perceived before. Wait. He utters it as if it were a life sentence, makes waiting a thing to be done to the exclusion of all else. It makes my breath falter, to glimpse his life from that perspective. How could it be, I wonder, to center one's life around someone and await his pleasure, to abide in the sole hope of being noticed, of being remembered, especially when that person has set you aside as a thing outgrown, unreal, unnecessary? How would it be, I wonder, and then I know, in a single word. Tom. Has he not been my sun, and I the farthest and coldest of the planets trapped in his pull? The pang of pain that rings in me surprises me with its sharpness. I shiver and open my eyes, pull myself upright. The faun releases me instantly. Coolness flows in to touch me where I have been warm against him.

The brightness of the day surprises me. It has always been a dreaming thing, this holding and comforting and loving, a thing I could pretend to myself in the darkness to counterbalance the harshness of my days. I curl into my pillow, clutching it to my chest, clinging to it as I can no longer cling to Tom. I cannot believe in such tenderness by daylight. I glance over at the faun, but he is looking at the water. In profile, he is a king, a conqueror, square-jawed, lips set, eyes seeing beyond my limited horizons. Then he turns to me, and the eyes that look into mine make me want to hold him, to shelter him against his pain. But how can I do that, when the pain is of my making?

He smiles, a martyr's absolution. "So I'll wait," he says. "And when you are ready, you'll come to me. Knowing that I'll be waiting still."

"Please," I say, not wanting this. It is too big a sacrifice at my altar, too foreign an experience for me. I am too used to being the one who does the loving. I am uneasy being loved this way, it feels false and silly, a saccharine thing even less believable than Steffie's period romances. I look at him with dismay.

He shrugs and glances away, and it is like drawing a blind down. He does not look at me as he says, "We will not speak of it again, if you prefer." His liquid eyes dart back to me, and away again. He laughs, but it is a brittle thing. "I would not have thought that devotion would make you want to flee."

He knows my thoughts before I do. I resettle

myself, only now acknowledging that I had been rising, had been on the point of leaving to escape his honesty. What is wrong with me, I ask, that I gallop so yearningly after Tom's love, but pull rein and turn aside from the faun's offer? What is so frightening about being loved?

I have no answers for myself. My mind leafs through the books on abnormal psychology I have read, trying to find a neurosis or psychosis, a trauma or organic imbalance to explain this flaw in myself. Nothing comes to mind. Being loved for being myself has been out of my reach for too long. I cannot believe in it now. But how can I explain it to the faun? It does not even make sense to me. Has the quest become dearer to me than the subject of it?

"Evelyn Sylvia," he says, making a title of my name. "I did not mean to make you think of all these things," he says softly. "I only wanted to explain what I had done, all those years ago. And to let you know that for now, I ask nothing of you. Nothing."

I look at him for a long time. Far away, I hear a car horn honk, incongruous in this setting. Pan glances in that direction, then back to me. It honks again, long screaming blasts like outraged geese, but at this distance the anger is impotent. "I don't even know what I'm doing here," I say.

"Exploring," he says, and makes the simplicity of the idea enough for me. "Come on." He rises and offers me a browned hand. I take it and he pulls me to my feet, but even when I am standing, he keeps my hand. I do not pull it away. I am doing nothing wrong, I tell myself, holding hands with an old friend, there need be no guilt in that. "I know where there are huckleberry bushes," he tells me as he ducks his head to pass the overhanging branches of a show currant. His horns clatter lightly against the twiggy branches in passing. "They're not ripe yet, of course, but later you and I . . ."

He leaves the thought dangling, and I do not need to nod. His hand is warm against mine as I duck my head and follow. I feel the soft rasp of the ridges of the skin of his palm against mine, a pleasant friction. We move with the forest and he shows me things, with very few words to come between us. Here is a hummingbird's nest, a painstakingly fine construction beyond the scope of human fingers, and there a waddling porcupine followed by her three youngsters, hair and quills brushed back stiff as crew cuts. She ignores us, taking no alarm at the faun or the human. My scent, I think, is masked in his; he loans me his kinship with the forest as I follow him.

I do not know how much time passes. He shows me things I had forgotten how to see, increases in my eyes the value of this forest so different from my Alaskan home. We nibble a yellowish mushroom whose name I do not know, but it does not need a name in our silence. We go deeper into the forest, working our way parallel to the stream, going ever so slightly uphill. He shows me many things, but my eyes linger longest on the curve of his bare shoulders, the nape of his strong neck, brushed lightly by his uneven brown hair, the curve of his smile all but hidden in his beard until the edges of his white teeth show. Under his tutelage, I remember my love for these wild, ungroomed places. And I remember more than that.

It is only when we come to a meadow, a wild place of deep grasses, that I realize that shadows are lengthening and the sun is no longer over our heads. With a jolt, time recommences for me. My laundry is in the washer still, probably mildewing in the heat, my sheets in the dryer, Tom and Teddy will be wondering about their dinner.

"I have to go back," I say, feeling a sudden anxiety rising in me as I realize how far we have come, how far I must go to get back home. It will be dark, I think, before I cross the cow pasture again. The darkness does not scare me, nor am I worried about losing my way. No, my sense of direction has always been good, I am already thinking I could make my way back in a straight line rather than following the wandering stream back. No, it is not the darkness nor the distance that makes the way back so long. I think of the questions my long absence will prompt.

And Pan asks me the first, most dreaded question

of all. "Must you go back?" he asks, and it is a genuine question, not a teasing or polite thing.

"I have a child," I tell him, and he nods, understanding rising in his eyes, and also a deep sorrow.

"I do not," he explains, and lets go of my hand for the first time that day. He turns aside from me, looks over the wild meadow with farseeing eyes.

I feel like a boat cast adrift.

"I have to go," I say helplessly. I want to grope after his touch, but I restrain myself. I start to take a step away, but he turns, springs back to me.

"I know a deer path," he says, his liquid brown eyes suddenly alight. "We can run. Come on!"

He catches up my hand, pulls me along like a stuffed toy. I stumble at first, then fall into stride beside him, run with him, run as I have not run in a very long time. I expect to puff and blow, to stumble and beg him to slow down, but I don't. It is easy, running has always been easy, I wonder when I began to think of it as too strenuous for me. We swoop back into the arms of the forest, and now we must duck, but only slightly, for the deer have trod out the best and easiest way, their antlers have tattered away most of the overhanging foliage, and we can run, me on Pan's heels now, heads only slightly bowed. The earth is firm beneath our feet, but kind, giving to the shock of each stride, and the air is almost cool in the shade of the trees. I am sweating now, but the wind of our passage cools me, and the musk of Pan's sweat is for me like a lure to a hound. I run, more behind than beside him, and the path begins to wend down the hill, and we go faster and faster, his hooves thudding, my sneakered feet slapping the earth in rhythm. We spook some larger bird, a pheasant or grouse, it rises too swiftly for me to identify it, clattering in its angry flight. Still he runs on, and I follow, feeling muscles in my legs stretch and loosen, it is like scratching an itch I did not know I had, and my lungs fill full and the rich air of the forest is heady and dizzying as I gulp it in.

The path winds, but gently, and other, lesser paths feed into it. At one such intersection a doe springs back in sudden alarm, crowding the fawn on her heels, but we

are past them and gone before she can take full alarm
and bound away. Pan laughs aloud, and I find that I, too,
have breath for laughter. "Come on!" he urges me
suddenly, and drags at my hand, and we are racing,
going as fast and faster than I dare, heedless of any
suddenly low branch or obstacle in the trail. The sleeve
of my shirt snags and rips, but I do not care, I am
keeping pace with him, right on his heels, crowding
him, daring him to go even faster. He does, and then,
"Stop, stop, stop!" he is hissing. Chortling nervously
around his warning, he slides to a stop, turning, his arms
opening wide, catching me before I plow into the
barbed-wire fence that suddenly springs up before us. A
deer could lift over it easily, and perhaps Pan could, but
I could not leap it any more than I can stop my headlong
rush. I crash into him, but he catches me easily and spins
with me, burning out my momentum in a dizzying whirl.

The world tumbles around me and halts suddenly. I
am holding to him, panting, gasping, scarcely able to
stand. My arms are around him and I can feel his lungs
working, his ribs floating in and out as he pants with me.
I laugh brokenly, around my quest for air, laugh in the
joy of the run, and he laughs with me. I turn up my eyes
to look at him, and his face is too close, his eyes too big.
I no longer have breath to laugh, cannot remember how
to pull more air into my lungs. I close my eyes as his
mouth falls on mine, I think I must not do this, but I
want this kiss more than I have ever wanted anything.
His lips are soft, his beard a rough caress against my
face, he clicks his teeth against mine, deliberately, I
think, like a deer battles its velveted antlers against a
tree. For one instant I am electrically aware of him, of
every place that our bodies touch, of every place where
I am bound by the constraints of clothing and our skins
are separated.

We spring apart at the same instant, two magnets
with poles suddenly reversed. He backs into the forest,
his dark skin blending with the evening light of the
trees, only his white smile like a beacon, drawing me.

I could follow him, right now, I could pull him to
the earth atop me, there would be no one to know but

me, no one to punish for such a secret sin. It could be a present I give to myself, a secret thing as sweet and remorseless as a candy bar eaten in private, away from your brothers and sisters. I would be depriving no one by doing it, taking nothing away from anyone, would only be giving myself something I need, need very badly. I take a step.

"Lynn-nnn!"

My name is ringing out over over the flatlands, over the chicken yard and the cow pasture, and I turn to see if I can see Tom, if he can see me, standing here at the edge of his world, teetering on the edge, ready to leap off it. But he cannot see me, he must be on the other side of the little house. The place looks squat and sheddish seen from here, a converted milk house, plain as day, not the cute little guest house Mother Maurie makes it out to be. And her big house is no more than a great box of timber plopped down on a flat place and painted white, I see how plain it really is, no cushioning of plants around it, the few shade trees and scattered bushes struggling alone to survive on that baked, bare place she calls a yard. How has she fooled me this long, made me think her home a large and desirable place? It is a box that shuts out the world, and I turn my back on it.

But Pan is gone, the path is empty and darkening. As clear as if he had spoken them, I hear the words, "Not yet."

Not yet. But soon.

"Lynn-nn!" The name rings out again, and I imagine I hear a doleful note in it, a questioning, a wistfulness. Tom. Teddy.

I open my mouth. "Com-ing!" I send my own cry ringing back to him. I step on the lowest strand of barbed wire, lift up the next one, and slip through. Back within fence, back among the cows.

# Twelve

*The Farm June 1976*

"Where the hell have you been?"

I am just inside the door, it is scarcely closed behind me, and already I am too hot, stifled by the tiny house. The long run has disheveled me, and my body is still throwing off heat from my exertions, heat that does not disperse in this house but clings and wraps around me like a piece of cellophane stuck on gooey candy. It is a breathless insulation, hermetically sealing me from Tom's anger.

"What the hell is wrong with you, anyway, taking off like that? You know I've got to work, and off you go, leaving me stuck with Teddy. Mom asks me when you're going to get your laundry out of the way so she can do hers, I have to say, 'I don't know, I don't even know where the hell she is.' How does that look to my parents?"

"I went for a run in the woods," I say as he draws breath, but he doesn't hear, he has only paused in his tirade. He goes on as remorselessly as a D-8 Cat rolling over saplings. I try to listen, but there is too much for me to try to match up. I feel like a severed limb trying to reattach itself to a body. Artery here, bone there, yes, yes, and a zillion tiny arterioles that don't want to match up. Maybe it's the wrong body. I don't want to hook back into this life, I want to turn and run out the door and

back across the pasture. Tom is still listing his griev-
ances.

"I come in, there's no dinner, the house is still a
mess, so we go over to Mom's to eat and Teddy has a
screaming fit, and ruins the whole evening for everyone."

Click. All the danger lights go red in my mind.
Immediacy rescues me from my disorientation.

"Where's Teddy?" I demand.

"In bed," Tom declares firmly. "Where he belongs.
Dad warmed up his hind end, and then I told him to go
to bed with no supper. That kid is getting totally out of
control, and it's no wonder, with you off . . ."

"What the hell went on while I was gone?"

Tom stops, dumbfounded. I don't blame him. In the
sudden silence it is as if some other person has spoken,
some third party neither of us knows interjecting her
fury into our conversation. Tom falters. I realize I am
glaring at him, that I am suddenly furious. I take a step
closer to him, and he sits down at the table.

"We were trying to eat dinner," he says defensively.
"Mom and Dad had been good enough to stretch things
out for us, so we were at the table. And Teddy asked
about the pony, and Dad had to tell him that it had
turned out the pony was a bad deal. The farrier told us
that he foundered last year and probably wasn't as sound
as he looked. So Dad decided against getting him for
Teddy. And besides, it wasn't a very good idea in the first
place, because what in the hell would they do with a
pony after we left again? Waste of money."

I am sick. There are two parts of me, a head part
that is hot and angry, and a stomach part that wants to
throw up on Tom, that wants to drench him with the
bitter acid churning within it. Betrayal. I stare at him,
daring him to go on with his little tale.

"So," he says, speaking more slowly. "Teddy started
crying, saying he'd promised, and it wasn't fair, and that
if he couldn't have a pony, he wanted to go home right
now. So Dad told him, go ahead, go home and go to bed,
brat, and Teddy said, no, he meant all the way home to
Alaska. And Dad said, fine, start walking, little baby boy,

because no one else wants to go back there. And then
Teddy shouted that Dad was a liar and didn't keep his
promises and he didn't like him anymore. All of this at
the table, mind you." Tom struggles to find a little
righteousness. "Damn it, we never were allowed to carry
on like that at the table when I was growing up!" He
looks at me for some confirmation, for me to be shocked
at Teddy's rudeness. I stare back at him, cold as a snake,
waiting.

"So anyway," he goes on, hurrying now, "Dad told
him to pipe down, and Teddy wouldn't and so Dad
spanked him and we sent him straight to bed." Takes
a breath. "The kid is getting totally out of hand, Lynn!
He . . ."

That voice speaks again. "If he ever touches my kid
again, I'll kill him." Yes, that's me talking, I idly think, or
at least someone I agree totally with. "Furthermore,
Teddy is right. If he's not getting a pony, I think we
should all go home. Right now."

Tom is staring at me. "What's wrong with you? You
sound just like that kid. Lynn, that doesn't make a bit of
sense! Just because Teddy isn't getting a pony is no
reason for us to pack up and leave!"

"No?" I ask. "Why not? It was the only reason I ever
had for staying."

Tom's eyes have gone round. He looks younger
suddenly, groping. Something fierce in me realizes why
he was so frantic when I wasn't home. He doesn't like
this any more than I do, he was as outraged, but he
cannot admit it. Instead he is angry at me because I
wasn't here to step between, to prevent it from happening, to draw the fire to myself. To protect our child. That
other fierce one sticks the knife in, twists it. Gladly.

"Your father was wrong," I say unequivocally. "He
promised and he broke his word. We've always taught
Teddy that was wrong. And we both know Teddy doesn't
need an animal in perfect condition. He's not thinking
about riding off into the sunset, he's thinking about
having a pony for a friend. The fact is, Tom, that your
dad doesn't want to spend the money. He made the offer
because he thought he had to in order to get what he

wanted. Well, now he's got it, you've said we'll stay. So he figures he doesn't have to go through with the bribe." I have him in the cross hairs now. "He's wrong, though. No pony, no commitment. Teddy and I are going home."

"Lynn . . ." He is strangling on disbelief. "You can't just leave me like that! What will my folks think? How can you do a thing like that? Don't I mean anything to you, doesn't our marriage mean . . ."

"You left me first," I say, and I know I don't have to explain it, the guilt is in his eyes, he has known it all along. I throw the words anyway, cold and sharp as chunks of ice. "It's in everything you've said. You never worried about where I was today. You only wanted me to be here to do the work you think is mine. Watch the kid, dry the clothes, make the dinner, get between Teddy and your old man. Funny. You used to be able to do all those things just fine. Back when you thought we were married."

I turn around at a soft sound. Teddy is behind me, wearing a grubby T-shirt and his pj's bottoms. His face is still smeared with dust and tears. Tom hadn't even bothered to clean him up for bed. It is fuel for this consuming, fearless anger. I crouch down to be on his eye level. He is frightened, and I realize he has never heard Tom and me quarrel like this, has never heard us clash without conciliation.

"Let's get cleaned up for bed," I tell him, and I take his hand and lead him into the bathroom. We wash our faces and brush teeth. I pull off his dirty T-shirt and drop it on the floor. Screw it. Screw being tidy and wifely and all that shit. This is Teddy and me.

"I didn't get any supper," he tells me, and the whole of his grief is in that statement.

"Me, neither," I tell him. "We'll just have a big breakfast instead." It's an I-don't-care-so-there act of defiance we are sharing, and some of the pain goes out of Teddy's eyes. Tom is still sitting at the kitchen table when we come out of the bathroom. He thinks I will put Teddy to bed and come back to finish the argument. He's wrong. I take Teddy into the bedroom. I throw open both tiny windows, to let in as much of the night as I can, and we cuddle up in the big bed, Teddy in the curve of my stomach like a much younger child. Teddy goes to sleep very quickly.

I make plans quickly, without remorse. I'll pack tomorrow. It shouldn't take more than an hour. Phone for a cab? But the only phone is at the big house, and I do not want to ask to use it. I don't want to see any of them at all, I don't feel I have to justify or explain what I am doing. Let them figure it out for themselves. No, I'll just take the old pickup and leave it at the airport. It may take them a while to find it in the parking garage, but that won't be my problem. I'll put the tickets on our charge card. I decide to get fifty dollars cash from the bank on the way, but to leave the checkbook here on the kitchen table. There is a savings account in the Fairbanks bank, with sixty or seventy bucks in it. It will have to be enough. I think, I can call Annie from the airport, she'll pick me up. It is all neat and tidy. I fall asleep thinking how much fun it will be to see our Bruno puppy again.

The funny thing is, I don't think of Pan at all. He doesn't come into it. At least, I pretend he doesn't. I try not to think that the only reason I have the strength to leave Tom is because I have someone else to run to.

I have no doubts that when I get to Fairbanks, he will find me there, in the summer woods behind my cabin.

I have heard that after a seizure, some epileptics feel exceptionally clearheaded and optimistic. I don't know if that's true. I only know I awake easily, coming alert like animals do, instantly, with no lingering drowsiness. Morning is still very new, and Teddy's body is a sweet warmth against mine. I sniff the top of his head, where the blond stubble is growing into a soft downiness again, smelling that indefinable child smell about him. I shift my body slowly away from his, tucking the blankets around him before the warmth can escape. It is cooler this morning, a promise of a gentler day to come.

I am halfway dressed before it all comes back. How

I saw the faun yesterday, how I am leaving today. I feel sorry. Something has ended. Something that was once very good is all done. But the sorrow doesn't change my resolve, doesn't even make me think about changing my mind. It is the same way one feels when sweeping up a treasured keepsake that is irrevocably smashed. I wish it hadn't happened, but it did. And the thought of leaving the Potter family farm is a cool stream of relief flowing through my parched soul. Pan is somehow a part of all this, so intrinsic that I don't waste time trying to draw lines between what is real and what is not. It doesn't matter anymore. Briefly I wonder if I'm crazy, and then I think that it doesn't matter, either. Because if doing this is crazy, then it's a hell of a lot better than whatever I was before I decided to do this.

I go out to the kitchen, fill the toy kettle with water, set it on the stove, and turn the flames up high, send them licking blue and yellow against the enamel bottom, then I go through the house, opening all the windows wide to the morning cool, letting it flow into the house and displace the heavy house smells of cooking and cleaning products.

The door is last, and I throw it open to the day, heedless of the flies that will come in. Let them buzz and make spots on the wallpaper and die, legs up, on the windowsills. I don't care. The sky is high and pale blue with a wispy tracery of high clouds. The air is moist with dew that will burn off too quickly, but now it makes it possible to smell the dry grass standing in the fields, the oil and diesel from the equipment, the chickens down in the chicken yard.

Someone is walking down the long driveway. He is like a figure out of a dream, bareheaded, blond in the new sunlight. His jeans are faded, his checkered work shirt is open. He is leading a fat black-and-white pony by a loop of baling twine. The crunch of his boots and of the pony's hooves remind me of chewing ice. The pony's ears are up, and he has an intelligent, friendly face. I stand still, watching Tom come, wondering.

He knows I am watching him, but his eyes do not meet mine. Not until he is at the bottom of the steps.

The twine is too short to tie to the railing, but he tries. Then he looks up and says, "The tack-and-feed won't open up for another two hours yet."

I stand still in the door, looking down on his upturned face, still wondering what it all means. "I had to wake the guy up to buy the pony," Tom tells me, trying to make his voice light. "Boy, was he pissed," and it is on those words that his voice breaks, everything breaks loose and comes out. "Please, Lynn, I was wrong. I've been treating you bad, I see that now. Don't go. I love you."

So this is winning, and as it stabs me, I know it is the only thing that can hurt worse than losing. Making someone you love break like this and plead, making those strong hands shake with fear, it is an abysmal thing to do and I have done it. Tears sting my own eyes. A cold part of me wonders in an aside if Tom ever feels this bad when he makes me give in, if Tom suffers at all when he forces me to capitulate. But somehow it doesn't matter if he feels it, because I feel it, and it's part of how I'm made. My kind of love does not seek mastery, does not want it. "Please stay," he is saying. "I'll try to make it right."

"Tom," I say, and come down the steps to take him in my arms. I hold him as if he were Teddy, badly frightened by a sudden fall. There is the same stiffness in his body, the same unevenness in his breathing. He holds me closer, as if he would pull me inside his body. This is real. I rub my face against him, and I know what is true. This is real, we are real, and though we nearly broke it, our love doesn't have to be broken.

"If you say I've lost you, Lynn," he says, and I know he is crying, "I've lost everything."

"I'm here," I say. "I've got you."

I hold his warmth against me, breathe his scent, feel the warmth of the sunlight like a gentler continuation of his body, I wish I could put on his love like a garment, wear it to protect myself.

And remind myself.

The pony butts against us, wanting to be included in whatever we are doing. He lips my wrist questioningly and we both laugh in relief. It's over, whatever it was. We've made it past another rapids, into quieter water. Tom rubs his face against my shoulder and hair. He straightens, sniffs once, and then smiles like the sun breaking through clouds. A wave of recognition washes over me, it's like he's come home after a long absence, healed after a terrible illness. "This is the one," I want to tell them all, "this is the one I married."

Gently, he frees himself from my embrace. He sticks his head in the door, bellows, "Teddy!" with mock severity. It takes a moment, but then comes the hesitant pattering of bare feet. Teddy comes as far as the living room, stares from Tom to me worriedly. For a moment I fear I will have to explain, and then the pony, curious, sticks his head in the door. He has his front hooves on the narrow steps and Tom has to block him to prevent him coming the rest of the way in. He doesn't want to back down off the step, and it takes Tom pulling and me pushing before he is on level ground again. Teddy is agog with wonder. He holds back, looking up at the pony that suddenly looms for him large as any mountain.

Tom puts the string into my hand and picks Teddy up, sets his pajamaed legs and butt over the wide black-and-white back. Teddy sits very still. Only his eyes move. Then he timidly reaches down and pats the pony's shoulder. The pony turns his head to look at his new rider. Up to now he has seemed unaware of him. Teddy squeals when the pony lips at his bare toes and pulls his feet up out of reach of the green-stained lips. The pony is surprised, but his ears remain pricked forward. He gives a lick to his own shoulder and then turns back to Tom.

"Hold on to his mane, like this," Tom says, and puts Teddy's small hands into the coarse hair. "Grip with your knees. You know, squeeze him with your legs. And here we go."

And they are off, at a decorous walk. Teddy concentrates on the double handful of mane he grips, shifts slightly on the pony's back as the stiff horsehair prickles through his thin summer pajamas. "Hang on now," Tom warns, and increases his stride, finally drags the reluctant pony into a trot. Teddy bounces wildly, but clings gamely to the mane and tries to make his short legs wrap around the pony's round barrel. Around the yard twice, and then "Dad! Dad!" Teddy is shouting as he starts to slide down one shoulder. I start forward, but Tom is already there, catching him and pushing him back into place.

"That's enough for right now," Teddy tells him, and Tom helps him down. Teddy walks all around the pony in a wide circle, then ventures back cautiously to look up at him. The pony is not so shy. He pushes his muzzle abruptly into Teddy's chest, nearly knocking him down. When Teddy retreats, the pony steps after him, lipping at his straw-colored hair. "Hey!" Teddy squeals, and tries to retreat again, but Tom catches him by the shoulder.

"Look, son, don't run away. He's just trying to get to know you. You've got to stand still and let him sniff you and let him know who he belongs to, now. Here." He puts the thin baling-twine lead into Teddy's hands. Teddy presses up against Tom, but holds his ground as the pony sniffs him this time. He pets the white nose and giggles nervously when the pony blows out against his hand. Tom hooks an arm around me, pulls me up against his side. He is warm and solid. I lean my head against his shoulder. Contentment and safety wrap me. I sigh, and it is as if I had been holding my breath for days and suddenly let it out. He squeezes me again, and I look up into his eyes, and he is looking at me with love. I find myself clinging to him as he kisses the top of my head.

Someone clears her throat nearby. I startle and pull back from Tom, but it is only Steffie. "Well, well, what's this?" she asks Teddy delightedly. Her eyes go quickly to Tom's and congratulate him silently.

As she approaches, Teddy grips the pony's string possessively. "It's my pony," he tells her proudly.

"It sure is, Cowboy. Looks like a pony that could use a bridle and bareback pad."

"A red halter," Teddy says decisively.

"That's just what I was thinking," she says. "You mind?" she asks Tom suddenly.

"Mind what?"

"If Teddy and I go buy a few things for the pony?"

"Not at all."

She comes to Tom suddenly, hugs him hard and quick, then steps back and says, fast, "You're right. It's going to gripe his ass, but you're right. And I'm glad you did it." She turns suddenly to Teddy. "Tell you what. Let's put your pony in the chicken yard. That fence ought to hold him, and he can get a drink out of the pond, while we go get him a few things, okay?"

"Okay!" Teddy agrees happily, and they are off, Teddy leading the pony by the string while Steffie keeps a grip on his mane and walks beside him. I gaze after them, seeing what I have not before. That Steffie really does care about Teddy, enough to risk her father's wrath by subsidizing Tom's revolt in the only way she knows, by shopping for the pony's clothes. I am surprised, and surprised, too, by the bond between her and Tom. I realize I have been seeing her as an extension of her mother, as a remote-controlled unit of Mother Maurie. It is the first time I have glimpsed Steffie doing something on her own. It makes her seem both younger and older. I am still staring after them when Tom takes me by the shoulders, turns me to him.

We don't speak. He holds me for a while, and then we are walking back to the little house and into it, back to the bed, where we make love like demented teenagers, around and through our clothes, his jeans pushed down only to his knees, mine still on one leg, my bra still tangled around one shoulder. Afterward we fall asleep together for perhaps an hour, arouse, make a more leisurely kind of love, and then arise. The day passes like a dream. Tom does not go to work at all, and by some miracle his parents do not come looking for him, asking why. Instead, we go into town, have cinnamon rolls for brunch, and then wander from store to store, looking at everything, buying nothing. We run into Teddy and Steffie. They have bought a riding pad, a red bridle with silver stars on it, a brush and currycomb, a new cowboy hat for Teddy with a red bandanna and a length of red ribbon. I can see Teddy is uncertain about the red ribbon, but Steffie is talking persuasively about how the pony will love being dressed up with ribbons braided through his mane. Tom asks them if they want to go to a movie with us, but they are both anxious to get home and play dress-up with the pony. They leave, and suddenly I realize how quickly the day has flown, for we have just enough time for dinner and then we go to a movie. We pick one by the title and poster outside the movie house, for neither of us has any idea what any of them are about. Tom has been too much into his tractors, I have been too much into myself to pay attention to current movies. We get a very trivial comedy, full of lovers' misunderstandings and impossible situations. Tom watches it and I sit beside him in the darkness, listening to him chuckle now and then, sharing his popcorn, leaning on his shoulder, having him to myself.

I sit close to him in the truck all the way home. When we pull up, there is a single low light shining from the little house, and inside we find Teddy sound asleep on the couch and a note from Steffie that they had a great time today. We go to bed quickly, and once more we make love. Tom holds me afterward, and falls asleep with his arms around me. I lie still in his circle of warmth, his arm heavy across me.

I keep closing my eyes, but they keep opening again. I want to fall asleep fully contented, warm in his embrace. But I find I cannot trust this day, this miracle. I keep going back to this morning, when I was ready to leave. I am glad I didn't leave, glad Tom brought the pony, glad I decided to stay. But there is a spark of anger there, still. Does he think this is enough? the bitch in me asks. One day of his precious time, one day of carousels and candy apples in a summer of dust and gravel roads? Does he think I am a small child, bribed so easily to forget how he has ignored and hurt me? I try to ignore the hateful voice. Love is patient, is kind. Love does not envy, I recite to myself. Bears with all things, believes all things, hopes all things, endures all things. Love or idiocy, it's one of those two that does that. When I was a child, I spoke as a child, I felt as a child, I thought as a child. So what am I now, I'm sure as hell not a man? I can't turn off the internal dialogue, I can't sleep. I steel myself, admit a part of me is angry we made up, angry that I lost my chance to leave. A part of me wants to fight with Tom, to be hateful, to malignantly devour our relationship. But there is a part of me that loves his clean smell, his warm arm across me, loves possessing this desirable man for myself. I am too tired. Like Scarlett O'Hara, I think I will wait for tomorrow and another day.

# Thirteen

*The Farm June–July 1976*

The next morning, Tom gets up and goes to work at the dealership earlier than usual, to make up for playing hooky the day before. It doesn't bother me. He wakes me gently before he goes, by stroking his fingers over my face, tracing the lines of my brow, my nose, my jawline. I come sleepily awake to his light caress, in time to receive a warm kiss before he leaves. "See you tonight," he promises, and I drift back to sleep, secure, loved.

Teddy awakens me the second time. He is already dressed, his new cowboy hat on his head. The ring of milk around his mouth and the stray corn flake glued to his chin tells me he has already helped himself to breakfast. "Mom, wake up," he tells me urgently. "We gotta take care of my horse."

I drag myself out, get dressed while he is washing his face, make a cup of tea and wipe up most of his mess while he is brushing his teeth. I ache from too much sex. Sex hangover, I tell myself, and try to smile about it. I drink the cup of tea while he is assembling his "horse stuff." We have to carry it all with us as we go out to the chicken yard; the pad, the bridle, a length of rope with a clip on it, the currycomb and brush, the carrot from the refrigerator. "Watch me, now," Teddy cautions me as we approach the chicken yard. "I'll show you how to do it."

And to my amazement, he does. The pony comes willingly enough for the carrot, and Teddy quickly clips the rope to his halter and ties him to the fence. Yesterday's shyness about the animal has already mutated to a casual confidence I don't share. "You put your hand on his butt when you walk behind him, so he knows you're there. Aunt Steffie says so," he tells me, walking briskly past the deadly hooves. "And be careful of his ticklish spots when you brush him," he goes on grandly, and spends a diligent five minutes brushing one side of the pony up as high as he can reach. He needs my help with the bridle, for although the pony accepts the bit casually, the buckles of the new bridle are stiff. Teddy is very fussy about the bareback pad, and no matter how I fasten it, he keeps insistening it isn't tight enough. I am still struggling with it when Steffie appears. "Need help?" she asks, and I step back and let her. She settles Teddy onto the pony and passes him the reins. "There you go, Cowboy," she tells him, and he proudly rides off across the chicken yard. I watch him go, trying not to show I am anxious. Although the yard is fenced, it is still nearly a full acre for Teddy and the pony to wander. I wish they were more confined.

"He'll be okay," Steffie says quietly. "I think it would take a stick of dynamite to get that pony up past a trot. He's fat as a pig."

I nod silently, watching Teddy and the pony.

"Dad say anything to you guys yet?" she asks.

I shake my head as I turn to face her.

Steffie shrugs. "He probably won't, then. He was really burned up yesterday, but no one said a word about it to him, and he won't talk about it. He's like that. As long as no one says anything about the pony and as long as it's not trouble, it'll blow over in a few days."

"Oh," I say, not knowing what else to say. The silence grows long. The pony reaches the fence on the other side of the chicken yard and halts. Teddy pulls on the reins and kicks its fat sides ineffectually. The pony ignores him and lowers his head to graze. But Steffie has come prepared. She whistles between her teeth and holds up a carrot. I try not to show how amazed I am. This is a Steffie I have never seen before. Despite the long golden legs, the ice-white shorts, the yellow-and-white tank top that matches the yellow-and-white sandals she is wearing, despite her perfect hair and manicured nails, her flawless makeup, her mannequin stance, she is acting like a real person. Pony begins his plodding journey back.

"You seem to know how to handle horses," I say.

"I used to ride a lot, during high school. I was in 4-H and Future Farmers of America. I used to think I'd be a horse breeder, or a veterinarian when I grew up."

"Oh?" This is all news to me. Steffie, with ambitions. I try not to sound too surprised. Mother Maurie has spoken of Steffie being interested in interior decorating, in modeling, in ceramics and decoupage and macrame. On Tuesday and Thursday evenings, they go together to classes in tie-dyeing and candy making. They go to bridal shows at the mall, order fifty dollars' worth of Avon products a month, and spend endless hours studying clothing catalogs and fashion magazines. Veterinarian?

"Yeah. But it's almost impossible to get into vet school, and Dad says there's no money in horse breeding anymore. Not unless you go into it in a big way. I talked it over with Mom and Dad after I graduated high school. I could have gotten into a veterinary assistant program at the community college, but there's not much future in it. Dad says all you do is clean kennels and throw away bandages."

He would. "So," I say lamely. "Think you'll ever do anything with it?"

"Only if I marry a rich guy," she says lightly.

I laugh. She doesn't, so I change it into a cough. Teddy and the pony finally reach us. "Looking good, Cowboy," she tells him as she gives the pony the carrot. Steffie takes hold of the cheek strap. "Want me to make him trot for you?"

"Naw." Teddy is elaborately casual. "It's too hot today to make him go fast." So he isn't quite as confident about the pony yet as he'd like to be. I am glad Steffie doesn't insist. She merely turns the pony's head and gives him a slap on the rump. Teddy and pony amble off on a circuit of the chicken yard.

"So, where'd you go the other day?" Steffie asks me.

"Just out shopping. You know. Movie. Dinner."

"No. I don't mean yesterday, I mean when Tommy couldnt' find you."

"Oh." I feel a sudden reluctance. "Back in the woods," I tell her, gesturing vaguely. "Just for a walk. It was cooler back there. I didn't mean to be gone so long."

"Yeah. It's easy to get turned around back there." She glances at the woods, a vague frown on her face. "There's animals back there, too," she confides to me.

"I'll be careful," I promise her.

"Actually, you probably shouldn't go back there. Not alone."

"I'll be okay," I assure her.

"Well, next time you want to go, why don't you tell me? We can take Teddy and a picnic. I'll show you where we used to pick huckleberries when Tommy and I were kids. It'll be fun."

"Yeah, okay," I lie noncommittally. My mind is suddenly busy. How will I manage to slip off on my own again? If I ask someone to watch Teddy, they'll want to know why. And I can't just leave him, not like last time. Nor can I take him with me. My mind works swiftly, furiously.

". . . today?"

"Huh? I'm sorry, I guess I was daydreaming."

"I guess so! I just asked what you planned to do today?"

My mind flounders. "I don't know. Uh, I'd better get the laundry I forgot day before yesterday."

"Ellie finished it for you. I think she even took it over and put it away for you."

I am left speechless again. "I'll have to thank her," I mutter.

"Oh, she didn't mind. She said it looked like you could use a hand to give the guest house a good cleaning, wax the floors and stuff. She'll probably ask you when you want to do it in the next few days. So, what are you doing today?"

"Uh, probably housework." Sheer dread envelopes me. Spend a day with Ellie, helping her clean up my own mess. I have seen her take a toothpick and go after trapped wax buildup in the linoleum. She dusts the bottoms of the kitchen chairs, and the light bulbs in the lamps and the tops of doors. There is only one way to stave her off. "I need to catch up on all the stuff that didn't get done yesterday. And Ellie is probably right that the place needs a good cleaning. But she shouldn't have to bother with it. I'll get started today."

"Oh." Steffie sounds almost disappointed. "You and Ellie. That's all you guys seem to do."

That's about all there is to do, I think, but I don't say it out loud. Somehow, I don't even want to know what she has planned for the day. I am saved by Teddy and the pony.

"Well, I better rub him down now," Teddy tells me as the pony saunters to a halt. Steffie catches him as he slides off. She looks sure and competent as she helps Teddy take the bareback pad and bridle off. I catch myself wondering who the hell she really is. From this to Mommy's little helper at the dealership, to the long-legged beauty at the mall, to a would-be veterinarian. I think maybe I don't know her at all. Hell, maybe she doesn't know herself. It's not my problem, I tell myself. "I'll help Teddy clean up Houdini," Steffie tells me.

"Houdini?" I ask blankly.

"That's the pony's name. Weird, huh?"

"Yeah. Well, I'd better get back to my housework," and I leave them brushing and currying and discoursing learnedly about ponies.

Back at the little house, I Pledge and Windex and Fantastic my way through the rooms, determinedly eradicating every trace of our usage. The sweet elation of yesterday has evaporated, leaving me discontented and surly with myself. So what? I ask myself whenever any thought occurs. So I'm a pig, and I've made a sty of the cute little guest house. So what? So Tom wants to make things work? So what? It doesn't mean he really wants to change anything, he doesn't want to go back to Alaska, he just wants to change things enough to keep me here. Did I think I had won something yesterday? Hell, all he was doing was keeping the promise his chicken-shit dad had broken. For this I'm supposed to be meltingly grateful?

I was yesterday, pathetically grateful. Yesterday I was in love. Today, I'm angry again. This doesn't make sense, not even to me. I make a cup of tea, sit down on the cozy cushions in the stiflingly hot little house. Dust motes are dancing in the white light pouring in the windows. My thoughts waltz with them, and I let them go, knowing that if I do, they may lead me back to the truth. It comes to me, in elusive bits. Yes, I love Tom. But I'm angry with him. Because if you love someone, it should be easy to be faithful to them. And it isn't. No matter how I ignore them, my thoughts caper with fauns, with brown polished horns and white teeth, with sleek flanks and roundly muscled bronze forearms. Yesterday I had an excuse. I was a neglected, mistreated woman, and the faun was offering me comfort. Today, I don't have that excuse anymore, not really. Yesterday's kiss can be explained away, to myself at least. But if I leave the house today and go to him, it will be because I want to go to him, not because Tom has hurt or slighted me. Only because I want to be with him.

I examine my two loves, and they are two different things. Neither cancels the other, neither makes the other any less necessary to my soul. All the cheating country-western songs I have ever heard go schmaltzing through my mind. "One has my name, the other has my heart," "Yore cheatin' heart will tell on you," "You picked a fine time to leave me, Lucille!" I slam a fist down on a yellow cushion, launching an explosion of dancing motes. It isn't like that, like some stupid song, it's not beers and tears.

So what is it like, then? I ask myself.

"It's a lot more dangerous."

I hear myself say the words aloud, hear them swallowed by the cuddly little house. I wonder if I'm crazy, talking to myself, seeing fauns in the forest. No, I deny it quickly, but then I force my mind back, force myself to reexamine the day, try to find one shred of proof I can offer myself that yesterday I spoke with a faun. There is nothing. I touch my fingers to my lips, feel again that press of warmth, that clash of teeth. No. There is nothing, and everything.

But I don't need to worry about it, my sensible self tells me. No, not at all. Because all I have to do is behave myself. If I stay home and be a good wife to Tom, as I know I should, then I don't have to worry whether or not the faun is real. Because I won't see him. If I see him again, if I am crazy, it will be because I have been unfaithful first, because I have gone where no good woman would go, because I have deliberately put myself into an occasion of sin. Occasion of sin. I haven't thought of that phrase, straight from the Baltimore Catechism, in years. I think I finally know what it means.

I also think I am probably the last person on earth who cares what it means. I think of my college roommates and their casual sexual liaisons, Jenny, who believed that "if it feels good, do it" to be the highest attainable wisdom, and Stacy, whose speciality was virgins because "you never know what they'll do or say." Either of them would have slept with Pan yesterday. Slept, hell, they'd have rutted, fornicated, and copulated with him. Not for them these verbal niceties. Except that neither of them would have seen him. Because neither of them would ever let their heads get as screwed up as mine was.

Teddy comes clattering into the house, horse gear scattering in his wake. "Here," he tells me, "for you," and gives me three frail white trilliums, the small three-petaled flowers that grow in the shady parts of the deep woods. Their stems are crisp, their heads unwilted.

"Where did you get these?" I ask him, knowing already that I will have to apologize to Mother Maurie, that Teddy has desecrated some garden corner I was unaware of.

"Outside," he says vaguely, waving a hand. He takes off his cowboy hat, tosses it to the couch. "I saw a brown man leave them on the steps. Me and Steffie are going down to the river, wanta come?"

"No," I breathe.

"Why not? It's cool down there, and Steffie says there's a safe part where I can wade. Wanna come?"

"I'm going to stay here," I promise.

"Okay," says Teddy, and races off to the bathroom. He appears a moment later, with one of Mother Maurie's pale blue guest towels and a pair of his cutoffs. "Byebye," he says, and is gone. I hear the slam of a car door outside, hear the engine starting. I am a fly trapped in amber, frozen in the stiff white sunlight spilling in the windows. The trilliums are on the glass-topped end table. I know they are a near scentless flower, but the heat in the small room is leeching out their soft sweetness, polishing it over my Pledge and Windex smells.

I pick them up, feel their coolness against my fingertips, slender green stems, soft petals, as I carry them across the room. I open the cabinet under the sink, drop them into the waste can under there. I will not keep them, will not put their delicate stems in a glass of cool water, will not let their scent spread throughout the little house. I will not wonder what Teddy saw.

A few moments later I open the cupboard under the sink, peer through the gloom into the waste can. They are still there, white against the darkness, and the stink of banana peel and coffee grounds cannot conquer their sweetness.

No, I bid myself sternly, as if I am a two-year-old caressing a can of Drāno. No. I shut the cupboard door firmly.

I attack the housecleaning. I empty cupboards, put down new shelf paper, replace the cans and boxes in a frantically controlled order, boxes of cereal grouped together, canned goods ordered by size, convenience dinners grouped together. It will never stay that way, it makes no sense to do it, but I stock my cupboards as if I were stocking the shelves of Annie's store. In the bedroom, I empty the closet, rehang every garment, so that all of Tom's shirts face the same way and are completely buttoned on the hangers, and grouped by color. I dump the drawers on the bed, and am arranging his underwear in neat stacks when I hear the truck horn blow.

The fourth time it blows, I rise and go to the kitchen window. The pony is standing in the driveway, looking bemusedly at Tom's father. Tom's father is sitting in his pickup truck, blowing the horn. His face is very red, even at this distance I can see the beads of sweat forming where his hair has receded. Yet the look on his face is not annoyance, but righteous anger. I feel like I am six and have left my tricycle in the driveway.

The pony is not eager to be put back in the chicken yard. Nor is he afraid of me. I take hold of the cheek strap on his halter and pull. He braces his sturdy legs and rips his head free of my grip. And stands there. I slap him firmly on the haunch, tell him to "Move along!" He shifts two steps, moving closer to the idling truck. Tom's father sounds the horn again, a blaring accusation not three feet away from me. I flinch involuntarily. "I can't get him to move," I hear myself calling over the idling truck, as if he cannot see this, as if telling him that I am trying will make a difference to him. He doesn't say a word, doesn't even roll his window down, but only sounds the horn again. I glance around, but Steffie is gone, down to the river with Teddy, and Ellie regards us without curiosity as she flicks out her dust cloth on the kitchen doorstep. I know nothing of ponies, I suddenly realize, know very little about domestic animals at all. If Houdini were a black bear, I could get him moving, or a wolf dog, or even a lynx. Those things I know. This pony has no respect for me at all. I grab the halter by both cheek straps, brace my feet, and try to drag him forward. He resists, and then suddenly comes toward me, leaving me stumbling backward, nearly landing on my ass in the driveway. He takes another step before I can recover myself, and then, as I am scrambling backward, when there is, perhaps, maybe, barely enough room, Tom's father guns the four-wheel drive pickup truck and spins out gravel as he shoots around the pony's rear end. Houdini comes toward me in earnest then, and I stumble backward, trampling Mother Maurie's flower bed before I regain my balance. The pony obediently follows me into the flower bed and, the moment I release him, takes a culinary interest in the marigolds.

I grip the halter again and tug his head up. He nonchalantly rips his head free of my grip, tearing one of my fingernails across as he does so. I jam the injured finger in my mouth to keep from screaming, and watch as he resumes grazing. Then I do what Steffie, perhaps, would have done in the first place. I go back to the guest house and get a carrot from the refrigerator.

At the sight of the carrot, wagged enticingly before his nose, Houdini becomes very reasonable. He lets me clip the lead to his halter, and follows me docilely back to the chicken yard. The gate is firmly shut, the latch in place. I have no idea how he got out. I wonder, briefly, if Steffie and Teddy took him out and somehow forgot to put him back. That makes no sense to me, but I resolve to ask Teddy about it.

I go straight back to the guest house. I have no desire to go up to the big house and apologize to Tom's father for the pony being loose in the driveway. Instead, I dive back into my housecleaning. I move all the furniture to one end of the living room. When the Mop & Glo is dry, I put it all back, one piece at a time, each piece dusted, each cushion vacuumed before it goes into place.

I have taken all the sheets, towels, and pillowcases out of the laundry cupboard, and am refolding them before I organize them carefully into sets when Ellie walks in. She doesn't knock, no one knocks, after all, this is the family's guest house, and just because I am staying here, it doesn't make it any less their rightful domain. Ellie walks in, to casually announce, "Your pony's ruining Mom's azaleas. Not eating them, just walking on them. Oh, you know what, you know why your sheets are like that?"

"What?"

"'Cause you're using the wrong detergent and bleach. I noticed it the other day, when I was doing the laundry for you. I ended up washing everything a couple more times. You probably noticed that all the skid marks in Tommy's shorts are gone now. It's the water here. You've gotta let the enzymes in the detergent work for a while before you add the bleach. And Tide's about the only stuff that will suds in this water. The rest of the detergents, they just make a few bubbles and sort of die. Gotta use Tide and Clorox. Want me to show you how?"

"Uh. Sure. What about the pony?"

"It's in the azaleas, the ones planted along the chicken-yard fence. Daddy says he doesn't know why the hell you didn't put him back in the chicken yard. He thinks maybe you think it's okay for him to graze on the lawn, but actually the shit will pile up something fierce, and the only thing worse than horse shit on a lawn when you're trying to mow it is dog shit."

"I did put him back," I explain, but Ellie just looks at me, her eyes gently rebuking my lie.

"I'll put him back in the chicken yard," I say dully, and go to the refrigerator for a carrot.

Houdini is reveling in the azaleas, rolling luxuriously in their scratchy branches. Several are squashed totally flat, but most have sustained only minor damage. Once more, the carrot works its magic and he follows me sedately back to the firmly latched gate. I slap him on the rump as he plods through it, and follow him, latching it carefully behind me. I make a complete circuit of the chicken-yard fence. Nowhere is it broken down or torn loose from the posts. Nowhere. I study Houdini's round grass belly. He stops his grazing and lifts his head to gaze at me complacently. No way. No way that pony jumped this fence.

I make a second circuit more slowly, looking for tracks. It soon becomes plain that Houdini has followed this fence line more than once or twice. I doggedly continue, trying to find some clue as to how he is getting out. There is nothing. But in the far corner of the chicken yard, there are other tracks, overlaying the pony tracks. The marks of cloven hooves. Deer tracks, I tell myself firmly, and listen to how achingly quiet it suddenly is. No chirr of insects, only the far clucking of the chickens in the shade of the chicken house. The domestic animals are speaking, but the wild things, the bugs and the birds and the rustling of mice in the tall meadow grass beyond the chicken yard, all that is stilled. Stilled and waiting.

After a moment, how short or long I cannot tell, I come to myself. I stop my listening, and scuff over the deer tracks with one sneakered foot before I move on. I finish the circuit of the chicken-yard fence with no more idea of how the pony gets out than I had when I started. I am sweating, the sun is beating down on the crown of my head. Within the forest, it would be cooler, air would be moving, shadows and moisture would be trapped beneath the trees, breathable air. I latch the gate firmly behind me. The pony is peacefully grazing. Evidently his mind is no longer focused on escape. I leave him and go back to the azaleas.

Carefully, I gather up the broken bits of branches from the low, bushy shrubs. I snap off the ones that are only hanging by shreds of bark. It's not hard, the branches are dry and almost crisp, Mother Maurie has not been watering them enough during this dry spell. I decide that all but one of the azaleas will probably survive. The one casualty has been snapped off cleanly at the main trunk. Even this one, given plant food and water, will probably come back from the roots. I dispose of the dead branches in the moldering yellow pile of lawn clippings behind the toolshed. I check the pony one more time before I go back to the little house.

My sheets and towels are gone. I check the laundry cupboard. It is empty, but smells of bleach where the flowered contac paper has been freshly scrubbed. Gone, too, is the mop and bucket I had casually left in the corner of the kitchen. I find them by the back steps, the mop bleached and hung to dry in the sun, the bucket scrubbed and left upside down to drain.

I pace the small house. There is no real choice, I have to go over to the big house. To apologize for the azaleas, to find the sheets and towels. To thank Ellie for correcting my abysmal housekeeping. To grovel before my in-laws. I think about having a cup of tea first, but decide against it. I will have a cup of tea afterward, will save it as a sort of reward for myself for having done what needed to be done.

And suddenly I am determined to do it right. I will go over there with a cheerful expression, will admit that ponies baffle me, that I don't know how to get my sheets whiter and brighter. I will chuckle with them over my ignorance. I will even ask Tom's father for his advice on how to keep the pony fenced. I'll apologize for it being loose, and for the damaged azaleas. I will offer to water them and give them special care until they recover. I will be the model daughter-in-law, and Tom will be proud of me. When he gets home tonight, he will hold me and kiss my hair, and we'll be in love with each other, just like yesterday.

I look around the house, and in a few moments I realize what I am looking for. A gift, a peace offering. A platter of fresh-baked cookies, a white cake decorated with pink flowers, a bouquet of long-stemmed red roses. Something to share, something to say we are one family. But I have nothing.

Nothing I want to share.

But I go to the sink cupboard and open the low doors. Sweetness wafts out to me from the garbage pail. I reach in and get the three trilliums, brush a few clinging crumbs of coffee grounds from their purity. I feel as if I am sacrificing my first born on an alter as I carry them out the door and across the dust and white light and heat of the yard. I start to tap on the kitchen door, then remember that I am no stranger here. I must stop acting like a stranger if I wish to be treated as part of the family.

Tom's father spills the coffee he is pouring as he jerks around to see who has come in. "Oh. It's you. Startled the hell out of me," he observes, and walks out of the kitchen. I follow him into the living room. He sits down on the Naugahyde La-Z-Boy recliner. Mother Maurie is sitting on the sofa, working on a latch-hook kit. I suddenly wonder who's running the dealership while they are coffee klatching here, during the busiest time of the year when they really need Tom to stay to give them a hand. They both look up at me questioningly.

"Hi," I say.

"I expect you're looking for Ellie. She took all the sheets and towels into the basement. I wish you'd told us you didn't know how to get them clean before they got into such a state." Mother Maurie prims her mouth over her sewing.

Clean? They had looked clean to me. I swallow. "I guess I'm just not used to this kind of water. Ellie said she'd explain it to me. I'll go see her in a minute. Uh, I actually came over to say sorry about the pony being loose and all. I've put him back in the yard. I'm not real sure how he keeps getting out. I don't know much about ponies."

"Appears to me you'da thought about that before you told Tommy to buy him or else." Tom's father has eyes like a snowman, black coal set in ice. An elevator shaft has opened in the pit of my belly and my stomach has fallen into it and is sinking, sinking. Of course, I tell myself, of course. I can even hear Tom's voice, the way he'd phrase it, "Hell, Dad, you know how women are? What the hell was I going to do? Get the pony or I leave, she said, and I don't need that kind of a scene right now, with Teddy involved and all. So I got the pony. What the hell. I'll never understand women, maybe it's her time of the month or something." I have no place left to go, nowhere to hide.

Tom's mother has said something, is saying something. I try to hear her, but I can't make sense of it. It is words, one after the other, and I hear them, but I can't get the sense of the sentence. I'm mentally ill, I think, this is what they mean by psychosomatic deafness, I can hear her but I don't hear her because subconsciously I don't want to, and I am so busy with this thought that when she stops speaking, I can't remember even one word of what she said, have not a single clue as to what she has said. She is looking at me expectantly.

It doesn't matter. I know what I have to say. I don't have to build on their conversation, don't have to lace my words and thoughts in and out of theirs. I don't have to reply to what Tom's father has said and knows about me. "I'm sorry about the azaleas," I say. "I think most of them are going to be okay. But I'm going to go to the nursery and get some plant food and give them some extra care until they're doing well again. Um, the corner one is the only one that might not make it. It got snapped off pretty close to the ground."

"Oh, no!" gasps Mother Maurie. She lets her latch-hook work fall into her lap. I can see the motif, it is a little blond girl sitting on a potty. I feel vaguely ill, it must be the heat.

"I got that for Mother," says Tom's father heavily. "For our twentieth anniversary. It's a what-do-you-call-it . . ."

"Exbury Azalea," breathes out Tom's mother, and I am so relieved that I can hear her again that I smile at her. She stares back at me. "It's never bloomed. This year it had buds. I've waited six years for that plant to bloom."

"Maybe it needed plant food," I say inanely. "I understand azaleas like an acid soil. I used to know a lot about plants. I was going to be a botanist, you know, and I had to do a lot of work in the campus greenhouses. I know a lot about plants."

They are looking at me as if I have two heads. It cannot get worse, so I keep talking. "I brought you some trilliums. They grow back in the woods."

"I know." Mother Maurie speaks coldly. "I've heard that if you pick them, they die. But I'm sure a botanist like you knows that."

I look down at the wilted flowers in my hand. They have gone totally limp in my warm fist, lax as a dead bird, their heads dangle over my knuckles, the white petals are already going brown. I resist the urge to hide them behind my back.

"Too bad, Mother, that when you were young, you didn't have time to go picking flowers in the woods," Tom's father says heavily.

Mother Maurie says something in reply, but it is gone, my ability to hear her. The words are there, and I catch each one, try to restring the sentence in my own mind, but it is like trying to catch beads as they fall off a string, you get a handful but there is no telling what order they were in. Flowers, sheets, pony, mess, are, you, at least try, I get those bits, but I don't know if I have just been rebuked or encouraged. I smile witlessly. "You're probably right," I say, one of her favorite phrases, one I've heard Tom say to her a hundred times. "I'd better go talk to Ellie now," I say, and turn to go, but Ellie is coming into the room.

"Someone tracked all over my kitchen floor," she says, and we all look at my sneakers, spattered still with mud from the chicken yard.

"Sorry," I say determinedly. I will be good, I will be good, I will be good. "I'll clean it up. And I came over to wash the sheets and towels, just like you said," I add.

"They're already in the washer," she says, "and I already wiped up the mud."

"Oh," I say. Just oh. I look at the wilted trilliums in my hand. I don't know why I am not angry or crying. I am just so empty, it's like being in a big black room with no furniture or walls, and trying to feel my way in the dark. Nothing touches me. "Well. I think I'll go check on the pony, then. You know"—I turn to Tom's father and smile disarmingly—"I don't know much about ponies. I'd appreciate any help you could give me in figuring out how to keep him penned up. Maybe I could put him in with the cows?"

"And I can keep your pony in grain for you, huh, have him eating all the grain that's supposed to go to the cows, I suppose? No way! You should have thought about all this before you got the pony. There just isn't room on this place to keep a horse."

He is getting angry. I don't know why.

"Well, uh, when you were talking about getting him for Teddy, where were you going to keep him?"

"Why the hell did you think I decided not to do it! Damn, dumb kids!" And with this he indites both Tom and I. "A pony is nothing but trouble around a place. All they do is eat and shit. You mark my words. Teddy'll think that damn horse is great for a week or two, and then he'll forget all about it, and I'm stuck with it. All they do is run up bills, shoes, vets, worms, feed. If Tommy weren't so pussy-whipped . . ."

"Father!" cries Mother Maurie, shocked, but the

old man only chuckles wickedly. He has evil black eyes, lecherous eyes, not lusting after sex, but after hurt and control and reaction. His eyes are snapping at me, hoping I will flinch, will react in some way, but I cannot, I have no idea how to react.

"I'd better check on that pony, then," I tell them all. I have my favorite sheepish grin on my face, my oh-dear-you-saw-my-T-shirt grin, my go-ahead-and-despise-me,-I-probably-deserve-it grin. It has gotten me through many a bad situation, but I think perhaps this is the worst. It only grows wider as Mother Maurie starts talking. I resist the urge to watch her mouth move, see how her lips go to shape all the sounds that I can no longer resolve into words. I turn and leave. As I go out the kitchen door, I drop the wilted trilliums into the wastebasket there. They wouldn't talk to you like that if Tom were here, says a part of me. Go tell on them. No, don't, that's what they'd expect you to do, so don't do it. The only way to win is not to do what they expect you to do. That sounds stupid, even to me, and as I go down the steps I let all my thoughts go.

I actually do go to check on the pony. Houdini is gone, of course. I walk all around the big house, but he is not there. I do not call "Houdini, Houdini!" I know he would not come, and besides, there is something in me that has made me go silent. Thrust a knife through me right now, I'd fall without a sound. The silence is not a bottled thing, but a relief somehow. It is recognizing there is nothing to say, no one to cry out to.

Houdini is not in the yard, not in the chicken yard, not behind the barn, not in the cow pasture, not behind the guest house, not in the driveway. I walk the long dusty driveway all the way out to the highway, right past the dealership and the huge metal building that Tom is working in. I don't pause. I look up and down the highway, but Houdini is not there, either. I walk back, past fields tilled but left fallow, green fuzzed now with dead nettle and the beginnings of St. Michael's wort, stink chamomile and wild violets. The wild plants do not mind this heat, do not wilt and brown, but squat bravely beneath the sun, knowing that all sunshine in Washington is at best a temporary thing. This heat and light will pass. If the truth be known, all things are temporary. All pains are temporary. Confine me to a wheelchair for the rest of my life, it's still temporary, only one drop of moment in God's eternal time stream. If there's comfort here, it's a sparse one.

I look all the places I have looked before. The pony is still not in any of them.

I think I know where he is.

Cool water and crisp green things to bite. Scratching his dusty rump against a tree. Brown hands unbuckling the harness straps, rubbing the halter marks off with handfuls of moss, wiping away his tameness with the wild woods.

As I go through the barbed-wire fence, I know it is not a good idea. Soon Ellie will be walking into the little house with her arms full of whiter-than-white sheets, with stacks of towels perfumed from fabric softener. She will wonder where I am, she will tell her parents I am gone, and they will tell Tom.

It is not that I don't care. It is only that I am silent inside.

There are hoof marks beside the stream as I follow it, of hooves both cloven and shod. When I come to the halter, I pick it up. I find it is heavier than I knew, the leather is damp with sweat and the metal pieces are cool and smooth to my touch. I drape it over my arm, and it weighs it down. I try to imagine having it on my head.

The air is cooler under the trees. I pluck my shirt loose from my sweaty back and feel my body cool. My feet are so hot, the path of packed earth looks invitingly smooth and cool, but I do not take my shoes off.

I do not have to go far. The pony is in a small, sun-dappled clearing. Grasses have been laced through his mane and tail, woven into the shining braids. His coat has been cleansed of dust, even his hooves shine. I come toward him slowly, one hand outstretched in a friendly way. I smell the wild mint that has been wiped over him.

When I am within range, I grip his braided mane, firmly, suddenly, but he does not flinch. He stands docile beneath my touch. He does not toss his head as the leather is settled over his brow and muzzle, does not pull away as I fasten the stiff buckles. My hands shake as I comb them through his mane, pulling the braids free of the knotted grass stems that held them, dragging my fingers down the coarse hair so that the grasses and flowers shower loose from the braids and fall at our feet.

When I am finished, I look around the clearing, at the straight trunks and uplifted branches, at the buck brush and the wild roses. I have something to say, but no one to speak to. I say it anyway, speaking to one who is not there but who will hear me anyway.

"No," I say. I repeat it to be clear. "No."

The pony does not resist me as I lead him home.

# Fourteen

*The Farm July 1976*

When I get back, I put the pony in the chicken yard. Then I get my purse from the house and check the cars in the yard. There are three, Ellie and Bix's huge clunker, Mother Maurie's shiny sedan, and Tom's father's four-wheel drive red pickup. The keys are in the ignition of the sedan, so I take it. I don't ask permission. The silence inside me wouldn't let me.

At the hardware store I buy nylon line and shackles, a long metal rod and a swivel.

When I get home, I take a sledge from the shop, and drive the metal pole into the ground of the chicken yard. I put the swivel on it, and then peen the head over. The line and shackle fastens to the swivel, and finally the swivel clips to Houdini's halter. He is not pleased, and immediately checks out how long the picket rope is. He backs up and pulls steadily on it. I watch long enough to be sure my rod isn't going to pull out of the ground, and then I go put the sledge back in the shop. Houdini still has the picket line stretched tight when I come back. I ignore it. He'll get tired of it soon enough.

I go back to the little house and go straight to the laundry cupboard. The sheets and towels are there, in precise white stacks. A little stick-on-the-wall deodorizer has been added to the cupboard. Lemon-spice flavor. Oh, goody. I shut the cupboard doors.

Teddy comes home from swimming, hair slicked to his small head. Tom comes home later. We eat dinner. Teddy runs back to watch Disney with Steffie. Later he comes home to go to bed. Later Tom goes to bed, and then I do. He sleeps. And no one notices my silence, no one comments on it, or asks if I am all right, am I angry, am I sad? I think perhaps it has been a long time since they really heard me. And it doesn't bother me. If Tom's parents have said anything at all to him about me or the pony, he does not mention it. I cannot believe they haven't said anything to him. Before today, I would not have believed that they could complain to him about me and he wouldn't tell me about it. But now I can imagine it, how they talk together, how he shrugs his shoulders over me and says, "Well, Dad, I just don't know what to do about her." I wonder what else he has discussed with them, if any of our quarrels have been private. It makes the emptiness inside me a little colder.

I listen to the wind blow, and feel the house cool. Before true dawn, the rain begins, falling steadily in a drenching, cooling flow. I cook breakfast to its music. I find that words and silence are not mutually exclusive. "Over easy?" I say, and "More coffee?" and "Your clean socks are in the top drawer now," and still my silence is undiminished. It holds when Teddy and I go out to give the pony a bucket of water and some grain.

Houdini stands in the rain, looking abjectly miserable. "Can't we put him in the cow barn?" Teddy asks, and I have to shake my head no. No sense in even asking. "He's used to being in the rain," I tell Teddy, and I know this is true, for his old owners left him out in that one pasture, rain or shine. He has already made a circle of trodden mud at the limits of his picket rope.

The rain lasts five solid days. After the second day, Teddy doesn't want to go out in the rain and mud to feed and water the pony. So I do. By the third day Houdini has worn a great brown circle in the chicken yard. I have to pull up the rod and move his picket line. It is difficult dirty work, mud splatters up in my face as I struggle to drive the rod into the ground, but I don't ask anyone for help. I can't think of anyone I could ask.

I can't even think of anyone I can talk to. I now know that talking to Tom is like talking to his parents via satellite relay. If it isn't something I want to say to them, I shouldn't say it to Tom.

There is nothing I want to say to Tom.

On the first sunny day, Teddy suits up in his cowboy clothes and rides Houdini for an hour. The next day he rides for fifteen minutes. The next day is Saturday, and he goes to watch cartoons with Aunt Steffie. The next day is Sunday, and he wants to sleep in. He no longer helps me feed and water the pony each morning. I don't really blame him. Houdini is not exactly a bundle of personality. He is to Trigger, Fury, and the Black Stallion what Cream of Wheat is to Super Sugar Puffs.

The summer days are as rainy now as they have been hot before. The days drip by, interspersed with clear spells when the sky is incredibly blue and the wind blows fresh over the green fields. My life drips by, spells of grey interrupted by brief moments of clarity. On the grey days, I move Houdini's picket line from his current circle of mud, and wonder with trepidation when Tom's father will pounce on me about the ruin of his chicken yard. I feed the pony, and water him, and groom him, as if he were my own. Everyone refers to him now as Evelyn's pony. It is a household joke. I am a household joke. It doesn't really bother me. All I have to do is keep going from day to day. I have come to understand Ellie's obsession with housework. There is always something to do, always something to busy the hands and dull the mind. It is wonderful, how every day there are more dishes to wash, more dirt to sweep, more clothes to wash. An endless supply of busy boredom. The clear spells are much harder to deal with. I awaken in the middle of the night, weeping, and have to go huddle in the darkened kitchen so that the shaking of my body will not waken Tom. I do not know why I weep, whatever I dream hides itself from me. When the fit passes, I look out the window into the darkness and hate. Hate Tom for trapping me, hate myself for submitting to being trapped, hate Pan for giving me up so easily. Why does he not come to my windowsill, push open the window

from outside, offer me a hand to take as I clamber over
it and outside to freedom? Why don't I climb out on my
own? The second question is the most painful one. The
only answer that I can seem to find is that if I just walk
away from it all, I will have lost everything I ever cared
about keeping. I try to believe that if I just hang on,
withstand this battering and hang on, in the end it will
get better, and that when I leave, I will leave a winner,
taking what I care about with me.

After one such spell, I resolve that I will at least
have Teddy. The next day dawns clear and blue, and I
devote myself to him with a single-mindedness that is
devouring. My favor shines on him like a spotlight on a
deer. He cannot escape me. I start with pancakes shaped
like teddy bears and swans. I have him wash the dishes
afterward, while I stand beside him and dry them. Then
we go out together, into the new washed day. I insist he
help me feed the pony and brush him, ignore his
resentful silence and his unsubtle hints about the morning cartoons at Grandma's house that he is missing.
Without his help, I saddle Houdini.

"Today," I tell him, "you're going to ride him
outside of this stupid chicken yard." And this is enough
of a novelty that it wins his attention. I lead them up the
long driveway, my grip on the bridle firm, and then, on
the way back, I say, "Hold on now," and let go of the
leather and give Houdini a determined slap on the butt.
Houdini has come to respect me over the last few weeks,
and he jolts into a determined trot. "Grip with your
knees," I call to Teddy as I run along beside him. "Toes
toward his nose. Hold the reins with your thumbs up,
like you're holding ice-cream cones. Move with him,
now." Wisdom garnered from a hundred horse books
read when I was a kid, rules I've never applied, telling
him to do things I've never done. But he listens, and
tries, and suddenly, halfway down the driveway, instead
of being spanked up and down by Houdini's back, he is
riding. And that fat little devil of a pony, from some
unsuspected depths of his soul, remembers what it was
like to be ridden, and actually launches into a canter.
They outdistance me rapidly, and to my horror, when

they reach the chicken yard, Teddy actually reins him around in a circle and they come cantering back toward me. I stand my ground as they come toward me, that four-legged liar and everything I still care about on his slippery barrel back. I will not let them past me, will not let him carry my last hope and joy out onto the highway and into the path of some determined chicken truck.

But Teddy hauls back on the reins as they approach, and Houdini actually slows, then halts. Teddy launches at me and I catch him, barely making out his shrieks of "I did it, I rode like a real cowboy!" I hug him tight, swing him in a circle, and then he is kicking free of me, running back toward the pony. He hugs the cussed little beast, and Houdini actually appears to enjoy it. Maybe he was just sick of plodding around a chicken yard, I think to myself. Teddy still needs a boost to scramble up, and then they are off again, this time Teddy leaning forward and urging him to even greater speed.

On the third time down the driveway, Teddy slips off at the turn, and lands with a thud I can hear. But even before I can get to him, Houdini is standing over him, sniffing him concernedly. There are no hard feelings, but that is enough riding for today. For the first time since Teddy got him, there is actually sweat on the pony's hide when he rubs him down.

"I gotta tell Steffie!" Teddy exclaims.

Guile rises in me. "Later," I tell him. "Maybe this evening. But right now we have to pack our picnic lunch."

"Picnic?" asks Teddy, and I nod and grin, showing all my teeth in a wolfish smile. Mine, mine, all mine.

I have not planned for a picnic today. No matter. Eggs, there are always eggs in the chicken house, and we "rustle" six, giggling and poking each other in the wild joy of theft. Back at the house, we make deviled eggs, and peanut butter and jelly sandwiches, and a thermos of Kool-Aid. We don't have a basket, but a brown paper sack will do. At the last minute, an ancient memory surfaces, and I add a plastic mixing bowl and a small kitchen knife.

"What's that for?" asks Teddy, but I shake my head mysteriously, and lead him out of the house.

And across the cow pasture.

And into the forest.

When I was twelve, I was a poet for at least six months. An ancient snatch of it comes back to me. "As the sun was breaking, I slipped down the lane. Back to the arms of my forest again."

Back to the arms of my forest again, bringing my son. He follows behind me, as a fawn follows a doe, as porcupines the size of croquet balls waddle after their armored mother. He follows me down the narrow path, stooping when I do, slipping under the leaning branches, stepping over the fallen limbs. We move silently, as one. I glance back at him once, and his eyes are shining. I only wonder that I have never done this with him before.

We scarcely speak, except for my giving of names. "Show currant," I tell him, and "Alder." "Russian thistle, watercress, here, taste some, wild mint, taste this, too." It becomes a litany of introductions, a presentation at court. "Club moss, fly agaric, Saint-John's-wort, liverwort, witches butter, buttercups." Pouring it into his head like cake batter poured into pans, to bake and set and live on for the rest of his life.

Soon he begins, "What's this? What's that?" and soon I am admitting that there are many here I do not know, and promising a trip to the library or even into the mall to a bookstore to find out.

We usurp Pan's glen, spread our picnic on his moss by his stream. Does he watch us? I refuse to think about it. Instead, we eat, deviled eggs dipped into salt from a twist of wax paper, peanut butter and jelly, sharing the thermos cup of Kool-Aid, and it all tastes much better than it really does because it's a picnic. Teddy rolls up his jeans and wades in the stream. Sediment swirls up around his pink bared feet and flows away. A startled fingerling flashes past him, brushing a scaled side against his skin and jolting an exuberant shout from him. He pursues the fish with much splashing and shrieking. It is midafternoon when he tires of the game and comes out, to eat the last deviled egg and stretch out on the moss for the sun to dry his bare legs. He falls asleep there on the bank, and sleeps limply as do all wild things on a warm afternoon in the forest. His pale hair and tanned face contrast with the moss that cushions his sleep. I sit and watch the water flowing, the birds flitting from branch to branch, and my young son sleeping. Restlessness and urgency depart me, and I breathe slowly, in a kind of open-eyed sleep. The glen has a wholeness to it that cannot be broken, so that I see it all when I look at one damp pebble, and see each stem of grass, each frond of fern, when I let my eyes go wide and unfocused.

And, of course, he is part of it.

I watch him come, stepping with ancient elven grace, hooves entering and leaving the stream without so much as a splash. Slanting sunlight through the branches gleams his flanks, polishes his high cheekbones, is swallowed in the darkness of his eyes. When he moves his head, light ricochets off his horns. I do not move or speak. It is not me he has come to see.

He steps all around my boy, his nostrils flaring and working as he takes in his scent. His cloven hooves cut deep into the moss, scoring into the rich earth below the green carpet. My boy sleeps before those sharp-edged hooves, and a stiffening of apprehension runs through my muscles. It is no longer the friend of my childhood who stands there, but the forest god, the hooved and horned one beholding an intruder in his domain. What rules bind one such as that? My breath slows in my lungs, pauses. He cocks his head as he studies my son, watches the slow rise and fall of his chest. I see Teddy as he does, the dark lashes of his closed eyes, the round curves of his cheeks, the small lips that move slightly in some dream conversation.

Pan lifts his eyes to me, then looks back at my boy, and I see him making the connections, finding the lines of my face traced in Teddy's. Finding also the alien configurations of the man I have given myself to, Tom's brow, Tom's long lashes, Tom's soft pale hair. He glances back to me suddenly, a harder look, but I take it calmly and hold my ground, returning it levelly. This is where we are, I think to myself, and also, perhaps, to him. This is how it is, and no changing that. For a long time our eyes are locked, and then his face changes, slowly, softening with both pain and acceptance of the pain. When he looks back to Teddy, I know he is seeing him differently, seeing him as a separate entity, as himself, as a young boy asleep in the faun's glen. Teddy sleeps brown and gold as any offering, and I see Pan consider him. There is the place in Kipling's *Jungle Book* when Mowgli is presented to the pack, and the cry rings out, "Look, look well, O Wolves." When Pan nods slowly, and a curving smile bares his white teeth, I know my boy is free to both field and forest, and I am glad.

He looks to me once more, a look I cannot read, and then he turns aside. He leaves as he came, not a drop of water splashing at his passage, not a leaf rustling. Only the track of cloven hooves remain, and I touch them with one finger, feeling the realness of sheared earth.

Not even his scent remains in the dell when Teddy awakens. Teddy does not notice the tracks all around him, nor do I call his attention to them. Instead, we take the bowl and knife and venture deeper into the woods. "When I was little," I tell him, "my mother taught me all about mushrooms. We'd go out every good damp morning and look for them. She showed me the ones I could eat, and the ones I couldn't. And when we came to one we didn't know, we'd take it home, and look it up in a book. Sometimes we'd make spore prints from the mushrooms by setting the caps down on white or black paper and leaving them there until they'd dropped their spores. Spores are like mushroom seeds, sort of, but very tiny. They make a lovely pattern on the paper, like the spokes of wheels or the ribs of an umbrella. There's one. This shrively black kind is called a morel. They mostly like burned-over places, but sometimes they grow in the deep woods, too."

We look for mushrooms together, and though we do not find many, we have a few morels, two shaggy manes, and six small puff balls to take home with us. As we pass back through the faun's dell, we pick up our sack and thermos.

"My mother knew as much about mushrooms as anyone in Fairbanks. When the time came for the Tanana Valley Fair, she used to take me into the woods, and we'd gather moss and sticks and layers of fallen leaves, and cover a display table with them. Then we'd gather fresh mushrooms at dawn, for every day that the fair was open, and we'd set them up in the moss, with little signs saying what they were, and if you could eat them or not. I didn't care much for the fair, but I loved the early mornings with my mother. We'd take the bottoms of beer boxes, and put a long string from one end of them to the other, and hang the strings around our necks, so the boxes stuck out like trays in front of us. We'd gather each mushroom whole, and carefully set it on the tray, so that when it got to the fair, it wouldn't be bruised or crumpled. My mother knew so much about mushrooms that once, when someone had to go to the hospital after eating the wrong kind, the hospital phoned up and described the mushroom to her, so she could tell them what it really was and what kind of poison was in it."

I think this is the first time I have ever spoken to my son about his other grandmother. I am surprised at how sharp the images are, how easily the words come. When I tell him, I can see her, wearing a baggy, hooded sweatshirt, the sleeves pushed up nearly to the elbows, the lines in her weathered face undisguised by makeup, proud of her years. A flood of affection washes through me for the woman who gave me to the forest. As now I give my son.

By the time we get back to the house, it is time to make dinner. We clean the mushrooms and fry them beside the hamburger patties. Tom won't eat any. He has never trusted my ability to identify edible ones, and plainly does not approve of my risking Teddy's life by feeding him fungus things from the forest. Teddy and I pay him no mind, but eat well. And after dinner, I do not do the dishes, or even clear the table. Instead, we sit on the couch, and I tell him stories of what Fairbanks was like when I was a little girl. I tell him of duck nests, and baby rabbits so small they fit in a teacup, of chewing on the new green bundles of spruce needles before they turn dark green, of a squirrel nest made of someone's old nylons, of moose walking past me by moonlight. He laughs when I tell him about how, for two months straight, I walked someone's trap line every day and sprang every single trap, because I didn't want anyone trapping so near my slough. Tom clatters the dishes a great deal as he clears the table. He dumps them into the sink, but doesn't wash them. "Honey, where's the coffee?" he demands a short time later, and I say, "In the bottom left cupboard," but I do not rise to hurry over and make a pot for him. Instead, I tell Teddy about swimming in gravel pits, and unwinding paper bark from birch trees, of picking rose hips and stoning wasps' nests. I tell him about Rinky, and our log house, and sword fighting with my brothers with the long icicles from the eaves. When he lies down to sleep, his eyes are full of stories.

I go to bed without Tom. He comes in later, and wants me, and I do not care. It is a simple coupling, with little foreplay and no whispered words or long kisses. No more difficult than doing the dishes or sweeping the dirt or washing the clothes.

"Sorry," he says some moments afterward. "I guess I came too soon. Tired, I guess. Next time will be better." Then he goes to sleep. I am somewhat surprised that he even notices that I did not climax. I had not paid much attention to it, myself. I have other things to think about.

The next day is more difficult, for I know it must be as good as yesterday was. Teddy helps me make a coffee cake for breakfast, with cinnamon and raisins. But it takes too long to bake, and Tom and Teddy both eat bowls of cereal before it is finished. Tom leaves early, and Teddy and I have a leisurely second breakfast of coffee cake by ourselves. I leave the dishes again. I know I will have to do them later, but I don't want to risk Teddy getting bored and slipping away from me while I am washing dishes.

Houdini's whole attitude changes as we approach

him. Head and ears go up, and he shudders his whole coat as if to prepare himself for the bareback pad. Teddy slaps his shoulder with affectionate fearlessness, and saddles and bridles him with minimal help from me. This time I do not lead them out of the chicken yard, but merely open the gate and stand aside as Teddy reins him through.

Although my heart pounds, I force myself to lean casually against the gate as Teddy trots Houdini up the driveway toward the highway. I have to believe in him so he can believe in himself, I tell myself. And at the highway he turns him competently, then leans forward and I see his knees tighten, his small hand rise and fall. They come toward me at a gallop, growing suddenly larger like a locomotive in a cartoon, and then they are sweeping past me in a gust of horsy wind, going all the way to the end of the driveway before Teddy reins him in. Teddy turns him and rides him slowly back toward me. His face is flushed with pride and Houdini tosses his head willfully as if he were the Black Stallion. Little shits.

I hear the sound of clapping from the screened porch of the big house. Even before Steffie steps out, I know it is her.

"Well, Dad told me about it, but I just had to see for myself," she exclaims as she crosses the yard toward us. Teddy halts Houdini beside me and sits grandly awaiting her praises.

"Your dad?" I ask bewilderedly.

"Sure. He said he saw Teddy riding yesterday and was impressed with what he could get out of that fat little hay-burner. Said he almost wished he'd bought Teddy a real horse instead of that pony. Dad and Mom both said Teddy's inherited the Potter way with horses, and they're right. That kid sits that pony like he's been riding for years."

Damn him! "Tom bought the pony for Teddy," I point out quietly.

It goes past Steffie. "Well, sure, but you know what he means. Hey, Cowboy, you know what would be fun, now? Sign you up for 4-H with one of the horse groups. You get to learn all about horses, and when fair comes, you go to Puyallup and sleep in the barn with the horses and the other 4-H kids and show what you know and win ribbons and stuff."

Teddy's eyes grow big.

"Oh, hey, you know what would be really great!" Steffie's eyes are glowing too as she includes me in this wonderful idea. "I could borrow a horse from Clemmons down the road, and Teddy and I could go riding some of the back trails. The survey cuts go for miles, you know . . . hey, Cowboy, we could take a picnic and be gone all day, even."

I'd like to drive a stake through her heart. I'd like to tell her, "Hey, go have your own kid instead of trying to steal mine." But there is something in her words, a veiled sort of desperation. Steffie, so beautiful and perfect. So caged and so bored. Waiting to be a model, an interior decorator, an artist. Waiting for a handsome, rich young man to come into the equipment dealership, see her and marry her and take her off to raise horses. I don't think she's ever had a job in her life, other than working for Old Man Incorporated. Her high-school friends have gone off to college or gotten married. None of them have time for Steffie, trapped in the amber of an eternal Senior Sneak Day. Her makeup is flawless, there is not a chip out of her enameled nails, no two eyelashes are stuck together, all her hairs are artlessly but perfectly touseled back from her face, there is not a scratch or scuff on her long, tanned legs. The long-stemmed American Beauty has reached dewy, hothouse perfection. She has it all.

It would probably be the high point of her summer to take a little boy on a trail ride.

I can't hate her like I hate her parents, and I know this is a chink in my armor. It is through Steffie that they will stab me dead and steal my boy away. But it is like the way I love Tom, a thing I cannot deny, and I find I am nodding up at Teddy, watching the wonderment in his face break out in his excited grin.

"Okay, now, okay!" Steffie says, a little breathless. "Don't get too excited, Cowboy. It's gonna take me a while to get this set up. I'm not sure who's doing 4-H anymore. And I have to go down to Clemmons's in person, if I'm gonna talk Dougie into loaning me a horse."

Wickedly I imagine how she will look at that poor stump rancher, how she will smile and turn in her high white shorts as she asks to borrow the Morgan that is his pride and joy. She'll get it, I know, for I've seen how he looks at her when he comes to the equipment dealership for parts for his old back hoe. It is pathetic to me that she will vamp that poor bastard to borrow his horse so she can go out with my five-year-old son. Pathetic, but at least human.

Impetuously she hugs Teddy, the pony, and me before I can sidestep her. Her little white sandals clatter over the driveway gravel as she races back to the house and the telephone, to find out who is 4-H'ing this year. Purpose replaces her usual languid stride with the scuttle of a banty hen. Teddy and I exchange looks. "Well. She certainly seems in a hurry," I remark, and Teddy surprises me by giggling. "You want to go riding with her?" I ask, already knowing the answer, not even hoping he will say no.

"Sure," he says, and by way of punctuation he reins Houdini's head up and turns him up the driveway again. Off they go at a trot that becomes a canter, and he turns the pony in a whirl of mane and tail and brings him back. He reins him in smartly beside me this time, to ask worriedly, "After we ride today, we're going back into the woods, aren't we?"

"You want to?" I ask, a little surprised.

"'Course." He looks down at me as if I'm a little crazy. "To the stream," he adds, as if fearful I would not know that.

He makes another trip down the driveway and back, pauses to ask, "Can I build a fort back there?"

He doesn't even wait for my answer before he is gone. I know the next question before he brings it to me, in a clatter of hooves. "Am I allowed to go back there alone?"

"Of course," I say, feeling the rightness. "There's nothing back there that will hurt you."

How could I have forgotten the fascination that moving water holds for small children? That afternoon I let Teddy lead, watching with a small sense of awe how easily he takes us by exactly the same route we used yesterday. He is not even conscious of having memorized it. The practical side of me makes him stop several times and look back the way he has come, see the stump with the broken limb, see the three madrona trees together, see the fallen trunk with three saplings growing out of it, to be sure he can recognize the way home. He is impatient with this, just as if I had asked him to turn around and look back down the driveway to the house. Of course he knows the way home; it is too simple to even talk about.

For now, the stream is all he asks of the forest. It is an incredibly rich place, brimming with life and movement and light. He enmeshes himself in the network of the glade, lying on his belly to let the stream flow over his hands and arms. The underwater plants that bow to the flow of water, the frogs that boldly stroke upstream against it, the water itself that is the movement, all this he touches and explores. He droops his head to the passing rush of water, opens his mouth to it and becomes one with the movement, the moisture, and the life. The sunlight breaking through the tree branches strokes his smooth browned back, bounces off his pale hair in the same dazzling way it breaks off the moving water. He has found his niche within the forest, beside this moving water, and now is part of the whole. I've done all I needed to do. It is all assured now. I could not tell what it is that is assured, but I know that it is safely accomplished. And that is a satiation of sorts. I lie back, the dappling shade against my thighs as soft and warm as a lover's hand. I feel more at peace than I have felt in months.

Ultimately, this is what Teddy gives me. A peace at the center of things. Tom's bitching becomes more overt, and before many days pass I am back in my routine of washing the dishes and doing the laundry and sweeping the floor. Steffie does borrow a horse and does take my boy riding. And he has a wonderful time. But the very next morning, long before the sun is high, he is gone again, back to his woods and stream. I know they will never hold him now, for like the giant who had no heart in his body, Teddy's heart is hidden from his enemies under cool moving water in the depths of his stronghold. The forest teaches him, and I eavesdrop on his lessons when I empty the pockets of his shorts each night. An acorn, the delicate sun-baked skeleton of a frog's leg, a water-smoothed agate, a curl of birch bark, an alder cone: all notes from the anatomy of the forest, all elements of the grand equation. I smile foolishly over them, and group them carefully on the glass-topped table in the living room, for him to do with as he will.

The raging heat of July burns past me in a sort of dream. There is the noisy orgasm of fireworks spattering against the night sky, but they are quickly forgotten in the high heat of summer, in browning grasses and ripening berries. He brings buckets of berries to me, handfuls of mushrooms, pinches of watercress and mint. One evening I am gifted with a tiny boat fashioned of a curl of bark with a leaf for a sail. Pan and I used to make these, I think fondly to myself. I smile over the memory as the dish suds slide down my forearms into the steamy sink, and Tom's grousing about a late parts shipment and water in someone's hydraulics are like a radio in a different room.

Tom and his family have retreated. No. They are where they always were, quarreling, boasting, dealing, figuring, and scheming. But I have a distance around me now that they cannot broach. When Mother Maurie clucks over how the sun and wind have ruined my hair, I can shrug it off. When one day Houdini is surreptitiously moved into the cow pasture, I can take it with equanimity, as I do the new red saddle that delights Teddy from his grandfather's hands. Now that Tom's father takes pride in his grandson's riding ability, the pony is accepted and necessary. When Steffie carries

Teddy off to an evening 4-H meeting, to later bring Teddy home and then leave again with the young man who oversees his group, I can smile to myself and even take a vicarious pleasure in her interest in him. All of it, somehow, is tolerable now. They cannot hurt me now, I think.

I will never be so wrong again.

# Fifteen

*The Farm July 1976*

It starts on Ellie's birthday.

Ellie's birthday is no big deal. All it means is all of us having dinner together at the big house. Ellie cleans up the house, puts a cloth on the table, makes a nice meal of roast beef and mashed potatoes and green beans, and lots of coffee. She bakes herself a nice cake, chocolate cake with white frosting. We sing "Happy Birthday" and she blows out the candles. She opens presents. Nice presents. An apron with a big white goose appliquéd on it from Steffie. A cookbook from Mother Maurie. A dozen little canning jars, with special decorated labels that say, "From the Kitchen of Ellie Bishop," from Bix. I wonder if the labels are to help her remember her last name is the same as his. From Tom's father, a bottle of special spray solvent. "New kinda stuff," he tells us when Ellie unwraps it. "Guy at the store says it'll cut through the crud on range hood fans, barbecue grills, oven spills, baked-on greasy stuff, just like lightning! Gotta wear rubber gloves to use it, though. Should make things a lot easier for Ellie."

He is obviously proud of his gift, of his practicality and thoughtfulness. Ellie beams at him. "Thanks, Daddy. I didn't think anyone had noticed what a time I have with that ol' range hood."

The last present is from Tom. He has picked it up in

town that afternoon. I have no idea what it is. Ellie
opens a white box, unwraps tissue paper endlessly. A
ship in a bottle. She holds it up and we all look at it.
Then we all look at Tom. Except Ellie. She looks at the
ship inside the bottle.

"What the hell?" says Tom's father.

"Remember," Tom says, his voice ineffectual in the
quiet. "When Steffie and I had measles, and Ellie read
*Treasure Island* to us? We'd never heard anything like
that before. And remember, Ellie said that when she
grew up, she was going to get a pirate ship of her own.
So, well, I saw that in Ardinger's window, and I got it for
her." He tries a laugh. No one joins in. "Her own pirate
ship," he explains. He laughs again. Alone.

"Oh, yeah," Steffie says belatedly. I can almost see
the light bulb go on over her head. "I remember that.
Long John Silver and Tom Hawkins, or something.
Yeah, the kid in the book was named Tom, like you,
wasn't he?"

"Jim," I mutter, but no one notices. Tom is getting
pink around the ears. His father looks confused.

"Ellie can always keep it on her dresser," Mother
Maurie announces brightly. "It's amazing how one unusual thing can liven up a room's decor."

I giggle into my coffee, turn it into a choking fit,
which everyone politely ignores. This room couldn't get
much livelier, then, I want to say, but I don't.

Tom's father is still miffed, offended somehow by a
gift he cannot understand. "Well, that's a peculiar thing
to give your sister for her birthday, but I guess it's some
family joke I'm left out of," he concludes. I am so glad he
has explained it for us all. Steffie looks uneasy, as if
Teddy has asked her to explain incest or the hickey that
peeks over the collar of her shirt. She shifts uncomfortably. Ellie is still looking at her ship in the bottle, but for
once her angular face does not look gaunt to me. Her
eyes are dark and sharp, I notice, and those planes and
lines could have framed a scholar's mind, that large skull
beneath her severe hair could have housed the brain of
an archaeologist or historian. For a moment I imagine
her weathered hands sweeping dust from artifacts in-

stead of knickknacks, see her pulling the lines of a sailboat instead of a clothesline. Could have been. Lucky she married a big dumb farm kid and settled down to housecleaning before she ruined her life.

"The brown man can make those, only real," Teddy says. He shovels more cake into his mouth.

"What?" Tom's father asks sharply. I have an uneasy feeling he is grateful for this diversion.

"Brown man," Teddy explains, a few cake crumbs flying with the words. "Makes those out of wood and stuff."

"What brown man? Makes what?"

Teddy swallows like an ostrich. "I said," he says with an effort. "That my brown man can make boats like those. With sails and strings and stuff. But his really float. Until I bomb 'em. Then he gets mad and throws water at me!" Teddy giggles and shovels more cake in. I feel suddenly cold.

"What 'brown man'?" Tom's father demands indignantly. "Ain't no niggers live around here that I know of."

I sip my coffee, my lower teeth tapping twice against the rim of the mug before I can get it to my mouth. Stop shaking. Be calm. Think of something else. "Ain't" and "niggers" in one sentence. Must be wonderful to be able to sling fluent Redneck like that. I hope that somehow the subject will die. But they are all waiting for Teddy to finish chewing. Instead, he flushes the mouthful down with a glog of milk.

"The brown man in the woods," he explains patiently. "Back there." He waves a laden fork in the general direction of the chicken yard. Cake goes flying.

"Teddy," I warn maternally. "Better clean that up, honey, and stop telling stories."

"Okay," he says noncommittally, and I start to breathe out.

"Ain't no niggers back there. That's the govamint land back there," Tom's father explains.

"Teddy, you been playing with someone back there in the woods?" Tom asks his son, while Steffie asks, in general, "He goes back in those woods alone?"

"Only the brown man," Teddy says to the floor. He is gobbing up the cake with a paper napkin. "And only sometimes. He's got real hairy legs, you know," he adds, as if that should explain it all to us.

"I don't want my grandson playing in the woods with some nigger kid," Tom's dad announces grandly. "Teddy, you listen to Grandpa. You stay away from niggers, you hear me? There's none live around here, and if there's one back there in the woods, it means he's up to no good. Next time you see that nigger, you come and tell me right away, all right? I want to have a little talk with him."

"You don't think he'd harm the boy, do you?" Mother Maurie whispers in awe.

"I don't know." Grandpa is manifestly annoyed with his womenfolk's naiveté. "Who knows? He's got no business back there. Teddy, you remember what I said. You hear me, Teddy?"

"Yes, Grandpa." He finishes wiping up the cake and scratches a mosquito bite on his ankle. Then he climbs back up to the table. I try to catch his eyes, but he is concentrating on a second piece of cake that Aunt Steffie is dishing up. I have an eerie feeling that he doesn't hear his grandpa at all. No more than I do. The evening becomes more congenial now. Uncomfortable topics, like Ellie's birthday and ships in bottles, have been forgotten, and the conversation escalates into wicked-niggers-I-have-known stories. Everyone gets into it, with each story more lurid than the last. I can sense the family drawing closer around their shared values. Better than ghost stories around a campfire are these depraved darky stories, only I cannot seem to keep my ears tuned to them. The voices and words fade in and out like distant radio stations on a piece of winding road. Sort of like the day the pony rolled in the azalea bushes. I try to pay attention, only to realize I have been concentrating so hard on forcing myself to listen that I have forgotten to make sense of the words. "You remember what Grandpa told you, now," is Grandpa's good night to us, and perhaps no one but me notices the uncharacteristic hug that Ellie inflicts on Tom.

Later that night, as I tuck Teddy in, he asks me, "What's a nigger?" I realize it is a word he has not heard from Tom and me. It is a word, oddly, that I have never heard Tom use, not even in jest. I don't want to tell Teddy it's a rude word for a black person. The stories are too vivid and recent, and Teddy will innocently carry my definition back to Grandpa. So I shrug. "Never met one," I tell him.

"Then the brown man's not a nigger, 'cause he knows you."

Teddy rolls over and goes to sleep.

I do not sleep. I lie awake and try not to worry. What has the brown man told Teddy about his mother? What will Teddy tell everyone else? I dare not ask him not to tell. Secrets are too large a burden for his little shoulders. Especially secrets that make me feel guilty. Not that I have any reason to feel guilty. I have done nothing amiss. A single kiss? What's that, between old friends? Nothing. And everything. I do not realize Tom is awake beside me until he says, "Honey, it's normal for kids to have imaginary playmates. Teddy will forget this 'brown man' thing as soon as he starts kindergarten."

I am surprised that he has even known I am awake. As surprised as Ellie was by the boat. "I guess so," I answer. The immensity of the things I could confide in him swell within me, but I swallow the words, hoard the knowledge. It's nothing he'd want to know, anyway. "Teddy will be fine," I finally say. This seems to satisfy him, and I do not resist when he reaches over and drags me under him. In fact, I hardly notice.

Later, while he sleeps, I try to figure out where we are these days. If I don't care about him, I could leave, right? Just take Teddy and go? But I cannot say I do not love him. I cannot even bring myself to try the traitorous words on my tongue. It is so much easier to whisper, "I love you, Tom," to the unhearing night. I try to feel that, but it is buried inside me, a thing put into storage, a bright summer dress set aside in mothballs until the long winter passes. I know it was true once. I have the feeling that if I can last this out, there will be a someday when we live on our own again, and I will be in love with him again. I will want him again, I will wake him up in the middle of the night and lead him by the hand to the grove of birches behind the cabin and make love to him on the deep moss with the night wind against our skins.

It is too much like a fairy tale.

The next morning Teddy is up early. He gallops Houdini around in the cow pasture while I am doing dishes, dusting and waxing and other fascinating chores. Now that Teddy's riding is a thing for Grandpa to brag about, he is allowed to ride in the pasture. I go to the window and check on them every ten or fifteen minutes. Even so, Houdini is unsaddled and grazing the next time I look, and Teddy is nowhere in sight. I sigh a little, knowing where he is, and wishing I were there. Hoping, too, that the brown man will say nothing of me to my son, and that my son will say no more of the brown man.

Such hopes dare the fates. I know when Teddy returns. I hear him long before I see him. He announces his arrival with shrill tootling on a three-note willow whistle. I do not need to ask him who carved it for him. I do not even get the chance, for Grandpa intercepts him as he comes across the yard. Seemingly, he does not have to ask Teddy, either, for his words come clear to me inside the house. "Young man, what did I tell you yesterday?"

I see the sunshine fade from Teddy's face as he squints up at his grandfather. I do not hear his words, his child's voice is too soft. I turn away from the sink and the window and go to sit on Teddy's bed/sofa. It is a terrible feeling to not be able to protect one's child. A gutless feeling to wait while he weathers the storm of his grandfather's disapproval. But I know if I went out there, anything I said would only make it worse. Better to wait, to be ready.

He comes in, after years of waiting that last about twenty minutes. He sits solemnly beside me. He is bereft of his whistle. From some distant past, I hear my own grandmother's hiss in my ear, "Wash that fruit before you eat it. A black person might have touched it."

"Hello," I say noncommittaly.

"If you're brown, you're a nigger," he explains to me.

"Oh," I say. Inadequate.

"I really like the brown man."

I nod my agreement. I could give him a lecture about how it's rude to call brown people niggers, and that there are many different kinds of brown people, and that they are not at all like the nigger stories that were told last night. I could expound at length on race relations and brotherhood. But he already knows it all. He has met one brown man on his own, and he will never buy the nigger myth now. Too late, Grandpa.

"Let's make cookies," I say instead.

"Brownies?" he asks, and when I innocently agree, he bursts into laughter.

"Niggeries!" he chokes. "Grandpa won't eat them!"

The brownies are baking in the oven before Teddy remembers to dig in the pocket of his shorts. "The brown man made one for you, too," he explains as he shows me the willow whistle.

Somehow I cannot touch it, cannot take it from his innocent hands. It would be admitting something. Whenever Teddy speaks of the brown man knowing me, a coldness shivers inside me, like a hidden guilt roiling through my stomach. I want him to know his brown man. I do not want him to know of the brown man and I knowing each other. So I say, "You keep it for me. And play it. To make up for the one Grandpa took."

He looks at me gravely, then nods slowly. "I'll only play it back in the woods," he tells me. I wonder if I am teaching him deception, if I am doing untold damage to his tender psyche, poisoning his relationship with his grandfather. Then the oven timer goes off, and the brownies are done, and I have an excuse not to think about that anymore.

Tom comes in late that night. We have finished our dinner, and I have already done the dishes. Usually when he is that late, it means he has already eaten dinner at his parents' house. But tonight he comes in and vultures through the refrigerator, poking disconsolately at the meager leftovers until I get up and concoct something resembling a dinner for him. I make him a pot of coffee to go with it. I have been sitting at the kitchen table, drinking tea and reading one of Steffie's romances while Teddy plays Legos on the living-room floor. There is no graceful way to get up and move while Tom eats. So I resume my place there, and as he eats, he talks.

"Time to make hay," he tells me between mouthfuls. "Me and Bix are gonna help out the Clemmonses this year. We always did when we were kids, so it's kind of, you know."

I don't know, but it doesn't matter, as long as I glance up and nod.

"Bix's shoulder is a lot better now," he adds belatedly.

I look up at him, wondering why he sounds abashed. Oh. Now I remember. We were supposed to stay here because Bix's shoulder was hurt and he couldn't work. So Tom could help his family out. Somehow it seems long ago. Having lost that battle in those ancient days of caring, it is hard to find anything to feel about it now. Does he really think I am so stupid that I haven't noticed Bix has gone back to his regular routine? I shrug, and try to remember where on the page I was.

"Dad thought Teddy might like to go with us this year. See how it's done, ride on the hay truck, maybe even ride on the tractor?" He pitches this to include Teddy in the conversation. Teddy gets up and wanders over to the table, Legos in hand.

"All day?" he asks.

"Probably." Tom eats another bite. "Usually we hit it early, after the dew's burned off but before it gets too hot. Mom can pack you some sandwiches, and Bix and I will make sure there's some root beer in the cooler. Okay?"

"Grandpa doesn't want me to play with the brown man," Teddy explains for anyone who might have missed it. "Is Steffie gonna help?"

Tom glances at me, shifts, shrugs. "She might. She might drive the hay truck. Dougie asked her to come." Tom eats another mouthful, glances at me. "Hey, listen,

Cowboy, you want to make hay with us, you can. You don't want to, that's fine, too. Uh." He fishes in his shirt pocket. He lays the willow whistle on the table. "I think this is yours."

"Yeah." Teddy pockets it matter-of-factly.

"That's a pretty neat whistle. You make that yourself?"

Teddy just looks at him.

"When I was little," Tom says slowly. "I had a friend named Georgie. Georgie could fly." Teddy's eyes get big. "Because Georgie was pretend," Tom says laboriously. "But he was still my friend, and I still liked playing with him. Even if Grandpa told me to quit telling lies. Georgie was still my friend, and my only friend until I went to school. Pretty soon you're going to go to school, and you'll meet all the other kids from up and down the highway, and you'll go to their houses and they'll come to visit us. And your mom will be friends with their moms, and she'll go to PTA, and oh, there'll be all kinds of real fun to have. Field trips with your class, and birthday parties to go to, and spending the night. All kinds of things. You'll like it. But until then, I don't mind if you play with the brown man. Only, let's not get Grandpa all upset about it, okay? Because I don't think he ever had friends like that, you understand?"

I wonder why Tom is looking at me as he speaks, instead of Teddy. He seems to be waiting more for my nod than for Teddy's. I nod in a rusty, reluctant way. I feel faintly giddy, I notice abstractedly that my heart is pounding. Too close, we are getting too close to truth, and the truth Tom must never have is that the brown man was my imaginary friend before he was Teddy's. I wonder briefly at this shared insanity, the common delusion, is it genetic, have I passed my defects on to my son, and then my body is rising, my voice is asking Tom, "More coffee, dear?" and Teddy is escaping to the living room, flashing away like the little silver fish in the stream flash away from his fingers.

"Yeah, please," Tom answers, and then calls after Teddy, "So we going haying tomorrow, or what? Something to think about is this. Haying only happens once in a while, and it's kind of fun, even if it is work. You might not want to miss it."

"I'll go haying," Teddy says, and shoots me an oblique glance. Tom does not miss it. His eyes grip mine for a minute, and I see hurt in them, but I dare not wonder what it is that gives him pain.

They are up and off early the next morning, a brown bag of sandwiches and brownies clutched in Teddy's hand, Teddy's other hand clutched in Tom's. "Don't forget to check my pony and other stuff," Teddy calls back to me. I nod reluctantly. I should not check his "other stuff" but already I know I will.

I do each dish carefully, ignoring the hammering of my heart. I try not to think that today I am alone, that today no one will notice if I slip away. I won't stay long, I promise myself as I shake Houdini's grain into its bucket. He comes at a gallop, whiffles up his grain, and then plods off disgustedly when neither more grain nor Teddy appear. The feed shed is dark and cool as I put the bucket away. There are goose bumps on my arms, and a shiver in the pit of my belly. When I come out, the strong sunshine strikes right through my clothes and warms my skin instantly. It is a perfect day, warm, with a small hint of wind. A beautiful day. I keep wiping nervous smiles from my face. I make myself do all my chores before I go.

In the few short weeks since I showed him the way, Teddy's feet have worn what was scarcely a rabbit trail into a recognizable footpath. With every step I take, there is more spring in my knees, and my heart grows lighter. I don't notice when I start running, it is only when I am standing by the stream, catching my breath, that I realize how I have hurried. I crouch to palm cool water up to my mouth, and then straighten and glance around. It annoys me vaguely that he is not here waiting for me, even though there is no way he could have known I would come today.

After I drink, I sit down on the bank to wait. Hurrying here has made me sweaty. I pluck my shirt away from my body, let cooler air slip up under it. The day is clear and still and warm, humming with tiny lives.

The sun is bright on the moving water. I stare at it for too long, close my eyes to stop their watering. I lie back, putting my head into cool shade while leaving my body in the dappling sunlight. A bird calls, distant and sweet. Another answers it, echoing the melodious challenge. I breathe deeper, feel myself starting to drift on the slow spirals of midmorning sleep.

When I scent him, I am too deep in relaxation to react. I lie still, feeling the sun, the air, the damp of the moss beneath me, breathing him with the other earthy smells of the forest. I know when he reaches the clearing, I can feel him looking at me, and it makes my skin tingle and tighten to know his eyes are on me. He breathes across his pipes, a trailing scale as I open my eyes to him. The sun is too bright at first, he is no more than a dark silhouette, horned head atop muscular shoulders, against the brightness of the sky behind him. I lift an arm, peer up at him from the sheltering shadow of my forearm. He grins at me, teeth so white against his tanned face. I smile up at him.

He stoops to take my hands and pull me to my feet. It is not a day for talking, I know that instinctively. There is nothing to say in words, anyway. This is one of those days stolen from the dream time, when he will lead and I will follow, without question. Like crossing a line, I enter his world to abide by his rules, to see with his eyes. One of his hands keeps hold of my hand. The other hand is for his pipes. He breathes across them lightly, almost inaudibly as he draws me off into the forest, a different path this time, one that follows the water upstream.

We walk beside the stream for a way, and as we follow it uphill, the forest walls close over us, roofing us with the shade of the trees that arch over the stream to tangle their branches over our heads. The stream is a strong, steady flow of water, cutting its own trail down the hill. In places we are walking through a ravine, and several times it gets so narrow that we walk in the stream itself. He breathes over his pipes, echoing the susurrus of the water over gravel, and when it makes me smile, his fingers tighten on mine. He has not even needed to

turn back to see my face, but now he does. He pulls my
captive hand around him, hooks it on his goat-haired
hip, and then, both hands free, begins to play the day for
us. He plays it sweet and long, almost sleepy in the
dappling of bright light and cool shade. We are walking
in the stream again. I envy Pan the way the cold water
beads off his hairy ankles. My sneakers are soaked and
squishy, my wet jeans slap against my ankles when the
channel of the stream finally widens and we are able to
walk beside it again. My arm is still around him. I walk
in the circle of his scent and warmth.

I am beginning to see beaver sign, the gnawed
stumps and nibbled trees. When I look up, I see sunlight
ahead of us, and suspect what it is he has to show me. He
breaks off his playing, lets his pipes fall to dangle from
the thong around his neck and bounce against his bare
chest. He takes my hand again and hurries me from the
shadowy forest into the open clearing of gnawed stumps,
to the place where the stream sings and gurgles from the
dam.

The dam is a wonder of natural engineering. Twigs
and branches thrust in every direction, grasses and small
plants grow from the soil trapped in every nook and
cranny. So disorganized and so perfectly constructed. It
cradles a beaver pond of blue sky and reflected trees, of
tall reeds and the arrowhead trail across the water that
shows where someone has just dived to escape the
scrutiny of intruders. I know from experience that life
will cluster and thrive around a pond such as this. It is a
biological maxim that the greater the variety of life in an
area, the more niches there are for other life forms. This
beaver dam and pond are like the hub of a wheel that
spreads out in all directions, beckoning life, providing a
place for frogs and fish and insects to lay eggs in the still,
warm water, nesting sites for water birds, and good
hunting for foxes and coyotes. Here deer can come to
water, and hawks can get a clear shot at the mice and
moles that make their narrow paths through the grasses
of the meadows. And the beavers are the custodians of
this ecosystem, opening their dam to release water,
building it higher, cutting back trees to open the

meadow. I feel dizzy thinking about it, like a kid looking down at a carnival with all its random clockwork movement and music and teeming life.

We explore. Tiptoeing gingerly across the top of the dam itself, balancing like acrobats on the high wire. Skirting the edges of the pond past a heliport of dragonflies and darning needles, sending a flotilla of frogs launching themselves into the water, until I give in and take off my sneakers and socks, and knot the laces so I can sling them over my shoulder. Then we wade together, bare legs and goat legs, out into the lukewarm water, sending pollywogs and fingerlings scattering into the reed-choked recesses of the pond. We emerge to find the green bones of a winter-kill deer, and birds' nests right on the ground or woven into the low bushes. A wasps' nest sends us both floundering back into the water, which is suddenly deeper than I expect. From knee deep to hip deep is but one step, and as I lose my balance I see his grin and know he has known all along I'd end up soaked. I go under, the water closing tea-brown over my head. I struggle back up, spitting and blowing. The water is thick with plant life, carpeted with tiny single leaves with trailing white roots, or clusters of flat green leaves and waxy yellow spatterdock flowers. It all seems to cling to me as I gain my feet. Water streams down my face from my hair and the plants clinging in it. I reach out a hand for him to help me out, then set my feet and drag him in. He ducks me as he goes down, and we both surface spluttering and gasping at the coldness of the deeper water. When we wade out, we are both festooned with plants and shivering despite the heat of the day. One sock has come out of my shoes, and I see it float merrily away on the invisible current of the pond.

We retreat from the pond until the meadow sod is dry and firm underfoot, and then sit down, neck deep in the tall grass. I drag my hair forward over my shoulder and wring it out. Pan helpfully lifts a dangling strand of duckweed from my hair. A long green beard of algae drapes his shoulder. I wipe it away, fluff tiny leaves from his hair. His fingers deftly pluck clinging watercress plants from my shirt. His touch is lighter than a tickle,

and combines with my damp clothes to send shivers
running up my back. When he finishes, he lies back in
the meadow sun, closing his eyes to the sky. I flop back
beside him to let the sun bake the wet from my clothes.
I cushion my head on one crooked arm and stare at him
as he dozes. The wet curls of his hair spring up as they
dry in the sun. His lips are very slightly ajar as he
breathes deeply and evenly. Magic and forest and animal
all, myth and archetype and friend of my childhood. He
is better than anything Edmund Dulac or Kay Nielsen
ever drew. I love all of him, hoof to horns, every graceful
line of muscle, the unguarded awkwardness of his sleeping sprawl. Watching him, I doze off, more safe and
content than I have been in a long while.

From being truly asleep I pass to a stage where I am
dreaming the light fingers on the buttons of my shirt,
and then to a place where I am achingly aware of their
every touch, of the hushed breathing of his open mouth
as he leans over me, but I do not stir, I refuse to admit
I am awake. As long as I am asleep like this, then this is
a thing he is doing to me, something I don't have to
decide about. He lays my shirt open as precisely as if he
were doing a dissection. As he leans forward over me, I
feel his shadow blotting the sun from my closed eyes.
His lips graze my eyelids, settle on my mouth. I lift a
hand, put it against his shoulder, wanting but knowing I
must not have this. I push him away.

But the day is too warm, the smell of his musk too
sweet, his mouth too knowing. He simply braces himself
against my hand, uses it for support as he smells my
flesh, and then tastes it, a cautious lapping of warm
tongue. Heat bursts in me, and I want him as I have
never wanted anything else. I lie back, my breath
coming hard, let him do whatever he wishes.

He does not make love like a man. A human. I am
aware of this as he fumbles with clothing catches any
man would know, as he takes as great a pleasure in
scenting me as in touching me. The knowledge that this
person who nuzzles at my breasts is not even of my own
species builds in me, creating tiny discords in the
thrumming melody he plays upon my body. I put my

hand on the back of his head, draw his mouth to mine, kiss him deeply to try to drown my uneasiness in him, but my fingers find the hardness of his horns, the knurled bases of them hidden in his hair. This is not a man at all. The musky smell of him is all around us, he rubs against me anointing my skin with his scent. That is the act of a beast, wrong and foreign, but the smell of him is compelling, rich and spicy and good, so good, I know as long as I ever breathe it I will desire him. It is like catnip to a cat, this scent, and I rub against him, for all the world like a cat in heat. He touches me as I have never been touched, awakening instinctive reactions I did not know I had. Making me respond like an animal. Coarse-haired beast legs are parting my thighs. Sex with an animal. A goat. The thought jolts my eyes open even as his goat legs are kneeling, bending in the wrong direction between my pale hairless legs. His hovering penis is not a man's.

Revulsion jolts me as it nudges at my flesh, and my belly muscles jump like a frog as I jerk away from him. Panicky, shaking, "No!" I say, as hard brown hands hook over my shoulders and force me down again. For one terrifying instant I think he will defy me, will hold me down with his greater strength and plunge inside me regardless of my denials, be the animal I am seeing. But he doesn't.

Instead, he remains poised over me, holding me down, yes, but touching me only with his hands. I look up into his face, try to read him. And for once his forest-deep eyes are not a closed place, he is not hiding in their depths. He looks deep inside me and his own eyes drag me into their depths, back through a hundred days and times we have been together, and I suddenly see that every day, every moment spent with him was a countdown to this day, this moment, this act. There is no animal in his deep eyes, at least no more than in my own. There is only Pan and whatever he is, not man, not beast, but his own faun self as I have always known him and the wordless promises we have repeated to each other a thousand times. Whatever he is, he is more like me than any other creature I have ever encountered.

Our kinship goes too deep to be denied by dissimilar bodies. We know each other too well for any wall to stand. Whatever we do here is beyond the rules of any of our kinds. It is ours. The doubts are gone, leaving only the need.

I put my hands on the slim goat haunches and pull him toward me. His hide is silky, the muscles beneath the hair hard, my hands slide on his pelt, I cannot get a good grip. He calmly resists, making me admit this is my own demanding I am satisfying. No graceful way to give in and simply let him proceed. This has to be my own doing. I give in, and tug harder at him, digging for a grip with my nails, and still he holds back. I glare up at him, frustrated and angry at his delay—is he mocking my need?—to find him smiling down on me. It is not, his smile seems to say, so grim a thing as I am making it. No earthshaking decision, no cataclysmic action. It is, after all, only mating, and the summer world around us is alive with the sounds of other lives doing as we are doing. The humming of the insects, the songs of the birds, the croaking of the frogs, this is what all those songs are about. We have come to a center of a circle of life, and in this place, this thing is to be done. There is no hurry, we have the whole day. His mouth comes down on mine, sweet as flowers, pungent as herbs, warm as summer. I give myself up to it, ignore the angry buzzing of an insect by my ear, ignore even the sharp jab of its stinger in my bared shoulder, so caught up in the touch of my mate that the penetration of the animal's stinger is lost. Pan slips into me, warm, wet, and the surging goat hips beneath my hand, the rasping of the coarse hair of his legs against my inner thighs as he plunges and butts against me, are all as it should be, all as I always knew it would be.

# Sixteen

The day is cooling. I shiver and shift, trying to get more of me under the warm weight of his body. Vaguely I am aware that we have both fallen asleep in the act of coupling, how rude of me, I think, smiling, for we are still limply joined, he is as contented as I am. Even as I shift under him he is aware of me, his grip on me tightens, and his new arousal seems instantaneous. I feel him swelling against me yet again. Some part of me knows that tomorrow I am going to be very, very sore, but I pay no attention to that as I reach my mouth to his. He starts a very lazy rhythm, sex for sleepyheads on a sunny day, a slow reciprocation that brings us both languorously and effortlessly to total satiation.

He collapses heavily onto me, and "Off," I grunt graciously, poking him gently in the short ribs.

"Make up your mind," he replies, but eases himself off to one side, allowing me to take a deep breath again.

I pillow my head on his hard shoulder, speak into his neck. "I'm going to have mosquito bites all over."

"Probably," he concurs. His voice sounds sleepily satisfied, but when I look up into his face, his eyes are open and alert, deeply pleased about something.

"What?" I demand.

"It's funny. It's always better than you remember it, but you only remember that about it afterward. And"—he turns his face to me—"it will only keep getting better and better." He kisses me, mutters into my mouth, "Though first times have a very special charm of their own."

I am not pleased, either to be compared to others, or to be given a sales pitch. He senses this through my silence. After a moment he adds quietly, "Though perhaps my opinion of my performance isn't shared?"

I think he is being sarcastic. I pull back, glance warily at his face. There is genuine uncertainty in his eyes. "No lovemaking has ever left me feeling like this," I tell him, and he does not mistake my meaning. "I just don't like to be reminded there have been others before me."

"Um," he says, and his eyes go soft and unfocused, meandering through his own thoughts as I wonder where and when and who else he has held.

"Not for several generations," he muses aloud.

"What?"

"Racial memory," he tells me, smugly superior. "Something your people only speculate about. But, looking back, I can recall that not for several generations in my line has there been such a mating. And even then," he adds wickedly, "I don't think my ancestor did as well his first time as I have done today."

There is too much in his words for me to digest it quickly. Racial memory? Sharing the memories of your ancestors? The "your people" acknowledging aloud that we are different from each other, putting up a tiny wall. I gloss past that, consider the rest. "This is the first time you've made love," I say slowly.

He shrugs, jogging my head on his shoulder. "In this body, yes. But I've the expertise of the ages. Shall I show you?" Tanned brown fingers skate down my body, lazily circle one of my breasts.

"No," I say, but do not move to avoid his touch. "Tell me, instead. Can you really remember your ancestors' lives?"

"Certainly. Well"—he pauses, flicks teasingly at my nipple—"there are limits to it, of course. Just as it's easier for you to remember what happened last week than what happened twelve years ago. The last three or four generations are the clearest. After that, things run together a bit, unless one chooses to really concentrate. But some things"—swift as a snake he moves, darting to fasten his mouth to my breast—"one never forgets," he says through firm teeth. He is already hard against my thigh.

"Don't you ever get enough?" I ask him, and he shakes his head minutely, his eyes merry with lust.

"Well, I do," I declare, and shake free of him, leap up and run. I get as far as the pond's edge before he overtakes me, and we are both laughing wildly as we wrestle and splash into the water. He catches my wrists, not ungently, and forces me down in the shallows and makes love to me yet again, unmindful of the mud and warm lapping water. Afterward we wade together into deeper, clearer water, to rinse mud and small clinging plants from each other's backs and faces. Then I turn slightly aside from him, unreasonably shy, and as I wash myself I can feel I am swollen, tender from all the sex. He comes closer, murmurs, "Shall I do that for you?"

"No," I say firmly, backing away, more than a little intimidated by his endless capacity for sex. He shrugs those muscled shoulders and watches with frank interest as I finish washing myself. I know that if I turned back to him, showed the slightest hint of receptivity, he would come for me again. And again and again and again. It is a daunting thought, a sobering thought. When I wade out and dry myself on my shirt, I notice the longer shadows of the trees shading our sunny coupling space. Daylight insects are quieting, the high heat of full day fading. We both know, without words, that it is time for me to leave.

Tom and Teddy may even be home already. The thought comes unbidden, and with it a huge weight of . . . something. Not quite guilt. More like suddenly remembering that your term paper is due tomorrow and you haven't been to the library yet, or that guests are coming for dinner in an hour and you haven't even taken the meat from the freezer yet. A suffocating press of things that had to be done, immediately, right now, the choke chain of adult responsibility snugged up suddenly and tightly. I struggle with the burden, try to find some way to justify this day I have stolen, the gluttony of pleasure I've wallowed in. This day does not match up with what I thought I knew of myself, the painstaking picture of myself that I've created. Aren't I the faithful one, the unswervingly loyal one, practical, honest, dutiful: the list of my supposed virtues reads like the *Boy Scout Handbook*. So how have I come to be dressing in the woods after fornicating with a faun? In the sequence of my life, the images of our couplings are like Tarot cards interspersed with the family portraits; oh, look, here's Micky and Bobby Sue and your cousins, and Grandma and Grandpa with Frisky the cat, and this one's the Hanged Man . . .

"You could stay," he says.

My underwear is damp, it clings to my thighs when I want to pull it up. Want to feel ridiculous, try getting dressed in front of a satyr whose erection is still pointed your way. My jeans are too tight, they seem to have shrunk from drying in the sun. Where the hell's my other sock, oh, yeah, at the bottom of the pond by now.

"You don't have to go back," he says it again, a different way.

I shake my head, mute, my throat suddenly closing tight, choking me with unsheddable tears. I throw my sock away, jam my bare feet into soggy sneakers. I can't find my bra, there it is, some twelve feet away, I'll never know how it got that far. I walk over to it, stoop down to untangle it from a Russian thistle. I try to put it on gracefully, such a ridiculous garment, and for me, anyway, serving no purpose at all. A pretense at civilization.

"Why do you have to go back?" he asks softly.

From anyone else it would have been some kind of accusation, or a veiled plea to change my mind. From him it is only a question, and the gentle way he asks it tears at my heart. Because I long to stay. I shrug my shoulders stiffly, pick up my wet shirt. "Teddy," I say, and then force myself to complete the honesty, "and Tom."

"Oh," he says. Not "I see" or "I understand" because he doesn't. Just "Oh," because he knows I'm telling him the truth. I do have to go. I button my shirt, waiting for him to ask me if I will come back again. But he doesn't, and after a while I know its because he knows that I don't know. Not yet. I probably won't know until I do come back. Or I don't. I don't want to say good-bye, don't want to make any parting gesture at all. Neither, it seems, does he, for when I glance up from my buttons, he is gone. And I am grateful.

Easy enough to find my way home. Parallel the stream through the cooler shadows of the trees, through the thickening evening, hell, it must be past five already, they're all going to be home. There will be questions. Again. Probably another quarrel. I'll say I fell in the beaver pond, and they'll believe me. Just another detail in the family legend of Evelyn's weirdness. Stories will probably be passed down about me for generations. The Daughter-In-Law Who Stared at the Chicken Yard By Moonlight. The Daughter-In-Law Who Couldn't Get the Sheets White. The Daughter-In-Law Who Fell in the Beaver Pond.

My insect bites are beginning to itch, and I realize ruefully that some of them are in embarrassing places. Explain that, Evelyn.

I stride along, every step carrying me closer to confrontation. Part of me knows there is no justification for what I have done today. Part of me doesn't care. Part of me is childishly optimistic that no one will notice anything. Perhaps it is that part that makes me run my fingers through my bedraggled hair, pulling out bits of moss and leaves and twigs. Noticing my shirt is buttoned unevenly, I redo it, and tuck it firmly into my jeans. By the time I emerge from the forest and climb through the barbed-wire fence, I am as respectable as possible under the circumstances. I cross the cow pasture, feeling as if there were a cross hairs on my chest, expecting a shout at any moment. Houdini lifts his head, recognizes me, and goes back to grazing. That's all.

I come out on the driveway, glance about, and cannot believe my luck. I've hit the jackpot, won the big prize. There isn't a vehicle in sight. They are all gone, every one of them, which means that no one is home yet. I am saved. I glance up at the windows, expecting to at least see Ellie peering out from the upper story, but all the curtains hang straight and white. Home free.

I step out of my wet shoes at the door. I am shedding clothes as soon as I am inside the door of the little house, not scattering them, but dragging them off and bundling them under my arm. They smell unmistakably of sex. I bury them deep in the laundry hamper and jump directly into the shower. The hot spray hits my body and for a few moments it just seems to intensify his musk on me, the whole bathroom reeks of sex and faun. But the scented Avon soap that Mother Maurie provides soon cuts through it, and for once I am glad of its Whorehouse-in-June pervasiveness. I shampoo with Prell, and watch in a sort of awe the brown stream that trickles down my shoulder and belly. I hadn't realized I was that dirty. I lather up twice before it rinses clear. I turn off the shower, wring out my mop of hair, and bundle it into a towel.

I make a careful inspection of myself in the bathroom mirror. There are plenty of insect bites, a few scratches, but no hickeys, no rakes of nails nor love bites. He has left no outward trace at all upon my body, and but for the tenderness between my legs, I might have imagined the whole thing. Now that is an unsettling thought and I hastily chase it away. I am not *that crazy*, and besides, Teddy has seen Pan, too. He's real.

I go to the bedroom, dress quickly, loose shorts this time, jeans are too uncomfortable against me, a tank top and one of Tom's cotton shirts thrown on over it. Dry shoes, sandals have to do, and there I am. I drag a brush ruthlessly through my hair, then braid it back in a long tail. It will pass. And ta-dah! I'm ready, you can all come home now.

I go to the living room, sit down for an instant, then jump up and go to the kitchen. Dinner, I should be cooking dinner, but even as I rattle out pans and drag out ingredients, it occurs to me that if it is this late and they are not home, they are probably eating dinner at the haying place, probably part of the fun, all get together to work, and afterward eat and drink together and sit around and talk. Belatedly I notice that I was not invited. A few weeks ago that would have incensed me, a few days ago it would have depressed me, but today I feel nothing about it. No, I feel almost good about it. They have theirs and I have mine. That they have excluded me once again excuses in some small measure what I have done today. So.

I put back the pans, and instead fix myself a sandwich, find a handful of softening potato chips in the bottom of their waxed bag, put together a cup of tea, and sit down with a book. But in a few moments I am up again, pacing, the half-eaten sandwich languishing in the heat beside the soggy potato chips, the book tossed aside. I cannot sit still. I want Tom and Teddy to come home, I want all of them to come home, because I need to find out what I will do. Different scenarios keep playing through my mind. Will I cast myself at Tom's feet, confess all and beg forgiveness? Or will I coolly pretend nothing has happened, be all wifely dutifulness and deception? Will I be cold and uncommunicative, leaving him to wonder what has happened? I don't know.

Worse, I cannot even concentrate on wondering. My body keeps remembering his touch, his scent, the taste of his mouth. I am too full of him to think of anything else. Too full of him to think about the guilt that has begun to crawl along the edges of my nerves. Incredibly, I want him again already, as if his constant ready lust is a thing he has infected me with. I think of all we did, and wait for shame or guilt, but get instead the warm itch of arousal. Is this what sets an animal in heat to yowling?

I pace the small house until grey evening becomes true dark. I throw the sandwich and chips into the kitchen garbage, dump the cold tea down the sink, and make a fresh cup. This one I take outside into the coolness. I wonder what he is doing, if he is lying under a tree somewhere, piping and thinking of me. But there are no breathy notes hanging on the evening air to tempt me. Instead, I notice a peculiar thing. No lights. Only the big mercury vapor light high on its pole is on in the yard. The big house is dark and still, totally bereft of life. I have never seen it so. Even if the Potters Senior are gone, Ellie and Bix are usually there, and even if Bix is still out haying, Ellie should be there. Something cold turns over in the bottom of my stomach.

I go back to the little house, measure it with my steps. Where are they all? Did they all get together and decide to go out for dinner and then leave without me because I wasn't here? That could be it, but it's not likely. Tom's father is too wary to get stuck buying dinner for that many, and Tom and Bix simply don't have the money. No. Probably all of them have just gone off in different directions. Or maybe spending the afternoon with a faun has cast an enchantment on me, I am now completely in his world, and I cannot see or hear or feel the people from my old world even though they are right here around me. Just as I couldn't hear Mother Maurie, maybe that was just the beginning of this. Maybe they are all around me, talking, eating, doing the books. I get a cold shiver up my back, push the thought away. Teddy, I'd always see Teddy, because like me he touches both worlds. If Teddy were here, I'd see him.

So. There is the logical thing to do. Phone Clemmons's farm, ask if Teddy and Tom have left there yet. Feel a fool, maybe, when they tell you, hell, they left hours ago. Feel even dumber if the voice says, hell, yes, they're here, hey, Tommy-O, the old lady's on the phone for you. Then what do you say? Forget it, it's all a pipe dream anyway, I don't have a phone, the phone's in the big house, and there's no one there to say I can use it.

I hold out for an hour, an hour of pacing, of making cups of tea and setting them down in various places around the house, to discover them, cold and congealed, only after I have made a fresh cup. Finally I put on a sweater, for the night outside has chilled, and there is a coldness, too, inside me. No one in the Potter family stays out this late, let alone all of them. It is almost ten.

I cross the yard, furtive as a raccoon crossing a freeway, waiting for the sweep of headlights, the blare of horns. The doorknob to the back door is cold under my hand, and does not turn. But the secret key is in place on the lintel. I thieve it and push it into the lock, twist the knob, push the door open. Quickly I put the key back, thinking that if I hear car noises in the driveway, I will quickly leave, locking the door behind me so they will not know I have been inside their house alone, will not demand of me, "What were you doing in here?"

I ghost through the house, but of course no one is home, there is only the grey light from the yard light falling in window squares on the floor, the smell of stale cigarette smoke and the oversweet bug-spray fragrances of Avon products. Nothing is alive here, nothing is out of place. It looks more like a hotel lobby than a home. The newspaper, *Sunset* magazine, *Reader's Digest* are fanned on the coffee table. The cork coasters are in their holder. No one ever leaves his slippers by the couch, no one forgets a crumpled tissue, part of a cookie, no, not in this house.

The phone is on an end table beside a huge fat lamp. I hate to do it, I squint my eyes against it, but I turn on the lamp. I cannot find the phone book without it, but I soon find I cannot find the phone book with it, either. I discover it at last in a drawer in the other end table. I try to look up the number, but find I don't know first names. I search fruitlessly for some scribble in Tom's hand, some note, was it Clemmons or Cullens they were going to hay with? I can't remember the last name, let alone the first. The phone book is useless to me, and there is no scribbled hint.

I put the phone book back carefully, exactly as I found it. I click off the lamp, stand in the sudden rush of darkness, thinking. The phone erupts suddenly beside me, jangling shrilly, sending me leaping, stumbling, irrationally grabbing at it to still its scream. My jerking hand dislodges the receiver, oh, shit, there's nothing for it but to answer it now, I cannot simply hang it back up, maybe it's even one of the family.

"Potter's Equipment," I say. It is what they always say, at home or at work, for the number is the same.

"Hello?" says a woman's voice uncertainly. A soft country voice, uncultured but not unkind.

"Hello?" I reply, my voice shaking in spite of myself.

"I . . . I just . . . I know it must be a bad time, to call like this, but I just wanted to say how sorry we all are. To hear about it."

"Oh," I say stupidly, not knowing what else to say. I can not ask what the hell she is talking about, that is too weird, so I say, "Uh, who is this?"

"Jenny Snow. You know, I helped with his 4-H group. And I was just so shocked to hear, and I just wanted to say . . ." She is weeping now, but I am very still, very cold, all is going dark around me. "We're so sorry to hear about it. Just when he was getting so good with his pony, too. It's just such a, such a waste."

She falls silent. I cannot say anything. But I suppose I have, I hear someone whisper, "Teddy," and the sound hangs in the air.

"I, well, I just can't tell you how sorry we are. That's all." The voice on the other end is unabashedly weeping now. "I just wanted the family to know," she says, and then "good-bye."

And she hangs up, but I hold the empty phone to my ear, gripping it hard.

Time passes so softly in the darkness and stillness. I set the phone down, sometime, very gently, joggling it back into its cradle. The handset is wet. I wipe my cuff across it, stand up, I do not remember crouching down, but my legs ache almost as much as the hand that gripped the receiver. Quietly I move through their house, as silent as drifting smoke, needing no light to avoid any of their obstacles. I push open the kitchen door. My wakeful hand finds the button, locks the door before it tugs it shut behind me. I let the screen door close over it, and then sit down the top concrete step.

The night is very beautiful. There are stars out, so bright that not even the mercury vapor lamp can drown them. The night land smells of animals and crops, with only a trace of diesel drifting up from the shop. It may be only my imagination, but I think I can smell new-mowed hay. It is a new scent for me, for in Alaska I lived near the forests, not the fields. But I think that is what I smell. Maybe I am imagining it.

I replay the call a thousand times in my mind. I hug

myself, grip tight on my shirt, feel my ribs through the fabric. So. What do you really know? That it's Teddy. Teddy is . . . hurt, maybe, perhaps. Oh, really. Do neighbors call like that about a hurt child? Only if the child is hurt really, really bad. Or dead.

Dead?

Let's not play games, Evelyn, that's sure as hell what it sounded like. A condolence call.

But wait. How? Where? Where would they all be, if it happened a while ago, long enough for word to spread, they'd be home by now, wouldn't they? Wouldn't they?

Hospitals. Morgues. Funeral homes.

NO!

A part of me wants to get up and run, run so far and so fast that moving my body would take up every thought space in my mind. That part screams and races around the walls of my head like a cartoon mouse. The rest of me just sits there, on the cold concrete steps, and thinks stupid things, like this is a great way to get hemorrhoids, the mosquito bite on my ankle itches, I wonder what time it is, maybe they all went out for ice cream and got a flat tire, maybe the phone call was a bizarre wrong number. I will into existence Teddy with chocolate ice cream dabbed on his chin, jumping out of the car, saying, "Mom, where were you?"

My magic must be stronger than I know, for in response headlights are turning down the driveway, one, two, three sets of them, here they all come, in a row, like a funeral procession, no, like a parade. I stand up, dusting my chilled rump, and moved forward to meet them, go hastily, actually, to stand by the porch of the little house, I don't want to look too much like the family dog waiting to be let in. They sweep past me without a pause, pull up and park in their regular spots. Engines turn off raggedly, headlights blink out. For a brief instant silence holds, and then Ellie and Bix are getting out of the station wagon, Tom and Steffie hop out of the truck. No sign of Teddy, yet, but they are all converging on the sedan. He is probably in there, riding with Grandma and Grandpa. I take three stiff steps forward, then find myself striding up to them as Tom's father gets out of the car, says, "Bix, you get the door, Tom, you help me with your mother."

They ignore him, all of them getting in one another's way as I stand at the edges, asking timorously, "What's happened?" and "Where's Teddy?"

They don't ignore me so much as overwhelm me with their muttered directions to one another as Tom's father coaxes and then Tom stoops, reaches into the car, and lifts his mother out. She seems small in his arms, not the powerful woman she's always been, and her head lolls against his shoulder. "Where's Teddy," I demand again as Tom's father orders, "Turn on the porch light, for Christ's sake!" No one hears me or answers.

"Where's Teddy!" I cry, and even I can hear the edge creeping into my voice. "Teddy!" says Mother Maurie, barely lifting her head, and her voice trails off in a moan. "Shut up!" Tom's father roars at me, and then more softly, but not for my sake, "You're only going to upset her again. The doctor says she needs quiet."

The procession is moving past me, Tom is already edging his mother inside the door, I can hear Ellie within, clicking on lights, conferring low-voiced with Bix. I grab Steffie by the elbow, jerk her back as she starts to follow her father inside. "Where's Teddy," I ask, and my voice is low, this is no demand, there is a threat here.

She looks at me, her movie-star face gone flat, her eyes dulled. "He's dead," she says, without expression, and then, as if someone has thrown a switch, she drags in a deep ragged breath and tears come streaming down her face. "Oh, my God, Lynn, he's dead. I'm so sorry, I'm so sorry, oh, my God!"

I am staring at her, numb, when her father comes down the steps to take her from me. "There, baby, it'll be all right," he says comfortingly, and then to me, "Jesus, woman, can't you see she's had all she can take? Do you think I want to have to take her to the hospital to be sedated, too?"

They are leaving me, the screen door is closing before I can ask, "What happened?"

"Not now!" he snarls back at me. "It'll only upset her to talk about it."

I attempt to follow them in, to at least find Tom, but his father turns on me again. "Not now, dammit! Tom will be out in a minute. You waited this long, you can wait a little longer! You sure as hell didn't care about it when it happened!"

"Oh, Daddy," Steffie wails, and I can't tell if she is trying to rebuke him for his unfair words, or if she rails at the unfairness of the world in general. It doesn't matter, I stumble back down the steps as if pushed, and he shuts the door firmly behind them. The slam of it is a physical pain. My exile is complete. A fist in the face could not have stopped me better. I am left alone in the dark.

Aren't I always left alone in the dark?

I turn away from the house, now lit and surging with shadows of life, and trudge back to the little house. I go in, not bothering with lights. I walk surely through its too-familiar darkness, crouch down beside the wicker sofa. No, he's not here. Not here at all, hardly even a touch of him. A book or two, a blanket that still smells like his grubby little feet. That's all. It might have been better if it had happened at home, I think, where I could have knelt by his little bed, touched his special pillow, his stuffed animals, the cold metal of his Tonka trucks. Here there's nothing except his absence. Nothing to cling to.

I find *Where the Wild Things Are*, hold the battered book close to my chest, feeling its corners dig into me. That's all there is. And I wait. Tom will come soon. He'll explain it all, tell me how my Teddy died, where he is now, what happened. Everything. If I just wait. The need to know exactly how it all happened is a surging thing in me, that builds and builds until I think I will scream, and then suddenly subsides into a not-wanting-to-know, a dread of details and images. Whatever he tells me, I will know for the rest of my life. Maybe these are the last moments I will have when my images of Teddy are all images of him alive, running, laughing, being tickled, riding a pony.

Time is passing very slowly, I think. Very, very
slowly. Tom will have carried his mother upstairs, will
have put her down on her bed. Ellie will quickly shoo
him out, will help her mother undress. Tom will stop,
perhaps, to speak briefly to his father. I know this, and
then he will come hurrying to me. It is only the waiting
that makes it seem so long, not that much time has
passed. He will come swiftly. He will tell me the things
that will finally let me cry and grieve instead of sit here
and feel confused or stupid. He will come to include me
in the sorrowing, for it is, after all, our child who is dead,
our child who we have shared, and so the grief is a thing
we must share as well. I wait.

I wait for what seems like hours. My legs cramp, I
grow chilled, and the weight inside me seems to grow
heavier every minute. Slowly, I start to believe that all
this might be real. Teddy might really be dead, it might
not all be some odd mistake, some peculiar Potter error.

At three o'clock in the morning, I realize Teddy is
dead.

The knowledge comes after I stagger to the kitchen
to look at the clock. Three o'clock. Yes, it has been that
long. And the lights in the kitchen and the living room of
the big house still burn. Over there, they still talk and
grieve together.

I go to the door and open it. I go out on the porch,
down the steps.

I can't go any farther. This is as far as I can go toward
Tom. I don't know why, but it is so. I sit down on the
steps and wait. I am still not crying. I have never been
one to cry over the big things. Cry over a smashed
thumb, a ruined book, an insult from a boy you don't
even know. But not for your dog hit by a truck, not for
your parents. Not for your little son.

I try to think of Teddy dead, but I can't make it
seem real. Perhaps it won't seem real until Tom comes to
tell me.

A very long time later, the door of the big house
opens. Tom comes out. It has to be Tom, because it's not
Bix or his father. But it doesn't walk like Tom, it shuffles,

head down. It comes across the yard slowly, stops by the steps when it sees me.

"Oh, honey, what are you doing out here all alone?" he asks me gently, and gathers me up.

"Where else would I be?" I ask him, confused suddenly.

"I thought maybe you'd gone to bed, as exhausted as the rest of us," he says into my hair. He opens the door, clicks on the light. He is ten years older. Lines in his face, bloodshot eyes, his pale hair looks more grey than blond in the incandescence. His arms still around me, he walks toward the bedroom.

"What happened?" I have to ask. My voice sounds surprisingly steady.

"Oh, baby," he says, and chokes. "He . . . slipped. All the noise and the machinery. Fell, I guess."

I can barely decipher the words. He gulps them out, between suppressed sobs. He does not look at me. He takes several deep breaths.

"Mom . . . We had to take her to the hospital, too, when she heard. Doctor said it might be just the shock, or maybe her heart. We gotta be real careful of her for the next couple days."

Bedroom. Light on. He starts dropping clothes, walking out of them. Digs the bed open, climbs in.

"What happened to Teddy?" I ask again.

"Oh, Lynn!" It is an agonized cry, a plea. "I . . . I should have known better. I shouldn't have let him come. I should have left him with you. It's my fault. Is that what you want to hear me say?"

He starts shaking, huge running tremors that rattle him. I don't want to hear him say that. I don't believe it's true. But I am sure it is what his father has made him say a dozen times already, just as I am sure it is what his father wanted to hear him say. I feel like a heartless wretch, but I still have to ask, I still have to say, "I need to know exactly what happened!"

"I—ca-ca-ca-n't!" He is hysterical. The word they use in those old-fashioned novels. Beside himself. Our son is dead, and my husband has been so hammered that he cannot put three words together. His eyes are Teddy's eyes, wide, panicky, as he cannot take a breath, cannot breathe out, cannot form words, only sounds like the beginnings of words. I kick off my sandals, crawl into the bed beside him, put my arms around him, and rock him. And rock him. He shakes and cries, and I know that up to now he has been unable to shake or cry. They took that away from him and gave it to Mother Maurie and Steffie. They have been allowed to grieve for their grandson, for their nephew, but Tom has had to be strong and responsible and manly. So now, he, who was there, who saw it happen, can finally grieve. I cry with him as I rock him, but it isn't for Teddy. It's for him, and then it's for me. Crying because I cannot even grieve, they won't even let me do that.

He curls up, fetal position, but I hold on to him, put my warm belly against his cold back, try to shelter him, try to hold him. Toward dawn he grows still. I think he is asleep, but then he whispers, "I'll tell you about it tomorrow. Okay? Tomorrow?"

"Okay," I say softly, holding him still, and he suddenly goes limp in my arms. Asleep.

I lie in bed and wonder what has become of Teddy. And Tom. And me.

# Seventeen

I never did find out how Teddy died.

They think they told me. Every time I try to ask about it, they get angry. It is so simple for them. He fell, and was killed. Crushed by a machine? Hit his head on the way down? I don't know. Only that he slipped. I have gathered that from Tom's broken words, and perhaps it should be enough for me. But a part of me wants to know every scalding detail. Where was he? On the tractor with Bix, or riding on the hay truck with the bales? Did something lurch and he slipped, did a bale hit him and he fell? Was he being reckless, jumping about in the dust and the noise and the motion, or was he sleepy perhaps, in the heat of the day, the roar of the machines a dull lullaby to his numbed ears, slipping quietly down beneath the massive wheels? Did he cry out, and that cry went unheard in the noise of the equipment, or was it enough to startle the grown-ups, to make them glance about immediately and ask, "Where's Teddy?"

I play the scene a million ways in my mind. Sometimes he falls from the tractor, right under the big black wheels and is crushed silently, and they do not even notice. That is the worst one. Where the noisy machines pass over him and move on and he lies in the hot field under the immense blue sky and the white sun, and his last little bit of life sputters from him unnoticed. I see him crushed and discarded in the stubble, a pastel scene like Christina's World, a small bit of color in an

immense field where noisy machines work in the distance. The image makes me want to scream. I don't want
him to have died as I am living, unnoticed and unimportant to the great and noisy work at hand.

Other scenes occur to me as well, replay graphically
in my mind, swift counterpoints to one another. As we
were coupling in the grass, the faun and I, was that when
he was dying, blood leaking from the corner of his
mouth? As we splashed each other and laughed and
shrieked, did he call out for me, or was he already dead
and silent in the hot sun of the dry open field? Or was
the life crushed from him as Pan lay atop me in the
waters of the beaver pond and I rutted with him, as
animal as he? Why had I felt nothing, noticed nothing
when the keystone of my world was ripped from its arch?
How could he die and I not know it, go on merrily
fucking away under the bright forest sun? There is no
one I can ask these questions. No one even seems to
sense my anguish. They are all too busy, and I am
dragged into their frantic activity.

Teddy's death has become less an event than a
grand family project. There is not time for grief or quiet
reflection. There is too much to be done. They cover up
his death in all the doing that follows it, the errands, the
plans, the procedures. The next few days are a carousel
of activity, as if we are planning a party or a masqued
ball. No one has time to talk about what happened. They
talk all around it, take care of a thousand details arising
from it, but of that day, no one speaks. Not ever.

Tom and Steffie and I go to the funeral home to look
at caskets. Tom looks like a haggard hick, hair un-
combed, plaid shirt, rumpled jeans. Steffie looks like a
bisque doll, pale, but perfect in her grief. In her
subdued navy dress with the flat white collar, she
reminds me of a grieving Quaker. I don't know what I
look like. I don't think anyone can see me. The salesman
certainly doesn't talk to me. He confers with Tom,
low-voiced, and looks at Steffie's legs. I walk slowly
through the display room, touching satin linings, brass-
tone catches, studying cutaway views of caskets constructed from man-made wonder materials. None of it

touches me. I cannot understand what I am supposed to be looking at. How can any of this matter? I am back in my silence, alone, wondering.

Steffie breaks down, just after she selects a white casket with blue satin lining and the deluxe option package. She clings to Tom's shoulder, sobbing. Her foundation makeup leaves pale pink smudges on his shirt. The salesman drifts past me, keeping a discreet distance from the grieving woman, and mutters to me, "Poor lady. She's really taking this hard, isn't she?" I don't answer, and he doesn't notice.

And that's how it goes. Like a giant shopping spree. Florist shop, for flowers for the funeral. Plot of earth to dig the hole in. Headstone, so no one forgets. Dress for Steffie. Dress for Mother Maurie, who is still too weak to shop for herself, but has given Steffie a note on crisp white paper that tells her size and preferences. NO POLYESTER is printed plainly in her concise hand. Hats for Steffie and Mother Maurie, in black of course, and Steffie's has a wisp of black net on it. Plain black pumps. Black stockings. Guest book. Guests? I wonder wearily. Suit for Tom, for the funeral. Appropriate tie. That takes almost an hour. She picks out new clean clothes to dress our son's body in. We trail in her efficiently grieving wake. Sometimes, when no one is looking, I take Tom's hand and hold it between both of mine. It is always cold, so cold he does not seem to feel me holding it. And in each and every store, I have to let go of it soon, for in each and every store Steffie breaks down shortly after completing her purchase. She always turns aside from the counter or the salesperson and gives a few warning tremulous sniffs that are Tom's cue to come forward, to put his arm around his sister's shoulders and reassure her. Always she turns into him, resting her clear forehead on his shoulder, one slender hand on his arm, as she weeps. Like the salespeople, I stand and watch. Perhaps I am here to witness this, perhaps someday I will be called on to come forward and give testimony to how deep Steffie's grief was. I don't know.

I don't know anything anymore.

I don't see much of Tom. Not alone. When he

comes home, he sleeps, deep sweaty sleeps that leave his eyelids gummy and his eyes webbed with redness. Days he does the errands, talks on the phone, listens to Steffie and Ellie and his dad. At the big house. He spends his evenings at his mother's bedside, or at the table in the big house kitchen, settling details, writing checks, totting up expenses, handling it all with Steffie at his elbow. It seems to me they have become miniatures of their parents. Teddy should have been their son, the perfect Potter child, by Potter, out of Potter, with none of my feral blood to ruin him. How close they all draw to one another, how efficiently they close me out without even knowing they are doing it.

I spend my evenings alone, in the dark, holding a book and sitting on a wicker couch. I try to grieve, and cannot. It's like it's not my turn, so I wait. Wait for this to stop, for life to start again, for everything to go back the way it was before. It's almost funny, I thought I hated my life the way it was before, and now I long for it. All I can think about is going back to it. I can't seem to grieve, not the way I am expected to, and I know this angers Tom's father. I cannot weep endlessly, as Steffie does, or go about my housework muttering, "Teddy, oh, my little Teddy" like Ellie does. Instead I do stupid things. I feed and groom the pony. Houdini turns sullen and unpredictable when he is ignored, and I feel some obligation to Teddy to make the pony feel better. I wash and mend and fold all Teddy's clothes. What was once an endless round of a job has become a finality. All of his toys are finally in a cardboard box under the wicker couch. They stay there, miraculously, as they have never done before. There are no Tonka trucks lurking in the dark hallways at night, no plastic cowboys in the bottom of the bathtub anymore. I stack his books and wonder what to do with them. Do I tidy my child out of my life, close up the empty space by removing all these place holders? His possessions remind me of zeros in a math problem. By themselves they are nothing, but they stand for the value Teddy had in our life. They hold open the wound so I can probe it, and every day I touch what was his to keep the pain hot and real.

It occurs to me once that the faun probably wonders what has become of Teddy. I picture him waiting by the stream, but I reject the image. No. I do not want to imagine him concerned and caring. I want to think of him as sly and carnal. I want to imagine that somehow he tricked me into what I did that day, that somehow there was coercion, treachery, even violence on his part. But not even my fertile imagination can make any of that plausible. What I did that day, I did. And I did it while my child was dying, and that is what makes it wrong and shameful and dirty. I cannot make the one thing a consequence of the other; I cannot even imagine it as a punishment from God for my copulating with a beast. It is not guilt I feel. Only a disgust with myself that somehow, while my child experienced the agony of death, I was joyously and mindlessly rutting.

I wish I could sit very, very still in a quiet place and think. Very often I wish Tom were there to hold me, that we could sit quietly together, close, and think about our son and all the things he was. But Tom is always busy, his mother needs him, the funeral director called, the church maintenance man called, has anyone called Cousin Ed yet and told him the sad news? Tom has to do it all, and it all has to be done from the big house, and I can no longer go in there.

No one has said this to me, of course. No one has said I am not allowed there. It is simply something I cannot do, I cannot make my legs cross the dusty yard, nor my hand turn the doorknob. I know this makes me bad, for I have not gone to sit by Mother Maurie's bedside and commiserate with her on losing her grandchild. Sometimes I think no one but me notices that Tom and I have lost our son. As if the deep grief is some sort of honor we are unworthy of, so his parents have assumed it to themselves. No cars stop by the little house to ask how I am, to bring cold dishes and words of comfort. They all go to the big house, all day, coming and going, dusty station wagons and pickup trucks, women with casseroles and Jell-O salads, like emissaries come to bring tribute. I watch them come and go, sitting on the steps of the little house like a retarded child, silent and empty-eyed and ignored. As they roll past me in a puff of dust and hot air, they do not look at me. It feels like they know what I was doing that day, but of course they can't. I feel obscurely guilty at the way they ignore me, as if losing my son is a crime I have committed, and shunning is their punishment for me.

The big day finally comes. We get up early, we dress in dark clothes, Tom in his new suit, me in the dark skirt and jacket that I wore on the plane coming down here. We say very little, save for Tom telling me what time it is, how many minutes are left before we have to leave. Lately he has become very aware of time, counting down to this day, this hour. Tom has washed all the cars the day before, and they have little black pennants tied to their radio antennae, so everyone will know we're a funeral party. Steffie picked up the pennants yesterday from the funeral home; she made a special trip to get them. She's making sure it will all go perfectly.

Tom goes over to his mom's house to make sure everyone is ready, and to help get Mother Maurie from the porch steps to the car in the folding wheelchair they have rented for the occasion. I do not believe she really needs it; I think of it as a prop for her role of bereaved grandmother. I stand inside the little house, watch him load her into the car, his struggle to fold up the wheelchair and get it into the trunk. Everyone else is ready. Tom's father looks fit for a wedding; his white shirt is too tight and bulges of scarlet neck redder than a turkey's wattle layer over it. Ellie wears a black scarecrow dress that strains at her wide shoulders and flaps around her calves. Steffie should always wear black, she looks so elegant. Her little black dress is perfect for going anywhere, but especially to a funeral. She clutches a little black lace hankie in one hand.

Tom is driving his parents' sedan. He and his father are in the front seat. I am supposed to sit in the backseat with Mother Maurie. I stand for a long time, wishing they would go without me. Then I put down our copy of *Where the Wild Things Are* and go out the door to them. I had wanted to take it with me, had wanted to set it in the coffin and put his little hand on it. But I cannot find the courage to even do that.

I sit in the backseat with Mother Maurie. When I get in, she is staring out her window. No one speaks to me. I take the cue, and sit close to my door and stare out my window. Up front, Tom and his father talk softly, deep heavy voices droning like summer insects. They talk of people who have called, and people who haven't called. Tom's father mentions how brave Steffie is, and Tom agrees. They never once speak Teddy's name or say words like funeral or dead.

We go to the Baptist church. None of us are Baptists, but they have a very nice church, and Steffie went to school with the minister's daughter, so it has all been arranged. Steffie thinks it is better than the funeral home, I heard her tell Tom, because they have several funerals a day there, but Teddy's will be the only funeral today at this church. So it's more familyish and privatelike. Steffie thinks that's how funerals should be. Familyish and privatelike.

But the church parking lot is full of cars, the church packed with people. Potters are an old-time family in this valley, and everyone has turned out to honor them. They have left us parking spaces right in front of the church. The body has already been delivered and put on display, right on schedule. The flowers are exactly as ordered, but Steffie has to go up and move one vase a foot or so to the left. The front pew for the family has been roped off with black crepe-paper streamers. After the funeral and burial there will be a potluck in the church hall. The smell of baked beans and macaroni salad drifts in with the gymnasium smell of the hall and mingles with the women's chemical perfumes and over-powers the flowers. It takes me back to Parish Rummage Sales and St. Judith's Spring Carnival. I wonder if there will be a ring toss and a fish pond to keep the kiddies busy while their parents are eating and commiserating.

I have loitered, staring around, and I suddenly notice people are looking at me. Even Mother Maurie is in place, having been wheeled up in her chair like an Empress Dowager, and carefully aided to her place in the pew. They are all in the pew but me, and Tom glances back at me, and something like annoyance flickers over his face. I am doing it wrong, I suppose, but I have never been to a funeral before. Someone should have cue cards for me.

I enter our pew, kneel, and make the Sign of the Cross. Wrong-O! Tom's family is all sitting. They are here for a funeral, not to pray, and I am holding things up. I take my seat carefully. No one has given me a program. I have to watch for clues. Someone starts playing an organ, no hymn I know, it seems to be only a repetitive series of solemn chords. People rise and file up to look at the dead child in the box. I watch the people look at Teddy. Some merely glance in, with an "oh, hey, sure enough, it's a dead kid in there" look and file past. Others stare avidly, eyes roving over him until they are reluctantly forced to move on by the push of people behind them. A carny sideshow. That's what it reminds me of.

Soon everyone has seen what they came here to see, except for the family. Then we are rising and filing up, Mother Maurie eschewing her wheelchair this time but leaning heavily on her husband and Ellie. I follow them, still groping after procedure and protocol. Some part of me suspects that this has all been orchestrated by Steffie anyway, and that no amount of funeral experience would have saved me. I feel like an actor who hasn't seen the script, and as we approach the coffin, I am sure I am going to blow this scene.

Each has a little grandstand play. I wonder if they have planned them, discussed them, perhaps rehearsed them in the big house living room, using the coffee table as a coffin prop. The farther we go, the less real any of this seems. Bix goes first. He glances in at his little nephew, says audibly, "Damn it all, anyway," and moves on. Steffie pauses, reaching into the coffin to rearrange a lock of his hair and mutter something soothing, as if to a sleeping child. She stands there, unmoving, for just a moment too long. Then she begins shaking, and Bix has to take her arm and lead her away. Ellie, Mother Maurie, and Tom's father view him as a group. Ellie grips the side of the coffin, while Mother Maurie breaks into stifled sobs and leans into her husband's shoulder. Tom's father looks old and tired and bitter, but strong still, the pioneer father shepherding his family through hard times. He moves on first, taking his sobbing wife with him. Ellie trails behind them, wiping her eyes on a large white hankie.

Then Tom is looking into the coffin. Or not looking. I am right beside him, and I can tell he is not looking at the body, but is staring at a place on the blue satin lining of the box. I step up beside him, force myself to look in. A sudden wave of relief washes over me. It's not Teddy! I grip Tom's hand, squeeze it, force him to look at this child. It's not Teddy, there's been some awful mistake, but it's over now. Someone else's child is dead, not ours. The child is smaller, paler, the bones standing out in his face, his blond hair nattily wet-combed to one side, his legs skinny in black pants. This isn't our husky, hearty wind-browned boy. "It's not Teddy," I whisper to Tom and squeeze his hand again. "It's someone else."

"Evelyn," he says in an awful voice, full of rebuke. There is terrible anguish on his face as he reaches in to touch the small mark on the boy's hand, a mark like from the sharp edge of a can of dog food, a mark like Teddy had from when he was three and tried to feed the dog himself. I stare at it, trying to make it not enough, but it is. I look again, and this shrunken body is all that remains of our son.

It's real.

Now, this minute, my son is dead for the first time for me. Before I was just going along with them, making believe that what they told me was true, to be polite, because I didn't seem to have any choice. No, really, I thought I had believed it before this, but I didn't, not really. I hadn't seen the body. Teddy gone was not Teddy dead. I couldn't "feel" him dead, somehow he'd been still there, around the corner, in the barn, at the big house. Some part of me had not believed any of this, had thought it was some sort of elaborate torture, and that sooner or later they'd have to give him back. I hadn't believed he could be dead. But now I do. I can hear I am making some weird sound, not crying or laughing or hiccuping, just this weird animal sound. And Tom is closing the coffin, pushing me back from it so my fingers won't get shut in it, and his father has come up behind us and is saying, "Oh, for Christ's sake, Evelyn!" Like he's really totally disgusted with me this time. He grabs me by the shoulder, I don't know what he plans to do, but Tom is stepping between us, saying, "I'll handle it, Dad, just let me take care of it." And Tom takes me firmly by the arm and walks me down the dim aisle of the cool church, with everyone gaping at us, like a wedding procession in reverse, and out into the hot dusty day outside.

It makes it worse. This is summer, the day is hot and bright, no one could be dead today, death is something that happens at night in cold places, or it happens on TV, right before the commercials, but it never happens to the main characters, never to the important ones. How could it have happened to Teddy? And I can't stop making the noise. I'm not even trying. Tom takes me by both shoulders and shakes me. "Stop it," he says, and not gently. "Just knock it off. Damn it, I've got all I can handle already. So just knock it off. Don't you see we've got just this last little bit to get through? Just burying him, and that damn supper, and then it's done, it's over."

His words aren't making sense to me. Teddy is going to be dead forever. There is no way that doing these last few things will put an end to it. I stare up at him, trying to see him through my tears. His face mirrors his disgust. I know I must look awful, my nose always runs when I cry and my face blotches into red and white. My green eyes are bloodshot right away. I know I must look awful and disgusting, but Teddy being dead is so big and awful a thing that it shouldn't matter to him right now. Nothing should matter but that our boy is gone forever.

I grope for a tissue, find none, drag my sleeve across my face. That seems to be the final straw, for Tom releases me abruptly, turns away. "Shit!" he says, bleakly, without hope. I get myself under control, swallow the noises even though they make huge dents in my throat. Tom stares over the parking lot. Finally he turns back to me as suddenly as he had turned away. Something else is in his face, something I have never seen before. He is almost smiling, like sometimes little kids look like they're smiling when they're trying very hard not to cry. "Why are you doing this now?" he demands, his voice gone cruel but choking. His eyes are very bright. "To make a big show for everyone, show them how much you cared? Hell, you weren't even around that day! If he'd been home with you, none of this would have happened. Hell, if you'd even bothered to come with me, to at least keep an eye on him, none of this would have happened. But no, you had to have one of your sulks, go off alone, and leave Teddy for me to handle."

It is not true, not one word of it, and as I look at him in horror, I know he knows that it is not true. But some part of him is begging for me to admit it, the way he has had to admit it to his family every day since it happened. I can see how it was. In the Potter family, nothing bad ever just happens. It is always someone's fault, someone always has to take the blame for it. Flat tires happen because you drove too fast, or took the wrong roads, or hit that last bump too hard. Washing machines break because they were overloaded, or you used too much detergent, or you didn't vacuum under it. Teddy died because his father took him haying. Or because his mother didn't keep him home.

I think he is asking me for something. I don't think he knows it, but he is. He has nothing left. What was between us is gone, has been dismantled brick by brick over the last few months. His son is dead. What he has left is maybe his family. But only if he isn't guilty of killing his child. How they must have been working on him these last few days, I don't want to imagine. But it is all there, in the lines graven in his face, in the hair that is dead straw now instead of warm gold, in the eyes that are starved and flat. The shock of all this has made my own grief a distant scream in the night. I wipe my sleeve once more across my slimy face, see him wince in disgust again at my unladylike ways. He loved me once. How that must shame him now.

It's a little like shooting your dog. I've had to do that only once in my life. You see the crushed body the semi has rolled and humped over, and it's like your dog is trapped inside something that isn't part of him anymore. He's dying, but not fast enough. If death had a door, he'd be scratching and whining at it, he wants out that bad. And only you can let him out. So you jack your father's black military .45, and it makes the deadliest sound in the world. You hold it two-handed, and your fingers are barely long enough to trip off the safety. You flash for an instant that if there's a rock in the dirt under Rinky's skull, then that bullet may come flying right back up at you. But somehow that doesn't seen so bad, and you put the muzzle into the pink inside his ear, and it's stupid, how he can still flick his ear to try to dislodge it, like it's only a bug instead of cold metal, like something in his ear is more important than bone sticking out of his side right through the fur. And you pull the trigger. In love. In mercy. In a horrible explosion of stinging sound, and the gun leaps in your hand like a live thing and bits of Rinky spatter against you with a hot force like they're going to go right through you. And it's done and he's gone and you don't even have a good memory left of his wise eyes and broad skull and velvet ears under your hands, it's all gone to shattered bits and wet fur.

But it was what you had to do. What his subaudible cries had been begging you to do. So you did it. You destroyed what's left to set him free.

"I have a lover," I say. "I was with him when Teddy died. That's why I sent him with you instead of keeping him home and safe. So I could be with the brown man."

The day is hot and dusty and still, and the sun is white in the sky. There is too much light to see clearly. I think that is it, because at first I don't see his face change at all. Then it's like colors washing through an octopus I saw in an aquarium once. This is a flushing of Toms, many Toms flickering across his expressions, all taking a turn at looking at me out of his eyes. Some believe and some don't, some are hurt, some angry, and

at least once I glimpse one who knows exactly what I am
doing. But he is gone quickly, and it is the last one, the
outraged Potter, who steps forward and slaps me, hard,
so it throws me sideways up against the hood of the
sedan. When I can straighten up, he already has his back
to me and is headed into the church, back to his family.
The door swings shut slowly behind him, silent on its
pneumatic closer, until I hear the snick of the catch.

Good-bye Tom.

All of the Potter cars have secret keys in magnetic
holders under the hood. It takes me a minute or two,
because I can't figure out the hood catch, but I get the
key and I start the car and I drive away. The little black
pennant flies merrily in the breeze, and blood from my
nose and split lip drips off my chin until I open the
window and let the hot wind dry it on my face. Mother
Maurie will be upset with blood on the steering wheel
and road grit inside her sedan. Tom will probably have to
clean it up. Steffie will probably help him. Maybe it will
be then that he will confide in her, will tell her what it
was I said that explains why I left the funeral. She will
tell her parents. And they will all have been right about
me, and Teddy's death will have been all my fault. Poor
Tom. And life will go on for all of them.

The bright tackiness of the little house seems
sharper the last time I go into it. I move quickly, as if I
am a burglar, as if I will be interrupted at any moment.
Not by Tom and his family. By Teddy. The empty house
has a haunted feel, I almost expect to hear the light
rumble of a Tonka truck down the hallway, the clatter of
a dropped cereal bowl.

But there is nothing. I fill my overnight bag quickly.
It is a shoulder bag with lots of compartments, one of
those cheap under-seat pieces you buy through the mail
that never really fits under the seat of the airplane.
Jeans, underwear, shirts, socks. Not much to take,
really. Toothbrush, deodorant. Sheath knife, matches. I
change into jeans and a shirt, lace and tie my sneakers.
I leave my discarded clothing where I drop it. What
happens to it is Tom's problem. For a moment I consider
taking some of Teddy's things, the Mickey Mouse shirt

that still smells like him, the battered copy of *Where the Wild Things Are*. But in the end, I leave them, too. I think very seriously of setting the house on fire. But it is a brief thought, only occurring as I go out the door, not a revenge thought but a symbolic thing, to not only have it be ended but have it be cleansed by fire as well. But I suspect that not even flames could consume *Poems for the John*, the gaudy rooster plates, the plastic unreality of that house. I have no doubt that in a matter of days Tom will be back in his old room in the big house, where his high school pennants still fly on the walls. Steffie and Ellie will clean me out of the little house, and I'll be gone. Ellie's Clorox and Pine Sol and Endust are more effective than flames.

The bag is not that heavy on my shoulder. I have taken no money, other than a few odd bills and change already in my jeans. There is no money to take, it has all gone for the funeral, even the savings account in Alaska has been drained. Somehow that is fitting. I don't really care.

I shut the door firmly behind me.

I don't take the car. Mother Maurie would not hesitate to report it stolen. I'm not going to the airport, anyway. I'm not sure where I am going, but there are two places I am not going. One is the airport and one is the little clearing beside the stream. Because Teddy's death has ended that, too.

I reach the end of the driveway and head out up the highway. North. As good a direction as any, I suppose. It's a blacktop two-lane highway, ditches and brush at the sides. No sidewalks, no paths. Not the best place for walking. Broken bottles, litter, slipping gravel. Without thinking, I settle into an even swinging stride. The overnight bag on my shoulder thumps lightly against my hip with every step. Cars whisk past me, and occasionally a semi booms by me in a blast of wind and thunder. I don't think about what they must think, I don't wonder if any of the passengers turn to another and say, "Hey, wasn't that Potter's boy Tom's wife? Why isn't she at the funeral?"

The day is hot and soon I sweat through my shirt

and the bag strap begins to chafe. I transfer it to the other shoulder and keep on going. I wonder how many miles I can cover a day. I think briefly about food and sleeping, but right now I cannot imagine ever being hungry or sleepy. Only driven, as I am now, to physical exertion and distance making.

I am able to not think. This is very good. Even if what makes me able to not think is a splitting headache from the heat of the sun on my bare head and the bright light bouncing off the bare road ahead. Soon I am thirsty, too, and the dry dust that whirls up and coats me in the wake of each car doesn't help. It coats the edges of my eyes, dries out the lining of my nose and mouth, itches in my ears. I keep walking, concentrate only on what my body is telling me, on planning for only the next few hours.

I should have brought a canteen of water. I should have brought a blanket, too. I think about sleeping under an overpass, as I have heard about people doing, but it isn't for me. Sleep in the wash of headlights and the surf of passing vehicles? No. I will not go out on the actual freeway, will not ignore the NO HITCHHIKING signs that warn pedestrians back from the on-ramps. No. I think I will travel by highways like this, going north, until I reach the Alcan, and then I will follow it. All the way back to Alaska.

Part of me knows that is too immense a journey for me. Part of me is aware of buying food and sleeping somewhere and bathing somewhere. Part of me knows about crossing the border taking at least $200. Part of me knows all that stuff but it is a part I am not speaking to, because it is also the part that knows my son is dead and my husband no longer loves me and that there is no way to undo any of that.

I walk all day. Twice cars slow down to ask if I need a ride, but I just wave them on. In the evening I am still walking. I can feel blisters on my heels, and I am so thirsty I think my throat has dried up and cracked inside. When people start to use their headlights, I know it is time to move off the road. I wait until there are no cars in sight, and then I leave the road, clambering up the loose gravel wall of the ditch and through a barbed-wire fence.

I don't know why the land here is fenced, it is all replanted forest. The young trees are all Weyerhauser Spruce, no taller than my shoulder, most of them. But back from the road the old stumps still linger, showing how huge the giants were that once grew here. Some fallen trunks, rejected God knows why, still sprawl lengthwise. They have gone green with moss, soft with rot. They would make a good place to shelter for the night, sleeping up against one, but I am too thirsty.

I wish I had a dog's nose. I wish I had a wolf's eyes. It is getting dark, I am tireder than I knew, and eventually I know I am not going to find water as easily as I had hoped. Tomorrow, maybe. I sit down right where I am, it is as good a spot as any. I take a heavy denim shirt from my bag and put it on, and then use the bag for a pillow. I lie down, then sit up and toss a few twigs and sticks aside. I lie down again, pulling my knees up against my chest so I am curled up small. I close my eyes and try to sleep.

After a while, I open them again. I have not been asleep, only very still. It's dark, but not much time has passed. Sweat has dried cold and stiff on my skin, as if I have been damp-rolled in salt. I'm thirsty. The stars are out, looking at me. I distract myself by looking for the Dipper and the North Star. I find them, and then think about how they point the way home, and how far away that is. Impossibly far.

This has been childish. This whole thing. I cannot walk back to Alaska. And even if I could, then what? Walk into Fairbanks just as winter's settling in, no job, no money, no home? Beg Annie to put me up, give me work? No. It's stupid.

I have to go back. It's a matter of survival. What else can I do, wander around in these woods until I collapse of hunger or exposure or get shot for trespassing? I'm not a kid anymore. This is real life. I've had my tantrum, run off from my own child's funeral, quarreled with my husband, and packed up and run away like a little kid. Okay, so now what is left is reality. How long do I think

I can hike cross-country with no food or supplies? Five days? Seven? Hell, I don't even have a road map.

I have to go back. Back to Tom and the whole mess, back to Teddy being dead and his family hating me. Back to Tom knowing I've been unfaithful. I have to go back and beg for help, for shelter, for food. Beg them to give me enough money to go home. What will they do? The family lawyer will come in. The family lawyer went to school with Tom's father, Tom calls him Uncle Kenny. He won't let Tom make any merciful mistakes. That's what lawyers are for, I've heard Mother Maurie say, to watch out for your best interests even if you don't know what those are. It will be hard for him to figure out what he can take from me, but I'm sure they'll think of something. I have to go back.

I have to go back.

I can't. And that's a matter of survival, too.

I don't even want to think about any of it. Because the final conclusion is always the same, that I don't have anything anymore. No home, no child, no marriage. Nothing.

Except a faun.

No. I will not go back to him because . . .

My mind loops and runs like a rat in a cage, refusing to stop at an answer. At any answer.

Because I was with him when Teddy died.

Because I don't want to tell him about Teddy.

Because I want to go to him so very badly, because I think he could make me feel good again, and I know it would be wrong to feel good again when my child is dead. Because I want to feel bad?

What do I want?

I want Teddy.

Well, you can't have him. He's dead.

And finally I grieve. Weep the crying that shakes me and exhausts me. I cry myself to sleep. A fat lot of good it does me.

# Eighteen

It is raining. The cool drops are falling lightly on my face, washing away the salt and sweat and dust. I do not turn away from it or open my eyes. The shower ends, but a few seconds later it commences again, a light pattering on my face. I should get up before I am soaked. I open my eyes to Pan standing over me. The water is falling from his hands as he flicks wetness at me. He is not smiling.

I wave him away and sit up slowly. All the pains of yesterday come back, complete with yesterday's headache. I put my face in my hands, but he plucks at my elbow, pushes a waterskin into my hands. On the leather side it says BSA. Once that would have made me grin. I undo the plastic stopper and drink, then awkwardly spill some into my hand and smear it over my face. I sigh heavily, and Pan offers me a T-shirt from my pack for me to dry my face on. I take it, wipe my face, and drink again. I blink around at a day that is not quite here yet. Dark grey still.

He crouches down before me. He puts his elbows on his knees and rests his chin in his hands. It is a stance I remember from our childhood and I know he can hold it for hours. His cloven hooves are sunk deeply in the moss. I stare at them for a while, at the lines of grain and growth in the pale hooves, then look up at his face. His dark eyes meet mine unflinchingly. He looks so young to me suddenly, young as animals are always young. Sound of limb and lung, free of heart, immune to the things that follow humans from day to day to day. He waits in my silence, for a long time.

Finally, I say, "My son is dead. My husband doesn't love me anymore. I've run away."

He looks down, pursing his mouth gravely. When he looks up his eyes meet mine. No judgment. Simple comprehension, without questions.

Then he says, "So you've come to be with me."

"No," I say.

He continues to look at me. His nostrils flare lightly, as if reading the air. I feel my jaw set, feel the pain of my headache tighten into a sort of anger.

"Of course you have," he says, watching me, daring me to deny it. I think perhaps he is deliberately provoking me.

"Go away," I tell him, my voice gone harsh on the words.

He cocks his head and looks at me, as puzzled as Rinky had been when the recorded voices of wolves came out of the stereo speakers. He gets up and walks around me slowly. I see his nostrils flare as he takes in my scent, and for some reason that makes me even angrier, it is as personal as if he had laid hands on me, that kind of a touching.

"Leave me alone!" I roar at him, and it startles him into a goat leap, a sideways jerk of motion. His puzzlement wrinkles his brow.

"But you don't want me to," he protests. "And I don't want to go. I want to be with you."

There are many ways to interpret his words. I choose to take them sexually, to be righteously outraged by them.

"Get away from me!" I explode, shrieking. "I don't want you. I don't need you!" I fly at him, fists going, not the wildly flailing slapping hands of girl fights, but the short driving body punches learned a lifetime ago as the quickest response to my brothers. I actually land two on firm belly muscles before he leaps back out of my range. His eyes are as wild and white-edged as those of a kicked dog, teeth show in his mouth, he is breathing through flared nostrils. Not fear, not aggression, though. Animal bewilderment, the fight-or-flight response kicked in. I am panting, wild, disheveled. "I don't need you!" I scream again. "I can live in the real world anytime I want to!"

We face each other across a great gulf and the smallest of distances. I think perhaps he will come at me, hit me in the face, grab my hair and throw me down, hurt me, hit me, batter me into submission, be an animal to be. Part of me wants that, but it is not a sexual thing. I want him to be bestial and savage and low, so I can justify all the anger and hatred I am feeling. So I can somehow make everything be all his fault, and I can be poor, poor Evelyn, deceived and mistreated.

Like Tom, pops the thought, sudden as a fire-cracker. I want someone to blame, someone to hate so it can't be my fault. The realization is scorching, but I quench it with anger. I am not like Tom, I was deceived and tricked.

I really was, blinded by lust brought on by his goaty pheromones, used by him, that wasn't me, I wouldn't do that, I'm better than that. I'm a good mother, I would have known my child was dying, if it weren't for him. I loved my husband and child, I didn't wish for this, I didn't want to be free of them so I could follow the faun. It wasn't my fault, I didn't break some sort of magic circle of protection by opening my life to the faun. Betraying Tom couldn't have killed Teddy. "I don't belong to you," I shriek at him, my voice cracking on the words. "There was never any promise between us."

A great stillness comes over him. I can see it happening, it is like he was a painted image, and the watercolor artist has put a wash over him. A distancing that doesn't involve moving. "I've always known that," he says softly. And backs away, one cautious step after another, until the forest fades in around him and he is gone.

Again. So much like the last time.

And I am left alone, breathing hard, standing bolt upright in the forest of not-yet-dawn. I feel dizzy and woozy, as if awakened suddenly from a dream. Slowly I sink back down, find the warm spot on the earth where I had been lying. I pull the blanket back up over my shoulders and fall asleep again, sinking into blackness like a feverish child, fleeing these too intense feelings.

I awake again, later, to what seems like a different day. The light is clear and mild, high cloud cover gentles the sun. The air is moving over the young forest around me. Insects are chirring, birds calling. Life goes on, ignoring all questions and hesitations.

The waterskin is still beside me, and I drink from it. The blanket that has covered me is an odd thing, felted animal hair and wool in an uneven pad. Grass seed heads and a few burrs and twigs cling to it. Warp and woof of it seem to be some sort of reed or straw. It rolls up rather than folds, and a leather thong at one end seems to be for tying around it. I put the T-shirt back into my pack, and stuff the denim shirt in on top of it. I look around. Now what?

Logic rings up three choices. Go back to Tom. Go north. Wait for Pan to come back.

Would I come back? I ask myself. Repulsed, rebuked, would I return? No. But I am not Pan. He might come back. And if he did, what then? I have too many answers to that. I want to slap him, kick him, beat him bloody; both for what happened that day, and for the way he left last night. Perhaps for the way he left that summer day so long ago. But I also want him to hold me and comfort me, to make love to me, to curl up in his arms like a small child and be sheltered by him. There are too many things I want of him, too many things I want him to be. To be and not to be. To be part of my life. To be all my life.

Or to be nothing to me. To be free of him. To have him never have been real at all. As if that would make me free of everything else, of Tom, of Teddy, of death itself.

Like some awful trade. I'll give up the things that felt the best if you'll take away the things that hurt the worst with them. A kid's deal with God. Only God never believes in those trades.

For a time, I wait. I rise, I pace, and I settle again.

Waiting. Then, without really making a decision, I take the waterskin and the blanket and sling them onto my bag. And I go. Not back to the road. Deeper into the woods, following what the night sky showed me last night, going true north.

About noon I leave the Weyerhauser tree plantation and its shoulder-high trees, cross a small road, and enter true forest again. The shade is welcome. At a stream, I stop and refill the waterskin. I eat as I go, odd bits of things, not really enough to sustain me, not even because I really feel hunger compel me, but because it is what one does. Take food when you find it because you don't know when you'll next see it. So I eat a morel, a handful of fireweed shoots, a few wild strawberries no bigger than the tip of my little finger. My foraging does not take me aside from my path. Few things do. When I break out onto roads, sometimes I must veer to left or right to avoid houses and yards. But I cross pastures fearlessly, ignore NO TRESPASSING signs, and push north. Like a migrating animal, or a lemming in search of the sea, I don't pause to consider what I am doing, I simply do it. And I think. Because today is for thinking.

Thoughts go so fast, when you let them. Like a high-speed projector, they flicker uninterrupted, continuous, undisrupted by my eating a mushroom or stopping to crouch and pee. By the evening of the first day, I have replayed my entire childhood. My memories are like a melody atop the deep chords of my grief. The loss of Teddy is a constant pain, a theme that directs the way I recall my days. At the end of the day, I have considered things I have forgotten for years, the color of a crushed robin's eggshell, the necessity of my mother's hands, the smell of my father's pipe smoke in the intensely cold air of winter. All the small things that are so much more important than the big things because they are the true constants; these are re-possessed by me.

I am back in true forest by the time the sun is going down, moving among trees older than our country's name. Trees scoff at such human trivialities as giving names to areas of land. As if drawing a shape around something and giving it a different name makes it any less a part of the whole. As if renaming me wife or daughter-in-law or mother could redefine me, cut me off from what I had always been.

These are how the thoughts flow, how the passing connections are made. By the time I find a sleeping place between the root hummocks of a rosinous pine, I have reassessed my foundation and settled my life atop it once more.

The next dawn I do not hesitate when I arise. I tidy myself and my belongings and leave this temporary space. Today it is my adolescence that replays itself in all its pimply splendor. Sullen boys lurking in the corridors of my past, motorcycles on cool summer roads and locker-room slurs, the proms I never went to, the lies I told and almost believed myself. I come out of the forest in midmorning, onto another blacktop highway, directly across from a 7-Eleven. I wait until there is no traffic in sight before I climb through the barbed wire and out onto the road. The NO TRESPASSING sign that swings from the top wire tells me that I have been traipsing through a military reserve. It makes little impression on me. It was merely land to be crossed.

At the little convenience store, I use the rest room, tidy up myself, and then spend the bulk of my cash on candy bars. The glance I get from the cashier is only mildly curious. I offer no explanations. When I leave, I strike out down the road and have to travel some miles before there is again a wooded stretch that offers me northern escape. I eat a candy bar as I walk, and the sugar in my mouth is good. I have been hungry, but the chocolate is enough to make it less noticeable. Instead of being a pain in my gut, my hunger becomes a lightness I feel, a springiness to my joints, a bubble between the top of my brain and my skull. And all the while, I am reliving high school and college, examining crossroads and decision points of my life, saying if not this, then what?

The stretch of woods is narrow, it gives onto back pastures. I follow fence lines that go arrow-straight as far as I can see. Cattle graze in some pastures, in others hay is awaiting a second harvest. In one, yellow bales have been abandoned, rained on, and the green is growing up around them. I look aside, away from the good alfalfa hay left to rot in bales. It isn't time to think of that yet. I list my high-school boyfriends, put them in chronological order. Kerry and Steve and David and Larry and Steven and Brad and Eric and Bruce and . . . were there really that many of them in only four years? Yes. I try to think which one I would want to see again if I could summon one up. None of them. They were all disposable, interchangeable, and I knew it even then. So why had Tom become the permanent one, and when?

By the end of the day, when I am still following fence lines, I think I know the answer. I didn't choose him. He chose me and I went along with it. Until I believed I had chosen him. He was something to belong to, someone to be with when my parents stopped being. Somebody real to cling to, to show I could live a real life. So I had gone with him. Simply because he was so big and handsome I would have been crazy to refuse him. And good. Yes, admit he was good. He was honest and hearty and strong, laughing and true and brave. That part had been real, at least for a while. I am tempted to look for cracks in it, to somehow dull the shine by putting corrosion on my bright silver dreams. I could look at him with jaded eyes, with the malignancy of hindsight and impugn all his golden ways with tin motives. But it wouldn't be true or fair. And that is the point of all this. To find out what was real.

I sleep in the thin shelter of a brushy fence line. Myriad tiny birds are still hopping and bouncing within the brush as I drop off to sleep, pecking at dry seeds as they cling to twigs with unlikely weightlessness. All of me aches very good when I lie still and let the warmth of the earth flow up through me. Pan's blanket covers me, and I consciously go to sleep, climbing into the blackness with as much control as if I were climbing into a hot bath.

Morning comes and I move on. I wonder how many miles I have traveled, then dismiss it as unimportant. When I get there, I'll be there. Where is there? I'll know that when I see it, for my ultimate destination is no longer all that clear to me. I travel as much in my mind as I do in my body. When I get to a stopping point, I'll know it. Down all the years with Tom. Less than a decade, but it seems so much longer. Some of the days were so good. Sometimes I am smiling as I walk, and once or twice I even laugh aloud at shared silliness remembered, at smoky eroticism dissolving into puppy-ish roughhousing. It is like organizing a library, each volume handled carefully, catalogued and inspected and shelved, a thing done with. The days of the honeymoon, the months of the pregnancy, the time spent fixing the cabin, putting in the garden. Fixing the car on a dark cold afternoon in Fairbanks winter, fishing for nothing on the Chena riverbank. Trips to Manley Hot Springs, dip-fishing at Chitna with Teddy in the backpack.

And now it is finally time to think of Teddy. My baby, my boy. I go back to the moment when I decided I was pregnant, before any doctor told me. I cherish each instance I can recall. Careful as a miser I am, to miss nothing. I try for day by day, but often have to settle for a general idea of what we were doing season to season. The memories are jumbled as old photographs in a trunk, but I slowly shuffle them into an order I can understand. I leave the fence lines and pastures, walk through a small town and out of it, down a stretch of unpromising little lots with mobile homes and wanigans, ramshackle fences and abandoned cars, into a crossroads town consisting of a tavern, a gas station, and a gift shop, and over a bridge. On the other side of the bridge, I leave the road and go down, slipping and sliding in the gravel, and follow the riverbank north.

Travel is more difficult along the riverbank. The river is down this time of year, and the bank is littered with last winter's snags and driftwood. The river is a thick, silty grey-green, but it smells clean. Human litter on the bank is minimal. Probably the river's rise and fall cleans itself. Where there are reeds and grass, the grasses are rough and sharp-edged, and high enough to slice at my hands. Insects stir up in my passage, tangle in my hair, hum wildly in my ears. In their frantic buzzing is the message that rain is coming soon. I begin to think that following the river was not the best idea, but I make no effort to change direction. It flows past me, a dark grey-green beast, its song changing as its bed does, going south as I go north, not a true course, but close enough. Occasionally I walk past yards, past people's summer cabins and tidy lots fronting on the river. They politely ignore me and I ignore them. Public right of way and all that rot. I wonder idly why people would move out from the city to the country, and then spend hours changing a brushy riverbank into a rolling lawn, with white plastic furniture and tables with umbrellas sprouting out of the middles. What is the point of having a summer place in the country if you dress it like a suburban home, skirt it with lawn, belt it with pathways, manicure the bushes? The people are out on their ride-on lawn mowers, they are on their knees grubbing in the flower beds, they are refinishing the picnic tables, they are cleaning the rain gutters. All so busy getting ready to have a relaxing time at the country place.

I am glad when the river widens and the land to either side of it becomes more swampy. The houses dwindle and cease, and the forest moves closer to the banks. Raccoon sign here. Duck rises off her nest, in a flurry of air and feathers. I spook grandfather frogs into leaping out into the river's sullen shallows. So much more life going on here than along those manicured lots. Angry wasp in a hurry. A red-winged blackbird sings angrily at my intrusion. I realize I have stopped thinking.

I stand still. Deliberately I wheel my mind, bring it about, and head into it again. I think about the decision to visit Tom's family when the letter came about Bix doing his shoulder. I think about how excited we all were, an adventure, getting out of Fairbanks during the draggly end of a wet, cold spring, going to go Outside, Teddy would see the farm, the moo cows, and the roosters going cock-a-doodle-do. Packing up a box of our best homemade preserves, rose-hip jelly and blueberry jam, wild raspberry jam, sourdough sauce, mincemeat with real moose meat in it, the old kind. Pack it all up, roll the jars in newspaper so they won't crack and pack them in a beer box. Take new pictures of the cabin, of Teddy with his puppy, of the cache on its stilt legs. Tom buys the stupid Alaskan souvenirs, the plastic totem pole, the souvenir plate made in Japan, the "Moose-quito" made of shellacked moose turds and pipe cleaners. I should have suspected then, it occurs to me, what I was coming down into.

The first days of the visit went so well. They were so glad to see Tom, so proud of Teddy. Even me. I was so . . . interesting. I remember the introductions. "And here's the boy's wife, Lynn. I understand he caught her running wild in the brush up there, liked what he saw, and tamed her down to be his wife!" Laughter. "Is it true, Lynn, that you helped Tommy skin that big moose in the picture Maurie showed us?" "Hell, Jim, she did all the skinning, just ask Tom! He's real proud of his frontier girl."

The bragging family, talking about the wild girl they had taken into their midst, while I grow quieter and quieter. I suppose I was something of a disappointment to the guests. I could tell how I had been talked up by the Potters to their friends. Tom's crazy Alaskan wife. She'd rather live up there with no plumbing and forty below zero than in a real house. She's quite the squaw, kills the meat, tans the hides, splits the wood, and smokes the fish. They'd given me quite a buildup. Guess they'd had to, to explain why their son would want to live in that far-off, cold place.

So here I came. Nondescript. Quiet. No sealskin parka, no mukluks. Just a skinny, mousy woman. I could tell by the reactions of the people who met me that more than half of them had believed I was Eskimo. "What pretty green eyes!" they'd say, to cover the shock that I was not brown and black-eyed with wide flat cheeks. Even as a conversation piece, I'd failed the Potter family.

The shores of the river are narrowing as the banks become steeper. The going gets more difficult. I push through tangles of brush and emerge on a tiny beach with horsetail fern all over it. These are the big ones, old as dinosaur days, thick and dark green and high as my shoulder, no leafy fronds, just the vertical segmented tubes with each segment marked in black. The younger ones are a set of startling greens, all shades, with the segments less clearly marked. They are raspy and coarse, good for scouring out the fish-frying pan on a camping trip.

Finally, there is no shore left at all. The trees are right at the water's edge, leaning from the steep bank, some are half fallen into the water. Time to leave the river's edge. The brush is very thick, and I don't spot any animal trails at all. So I clamber up against the flow of the forest, the worst way to move in the woods, snapping branches, forging through blackberry bushes. There is cedar here, both old and young. One old fallen trunk provides me with a brief and treacherous pathway up the hill. The trunk widens as I go up it in a crouching walk, sidestepping what is left of its branches. I pass one of the huge anthills so common in this part of Washington. They always seem to be big reddish heaps of pine needles until you get close and see the life stirring all through it. The fallen trunk comes to an end in a claw of root and clinging earth. There are true ferns sprouting in the earth still trapped in its roots, delicate fronds studded with tiny brown seed spores on the backs. I think of eating fiddlehead ferns, gather the heads while they are still rolled and tight like the tuning pegs on a fiddle, rinse them and sauté them in butter. But these are all mature ferns, their fronds wide and somehow mysterious in the green under-light beneath the trees.

I cannot see the sky at all. Washington's rain forest, canopied almost like a jungle but without the lacing of vines weaving it together. I scramble down from my tree trunk, almost drown in the thick brush taller than my head. I pull my shirt cuffs down over my hands, for the hillside is steep, with patches of stinging nettle. The nettles are face high and I am climbing up through them. I know I will get hit, and I do, but I pick one of the thick fern fronds and squeeze out the sap to treat the sting. The nettle sting is oxalic acid, I think, like a bee's sting. Or, no, what is that acid that starts with an "f"? Or is any of that right? Names don't matter, the forest tells me, as the fern sap soothes away whatever it is that is burning on my skin. There are plants here in the green dampness that I cannot give a name to, huge leaved things with green flowers like the naked pistils of lilies, lacy little ferns I do not know, tiny plants with minute, petaled white flowers. Names don't matter. Only existence. I have to struggle and rip my way up through them, cracking branches, trampling crisp stems, leaving a wake like a hippo had wallowed up this hill. I am not proud of my destruction. It is not natural to leave this much evidence of passage.

I finally reach the top of the bank. I look back, but I can neither see nor hear the river. The brush is that dense. I am in cedar now, big fragrant trees. If one should fall, if a tree should crash down to lie supine on the forest humus, others will rise from her body in a neat rank. Nursery trees, they're called. It's life, I think. Use your body to live, or someone else will use it. Young trees, shelf bracken fungi, mushrooms, ferns, moss, all coat one fallen giant, take sustenance from its softening, sinking body.

I find myself thinking that this is a better way. They'd shot Teddy's body full of chemicals, and hermetically sealed him in a box. Kid preserves. Teddy jam. Like spiced crabapples in a jar. So pretty to look at. Then they'd taken that box, designed so carefully to keep the rest of the world out, and lowered it into a hole and buried it. I thought about his little body in its dress-up funeral clothes, alone there in the box, under the dark earth. How long would the embalming stuff hold decay at bay? How long before his body juices, what was left of them, began to work on his flesh, to try and turn him back into useful nutrients, to bring him back to oneness with the world? But they'd be defeated by the stout walls of the box, with its pressure-resistant layers. So lonely, alone in there. I remembered a story I heard a funeral salesman tell once. It was a long time ago, in Fairbanks, when I was little and those kind of sales were still made door-to-door. He'd been talking to my mother, pushing her to get land in a cemetery for a family plot or something while she stood in the kitchen, ironing shirts, and he sat at the kitchen table, telling her about these new coffins, how they never collapsed in on the bodies like the old ones did. And he told us what was supposed to be a shocking story about a widow who went to visit her husband's grave one spring, and found it all sunken in, and how she had grabbed a shovel and heaped dirt on the grave until it was level again because she just couldn't bear to think of what had happened down there. My mom didn't buy anything from him, but she let him talk himself out before she sent him on his way. She used to think doing stuff like that was funny.

Once Tom and I had talked about it, in a joking offhand way, and I'd told him to skip the funeral and just slip me into the compost heap beside the garden. I'd probably grow great tomatoes. It had been a joke, but now I see the merit. I can imagine setting Teddy into the warm black earth, a cloth over him, planting him like the root ball of some very precious flower, pushing the soft soil down over him, patting him into place. Somehow that would be better than the human selfishness of sealing up the remains, as if keeping the body out of nature's cycle will somehow preserve some essence of humanity. Preserve? It seems to me a very cruel setting apart.

I stop. The light pattering of rain sounds on the leaves overhead. I select a big cedar, move close to its trunk. I stand there awhile, waiting to see if this is just a passing squall. But the rain goes on, falling steadily, and now it starts to make its way down to the forest floor. The air cools perceptibly even as it comes alive with scents.

I sigh. My mind is a reluctant animal, reined back once more to the track, put again over the jumps.

If I had wanted to, I could have made Tom's family like me. That's what I have to admit. What I would have had to do, I would have had to change my external self enough for them to think they understood me. I should have been enthused about shopping, I should have begged Steffie to help me pick out some stylish clothes. I should have asked Mother Maurie about Tom's early toilet training. I should have asked Ellie which was better, Clorox or Purex. They would have loved me.

I didn't. Because I didn't want to. Because being me

was still more important to me than being liked. And that was where Tom and I had always differed. Being liked had always been more important to him than being Tom. At school, at our cabin in Alaska, at his home, he had always been whatever he had needed to be in order to be liked. I had once admired his wondrous ability to be whatever anyone wanted him to be. Now it seemed a lapdog's trick to me.

I tried to twist my mind about, tried to see our days in Alaska from Tom's viewpoint. How had he really felt the first time he shot the moose, how had he felt about working on the little cabin, grubbing in the garden, trying to keep a truck running all winter? I didn't know. He'd been too good at it, too good at being the Tom Potter I'd wanted him to be. I would never know the real Tom.

Maybe there wasn't one. Maybe he'd been pleasing others for so long that there wasn't any real Tom Potter left. Maybe he would spend the rest of his life now being whatever his family wanted him to be, Tom Potter's life determined by popular vote. It had always worked for him. Until he got a divided audience, and had to make a choice whom to play for. Hell, it was still working for him.

Slowly it dawns on me that he probably never even saw it as a choice. Probably never even stopped to think about it. Be whatever the majority of people want you to be. I was the one it hadn't worked for. Tom had quit playing to me, had opted for the larger audience.

I sit very still. The rain is falling on the branches and needles above me. Then it runs along their edges and falls again to the earth. If I listen very carefully, I can hear the pattering of the drops on the leaves and the different pattering as it hits the forest floor. The same rain, falling twice.

I suddenly discover I am finished thinking about Tom and myself. A strange relief, cool as the rain, comes over me. No more guilt, no more feeling bad about any of it. No point to trying to make high tragedy out of something that has only the makings for comic opera. We've been soap characters, the shrewish wife, or the much suffering wife, depending on who you're rooting for. The dutiful son, the dutiful husband, depending on which camera is currently on Tom. The all-American farm family, backbone of our country or the self-devouring incestuous horde. I am tired of all of it. And I am done with all of it.

There is only one thing left to think about. Teddy. And Teddy's death.

Teddy comes to me as sensations, not memories. Soapy washcloth getting the pine sap off his small fingers. Smell of his skin when he falls asleep on my lap in the truck on a long car trip and the absolute lax heaviness of his sleeping weight. Tying his shoelaces. The tight grip of his round downy arms around my neck.

It was and it isn't. It's gone. Like the wet footprints he'd leave on the bathroom floor, the handprints on the mirror, the sticky peanut-butter lipmarks on the rim of his milk glass. Teddy himself turns out to be as ephemeral as the tracks he left.

I balk, suddenly. No more. I am not ready to think anymore about Teddy.

Instead, I go back to my earlier lives and ponderings, pick up the one thread that has run straight and true through all of it. The one I have not had to think about these past three days; the piece that doesn't have to fit in the puzzle, for it is complete in and of itself. What is apart from my life and encloses it? Who has left his cloven tracks on every day?

I lean back on the big cedar, close my eyes. "It's okay," I say through the pattering of the rain. "You can come back now."

But when I open my eyes, I am still alone.

# Nineteen

I am safe. Even asleep, I know I am safe. Safety is something I smell, something that is warm and strong around me. It is safe to sleep now, safe to dream, as it has not been for a very long time. Like a swimmer plunging into blood-warm water I will myself deeper, feel the dream close in over me.

I am dreaming a summer day when I was nine years old, in the last of my one-digit birthdays. I am in the forest. It is the height of summer, and the forest is a sleeping animal. I walk over its skin, feeling its breathing all around me. I am sensing the wholeness of it, leaf and twig, bug and bird. I am tired of being an intruder here. I want to join it, to be within it and have it inside me.

It is a hot day, so very hot that I am unfastening my clothes and throwing them aside as I walk. I unbutton my shirt and throw it aside, pull my undershirt over my head and toss it over a branch. My pale skin looks dead, unnatural, but in a matter of moments the sun browns my chest and back and belly, until they are as dark as my hands. I stop briefly and skin out of my jeans, baring white legs and flopping ape feet. But as swiftly as my sun-browning, hair sprouts on my offensive legs, cloaks and covers them. I feel a tightening and turning of muscle and bone, feel my feet contract into tiny graceful white hooves. And there I am, a faun, as free as he, finally truly belonging to the forest. I try my new legs, and I can caper and prance as elegantly as he can. I find the muscles and make my tail whisk, keeping time with my high steps.

Something occurs to me, and I halt suddenly, my hooves cutting skids in the moss. I lift a cautious hand to my head, grope through my hair until I find them. They are small yet, and it feels incredibly good to scratch all around the horn buds. I have a leisurely scratch, and then notice the position of the sun. It is almost past the time, I am almost late. My dream self does not know this, but I hurry her on anyway. Down the survey cut, over the boggy places, skipping and leaping over the water from tuft to tuft with a wholly new grace. This time it will be right.

I follow the flow of the slough, come to the place where a tiny creek feeds into it, follow the creek until it is running through a gully with steep-edged sides. The day is hot, but down here it is cool, for the alders and birches lean overhead and shade the smooth mud banks. Cool green ferns drip down the side, and overhangs of moss drape groping bared roots. Baby's breath is in bloom, tiny white flowers sweetening the air until it is almost too potent to breathe. I am going to a place I discovered last weekend, a smooth place on the bank that showed many hoof tracks and the fossillike print of a hairy flank pressed into the cool earth. I think it is a place where a moose calf sleeps away the height of the day's heat. Today I am going to catch him napping.

I come upon him now as I did then, with a suddenness that takes my breath away. He is sleeping, skin and flank pressed to the cooling earth, no moose calf at all, but the very young god of the woods. His lips are smudged red with berries. A few still cluster in his carelessly outflung hand. For a time I stand on my side of the creek, staring at him, just as I did so many summers ago. In that other time, I was afraid to awaken him, fearing both the wrath of the god of the stories and that he would flee and I would never again look on such a wonder. In that other time, I left him sleeping there, and came back, day after day, to look upon him sleeping until the day he awoke and found me and was not afraid.

But this time, I wade the stream, setting each hoof

carefully on the wet rocks that slide under my weight. I awaken him with a gentle tug on his curls, and he sits up, rubbing his eyes sleepily but unafraid. Then his sleepy eyes widen and he leaps to his feet. His eyes travel up and down my self with undisguised delight, and I know that he sees we are the same, that we belong together. He embraces me, the hard hug of the overjoyed child, and I return it, holding him so tight that I wonder if we will meld into one creature. He steps back from me suddenly. He waves his hand, and the wind strikes up, piping a wild tune through the branches of the trees. We take hands and begin the dance.

We move well together, doing the wild steps perfectly, spinning and prancing, dancing the years down around us. The seasons pass around us, gold autumns, white winters, pale springs, and verdant summers, and we grow together, my hair getting longer, his beard coming in. He gains height on me, but my new breasts jut more proudly than the shining black tips of his wicked horns. His chest and shoulders muscle from boy to youth, but my arms are as round and brown and strong as his. Step for step, I match him, as the dance pits us against each other. The muscles of his back move under my hand, and I feel him hold me as we spin, refusing to let the impetus whirl us apart. The dance brings us closer together, until we are dancing breast to chest, lip to mouth, eyes never closing, and the dance never pausing as I feel him enter me, forming the link that makes us one.

Relief sweeps over me that we can be one, that I truly belong at last. "I'm home, I'm back," I say into his mouth, and he laughs into mine. Everything that ever bound me and kept me from him is gone, swept away like debris carried away by the river's rising. I feel the force of the final thrust that plants me with his seed and suddenly there is earth beneath my back, and I am aware of my body, supine, sprawled, weight atop it. The world spins wildly around me as I reorient myself on its face, back down, the moon and stars and tangled branches over me. And his face, looking down into mine, eyes brighter than any stars. It is still a dream, I think, until my ears feel his voice so close, words warm with breath as he tells me, "Yes, you're home." It is as he withdraws, warm, wet, that I come fully awake.

I shudder, shocked at our sudden separateness, and it passes into a shivering I cannot control. But he holds me, and the strength of his arms, the warmth of his skin, are all I could ever ask for. Slowly the shaking passes, but I don't let go of him, and mercifully, he holds me firmly, safely. His embrace was the safety I dreamed, his scent let me know I could relax my guard.

Time slides by like a slow river. We are covered by his blanket, pillowed on my pack, enclosed by the great crotch of cedar roots where I had decided to sleep. Gradually I become aware of more things, of my jeans and panties tangled still around one leg, my shirt open, my bra pushed up. I don't wonder how I slept through it, I simply struggle free of them to lie skin to skin with him.

His eyelids are drooping, his breathing is deep and steady already. There are a thousand things I need to tell him, questions I must ask, apologies to make. I take a deep breath to begin, but his hand comes up swiftly, two of his fingers gently silence me. "Have you ever noticed," he asks of the night sky, "how much better it all is when we don't talk with words? For one thing, it's much harder to lie to each other when we don't speak."

I am very still, then I nod cautiously. He lifts his fingers from my mouth, skates them lightly over my face. I am motionless, hypnotized by his touch. "Sleep," he suggests, the word fuzzy by my ear, and I do, finding a sleep deeper than dreams can follow.

It is not morning when he wakes me. It is not even starting to be morning. But by the time he has mated me twice, the light is starting to change. I am dressed and have gathered my belongings by the time there is enough light to distinguish shapes. Pan seems to have no possessions other than the pipes on the string about his neck and the blanket we share. We move silently through the woods, trying not to disturb leafy branches heavy with dew and yesterday's rain. It is a black and grey world we move in, reminding me of old moody

films. There is not enough light for me to distinguish
color, but as my eyes become accustomed to functioning
in the low light, I find it restful. Shape and motion
become more important than color; I find my senses
strangely sharpened, and I think I am seeing more in
this half-light than I ever did in the sun's full dazzle.

Color and life slowly bleed into the day. We are
miles from where we slept before the birds begin to stir.
We strike a road, and follow it, not on the shoulder, but
paralleling it through the brush. He pauses once,
reaches back to pull me close to his back. "Stay right
behind me," he whispers in my ear. "In the wake of my
scent." I am puzzled, but I obey.

It is still too early for humans when we turn aside
from the road. He leads me boldly down a driveway that
winds for half a mile between tall poplars before it
widens out into a farmyard. There is a white mobile
home with pink trim, with a collie asleep on its rickety
porch. The dog doesn't even flicker an ear as we pass.

Behind the mobile home is the old barn, its boards
gone silver with age. Relic of a bygone era, there is room
within its loft alone for a winter of hay and straw. Its
stalwart indifference to the years make the trailer house
a cheap toy. The sheer size of it dwarfs us all, but Pan
doesn't even pause to look up at it. Mindful of his words,
I follow in his shadow, and when he finds a door left ajar
and enters, I follow him.

Within is a warm darkness flavored with the breath
of animals, with stored grasses and grains and the
droppings of beasts. We go past two stalled horses, and
then a sow in a box stall with a littler of piglets feeding.
None of the animals express any surprise or interest. As
certainly as if he were the proprietor, Pan leads me on to
a meshed room of chickens dozing on their roosts and in
nesting boxes. He motions me to stand still while he
enters, to thieve eggs from under sleeping hens without
stirring so much as a cackle from them. I hold out my
shirtfront and he fills it to sagging with small brown
banty eggs. Then we leave the barn as we came, but
from the farmyard we do not return to the road. Instead,
we cut across a field of corn, walking between the tall

stalks. He adds four ears of young corn to the load in my shirt, and in the next field, he harvests six carrots, their bright orange smudged still with damp earth.

He never pauses in his steady pace as we leave the plowed lands behind and enter yet another stretch of woods. This is a fairly young forest, one that has been logged off and burned over, but was never replanted. Trash trees and brush have taken it over, and it is more open and airy than the woods of last night. Its greens are paler greens, its trees delicate twiggy things, and the morning breeze sets every leaf to fluttering. When the sun becomes a presence in the sky, and the day birds and insects start to sing, he halts our trek.

We sit in a dappling shade, to suck the eggs and leave the empty brown shells in a mound. He rubs the carrots over the moss to clean them while I strip the husks from the pale corn. The kernels are pale but full, and very sweet, and so tender that Pan eats his cobs and all. He shares out the cleaned carrots, and they finish our meal. It is more than I have eaten in days, and with a mouthful of water from the canteen, I feel satiated.

I lie back on the mosses and sweet grasses, and it seems only natural for him to lie beside me. I close my eyes as he loosens my clothing and pulls it away. Sex with him is natural and easy. I do not even need to think about orgasm, it is a gift we share when the time is right. The mating is simple and straightforward. No time is wasted trying out inelegant and obtuse positions; we do not compete to prove which of us is more imaginative. Yet each enactment is endlessly varied; it will never become routine between us, there will never be a time when his touch is any less electric. Afterward, we sleep through the heat of the day, mate again as the shadows begin to lengthen, and resume our journey in the cooling grey twilight.

The burned-over forest stretches long around us. We cross a stream, where we drink and fill our canteen. I remove my shoes and briefly cool my feet in it, while Pan hovers and waits. There is no impatience in the way he stands, but I sense his urgency to be moving again, and I do not linger.

As the colors are fading from the day, I make a kill.
He sees the rabbit first, shows it to me with a jerk of his
chin. I freeze instinctively as he continues a casual walk
that will take him close by it. The rabbit is as still as I am,
ears up, body tense, but almost invisible in the shadowy
brush. Pan springs suddenly, too soon, he has misjudged
the distance. I see his hand slip over its hindquarters as
the rabbit shoots off and he tumbles face first into the
brush. Two bounding steps let me intercept its flight. It
runs straight into my hands and I clutch it firmly, one
hand closing over its furred head. I swing it up as it kicks
wildly, and snap it like a whip. The weight of its body
breaks its neck with an audible pop. It gives a few feeble
jerks and is still.

I stand there, gripping its head still, feeling the
weight of its body depend on it. It is a large rabbit,
weighing about as much as a newborn infant. I heft its
body, feel the warm loose weight of it. Alive, dead.
Quick as a snap. Fast as flicking off a light switch. Alive,
dead. Like that. But there's no going the other way. No
dead, alive. Here is this body, in perfect working order
save for a break in the spinal column. If it was a machine,
a mechanic could go in there, redo the connections, put
the protective couplings back in place, turn the key, and
hey presto, the rabbit goes again. But it's not. The finest
surgeons in the world couldn't take this rabbit, repair the
damage, and start it up again. Even if they fixed all the
connections perfectly with microsurgery, even if they
rewarmed the body, renewed all the fluids, they couldn't
start it up again. Alive, dead. That must be the weirdest
thing about the living things. Once the spark is gone, it's
gone, as if it had never been.

Pan takes the rabbit from my hands. He is looking at
me oddly. I look back at him and realize with sudden
horror how fragile he is. It's not in his sturdy body or
bright eyes, not in the softness of his hair or the curve of
his lips that his vulnerability lies. It's that he's alive, and
if that is interrupted, if the heart ceases pumping, the
brain stops firing, the lungs stop swelling—he's gone.
There's no fixing him. All it takes is a brief pause. He
reaches to touch my arm questioningly, but the contact

jolts me away from him. It's not safe to love him, no safer than it was loving Teddy. Fingerprints, hoofprints, the rain washes them all away just as swiftly.

I stare about me, suddenly seeing stumps and carcasses. All of it temporary, every leaf, every buzzing insect. Nothing permanent here.

Nothing permanent save the earth beneath our feet. Whatever falls there does not perish, but is sucked in and broken down, to be renewed, to live again as rhizome or spore, butterfly egg or speckled fawn. I shake my head abruptly, feel that foreign world view subside. I touch gazes with the faun, who slowly nods. I am convinced he knows exactly what passes through my mind. Once more, we move on, the rabbit dangling limply from his grip on its hind legs.

When full dark of night comes, we halt and make a tiny fire. I offer him my knife, but he shrugs, and snips a tiny incision in the rabbit's belly with his white teeth. He sets strong fingers in the tiny hole, widens it with a tug, and then rips the hide loose. He works his fingers in between skin and meat, sliding them up over the rabbit's naked body, gradually widening the hole he works within. His fingers are strong. I hear the sharp snaps as he breaks the forepaws and hind legs at the last joint, and leaves those scarcely meated parts inside the hide. He slips the rabbit free of its skin neatly, and with a final twist and jerk pops its head off. He is left with a rabbit skin with the skull and feet ends still inside it, and a bloody carcass with the guts still membraned inside it. His strong fingers claw the entrails out and separate the liver and heart. He offers them to me, but I shrug, so he eats them himself, a quick chomp and swallow for the heart, a more leisurely chewing for the tender liver. His lips and mouth are red, I know, but the jumping light of the flames shows them only as darker. He snaps and rips the rabbit into portions, skewers them on green sticks, and props them over the fire. He pauses to see they are secure; then he comes for me.

We make love while the meat cooks. Firelight licks his body with the wet sheen of polished wood, polishes mine to gold. His mouth tastes of blood, and his hands leave dark tracks on my skin. The smell of the fresh blood mingles with his own intoxicating scent, lending it darker overtones. I glimpse the legends as he takes me, the wilder side that panicked Roman maidens at the sight of him, the purposeful carnality of him. This is no prancing Disney faun; this is the satyr, penis apricked, from a hundred Greek vases and bas-reliefs. Abandoning all pretense at civilization, I pull him to me boldly, daring myself to embrace this darker side of him. For the briefest of instants he resists, and I know that I have surprised him, that he had expected me to draw back from this aspect of him. But I have not, and he laughs aloud, a sound of discovery as he surrenders control to me.

The fire has burned low by the time we get to the meat. I expect it to be burned, but it is more smoked than cooked. We devour it quickly, gnawing the small bones clean and then throwing them into the fire. I think we will make love again, but for once Pan seems content. He wipes his hands clean on the moss, and takes up his pipes. He plays very softly as the fire burns down, a piping that is a weaving back and forth, the music of life consumed by other life and fueling new life. I lie back and stare at the stars, and let the music console me. The pipes take the sudden cessations of life, the jarring halts of mortality, and weave them into rests in the music, soft pauses in a song that goes on and on. Nothing to fear, it says, the song itself will go on forever, though each note may be played but for an instant. Under the influence of the song, I surrender myself to the small death that is sleep without fear.

That first day sets the pattern for all others that follow it. Each day I am awakened by his lovemaking. We travel in the times of the changing lights, spending both the times of full light and the times of full darkness in rest. Always we travel, always north, though I have never spoken of any destination. Each day, we forage what we need, from gardens, from the forest, once from a roadside produce stand, even from a farmer's smokehouse. I grow leaner and lither, feel the years dropping away as every day I do no more than walk and eat and

make love. It is a simpler life than any I have ever
known, and sweeter.

The frequent coupling, four and five or six times a
day, seems a part of the rhythm. Whenever he touches
me, I desire him. So simple. I am aware, peripherally, of
the way his scent changes, how he masks our passage
through farmyards by exuding some neutral scent. A
part of me knows there is something in the way he smells
when he comes to me, some powerful attractant in his
spicy musk, that numbs any hesitations or inhibitions I
might have. Pheromones, I think to myself occasionally,
sleepily, and picture moths flying for miles to follow one
elusive scent. But like the trees of the forest, names do
not matter here. Pheromones or love, it all feels very,
very nice.

I lose track of the days very quickly, for each day is
now divided into two wakings and two sleepings. Likewise, I have no idea how far we have traveled. Pan leads
the way in a veering path that avoids all but the smallest
towns. Twice, he terrifies me by taking me straight
through small towns during the dark hours. Once it is
right down the main street, lit by street lamps, where his
hooves echo on the pavement. We pass a tavern that
snores out a blast of country-western music, and a little
convenience store where a bored clerk leans both her
elbows on the counter and stares out past us as we go by.
No one sees us, and I fall asleep that night wondering if
I am real anymore.

The second time is even scarier, for he takes me
down alleys and through backyards, up and over fences,
ignoring barking dogs roused by the sounds of our
passage. One Labrador sets up a baying at sight of us.
Even my dull nose scents the change in Pan's identity, to
a mingling of wolf and bear that sends the Labrador
backing under its porch even as a snarl wrinkles its nose.
Dogs all over the neighborhood go off, a siren of barkings
at the stranger scented in their midst. We drop into the
next yard, race across, and scramble up the fence even as
I hear the creak of a screen door and an angry male voice
exclaim, "Damn kids!"

But after that second town is left behind, we are in

the woods for days, skirting low hills, occasionally climbing over them. I miss the human gardens and hen
houses, but Himalayan blackberries are everywhere,
heavy with dark fruit. There are cloudberries, too, the
color of pale salmon eggs. Wild hazelnuts are ripening in
their green husks and rabbits are plentiful. Pan and the
forest provide.

He seems to know where he is going. Not just
north, even I could manage that, but when to follow a
river and when to leave its banks, when to climb over a
hill and when to go around it. He never takes us near
sprawling suburbs or big cities. Somehow, he wends his
way north through a patchwork of places left wild or
nearly so.

The nights are growing cooler. It is the aging of the
year as well as our northward progression that carries us
into a cooler world. Few words have passed between us
in our migration, but one evening, I ask him, "Do you
think we will get there before winter?"

"Get where?" he asks me.

We are under a cedar tree, sleeping in a huge
fragrant pile of dry needles we have scraped together.
My head is pillowed on his shoulder, and the front of me
is warm where I press it against him. But my backside is
cold despite the blanket over us. "Wherever we're
going," I reply. A small pang of worry hits me as I realize
I no longer have any fixed destination at all in mind.
Once it was Fairbanks, then it was Alaska—now it is up
to Pan. Each day I've been following him without
thought. His arm snugs me up against him and he turns
his face to kiss me gently on the forehead.

"Don't worry about it," he tells me. "Winter, fall,
spring, summer—it doesn't matter. I can keep you safe.
You're in my world now, and even though I may no
longer be counted a god, some things still bow to my
will." He pauses, then asks gently, "Why do you ask? Are
you getting tired?"

I have to think before I answer. He's right. The last
few days I have felt more weariness than before. It is
harder for him to wake me, and easier for me to drop off
to sleep, no matter where we are. My lower back and

legs ache at the end of the day. "A little," I tell him, somehow ashamed to admit the weakness.

"Don't worry," he tells me again, and holds me close, his hands moving soothingly over my back, easing the aches I had scarcely been aware of. "We'll go more slowly, if you like."

"I'm okay," I tell him sleepily. The varying pressure of his hands on my back is almost hynotic. A bubble of question rises in my mind. "If you're not a god anymore, what are you?"

"Sshh," he tells me softly, fingers treading my spine gently. "I am what I am," he adds, almost unwillingly. "Just as you are what you are."

"What am I?" I mumble into his neck.

"You, oh, you," he says, his voice going deep and purring, becoming almost a lullaby as he half sings the words, "you are a memory reawakened, a tie re-formed, the woman who kisses us fresh with humanity's lips. You're the life-giver, the warm breast, the cradling arms. You're what we need and what we love best, the forest in the woman, the woman in the forest . . ."

There is more, but the deep idling of his voice has spelled me, so that the sound of him speaking is more important than the words. I spiral down into sleep within his arms.

The next morning I come awake on my own. I have overslept, dawn is already greying the skies and the last stars are no longer visible. He is not beside me, and for a moment I know panic, not at sight of him, but at his absence. I start up, but there he is, by a small fire burning almost smokelessly. Spitted meat is toasting over it. He is carving something with my sheath knife. When he sees I am awake, he tosses a handful of whittlings in the fire. He comes to me, and I lift our blanket, inviting him in, but he only crouches beside me. "Hungry?" he asks, stroking my hair.

"A little," I say, puzzled at this break in our routine. He sees it in my eyes.

"I've been thoughtless," he tells me gravely. "Too demanding, for oh, your sweetness is hard to resist." He cups my chin in his hand. "Lie still and let me bring you food."

He brings me not only the meat, but berries, miner's lettuce and watercress, and some scrubbed roots I do not recognize. He sets it all out on a mat of maple leaves. I feel uneasy. He has obviously been awake for some time, to gather all this. "Aren't we going to travel today?" I ask him.

He smiles, and any fears I have at his unusual behavior melt with his smile. He knows me too well. "You don't like me gentle and considerate?"

"I do. It's just . . . why?"

"Why do the flowers open up in the sunlight?" he asks me, and again there is that singing tone to his voice, as if words are not enough for what he must say. "Why do plantlets uncoil from their seeds in spring's warmth?" He pauses, and laughs aloud, visibly delighted at my confusion.

"I want to be gentler with you," he tells me softly, reassuringly. "That's all. To take better care of you."

It is all very puzzling, but I know from past experience that I will get no answers from him until he wishes to give them. We eat together, but he allots me the lion's share, for the food seems to make me aware that I was, indeed, very hungry.

We do travel that day, but only for about two hours. Then he calls a halt. It is probably a hot day in the world of pavement and freeways, but here beneath the trees it is merely fine. The canopy of leaves and needles overhead gentle the sunlight to a restful dimness. When I sit down to rest, he sits beside me and pulls me to lean against him, but makes no move to mate me. Instead he lifts his pipes and plays for me. The tune is very sweet, and strangely familiar, but for once I cannot tell what it is he is playing. This seems to please him, for he plays it over and over again, ever softer and slower, until I drowse off to the notes softly breathed by my ear.

When I awake in late afternoon, there is food again, in enough variety that I am amazed at his foraging. We eat slowly, and then travel again. We strike a deer trail and follow it. The going is much easier than it has been, and soon I am aware that our pace is slower than it was before. "Is something wrong?" I ask his back, and he turns that smile on me once more.

"Everything is better than right," he tells me, and reaches back to take my hand.

And so we go on, stopping before night is truly black, near the banks of a river. I listen to it as he builds a tiny fire, and I know from the sound that it is swift and powerful. Rocks are grinding along in that flow. I wonder if we must cross it, and how. I think I should go and look at it, it is no more than a five-minute walk from the sound of it, but I am suddenly just too tired. I am drowsing off until he awakes me and nudges me into a nest of pine boughs. Instead of joining me, he tucks the blanket in all around me. He sits at my feet and, limned by the fire, lifts his pipes and plays again. He is a black silhouette against the amber glow of the firelight. Occasionally sap pops in the wood, and then sparks float up to join the notes of his music in the night. Tonight he plays the river, and a heron fishing the quiet shallows. The last thing I remember is hearing the notes of silver droplets flying from the struggling fish the heron lifts in its beak.

I awaken the next morning with a slight headache. Again there is a plenitude of food and solicitude. But my headache makes me snappish and critical. "Stop treating me like an invalid," I tell him as he crouches by the bed with food. "You make me feel as if I'm made of glass."

"Of crystal, dear heart, and amber, and shards of emeralds in your eyes," he tells me, and grins delightedly when I glare at him. I am sick of his coyness.

"What is the matter with you?" I demand angrily.

"Only that I am too delighted to quarrel, my love."

"Why don't you want me anymore?" I demand, and surprise myself by realizing that this is at the core of my anger.

"Not want you? Sooner would I not want air in my lungs. It is only that you are tired, and sometimes I am . . . overly enthusiastic."

"I haven't complained," I point out awkwardly. His poetics are starting to jar. I want to burst out crying, for no reason at all, and this more than anything annoys me and sets the headache to throbbing fiercely.

"Oh, my love," he says sympathetically, and the sappiness of his tone and the fact that he knows I have a headache without my telling him only make my anger grow.

"Stop it!" I command him.

"All right," he says meekly, but sits looking at me with eyes as dumbly adoring as a cocker spaniel's.

"I mean it!" I cry out, and hear my own shrewishness. But I cannot stop myself from pleading, "Please, just be like you used to be. Stop being so smarmy!"

"I'll try," he says earnestly. "I promise."

It is the best I can get from him.

# Twenty

He leads me upriver. The banks of the river are all large rounded rock and river gravel, with occasional narrow belts of sand between the gravel and the water's edge. The footing is treacherous, for hoof or foot. The river shifts enough in its course from year to year that there are no large trees close to it, only white snags that have been washed down it, and small brush and trees footed in silt and sand, doomed to an early death some floodtime. The bright sunlight glances off the water, dazzling my eyes and leaving spots of light flashing before me every time I blink. The river seems to possess a wind that blows along with it, and as the chill air races past my ears they ache. I put up my hands to cover them but drop them away when I catch Pan looking back at me anxiously.

I have always hated it when people are solicitous of my health. To me, it seems the ultimate invasion of privacy, and to find Pan so concerned smacks of betrayal. I feel patronized. What I want of him, I am finding, is for him to be one hell of a good friend. Yes, and a sexual partner who is in it for the wild and romping side of it as well as the slow erotic touches. His tender poetics and coddling grate on my nerves. It's a little like being with someone who gets sloppy, weepy drunk. No matter how much you like the person, the out-of-character behavior gets old in a hurry. But then there is something in me that wants to be touched by his careful sidelong glances, that appreciates the way he holds the branches that cross the trail so they will not whip back in my face. Yet another side of me hisses that he did not always think I was such an idiot that I'd let a tree branch hit me. Actually, I can remember times when, as children, when we were following each other, we'd deliberately try to snap each other. Friendships like that never really end, I comfort myself. Yes, but romances do. Lovers almost always quarrel and part, and then what becomes of the friendship they traded in for the romance?

Pan has halted and is staring out over the river. Here it is, the sign is plain, this is a place where larger animals sometimes cross. A gravel bar makes a foaming barrier across the current, and reaches almost but not quite to where another bar stretches from the other side. It can be done. The deer sign proves it. But Pan stands and stares at it long. Then he glances back at me.

"There's another place," he suggests. "A better ford, only a couple of miles farther upriver."

"This one looks fine to me," I reply contrarily. I know I sound brusque.

He looks at me quietly for a few moments, then reaches back to take the strap of my bag. "Let me carry that for a while," he suggests. "It looks heavy, and I know you're tired."

I am, I suddenly realize, drained and weary, just from this morning's brief hike. He tugs at the bag, and suddenly I am furious at my weakness. Human frailty, I scoff at myself, and already the satyr is thinking I am too weak, thinking I need to be coddled and comforted. Thinking I don't belong in his forest, his world.

"It's fine," I snap, and push past him on the trail, step and slide down a short bank of gravel and sand and out into the river.

The water is cold, glacier fed, and it closes around my ankles like vise grips. Gravel shifts treacherously under my sneakers as I wade out. The current is stronger even than I expected, and as the water gets deeper, I feel myself sway in its grip. "Evelyn Sylvia!" the faun breathes like an invocation, and suddenly he is beside

me, up current from me. "Hold on to me!" he commands
me.

"Hold on to yourself," I reply, intending the crude-
ness, and plunge ahead of him, out of his reach. The cold
water is near knee deep; the grinding song of the river as
it tumbles gravel in its bed is all around me. The silty
river shatters the sunlight and throws the sharp shards
up into my eyes. I take a step, and suddenly the gravel
slides loose around my foot, and I am in above the knee.
More than half the river is still before me. I feel Pan
catch hold of the strap of my bag. "Let's go back," he
shouts above the sound of the water. It's a bad crossing,
too many hot days lately. Too much glacier ice turned
into water."

I know he is right, but a madness is on me, I feel
compelled to prove myself.

"Hell, we can make it," I shout in tones of daring
and bluff camaraderie. "Don't be chicken!"

Another step, and I am thigh deep. My legs are
shaking, both with cold and resisting the flow of the
water.

"It's too deep," he protests, and I feel the drag of his
grip on the bag.

I take another step. It all happens at once, the rocks
rolling under my feet, the river seizing me, the strap of
the bag giving way. I lurch sideways, the sky seems to
roll, and then boiling grey milk closes over me. The icy
shock of the water on my torso squeezes a gasp from me,
and I snort in river water. Cold in my sinuses, funny
thing to think when you're drowning. I've never been
good with deep water, never learned to swim, but panic
triggers instincts, and I am striking out, flailing at the
water. My feet brush tantalizingly against gravel, I feel
myself spin in the current. My eyes are open, but the
thick silty water is opaque, I can't see a damn thing. The
strap of the bag is tangled around my arm, I can't get free
of it. Suddenly my whole body is washed up against a
gravel bottom. With a surge of adrenaline strength, I roll
to my knees, stand, and stagger into knee-deep water.

My hair is streaming into my eyes, all I can see is
light. I choke and sputter, trying to take in air at the

same time I gasp out water. Water and the roar of the river dampen my hearing. "Pan!" I call, shuddering off water like an animal.

The reply is a splash and a gargling shout. I rub water from my eyes, open them despite the fine grit sanding them. He is a dozen feet from me, in deep water, struggling against the current. I hold out my hands, take two steps toward him, into chest-deep water that sucks wildly at me. He flings himself desperately toward me, our hands touch and grip. Fear is wild in his face, and then his feet find the bottom, and like a galvanized frog leg he is leaping and jerking us both to shore.

Milky water streams from both of us. The thin sunshine of the day is impotent to warm us. I am shaking too violently to speak as we crawl, hands and knees, up the sliding bank to the sparse shelter of river bushes. At least here the wind is less. I sink down immediately, almost on top of Pan, angrily claw the bag and strap free of my arm. "Idiot!" he barks, the word rattling past his chattering teeth. "You ass! You nearly got us all drowned." He clutches me and pulls me tight against him. His skin is cold against my hands, but we hold tight to each other. When the shuddering becomes only shivering, we rise and stagger farther from the river, into an area of tall, sun-browned river grass.

The wind seems less when we sink down here, but I am still cold. Gritting my teeth, I pull off my soggy clothing, wring it out, and spread it to dry. Everything in the pack is soaked as well. I drag it out, spread it in the sun. Pan is still lying on his side in the grass, half curled, his eyes closed. His face is screwed up as if he's in great pain. I kneel by him, ask, "Are you hurt?"

His eyes fly open, and I have never seen such fear. "The worst moments of my life; of any lives I can remember! You went in and the only thing I could do was jump in after you, knowing it was useless." A shudder runs over him. "Evelyn. I can't swim. None of my kind can. I knew we were all going to drown."

I lie down beside him in the crackling, poking grass and curl around him. My belly is to his back as I put my arms around him and think about his words. Biblical. Greater love than this hath no man, that he lay down his life for another. Probably applied to fauns as well. It is not something I can understand, someone loving me that much. It is not something I can accept. I don't want it, it's too big a responsibility. "Don't love me like that," I tell him softly. "I don't know how to be loved that way." Being already asleep, he doesn't answer me. It takes a long time for me to doze off beside him.

When I awake, I am covered by the still-damp blanket. It is much the worse for its dip in the river, but at least it traps some of my body heat. I don't want to move, I feel achy and nauseous. But I force myself up and into my dank clothing. The jeans are still wet at the belt line and in the crotch, but the shirt is almost dry. My socks are still hopelessly soggy. Barefoot, I go looking for the faun.

He has made his fire on flat rocks by the river, from dry bits of driftwood. Several small fish are baking on stones by the fire. As I come up behind him, he is poking them with a bit of stick. His hair is still wet, and my denim shirt is across his shoulders. When I touch him, he leaps wildly. "Pan," I say soothingly, and for a moment he looks at me as if he does not know me. His face is more haggard than I have ever seen it. "Are you all right?"

"I'm . . . I am remembering. Reaching way back. If we go downstream, quite a ways, five or six miles, the river should fork. It used to be very easy to cross it there. Of course, that was a long time ago. . . ."

His words trail off again, and for an instant, someone I don't know looks at me out of his eyes. Evaluating me. He starts to nod, and suddenly he is Pan, my Pan again. It is an unsettling experience.

"Hungry?" he asks me.

"Yes," I say frankly. "You know, lately all I do is eat and sleep. I don't know what's wrong with me, but I don't feel like I'm pulling my share."

"Sure you are," he says, and smiles maddeningly. His eyes are warm with some secret. I refuse to be baited.

We eat the fish, him crunching them merrily, me picking through endless tiny bones for the flaky white meat. We drink from the canteen, for the river water is too thick with silt to be palatable.

Afterward, I go to him and, standing before him, put his hands on my hips. I am inches from him. His eyes search my face. "Aren't you too tired?" he asks softly. For answer, I reach and kiss him. I need him. Not for horniness, but for closeness. We go back to the spread clothing, and he draws me down on the damp blanket. His lovemaking is peculiar this time; his kisses barely touch me, he puts no weight upon me, penetrates me only enough to bring me satisfaction. It is a teasing, delicate way to touch, but the very tenuousness of our joining makes the climax surprisingly explosive. He collapses beside me rather than atop me. Together we stare up at a limitless expanse of blue sky.

"It's going to get cold tonight," he says suddenly.

"This time of year, it usually does," I concur.

"I've remembered a place for us." He pauses, then goes on apologetically, "It's still a long ways from here."

"Across the river," I say.

"I'm afraid so. And days beyond that, too."

"No big deal," I say casually, dreading it. "Shall we get moving again? We can get to your downstream ford with daylight to spare. I don't want to cross it in the twilight."

He shakes his head lazily. "No. Let's let things dry out, rest for a while." He rolls suddenly to face me. "Evelyn, if I lose you, I lose everything. Everything." He speaks quietly, but the words are so intense it is like a shout.

"Don't worry. You won't lose me." I speak casually, but the words stir a deep uneasiness in me.

"Promise me you'll be more careful," he demands.

"I'll be okay," I try to put him off.

"Promise me," he presses. The words are like a noose tightening around my neck. "Please," he adds, and the word cuts me. There should never be "pleases" between us.

"I give you my word I'll be careful," I compromise.

For a long moment we are both silent, both uncomfortable. The weight of a promise given hangs between us. It doesn't feel natural for me to be this important to him, for him to care so much. I feel as if I don't completely belong to myself anymore. Like I've given him a part of me to control and watch over. My heart squeezes when I wonder if I ever made Tom feel this way. If the times when he put me aside, fended me off, were because I was too unbearably close. I don't want to be responsible for anyone else's happiness.

"Hey," he says later, softly. I turn to him. After staring at the sky, my eyes are dazzled, I can barely make out his features.

"What?" I ask.

"Nothing," he says, and grins. But it makes it better. I get up and turn the damp clothing, shaking it out loose to try and speed the drying process. But it is late afternoon before the clothes are dry enough to fold and put back into the pack. They are still not dry through, and I resolve to spread them out again during our noon pause tomorrow.

We move back from the river and into the forest again for the night. Pan makes one of his small hot fires while I make us a bed of cedar needles and dry grasses. I think of the great apes building their bowers each night, and wonder if we are so different at all. He brings fish for us again, and after we eat, he sits by the fire, whittling. I stare at the flames and do not pay much attention to him until he rises and comes to sit behind me.

"Be still," he tells me when I try to turn and face him. I obey, turning back to the fire, and feel his light touch on my hair. In a moment, something snags in it, and he tugs hard.

"Ouch!" I complain, and reach back to where his hands struggle. "What are you doing?"

He lets his hands drop away, and my fingers brush against a wooden comb snagged in my hair. I pluck it loose and look at it. This is what he has been carving these past few days. The teeth are wide and smooth, the back bears a tracery of vine on it. I have never seen work so fine and intricate. "I had a plastic one already," I tell him, not at all what I mean to say.

He only smiles as if I have thanked him endlessly and says simply, "Wood is better."

I bring my hair forward over my shoulder and go to work on it. It is strange to think that I have not bothered with it for several days. Twigs and moss and seeds are in it, and one small patch of sap. I struggle with it for a while, but do not resist when he reaches to take the comb from my hands. Gently he pulls my hair back, and starts to work on it, from the draggled ends up. He is clumsy at it, but I endure the small tuggings for the sake of his touch on me. But after a few minutes, I start to feel uncomfortable with it. Selfish. Guilty that he is paying attention to me. I feel I should be the one to pay attention to him while he sits and basks. "In every relationship," I once heard my mother say, "there is the one who does the loving, and the one who is loved." Always before, I have been the loving one. I don't know how to sit still and accept his attention.

So I shift and turn, taking the comb from his hand. "Let me finish it," I say, and ignore his puzzled look. I finish my grooming rapidly, tugging out the snarls he was picking at so carefully. I start to braid it up to keep it out of my way, but he puts a restraining hand on my shoulder.

"Leave it loose," he asks me softly.

I shrug and let it hang. I set the comb aside and reach for him. I rub his neck and shoulders, searching for tension I don't find. He half closes his eyes with pleasure, then opens them again to tell me, "You're doing this to keep me from touching you."

"Maybe," I said grudgingly. I move around behind him and my fingers work down his spinal column to where it vanishes into coarse goat hair, and then down to the base of his tail. His body never ceases to fascinate me. My hands travel up his back again.

"Did you ever think that it might give me great pleasure to touch you? That for me, touching you might even be as pleasant as being touched by you?"

"No," I say flatly. It is both an answer and a denial.

My conditioning, I realize, goes deeper than I think. It would be vanity to think such a thing, and vanity is a sin. It would also be conceited and selfish, and that is rude. Strange. Sooner can I copulate with the goatman than admit that he can love me. Or that he can love touching me. Irrational tears sting my eyes. I feel cheated that I cannot believe anyone would ever really love me. I immediately suspect I am feeling sorry for myself, and that makes me angry.

"Ouch!" complains the satyr, for I have let my anger flow through my hands, and have squeezed his shoulder muscles harder than I meant to. He turns to me, and I know the firelight reflects off the water in my eyes.

"Dummy," he says, and there is such love in the word that I nearly sob. Instead, I pull back from him.

"It's not you," I hear myself saying, idiotically. "It's me. I don't know what's wrong with me." I hug myself and rock like an injured child. Why do I feel so bad?

"Nothing's wrong with you," he tells me gravely, and pulls me back into his arms. For a while he just holds me, the warmth of the fire on my face, the warmth of his body down my back. Then we go to our bed together. He holds me until sleep slips me from his grip.

I dream of Fairbanks. It is a mixed dream, of planting the garden, of fixing the car. I keep looking for Tom as I do these tasks, but he is never around. Somehow this doesn't bother me. I waddle from the garden to the cabin, for I am immensely pregnant. When I go into our bedroom, the old double bed is gone, replaced by a fragrant pile of pine needles and boughs. I am very tired, so I lie down on the bed. Then I hear Tom's footsteps in the kitchen. I don't call to him, for I know he will soon come into the bedroom, bringing me a plate of crackers and a few slivers of cheese. He knows it helps my morning sickness if I eat a few crackers before I get up. So I wait, and the footsteps keep getting closer, but they never come into the room.

I awaken. But not quite. I can feel the sunlight dappling my eyelids, but I don't open them. The dream wasn't right. Tom never brought me plates of crackers in bed. I used to keep a box of saltines on the nightstand.

My whole pregnancy with Teddy made Tom nervous, as if I had some sort of giant parasite in my body and it might be contagious. One night when I moved over so my swollen belly was against his back, Teddy kicked him right through my body wall. Tom had jumped as if electrocuted. I had laughed, delighted, but Tom had declared, "I hate that! It feels icky. Squashy. How can you stand it?" "It's our baby," I had told him, and at the time it hadn't bothered me. Now it does, suddenly, and I am a little surprised to find it could still hurt so.

I stretch slowly, hearing pine boughs rustle beneath me. A familiar wave of nonspecific nausea goes through me. Lie still, I tell myself, and it will pass. Have a cracker.

Then I open my eyes to the dark branches of spruce trees against a blue sky. Too much contrast, they're almost black. I know what my dream was really telling me. Wake up, conscious mind, and pick up on what you already know. You're pregnant.

It's all there. A little achy, a little puffy. The feed-and-sleep syndrome. I try to worry about it and instead find my hand flat on my belly, a foolish smile breaking over my face. And that seems the ultimate confirmation, for I went through my first pregnancy in a blur of bovine contentment. Even Tom had bragged to his friends that I was so mellow while I was pregnant, he could get away with anything. Pumped up with female hormones, I had wanted nothing more than to eat and rest and grow a child. I look back over my behavior over the last few days and nod to myself at how blindly I have been following Pan, how trustingly I have put my life in his hands. Even so.

So how far along am I? I don't know. I've lost track of the days since I returned to the forest, but I know I have not bled on any of them. Another thought stops me dead. Whose baby? Tom's? The faun's?

Neither answer is acceptable.

I don't want to have Tom's baby growing in me. Not when he doesn't love me anymore. Even if we had not parted, I would not want a child this soon, not right on the heels of Teddy's death. It would be a betrayal, somehow. Like saying, well, that kid's dead, better get busy and replace him. Just whip up a new one in the old womb, only take me nine months or so.

My belly is flat beneath my sheltering hand. Maybe I'm not pregnant, I tell myself. Maybe it's just the dream and your own imagination. I'm probably being silly. But I am not convinced. I check my breasts, find the nipples tender to the touch. Too much lovemaking, I tell myself. That's all. I can't be pregnant. Not with Tom's child.

How about the goatman's?

My mind shys away from such an idea. I don't want to imagine myself calving some hooved thing in a field somewhere. A hairy little body, half child, half goat, growing inside mine? What would I do with it? Where would I keep it, how would it go to school? It would have no place in my world. A freak. Worse, what if it looked like me, with no signs of its satyr father? What would I tell him as he grew up? Don't fall in love with a woman, you'll give her goat children? And if it's a girl?

And what if it's neither, not human nor faun, but some combination of the two? Goat feet on human legs, or a human child, goat-furred on its lower body?

I am on my feet suddenly, and I am stuffing my things into my bag. I move in a sort of frenzy as I gather jeans left slung over branches in the hopes of drying them a bit more. I thrust them into the bag, any old way, I just have to get out of here, I have to get away from this place and this idea. I know that I will carry my pregnancy with me wherever I go, but somehow I think it will be different if I am alone. Problems are always easier to solve if you are alone.

I am moving, leaving the campsite, when I become aware of him. As always, it is his scent that precedes him. And as always, it attracts me, but this time I fight it. I breast through it as if it were deep water, push myself on, back into the forest. He will be at the campsite now, I think, as I push a branch out of my way. I hear his voice, not a call, but a question, "Evelyn?" behind me. Clear as a bird's call, without being loud. I push on.

The very woods themselves seem to have turned

upon me. Blackberry tangles thwart my path, fallen logs delay me. My mind assembles pieces of information, and hands them to me. What did I think the constant lovemaking was about, if not an attempt to impregnate me? Did I honestly think he could find me that desirable? And he knows, he knows he has succeeded, that is what is behind all his sudden tenderness and solicitude. What did he say yesterday? "You nearly drowned us all!" Not both of us. All.

The sweet words and moments of caring seem suddenly an insidious trap, his pungent body odor a sort of lure to bring me in. He has used me, I think, and anger rises in me, but not as strong as fear. I won't be trapped again, I think, but at that very moment, I hear his voice again, soft as always, coming behind me. "Evelyn?"

I push on frantically through brush that catches at me, that slaps and tears at exposed skin and tangles about my feet. I know I cannot outrun him, but I try.

"Evelyn?" he calls again, and this time there is a note of fear along with the query. I break out of the brush, into a clearing. I bound across it like a hunted deer, running instinctively, not even watching for obstacles, but dodging or leaping over them as my body commands. And then I am back in the forest again, on a deer path, running.

I think I hear him behind me, but then the sounds fade. I don't look back, I can't, I don't even look off to the side when I hear some large animal take flight. Then his scent hits me, coming from ahead of me, no, beside me, from all around me. I jerk to a halt, panting, trying to choose a new direction, but the smell of him is all around me, calming and warm, sweet as new milk. I cannot make a decision, not enveloped in that calm. I stand, sweating and shaking as he comes toward me on the path. When he reaches me, I pull back like a spooked horse, but he sets a calming hand on my shoulder, puts the other to my cheek. "Evelyn," he says, locking eyes with me. "It's all right, my love. There's nothing to fear."

I feel myself slipping into the depths of his eyes. His hands are steadying me, I want to open my arms and cling to him. His scent is all around me, wrapping me like an airy blanket.

"Stop it!" I say, and slap his hands away. For an instant his eyes hold only astonishment. Then something like a glint of amusement comes into them.

"All right," he agrees, and steps back from me. I take deep steadying breaths of air that smell only of leaf mold and trees, of earth and plants. My head and mind clear. No panic, no fear, but no stupefying calm, either.

"I, uh," he says. I look up and he is grinning, but abashedly. "I didn't mean to do that. I mean," he falters, seeing I am not returning his smile.

"I don't believe you," I say coldly. "You've been manipulating me."

His face changes. "Just like you've been manipulating me."

"I have not!"

"No? Do you think I'm immune to your pheromones? You think it's easy for me not to touch you when your body is flaunting your fertility? Even now," he says, and takes a step back from me. "You stand there, defying me, scolding me for my scent." His face changes again, a foolish grin washing over his features. "How can I argue with you when your scent says, 'Protect me, defend me, shelter me from all harm, for I am pregnant with your child.' Do you think that's fair? Do you think it's not manipulating me?"

"That's how you knew I was pregnant?" I ask him, forgetting my anger for an instant.

He nods, his smile becoming tender, his eyes soft.

"Stop it!" I command him. "Besides, it's not like I'm controlling it."

"But you are. You just aren't aware of it. I am. I stand here, away from your scent, but every drift of it makes me want to calm you, to steady you, to protect the child you carry. Do you know how hard it is for me to resist that instinct, keep that inside? Do you even know what you're asking of me?"

I am suddenly tired and confused. I don't know who is manipulating who. I don't care. I just want to sit down and rest. Some of it must show in my face, for sudden alarm widens his eyes, and he almost fells me with his calming musk. "I just," I begin, and look for a place to sit down. There is a fallen log, mossed green and with a few ferns sprouting from it. I know his hand is on my arm, helping me to it, but suddenly I am grateful it is there. "I just don't understand," I wail suddenly, overcome by it all. "It isn't fair. You never said anything. I didn't even think about getting pregnant. I didn't worry about it, it didn't occur to me that I could. And now I am, and I don't know what comes next."

"It will be all right," he assures me, crouching by my feet. But the worried look on his face put the lie to his words.

"Then why am I so tired?" I demand. "I couldn't be more than a few weeks along, if that. I shouldn't even be able to tell I'm pregnant yet. But I'm so damn tired."

A wave of calming musk flows up from him. I feel I will drown in the scent. My intellect is warring with my instincts. This faun smells like safety, my body tells me he is protection and shelter, but my mind sees the deep worry in his eyes. The conflict agitates me, and I can almost see him quiver as his body responds to the scent of my worry. I rise, intending to move away from him, but he leaps to his feet.

"No. You sit still and rest. I'll move away." He circles out from me, stops about twelve feet away. For a few seconds he looks at the ground. When he lifts his eyes to mine, they are shining.

"Perhaps you understand, now, what it was like for me that day when I came upon you in the grasses, and suddenly you smelled like a mature female. Not fertile at that moment, but matable. And there was I, only beginning to remember the concept of male and female." He shakes his head, looks back at the ground. "It was like someone blowing a whistle right by my ear when I'd been deaf all my life. I had to run away."

I can't think of anything to say. He looks back up at me. "Who knows? Maybe that was when the bond was first formed. I only know you are not a fat ewe or a tall doe to be tamed and turned to my uses. You are my friend, Evelyn, first and always. And if I have used you, it was with your body's permission. It has always known why we were coming together. I thought . . ." he pauses, changes his words. "You always smelled as if you understood. I didn't realize you would need the words as well."

"Liar," I say flatly.

"Yes," he admits easily. "But only a little. I knew that sooner or later, we would have to talk like this. But as to bearing my child—I never thought you would object to that. Or fear it."

"You fear it." Strange, how easy the directness comes. These are more words than we have exchanged in our time together, but there is no hesitancy. We are too close to mince words between us.

"Yes, I do." He paces a few short steps, turns as if to come toward me, but then stops. "These pregnancies. Between our kinds. They are never easy. Bearing a faun's child is never easy for whoever does it. Whatever."

"Why?" I demand.

He lets out his breath raggedly. "Conflicts. Between the ways of your own kind, and the needs of what grows within you. A human baby takes nine months to grow within its mother. My child will take but six. Yet it will be fully as large as one of your own kind, sometimes larger. The growth rate is greater than your body is designed for. So you are tired sooner, hungrier, and often uncomfortable." His voice lowers on the last words. "My child will grow faster than your body can adapt to it."

The silence is long, but only between us two. The life of the forest goes on. A bird calls somewhere nearby, two notes. There is a light wind in the upper branches of the trees, the muted shush of the river behind us.

"It's going to kill me, isn't it?" I ask him. I know he will tell me true.

"No," he says in a low voice, but I hear that it is a plea, not a denial. He looks at me, sudden anguish in his eyes. "It cannot. I will not let it. Sooner would I die myself than wish harm on you."

"And your child?" I ask.

He does not understand my question.

"Would you sooner see your child die than me?" I ask him simply.

He stares at me, dumbly. Then he wets his lips, swallows. "I do not know, my love," he whispers. He takes a deep breath. "Would you?"

I blink my eyes free of his stare, and look at him anew. See him whole, standing there where the path splits the ceiling of the forest. The satyr, standing in the slanting sunlight of the morning forest, gilded by the sun's touch. Ruddy lips, dark skin, glistening eyes, hair atousle beneath his proud horns. His skin gleams with health and the sweat of pursuing me. Sleek pelted legs, strong hooves splayed on the beaten earth. He is too far away for his scent to affect me, but as I stare at him, love floods me. Not for Pan, for this particular one, but for what he is. Tag end of a myth, strange species, companion to my own for generations beyond telling. I had read of you before I knew you, had loved you, had worshiped the forest god in my own savage heart, beyond the reach of any civilized teaching. I had known you had to be. No amount of common sense could have dissuaded me from believing in you. I love you as I love wolves howling and whales blowing, as I love all that is wild and dwindling. How many of you can there be left in this world? Would I die to increase your numbers by one?

I suddenly know it is true. My body gave consent to this long before my mind did, but my heart is not far behind. I would do this thing. Not just for my Pan, but for what he is. On one level it is a payback of sorts. Ask not what your forest can do for you. He is smiling at me. I don't have to lift my eyes, to nod, to open my arms, I don't even have to smile. He knows. And he comes to me, not just a faun, the companion of my childhood, my friend. My mate.

# Twenty-one

We travel only four miles or so downriver before our path is slashed by a two-lane highway. A concrete bridge spans the river. After checking for traffic in both directions, we quickly cross. I jog, wondering if I can truly already feel the slosh of a child in my belly, or if I am imagining it. "This is new," Pan tells me, hooves ringing on the pavement as he trots hurriedly beside me. "I don't remember this bridge or this road."

As we leave the bridge, I nod wordlessly at the 1944 date graved deep in the concrete.

"Well," he shrugs. "It wasn't a personal memory. Let's just say it wasn't here the last time any of my ancestors came this way."

I roll my eyes at him, and we leave the highway's edge, clambering over riprap, then sliding down a gravel bank to regain the river's edge. We are working our way upriver on the grassy bank when we hear the whoosh of an approaching car. Pan pauses, turns, brazenly waves at a Volkswagen bug. An instant later we hear the screech of its brakes, but before it can back up, we have regained the edge of the forest. We stand in the masking trees, holding our giggles back behind cupped hands, eyes as wicked as children's. We stand still until the car moves slowly on. Then we stamp and laugh and gasp until we choke.

After we catch our breaths, he pauses. He lifts his head, regal as any stag, and slowly turns it as if homing in on a signal. "This way," he tells me, and starts off surely through the forest. I follow.

The pattern of our days changes even more. Now we walk more slowly, and pause more often for me to rest. He makes love to me only if I instigate it, and even then he is maddeningly careful with me. And often I am too tired to instigate it, for he has told me true. This pregnancy weighs heavy and soon upon me. Instead of scavenging or hunting as we go, he now does all the hunting while I rest in the evenings. Once this would have hurt my pride. Now it seems natural and right. When I think about it, I feel only relief.

Once I ask him how many miles we are covering a day. The question seems to have no meaning to him. I decide it doesn't matter to me, either. We do not travel in a straight line, but across the lower skirts of the mountains. There are waters to ford, and towns to circle, and natural obstacles to avoid. It is no longer north that we travel, but a zigzag course of his choosing. Pan becomes my compass, and it is he I follow, trusting.

Each night I fall asleep, wondering what tomorrow's weather will bring. Never has the color of the evening sky meant so much to me. But winter seems to hold back her hand. The days are mostly fine, if brisk. Cold I can fight, with steady-paced movement during the day and Pan's body heat by night. It is the rain that I dread, for it pierces me through with its icy silver arrows. When the downpours come, they are drenching, dragging the warmth from my body and ladening my clothes with its wet weight. My sneakers are worn and they slip on the steep wet paths. By the end of the day, the knees of my jeans are caked with mud from my frequent stumbles. On rainy days, we make but a few miles, and they are torturous ones, scarcely worth the extra effort. Snow is what I fear, but fortune favors us with a slowly dwindling fall. Almost I could believe it is the will of the woodland god I follow.

I only become aware that we have entered Canada when we brush the outskirts of a small town, and all the license plates on the parked and sleeping cars are Canadian. He takes me through a campground that night, and plunders someone's Styrofoam cooler left out on a picnic table. Milk, fruit, and roast beef with lettuce sandwiches wrapped in waxed paper. That night I eat it all and he watches me, smiling. From the same campground, he has taken an old woolen blanket, probably someone's picnic blanket. We bundle under it gratefully, for the nights grow ominously colder.

That night before we sleep, I ask him how much farther we have to go. Again, it is a question he cannot answer. He can only turn his head and stare off into the trees and shrug. His eyes grow distant as he ponders. I sense he is like a migrating bird, following some beacon of his own. I believe that he himself will not truly know we are there until we arrive.

But if he cannot answer my questions about miles and days, he has at least become delightfully open about all else. In the evenings, after we have eaten, he plays the pipes for me, or tells me stories. I come to prefer the stories. Few of them are from his own lifetime. Some are immeasurably ancient, and these are sprinkled with words I do not understand, for ideas he has no English for. Others are as recent as his father's time. His father, he proudly tells me, attended a school once. He took biology classes. From his father's classes comes his understanding of what he is in biological terms. When I dispute it, he launches into a complicated tale of two old-timers in a cabin, wintering over on their homestead outside Nenana.

"They were too old and they should have known better," he tells me. "I think they did know better, but they didn't want to admit they were old. The old man walked his trap line and cut the wood, while the old woman kept the fire going and cooked the meals and prepared the skins the old man brought in. They had an old truck, and a few times a year the old man would take out his wrenches and persuade it to run, and they'd go to town, to sell furs and bring back supplies. I suppose they had been doing it for years. My father had lived in that area for a while, and thought of them as his neighbors. Summers he helped himself from their garden and smokehouse, winters he raided their cache and the back-porch pantry where the old woman kept her preserves. Never too much, mind you, and only to get himself through hard times. He always suspected they knew of him, but they never seemed to mind what he took. Are you comfortable, my love?"

I shift against him, not answering. I am not comfortable. My belly feels swollen and tender already. If I lie on my side, its weight drags forward on my spine. If I lie on my back, I cannot breathe. Lying on my stomach is unthinkable. So I lean against him, cradling my belly in my hands. He strokes my hair and goes on with his tale.

"My father was in a habit of shadowing the old man as he walked his traps. Not on his trail, of course, but flanking it. On this particular day, the old man had a wolverine in one of his jaw traps. He shot it, it dropped, and he went forward to retrieve the pelt. But the thing was only stunned and it came up at the old man, trap and all, and tore into his legs.

"The old man managed to stagger back and luckily for him, the chain on the trap held. He shot the wolverine a few more times, killed it, and then collapsed himself. When it became clear to my father that he wasn't going to get up again, he went to the old man, lifted him, and carried him home."

He pauses, staring into the fire. I let him. I have come to know that he has to stop, to remember before he can go on with the story. Things seem to come to him in pieces.

"He didn't go in. Not that first time. He only opened the door and set the old man inside. He was gone before the old woman could get there and see him. But the next day there was a vacuum bottle of hot stew left for him on the back porch. So my father kept watch on the cabin, and as the old woman's wood pile dwindled, he worried, for he had not seen the old man for some days. Then one day he saw the old woman outside, trying to split some of the frozen log sections the old man had stockpiled all summer. She cut some, but barely enough to take her through the night. So that night my father went down, and took up the maul and split wood for her. And halfway through his chopping, she opened the door of the cabin, and a great finger of yellow light reached out and lay upon my father. And the old woman called out, 'It's a cold night tonight, and too dark for working. Beast or man, you're welcome at our hearth as friend. Come inside and be warm.' So my father went inside, and that was how they became friends."

I stir sleepily in the circle of his arms. "It still doesn't explain how he went to school," I protest. His fingers walk lazily down my spine, finding the aching spots and soothing them.

"The old man's legs were ruined. My father helped them through the winter, and spring breakup, and did his best to care for them until friends came to find out why they hadn't brought their furs to town. The old man had to go to Fairbanks to see what could be done for his legs. They were gone some time. So my father stayed in their cabin, and planted their garden, and even tended the old man's trap line while they were gone. When the old people did come back, the old man was on crutches. He only lasted a year or two longer. When the old woman had to sell the place and move up to Fairbanks, it was her idea that my father go with her. They used the old man's wheelchair to pass him off as her invalid nephew. He studied at home with her for a few years, to regain his reading and math skills . . ."

"Regain?" I ask sleepily.

"Of course. Living alongside your kind for so many years, we have to learn your skills. Languages and letters change slowly, but change they do, especially so when we travel long distances during one lifetime. The skills have to be kept up. Don't you think we use your road signs and posted warnings?"

"Oh."

"Anyway. A neighbor of the old woman's took an interest in her crippled nephew, and encouraged him to follow his interest in biology. The neighbor arranged for my father to attend some classes at the college, and he did quite well there, until he took to disputing some of their information about the natural habits of the local flora and fauna. Of course, my father felt he was in a better position to know than the professor. It was all downhill from there, and culminated unhappily when my father one day abandoned his wheelchair and ran away with a large Suffolk ewe from a nearby farm. He never saw the old woman again, but trusted her to understand that he had lived among humans as long as he could."

"An ewe," I ask sleepily.

"My mother. Go to sleep, now, love, I've kept you awake long enough."

I giggle and drowse off in his arms.

It is days later before our talk eddies around to that subject again.

"Whatever became of your parents?" I ask him. It is a subterfuge, really. We are on an uphill trail. A few weeks ago, I would have said it was not too steep. Now I feel as if I have been climbing an endless ladder. My calves are sore, my back aches, and I cannot seem to pull enough air into my lungs. Pan is walking effortlessly ahead of me, back straight, hooves digging easily into the black soil of the path. It is a cool grey day, mist is swirling through the upper branches of the great cedars that roof us, but I am sweating and hot. But I do not want to ask him to go slower. Lately he has seemed driven. He looks often at the sky during the day, and at night he seeks clearings to study the stars. Time or direction, I cannot tell what worries him, and my questions only bring soothing nothings from him. So I ask my question, hoping he will slow down as he considers it. "I mean, I never saw any sign of your father or mother when we were kids. Had you left them already?"

"My mother was killed by a lynx when I was still very small. Luckily, I was nearly weaned already. My father . . . well, it is not the way of my kind to keep their children close by for long. By the time I was four or five, I was ready to be on my own. My survival memories were almost fully awakened, and I could draw on what I needed to survive. It was time for me to have my own territory. As the adult, it was up to my father to move on. To have too many of us in one area swiftly becomes dangerous. Especially since the area around Fairbanks was fast becoming settled. But for you, I would never have stayed there as long as I did."

I halt, putting my hand on a tree trunk to steady myself as I breathe. "A lynx killed your mother?" I don't know if it is the cool way he says it, or the sudden idea of a lynx being bold enough to bring down a human.

"Um," he agrees. He halts, and glances back to where I am. He comes back down the trail to me, takes the canteen from the bag that he now carries every day. "My father had put her to graze in a clearing. I suppose I was fortunate that I was not with her at the time. He had taken me to a stream to bathe me. It was quite a shock to me when we returned. Not much left of her but wool and hooves."

"Your mother was a sheep," I say inanely.

He nods gravely. "I'd wondered if you were really listening the other night, for when I told you, I expected some reaction." He takes the canteen from my hands, drinks sparingly, and then slings it back on the pack. He keeps his head turned aside, fussing with it, as he speaks. "My father was birthed from a white-tailed deer. I remember that my grandfather caught her when she was scarcely more than a fawn, and raised her to trust him. Before him, sheep for several generations. They are easily turned to our purposes, as human shepherds well know."

I feel slightly ill to hear him speak so. It shows in my face, but I cannot mask it.

"Almost any large mammal," he answers my unspoken question. He is staring up the trail, as if assessing the path we must follow. "But we feel the greatest kinship with those with cloven hooves. And with humans. It is easiest, of course, to take a dumb beast. It asks no questions, and it makes few demands. Easy to provide for. And if it dies in the process, or not long after, the loss is easier to bear."

His voice is getting strangled, and he will not look at me as he speaks. I take his hands and draw him from the beaten path, aside, to a mossy place where I can sit comfortably. I ease myself down and he crouches beside me. "What is it you need to tell me?" I ask him.

He puts a lean brown hand over his mouth, squeezes hard, pinching his lower jaw as if to still a trembling. When he drops his hand, he takes a very deep breath. "That I—that the memories of a woman bearing one of our children are old, very old. We take our lovers, our true lovers, from your kind. They seldom conceive. But you have. Usually, when a human woman becomes pregnant with one of our children, she rids herself of it before the child comes to term. It has been a long time since a woman has chosen to bear one of my kind. And when your time comes, I do not know how much help I will be to you. The memories are very old. And not good. And if something should happen to you, in the process . . ."

A tear breaks loose from those dark and shining eyes. It is inconceivable to me, as if I were watching a wolf weep. The faun is not made for human fears and sorrows. From him I have come to expect the natural confidence of an animal, the acceptance of the wild world as it is. It frightens me, and I reach to wipe it hastily away.

"I've had a child," I tell him comfortingly. "I know what childbirth is like. I'll manage."

"It's going to be hard," he tells me naively. "I've started to wonder if it was wise. If this isn't a terrible mistake for both of us." It is the last thing I want to hear.

"Let's go," I say suddenly, struggling to my feet. "We're losing the daylight. And I'm getting cold sitting still."

He rises, but this time he does not lead. He lets me set the pace, and follows a few steps behind me. Waiting. Finally I ask it.

"This child. It won't be mine, will it? It won't take anything from me, will it?"

"Clone is the word you're looking for," he says softly. "No. The seed my kind plants is a complete seed, needing only nourishment from the mother. It will take nothing of you from you. It will be me again, as I am my father and grandfather and great-grandfather."

"But how?" I struggle with the words, try to keep walking. I feel as if I have lost something, have been denied something. Cheated. The path seems to get steeper with every step I take. I am reduced to taking three steps, pausing, taking three more. "How could it have ever come about?"

"It's almost enough to make you a Creationist, isn't it?" he asks dryly. Then, more seriously, "How did the cuckoo come about? Or mistletoe? I only know it's true, Evelyn, if there is a biological niche, something will fill it."

"That's about what I feel like right now. A biological niche, and you came along to fill me." I am breathing hard and the words come out sharper than I intend them. I hear him pause behind me, and I deliberately push myself to keep moving up the trail. There is light ahead, a clearing perhaps. I push on toward it. I still don't hear him behind me. He is deliberately letting the distance between us grow.

"You're thinking," he calls up to me, "that you're nothing but a walking womb. That I've used you for my own selfish ends. That I got you with child, my child, solely for my own satisfaction. Without regard to what you wanted or needed. Well, that's true!"

Clear-cut. I emerge suddenly onto the bald crown of the hill. One of the big timber companies has been here and scalped the forest. Not one sizable tree of any kind still stands, and the smaller stuff has been trampled by dozer tracks, obscuring our path. Not too long ago. The stumps are still raw, the ashes of the burned branch piles are still black and new. I feel naked and exposed under the grey sky. Some of the scrub brush will survive this mauling. Already, those ones are springing erect again, but even on them, the leaves are scarlet or a withered yellow. Winter lurks around the next corner. There is wind here, too, sneaking inside my loosened shirt and chilling my body, making my skin as cold as Pan's words have made my soul.

"Evelyn!"

He is suddenly behind me. His arms close around me, holding me firm. I do not struggle. I am dead wood in his grasp. A great stillness has filled me, filled me more fully than the child that already pouches my stomach. His two hands settle on my belly. He speaks over my shoulder, his mouth by my ear.

"I have a memory," he says. "A very old one. A very precious one. Old but so clear, so vivid, as few of the old memories are. It is no struggle to recall it. It came to me when I was a child, clear in my mind, with no effort on my part. Do you know what that means? It means it has been recalled often, has been taken out and handled by every generation since its happening. It comes to me as clearly as the memories for fashioning a pipe and playing, as fresh as my own self-made memories. Because it has been remembered so often, and so well.

"It is of a woman, Evelyn. Her hair is dark and curly, her eyes are immense. Her lips are always smiling, my love, and she touches me, so gently, so surely. All is right and safe in her arms. She sings to me, foolish little songs, as she takes the tangles from my hair. And then she lifts me and holds me on her lap as she opens her garment and puts me to her breast. A mother, Evelyn. The last real mother any of us have known. And do you know what she wears, Evelyn, what she opens to bare that warm, milky breast? A chiton. A chiton."

We stand silent on the windswept hill, in the midst of this man-made desolation, and he lets the words sink in. I think of a dark-haired woman, hundreds of years ago, standing as I stand now, in a faun's arms, heavy with his child. Did she know she would be remembered, cherished by generations to come? Nothing of her body continuing in the child she bore; only her memory and her image, handed down the spiral ladder to each succeeding generation.

"All who come after me will know you, Evelyn. As friend, lover, and mother. You are the gift I give to myself, a hundred times over, perhaps to the very end of this world. I will never be sorry for that."

His body warms my back and his arms steady me. A gust of wind slides past the bared hillside, chilling me. The sweat has dried on me and I shiver in his arms.

"We'd better keep moving," he says, but stands

still, holding me a moment longer. Loving me so I can almost feel it, like a coat I can wear. For a brief time, I imagine I can see as he does, not back down his line, but forward. I carry a hundred children in my womb. All will know my touch, or recall my rejection. It is like standing on a stage before them all, and looking out over all their upturned faces. All of them are Pan. All of them are waiting.

I look out over the clear-cut hilltop. The area seems smaller now, for it is but one hillside, and is surrounded by many that are still crowned with trees. It has been slashed and burned, but that is not what is permanent here. Fireweed will spread and seed across the burned areas. Bulldozed willow will send up new shoots, from the cedar stump new branches will sprout, a million tiny seeds that have waited for the soil to be opened to the sunlight will germinate next spring. This devastation is temporary. Life is what is permanent. Fragile, forgiving life is what we all must eventually answer to.

Then Pan steps clear of me, but takes my hand. He leads the way and I follow him, stepping over tangled branches and smashed and flattened bushes. The way is slow and difficult, but he leads me surely on.

# Twenty-two

We seem to have left all civilization behind. This part of Canada is made entirely of forested mountains, divided by lush valleys and cold rivers, and all capped with ice. These are young, lusty mountains, rugged and toothy against the sky. The beauty is breathtaking. So is the effort of crossing such terrain. Our path curls and twists as it threads its way through the mountains. We challenge no more than the foothills, but it is a daily trial I must face. The constant climbs and descents are a torment to me. Each day the snowline on the mountain peaks creeps lower. Nights are cold, and frost edges our blankets each morning. I never knew I could be so tired, so cold and uncomfortable, and still press on every day.

I miss humanity's food. Pan provides, and I trust him when he says the things he brings are edible, but most bear little resemblance to anything I've ever eaten before. There are scrubbed roots, some long and tough, some like handfuls of rice packed together. There are greens, but these are scarcer, more fibrous, and most have a bitter edge to their flavor. The meat is mostly hare, sinewy and lean. In the cold weather, I begin to long for fatty, greasy foods, for rich foods thick with calories. I dream of french fries and deep-fried chicken, of ice cream and cheesecake and chocolate bars. But the wild land yields up no such luxuries. The berries he finds are past their prime, shriveled by frost's touch, but edible. At one stream we pass, he finds the survivor of a late salmon run. The dog salmon is tattered and mossy-looking from its long sojourn in fresh water. Its teeth have grown enormous, giving it a monstrous prehistoric aspect. All spawned out, it lurks under a cut bank, waiting to die. And die it does, when Pan hauls it out triumphantly and it flops the last of its feeble life out on the shore. We cook it immediately. It is a large fish, but when we are finished, there are only bones and a few scraps of skin. Never has anything tasted so good to me. I am tempted to linger here in the hopes he can find another, but with an apologetic look, Pan gathers our gear and we move on.

We move slowly now, ponderously. Already I have felt the stirrings of the child within me. Something, elbow, small fist, tiny hoof, occasionally pokes out uncomfortably. Then I massage my belly as we walk, gradually easing it back into position.

My jeans are too tight. I can no longer snap them, and they only zip partway. I have used my knife to bore more holes in my belt, but soon I will run out of space on it. If I am this big now, what will I be when the baby comes to term? I don't like to think about it. My bra is too tight, but going without it is even more uncomfortable. I am not used to the weight of swollen breasts depending from my chest. The stretch marks are shiny and purplish, and extend up my belly like ragged ferns growing from my groin. The skin is being forced to stretch too fast. I try not to wonder what my body will look like when this is all over.

Pan continues to be solicitous of my health. He looks tired, for he has taken all tasks to himself. He is thinner, too, for he will not eat each evening until he is sure I have had enough. After a day of walking, while I am resting by a fire, he goes off to do his hunting and scavenging. Then he returns, to cook the food and to spend long hours rubbing my back, or gently massaging my belly. This type of touching has replaced sex between us. I am usually too tired to want more than this, and my swollen belly is not an easily surmounted barrier. So he strokes me gently, easing the aches instead. One evening he plays the pipes for me as I huddle by the fire wrapped in our blankets. He plays again that same mysterious tune that had seemed so familiar. Now I recognize it as the infant growing inside me in a muffled liquid world. The baby stirs as the music flows, and I put my hands on my belly, holding the child securely. For a few moments I can forget the discomforts of this pregnancy, the deep chill of the night, the daunting walk that awaits me tomorrow morning. For just an instant, we are a closed circle, we three. Everything I need is right here.

The next morning, Pan wakes me very early. "We have to get up and get moving," he tells me. "Now. We're running out of time."

He doesn't need to explain. The sky has lowered, disappearing the mountains, leaving us in a low-roofed grey world. There is wind above the trees that shelter us, and a damp edge in the air. Bits of branches and dry needles fall. I am already wearing every shirt I own, and it is not enough. Today when we pack, Pan keeps the two blankets out. He puts the woolen one around my shoulders, and wraps his, much the worse for wear, around himself. It is the first time I have seen him take any precautions against the weather. It is not reassuring.

We are on the trail for perhaps an hour when the first flakes start to fall. They fall as large clumps of tiny wet flakes, drifting down between the trees to quickly melt on the moss. If this is as bad as it gets, I think, we'll be fine. But the snow continues, and the temperature falls with it. Soon the snow is sticking, lacing the branches and forming a mosaic tracery on the forest floor wherever the interlocked branches overhead do not catch it. Our trail is uphill, as it seems it always is, and the snow makes slippery spots. Pan's hooves cut through the wet snow down to the moss and earth, but my worn sneakers are treacherous on the stuff. Mindful of how ungainly I have become, I set my feet carefully and move more slowly.

By noon we are still climbing. The tree cover has changed. The trees are shorter and more gnarled, natural bonsai, but still taller than we are. They bow away from the wind. Soon, I think, he will decide to stop and rest. I have been walking with my head bowed and the blanket up over my hair and ears. I watch little more than the path right in front of me. It seems to me that the snow is becoming thicker, that more often we are leaving tracks in it. Before, the pressure of my steps was enough to melt it down to the earth. Now it packs beneath my sneakers. I can feel the edges of my socks starting to get damp. These are the things I think of as I hike. Tired, wet feet, and surely we must start to go downhill again soon. No more than that. I follow Pan, trusting, not thinking.

But when Pan does stop and I lift my head and look around us, I am filled with dismay. We are leaving the tree line behind us. I am breathing hard, and I put a hand on his shoulder to steady myself as I look back the way we have come. I am looking out over an irregular bowl, lined with the tops of the trees. Down there is the sheltering forest. Up here is knee-high brush, rocks, lichen, snow, wind, and little more. I look back at him, dumbly questioning.

"Up," he says, gesturing with his chin. "We're close now, I think." The falling snow deadens his words, makes his voice dull.

"It's colder up there," I protest. Even this brief halt has been long enough for me to start chilling. My shivering will soon turn to shaking.

"No." He looks vague, tries to explain. "There's shelter up there. A warm place."

"A cabin?" I guess, looking up the treeless slope ahead of us.

"No." He pauses, furrowing his brows. "A cave. With water in it. But it's warm."

"I don't think that this is a good idea," I tell him. I am not feeling stubborn so much as impossibly tired. As far as I can see, the ground does nothing but go up, getting steeper each step of the way. "I don't like the idea of getting halfway up there, and not being able to go any farther. Can't we go back down, under the trees, and then start the climb fresh in the morning?"

He looks at me and then up, measuring my strength against what the sky threatens. "It has to be now," he says at last. "This snow isn't going to stop. If we don't get there by nightfall, we won't get there at all. We'll be forced back down, into the forest."

"Would that be so terrible?" I have wrapped my arms around myself to try to quell my shaking. Snow blows between us as we speak. It clings to his eyelashes and brows until he lifts a hand and brushes it away.

"It will soon be deep snow down there as well. Up there is the only place I know where we can be safe until spring." He turns, bows his head, and starts uphill again. For three steps I can only stare after him, stalled out by the enormity of his words. Until spring. Up there, somewhere, in a cave. For months. What will we do, what will we eat, what will we wear? Like a dash of cold water in the face, it hits me how completely I have been trusting him. And this is what he's been leading me to. A cave.

I spring after him, my heaviness temporarily forgotten, and hurry to catch up. I have too many questions, they are logjammed in my mouth, but before I can even clutch his arm, he turns back to me. "You'll have to trust me," he says, offering me his hand. "It will be all right. Believe me."

And I do. I try not to wonder if it is the pheromones or love or simple stupidity. At this point I decide it hardly matters which it is. If I go back down, I'll freeze. If I follow him up, I may freeze. But then again, I may not. And that is as good as I've got right now. I realize I have surrendered all control to him, that I have become so enwrapped in listening to the life growing within me that I have forgotten all else. How foreign, how stupid of me, I think, but there is no surge of the old anger to support such an opinion. Walking takes all my energy.

So I follow. His grip on my hand is sure, his fingers warm mine. We climb. The snow gets deeper as we go up, and the flakes seem to fall faster. We climb. It's colder up here, but not so cold that the snow stops falling. Maybe it's the wind, which is definitely stronger up here. I grip the blanket tighter under my chin, but the wind sneaks up under it and whips it out behind me like a cape, stealing my hoarded body heat. And still we climb.

My feet are completely wet now, and my toes are going numb. There is nothing I can do about it. Stupid to think about stopping and changing into dry socks. They'd be wet again one minute later. No, keep going, and trust to the exertion to keep the old blood pumping around, hell, I had numb feet a thousand times when I was a kid, frost bit hell out of them a couple of times. Don't think about it. Just keep going. Up. I keep following him, clutching his hand, watching little more than my own feet.

The wind lessens. A few more steps and it lessens even more. I am not aware of how much we have been fighting it until it drops, and the going seems almost easy for a while. Pan has taken us around a fold in the mountain. The wind whips past above us and I am grateful for that, but to me it looks as if the going will soon be even rougher. I lift my head and look around. To our left, the ground falls away, sudden as a knife slash. There is a deep gouge down the mountain, carved by a boulder-choked stream that runs moodily at the bottom of the ravine. Our path parallels the edge of the slash. We walk on an area that retains its thin skin of topsoil and stunted plant life. Only a few feet away to our left, that ends, and the sliding gravel and bare stony earth of the crumbling embankment begins. Tiny plants cling precariously in patches, but there is no real plant life nor roots to anchor the earth. I don't like walking this near it. I know that I am safe where I am, but I have an idiotic fear that somehow I will get too near and the edge will give way. I can visualize so well myself sliding on a carpet of moving pebbles, flailing and grabbing for support that isn't there, slipping irrevocably over the edge, falling free down the face of sheer rock. I've done it a thousand times in dreams. It isn't true, what they say about waking up before you hit. For me there is always the sudden bloody impact, and the shocked realization, beyond pain, that my body is ruined, that the little animal I live inside is shattered. That's what wakes me up.

"Only a little farther. Right up there," Pan tells me cheerfully, and moves on, his small goat feet tripping blithely along. I stare dumbfounded at where he has pointed. "Up there" seems to be where the water is trickling and dripping down the bared stone bones of the mountain.

"I can't do it," I say with great certainty. "I can't get up there."

"There's a path," he says reassuringly.

"I'm pregnant!" I tell him angrily. The baby picks that moment to attempt to stand up inside me. At least, that is what it feels like. Something slams into the bottom of my lungs while it treads firmly on my bladder. I gasp in surprise, and Pan is instantly at my side.

"Sit down a minute," he tells me, and tosses the pack into the snow for me to perch on. But sitting down is the last thing I want to do. I feel as if I'd never get up. And my guts feel crowded enough as it is, without folding up to sit.

"It's too soon for it to feel this big," I tell him, taking deep breaths. I have forgotten the mountain entirely and the climb ahead of me. The real endurance challenge is what is building itself inside my body.

"I told you. My child will develop faster."

"Not this fast. Something's wrong."

He blows out a shuddering breath. I know I am frightening him, but I cannot stop myself. I'm frightened. I see him swallow. "Please, Evelyn," he says desperately. "Let's keep moving. You'll be more comfortable up there."

The baby sloshes itself into a more comfortable position. I can take a deep breath again. "Okay," I say, surprising myself. Easier to surrender than to stand arguing on the side of a snowy mountain. He picks up the pack, starts slowly up the trail again. I slog along behind him.

The way does not get any easier. The afternoon light goes greyer in the snowfall, and then starts to fail completely. I am past worrying about it. My whole being is focused on taking step after step after step, following the sparse trail Pan breaks through the snow. The snow gets deeper, rising past my ankles. It is halfway up my calves before it finally quits falling. It seems darker without the white flakes catching the light as they fall. As the light goes, the world around us cools. The snow takes on a crispy quality as I wade through it.

Occasionally I lift my head, to look out on the huge expanse of mountainside and forested valley that we have left behind. I can feel how minute we are, tiny specks of life crawling up the mountain's impassive flank. The valley behind us is filling up with darkness. The light that bathes us now is gentle and has a pink tone. I blink once toward the sun. It has found a crack in the cloud cover and is sending us its last rays through a picket fence of mountain peaks, as if it knows how desperately we need the light.

"Come on," Pan calls.

Our path has taken us closer to the ravine. Indeed, we have almost come to the end of it. Another hundred yards up the mountain, it disappears under an immense scab of old ice. The dirty-looking glacier has been dusted with the fall of fresh snow, but that whiteness only serves to show the age of the ice beneath it. It reminds me of antique ivory, layers in various shades of cream, yellow, and brown. Below the slowly dripping edge of the glacier is a vertical drop of rock, cracked and tilted panels and chunks of stone many times as tall as I am. Their edges have been humbled smooth by the flow of water. In summer, when the ancient water of the glacier runs freely, a waterfall probably sheathes these rocks. Now cold has locked up the glacier and snow-pack water. Some planes of the rock are shiny with trickling ice. Others are edged in moss and slime. A few hardy trailing plants have found a temporary niche in which to flourish, but their time is nearly over. In one area, a thick yellow stain trails down the face of the rocks like a spill of paint. My nostrils catch a faint whiff of a smell like a struck kitchen match. Sulfur.

"There," Pan is saying, pointing. "See it?"

I see nothing except that he is pointing out at some spot on that cracked wall of rock. He glances at my face, grins at my disbelief. In the gathering darkness, I cannot read his eyes. I do not know if they are merry, or if their depths shelter doubts as vivid as my own. He pulls me close for a moment, tries to hug me, but my layered clothing and swollen belly are as effective as any castle wall. He frees me. "Here," he says, "I'll show you. It's not as bad as it looks."

No. It's worse. He walks cautiously across a strip of pebbly ground to where the bared rock begins. Tiny stones roll free from the earth's cold grip and go bounding into the depths of the ravine. He steps nonchalantly across a gap onto a huge tilted plank of stone. I hear a tiny scree as his hooves slip slightly, but he has the sureness of a goat and quickly he regains his balance. His hooves tack across it, and then he has reached the more vertical portion of the rock face.

His body puts it in scale for me, makes the immensity of those slabs of stone apparent. I have never gone rock climbing, and I begin to wonder if I have feared unnecessarily. He makes it look so easy. He stays close to the rock face, sometimes clinging to it, sometimes merely trailing a hand across its surface. He moves up and then down, following the contours of the cracked and tumbled rock. He gives me a bad moment or two, times when he ventures out onto steeply slanting surfaces. Twice I hear his hooves slip, and once he has to backtrack when he comes to a dead end of slick, straight stone.

He is working his way ever closer to the yellowish stain. I realize that I am squinting my eyes to follow his progress. The light is going, and rapidly. He clambers to the top of a steep slant of stone, skitters down it, and suddenly disappears. Before I can even catch my breath, he reappears, sticking his head out of what I would have sworn was solid rock. In the tricky light, it is hard to make my eyes obey me, and sort what is shadow from what is variegated rock from what is a deep vertical crack in the rock face. He reappears completely now, standing on a tiny lip of rock, and makes a deep, sweeping bow in my direction. It sends a chill up my spine. It is too surreal to bear, a goatman with a worn wild blanket for a cloak, bowing to me like a shamanic magician from a rock stage set high over nature's amphitheater.

He comes back to me, traveling more swiftly and surely. I see his eyes dart to where the sun is a bright smear between mountain peaks. I know what he is thinking. Bringing the battered bag that holds our belongings, I start out across the pebbly strip of crumbling earth toward him.

The first step is the hardest, and I force myself to take it before he can reach me. Some dormant sense of independence is raising its head. Despite my belly and weariness, I do not want him to coddle and coax me across this final stretch of rock. I want to go as I would have gone when I was twelve, following him, yes, but following him with no doubts as to whether I can duplicate his feat.

But on the first slant of stone, I discover why his hooves slipped. The fine misting of water sliding over the cold rock is turning into ice. I can get no purchase. Flailing my arms, I slide, my worn sneakers as smooth as skis. My shriek is an echo of Pan's hoarse cry as he comes bounding toward me, heedless of his own footing. I sit down heavily on the slick rock, landing with a jolt that rattles the full length of my spine. For an instant I can only sit, staring out over the ravine before me. I feel sick and swirly, the rock is tilting under me, I am sure I am going to go sliding down into that darkness. I close my eyes, will everything to stillness.

I hear Pan's hooves clatter behind me. His voice is husky with fear as he begs me, "Take my hand."

Eyes still closed, I shake my head slowly. But it is not stubbornness. I don't want to touch or be touched right now. "If I'm going across this rock face," I tell him, "I've got to do it on my own. It's the only way I can find my own balance. If I'm holding on to you, I know I'm going to zig when you zag, and we'll both end up falling. Just give me a minute."

He is silent, but I feel his grudging assent. He wants to touch me, I know, but knows the truth of my words. "At least let me take the bag," he suggests. I wave a hand at it, and hear the scrape of canvas over ice as he tugs it up to him. I open my eyes again. The light is dimmer already. No time to sit and gather courage. By the time I'm brave enough to do this, it will be too dark.

I reach past my belly to my shoelaces. They are wet, and half-frozen. My cold fingers tug at the knots. I grunt as I pull my shoes off, and then peel off my socks. I stuff the socks inside the shoes, then knot their laces together and sling them over my shoulder. My feet are cold, my toes numb, but even so I will get better purchase. I scoot back up the rock. Great. Now my butt's wet, too. When I feel safe to do so, I stand up. Cold bites my feet, but I have a little traction. Pan stands about six feet from me, on the next stone I must clamber. His eyes are very big and dark. "Just what I always wanted to be," I tell him, trying to break the tension. "Barefoot and pregnant."

He doesn't even smile. "Oh, be careful, my love," he tells me, and slowly moves over to make room for me.

I follow him, in fits and starts. From this tilting slab, to that flat but so narrow surface. From places where I can cling to the rock face, to places where I must go, hunched over, hands touching nothing, relying only on my cold feet. I dare not walk upright, but curl over my belly. My center of gravity is wrong, there is no moment when I feel surefooted and agile.

I am a shambling ape thing following his goat lead. His hooves find every possible purchase and he walks upright, while I come behind, gripping with toes and fingers. It is getting colder and darker with every step I take. Like dying, I think to myself, and out of nowhere, Teddy's little face swims before my eyes. I try to push the image away, but it clings to me every inch of the way. The baby in my belly churns uneasily, and my little dead son seems to cling to me also. He didn't know how close death was hovering, that day on the tractor under the bright hot sun. It came quickly for him, snatching him away and closing its bony hands over him. Not like this, where every step I take might be the wrong one.

I am at a very tricky spot. Both my hands are seeking purchase in an almost horizontal crack as I slide my feet across an unrelated slab of stone. My belly is up against the rock face, pushing me out and away from safety. I turn my head, but Pan is out of my sight and my reach for the moment. "Oh, Teddy," I say, like a prayer, as if my little son can somehow keep me safe. The deep aching loss of him bursts suddenly back into my life, as if I have wallpapered over a door and now he suddenly breaks back in through it. I feel as if I am walking a narrow path between two children. One grows and turns inside me, demanding a share of every breath I take, of every morsel I eat. His safety depends on my surefootedness right now. The other seems to hover at my shoulder, and his presence is like a rebuke to me. How dare I use my body to shelter another when I did not protect him that day? How dare I be so fearful of the false step and death, when, alone and unprepared, he has already plumbed that fearful chasm?

"Evelyn, Evelyn," Pan's voice reaches me. I am aware that I have stopped moving, that my sweating forehead is pressed against cold rock. My feet are numb except for one extremely painful area by my left heel. I assume I have cut myself, but there is no way I can look. "Evelyn!" he calls, more sharply.

"I'm okay," I lie, and take another breath. God, it's cold and I'm so tired. It's hard to remember why any of this is important. I only know that the longer I stand, the harder it is to move again. And it's dark.

"It's only a little farther," he says. "Please, love."

I turn my head, try to look around me, but I am pressed too close to the rock face. Impossible to tell how far I have come. I shuffle my feet a few steps, following the sound of his voice, and come to a place where I must let loose of my handholds. I feel sudden fingers brush my shoulder, and nearly scream. "It's okay, it's okay," he says soothingly, and prys my fingers free. "Hold my hand, now. I'll brace you." He steps back, away from me, but pulling me. He steps over a gap in the rock, from one slanting rock surface to another. And draws me after him.

I can't step over that empty space, not with my belly drawing me down like an anchor on a sinking ship. But I do, and he keeps my hands and draws me on, and suddenly we are skittering down a steep slant of stone. There is nothing to hang on to, and it is too dark to see much of anything, but before I can panic, he stops me with a jerk, and pulls me in close to the rock face.

"In here," he whispers, and the words echo. I take a few steps, following him into absolute blackness. My feet make light splashing noises, and suddenly the cut on my heel stings to vicious life. "Stand still," he tells me, and before I can protest, he lets go of my hand and steps away. I am left standing in complete darkness.

I glance over my shoulder. There is a jagged grey crack in the darkness behind me, no more than a brighter dimness where the dregs of the light are seeping in. It illuminates nothing. But in a few moments, I start to become aware of my feet. They tingle and ache and burn. The smell of sulfur is stronger, and I surmise that I am standing in the runoff from a hot spring, and that my feet are being thawed by the warmth.

I stand still in the darkness, letting the warmth seep into my feet, and listening to the odd sounds Pan is making. He is fumbling with something, cursing softly and thudding something about. I hear a clank, like metal against glass. A sharp odor I can't quite identify drifts to me, and then there is a sudden flare of light. I shut my eyes to it and turn away before I open them again. Then I turn slowly back, letting my eyes adjust gradually.

It is an amazing sight. Pan is holding aloft a small glass lantern that would probably bring a fortune in any antique store. The sharp smell was the kerosene from the Mason jar on the floor by his hooves. He brushes more dust from the glass chimney before setting it back on the lamp. He hangs the lantern from a metal spike driven into a stone wall and makes a welcoming gesture that invites me in.

I walk forward slowly, my curiosity overcoming my weariness. The lantern light is yellow and warm, but the cave is warm also. Much warmer than outside, and free of the wind. Deep in the recesses, I can make out the shimmer of reflected light. A pool, and the faint disturbance that makes the light waver on it is the upwelling of the hot sulfurous water. The warmth it gives to the cave is almost worth the rotten-egg reek of it. I am still standing in the shallow moving overflow from the spring. The light touches here and there on the stone walls of the cave, giving me an impression of a low ceiling that rises higher above the spring, but most of the cavern we stand in is left in shadowy darkness.

Yet it is not the natural wonders of this place that impress me the most. Instead, it is the very plentiful evidence of its former habitation. There is furniture, of a sort, of hewn slab wood, and two wooden chests. Closer to the entrance, scorched rock and sooted wall mark a naturally vented area for a fire. Pan deposits our pack on the table. It quivers with the burden.

"I don't think we can trust the table, do you?" Pan asks as he gives that rickety object a shake. The wood of it is damp and mossy-looking, and it gives alarmingly when he leans on it. Of wood, too, is a stoutly built bedstead laced with rope set not far from the table. Tattered scraps of faded fabric scattered across the ropes are probably the remains of a straw tick. "Make yourself at home," Pan tells me as he tidies up the fabric and bits of long rotted straw and dumps them in a pile on the fire spot.

"How did you know this was here?" I ask him, already anticipating the answer.

"Ancestral home, my dear. Hasn't been used in quite a while, but actually, more things have survived than I expected. Bedstead will probably be okay, if I put new rope on it and a new mattress for you. Cedar is forever. I'll get a fire going while you go through the chests and see what's survived." There is no mistaking how pleased with himself he is. He is as good as his word, efficiently breaking up the table for firewood. I eye the punky damp-dry wood with doubts as I reluctantly leave the stream.

The cave floor is cold against my bare feet. I stop to dry my feet and put on two pairs of dry socks. My sneakers are hopelessly soaked. I hang then and the wet socks from other metal spikes driven into the cave walls. I think I am too weary to do more than that, but my curiosity is strong. I pad over and sink down by one of the wooden chests.

It is made of cedar, hand hewn, and the cracks have been packed with oakum and sealed with rosin, like an old sailing ship. There is a brass hasp, green with age, but no lock. I have to use my pocket knife to pry the hasp up, but then the chest opens easily.

Dried herbs, gone to crumbles but pungent still, lie in bundles over a thick layer of brown paper. I lift the crackling paper away, to find beneath it thick homespun blankets, only a little musty, and beneath them a little knotted rug. Under them is another layer of brown paper, and then cast-iron cookware, a skillet, a pot and a kettle, heavily greased against the damp. Rolled and packed in thick layers of brown paper are four more Mason jars, large ones, gurgling full of kerosene. There is a knife with a bone handle. The wooden spoons have not survived; their wood has twisted and cracked with time so they are barely recognizable. Another layer of brown paper and more herbs. Below that, a leather garment and several animal hides have not survived. They are greenish and stiff, and have taken with them a patchwork quilt once stuffed with feathers. That is all for the first chest.

Pan has a small smoldering fire going, more for the comfort of the flames than for any usefulness. "A pity about the quilt," he says from behind me. "I remember it as being a pretty thing. I think it was what they call a Wedding Ring pattern. You would have liked it. But, come, let's get you comfortable."

There is a strange cadence and lilt to his words. I glance up at him, wondering which Pan I am speaking to, mine, or the one who lived here a hundred years ago. He understands my glance for he smiles abashedly. "Returning to a place like this, and finding it so little changed . . . it brings the memories back, so strongly I scarcely know who I am, or when. But then I look at you . . ." His voice trails off and his eyes drop from mine to my belly. When they come back to my face, there is a warmth in them such as I have never seen in a human man's eyes. I could be Helen of Troy, or Eve, or the Earth Mother for the adoration that shines there. "Let's get you comfortable," he says again, and makes the words a promise of Eden.

He tests the ropes on the bed frame, but the old hemp speedily parts. Shaking his head, he discards it onto the fire. "You get out of those clothes and go soak for a bit," he directs me. "I'll make up some kind of a bed for you."

He helps me to my feet. I am staggeringly tired. "I think I'd rather just sleep," I tell him, but he shakes his head.

"Come on," he says softly. He slips an arm around me as he leads me back to the shadowed pool. I am too weary to protest or help as he begins work on my buttons. I take off shirt after shirt, and soon become aware, despite the sulfur smell of the water, that I smell worse. Goose bumps pop up on my skin. While the cave is nowhere near as cold as it is outside, it is still no place to go nude. He skins my jeans down for me, and then drags off my socks as I lift each foot, exclaiming when he comes to the cut on my heel. "That's definitely got to be soaked," he tells me, solicitous as a mother hen. He gestures at the pool.

"It gets deeper, and hotter, quite gradually. Take it slowly," he suggests. And leaves me.

I wade in cautiously, finding it as he says. There is a mineral sediment of some sort on the bottom that I try not to stir up. I wrinkle my nose against the smell. I venture out, into darkness and warmth, feeling the hot water ease the kinks out of my feet and ankles and knees. When I am hip deep, the water is quite warm, almost hot. I sink down slowly, feeling the hot water take the weight of my belly off my spine. For a few moments, I wash myself, scrubbing at my pubic hair and the surprising growth of hair under my arms. My fingers gingerly explore the cut on my heel. Then I plant my palms behind me and lean back against them. I have never known hot water to feel so good. As I become used to the sulfur smell, it becomes almost unnoticeable. Muscles unknot, and the deep cold is driven out of my bones.

I am almost dozing when I feel the water move and hear the light splashes of his passage. Pan sinks down beside me. He sits behind me, bracing me, so I can lean back against him. His wet flesh is warm and firm and his arms come around me securely. His long-fingered hands settle over my belly, caress it possessively. For long moments we are still, and then his strong hands begin to move over me, massaging away the last of the aches. I move back closer into his embrace, only to come up against the jut of his prick against my buttocks. I find myself laughing.

"You're too tired," he says, moving slightly away from me.

"Are you?" I ask him, and my answer is the sudden spice in the smell of his musk as he leans forward and kisses the side of my neck.

"We shouldn't," he says regretfully. "The baby is so large."

But I turn to him and give him a push that inclines his body back into the water. He braces his hands on the pool floor behind him to catch himself, looking startled. I don't give him time to react. I straddle him, grip him, and guide him into me as I settle on him. I realize with surprise that it is the first time I have been so aggressive with him. He seems almost shocked. In the wavering yellow light of the kerosene lamp, his eyes are wide and incredulous. I have to smile and lean forward to kiss his mouth. It is a moment before his lips move under mine, and then he responds almost shyly.

I experiment, taking in only as much of him as is comfortable. Buoyed by the water and astride him, my pregnancy seems small hindrance. A different sort of passion seizes me, and my exhaustion drops away. I am suddenly determined to possess him, to have him as no woman ever has, to his satiation. I lean forward and kiss him, tonguing his mouth open, deliberately pushing his head back into the water, so he must push his mouth back against mine or go under. I use him as I have never used a man, brazenly putting my nipples to his lips, watching them tighten at the touch of his tongue, and then swell. The third time I kiss him, I feel him shudder, and the small echo of it inside me as he pulses to climax.

But I do not release him.

Some demon is on me, some urge, to territoriality, to possession, to dominance, to I know not what. Knee and thigh, I grip him, trapping him inside me. I grab the hair on the back of his head firmly, force his mouth up to mine. I kiss his eyes, taste the side of his throat, bury my nose against his hair and the scent glands at the base of his horns. I bring his mouth up to mine, kiss him deeply. He pulls briefly free of me. "Evelyn?" he says, and there is no disguising that there is an edge of fear to his wondering. An unease. He had thought he knew me.

I had thought I knew me. I was wrong.

"Remember this," I tell him. "For all time and for all children to come." And then his horns become my grips as I guide his mouth to my body. I ride him, through the lapping of warm water and yellow light against our bodies, ride him until I feel him yield his maleness to me twice more. Taking his energy, draining him as surely as a vampire at his throat. And still I hold him, clasped within my thighs and gripped within me, caring nothing for my own orgasm, but taking a different kind of release from his body each time I bring him to climax within me. I feel him trembling slightly beneath me, and I know I am shaking as with a fever. The day has been too long and arduous for any of this, I am hungry and tired and every muscle in my body should be sore and aching. But I do not let him go.

"Evelyn," he says softly, against my throat. "The child," and he is almost pleading.

"I know what I'm doing," I say, and almost, I do, for the firm grip of my thighs on his furred haunches keeps him from penetrating farther than is comfortable for me. I smile down at him, and wonder if the shadows can hide from him the cruelty that I know lurks in my smile. I fear what is driving me, but I cannot deny it. I bend once more to my task, running my hands over his body beneath the water, nuzzling his face, rasping my cheeks and breasts against his beard with animal abandon. He moves against me suddenly, startlingly, and for an instant I think he is struggling to get away. And then I recognize that, no, he is trying to unseat me and mount me again, to be over me once more.

I don't let him. He cannot take me without hurting me, and I know he will not do that. I take his face between my hands, burrowing my fingers through his curly beard, using him as I want to, controlling him, as I move sure and swift atop him, building his passion whether he will or no. He cries out aloud this time as I take him, an animal sound, almost of fear, that escapes past my wet mouth on top of his. I feel the spurt of his seed, hotter than the warm water that laps around us. But it is not that, but the feel of him suddenly flaccid, slipping away from my muscled grip, that brings me to cataclysmic orgasm.

I fall forward atop him, skinning my elbows on the rough stone at the bottom of the pool as we come free of each other. We move apart, both shuddering and panting, to lie back in the warm water. I hear myself mutter something, too soft to be true words, too quiet, not intended for the satyr to hear, and he doesn't. But the sound of them echoes in my own mind, and leaves me aghast.

"I win."

# Twenty-three

I awaken early, before the faun. We are sleeping, belly to belly, with the bulge of his child between us. Our old blankets are a pad beneath us, but the hardness of the rock floor is still very much evident. The thick homespun wool blankets over us smell of the pungent herbs from the chest. The folded rug serves as a sort of pillow. This rudimentary bed is warm, but it cannot begin to explain the immense sense of well-being I have.

I look into his sleeping face. When I study the features, there is something distinctly unhuman about them. Not inhuman. No. It is something, the slight flare of a nostril, the suggestion of a point on the tip of one bared ear, the whiteness of his teeth that show as he breathes through parted lips, something that suggests a closer kinship with the natural world. It is a balanced thing, for even as he can cope more readily with the natural world, he is equally dependent upon its largesse. Like an animal, he alters himself to fit the world rather than alter the world to suit himself. These blankets and the cookware are trappings of humanity that he has assumed for my convenience. Were it not for me, and the child I carry, I doubt he would choose this place to winter. Instead he would depend on his kinship with the natural world to get him through the hard times. That which grows within me, parasitically, will share that kinship. It will be born almost ready for its world, near as capable as any beast, without the long human period of helpless infancy. So he has said.

But whatever he is, beast or man, last night I mastered him. I try to be ashamed of the satisfaction uncoiling within me. I do not understand it, cannot fathom what drove me. Perhaps I had simply been his unquestioning follower too long, and felt driven to assert myself. Perhaps the worship so apparent in his eyes awoke some sadistic taste for mastery in me. Whatever it was, I cannot deny the enjoyment I took of it. He spoke little afterward, but when I came out of the water, he dried my body with one of my T-shirts and then made up a bed for me, tending my needs as if I were a goddess, all with a sort of dark wonder in his eyes. Something had changed between us, but I could not put a name to it.

Watching him sleep, I know my affection for him has not diminished. He is not slave nor pet, nor anything less than what I am myself. What has changed is that I feel strong and competent again. Capable of matching him, and sometimes beating him. Strong on my own, with or without his supporting me. It is a strange thing to base on a sexual victory, but I am obscurely pleased by it. My fingers trace the line of his jaw beneath his beard, and then I drowse back to sleep.

When next I awaken, I am alone. The blankets have been snugged down close around me. I rise, taking one blanket around my shoulders as a sort of cloak, and go looking for him.

The grey light of day reaches into the cave, dispersing its mystery and making it smaller somehow. I can see now that it does not extend much farther back than the farthest reaches of the sulfur spring pool. Already, I am accustomed to the sulfur smell. I notice more pegs driven into the wall, a teetery old bench in a small grotto near the pool, the remains of several rotted barrels, and other minor signs of his housekeeping. The second chest stands open now, contents scattered on the floor. Pan is gone. I go to the lip of the cave and urinate where the moving water will carry it swiftly down the rock face. I look out over the ravine and the far bowl of the valley, but there is no sign of him. All the trees have been dusted with snow, giving the scenery a Christmas card look. More snow will fall today, the grey clouds promise. Shivering, I return to the semiwarmth of the cave.

The second chest seems to have contained hardware of various kinds. There are several small jaw traps on the floor, gleaming with grease. An extra lantern. A stack of thick white lamp wicks wrapped in heavily waxed paper. Hatchet and rough saw. Both of those need new handles. A paper of needles, some of steel and two of bone. Two tin plates, battered but usable. Two wooden bowls, one cracked. A single mug of heavy blue-glazed pottery. A whetstone. And, set aside, on a separate paper, in a box woven of cedar, a string of tiny blue beads, and a handful of drilled shells, and a fine silver ring.

I step back from it, feeling as if I have been reading someone's diary. I suddenly know that whatever satyr lived here was not always alone. It had been made a fit place to bring a human mate. That is why he chose it, why we trekked here. A sudden streak of jealousy chills me. I wonder if this place stirs memories of her for him. Was she dark-skinned and deep-eyed, did her skilled hands weave that box? Or was she some settler's daughter or trapper's widow, stitching the patchwork quilt by the yellow lantern light? And then I smile, wondering if this was what I sensed last night. For I know that last night I marked this place and this satyr, at least, as mine, in a way that will not be forgotten, not to the end of his line.

I pause in that thought, amending it. For the child I carry now will not be marked by that memory. I wonder where the link of memory is forged. Will he remember the moment of his own conception, and then have a blank of six months until his own birth? I will have to ask Pan when he returns. I think of the child having the earliest memories of his mother be of mating with her in a forest glade. It unsettles me for a moment, as I imagine looking into infant eyes and sharing that memory. Then I push it aside. I will ask the faun about it when he returns.

In the meantime, I decide to be domestic. I take every scrap of clothing I own, and the old wool blanket,

and carry them to the sulfur pool. I have no idea what
the mineral water will do to the fabrics, but it can
scarcely make them smell worse or be scratchier. I wade
out with them and dump them in the pool. One at a
time, I slosh and rub them and scrub them out in the hot
water, and then wring them out and drape them as best
I can over the bed frame.

I realize belatedly that I have left myself nothing to
wear. I end up fashioning a very heavy sari from one of
the homespun blankets, and going barefoot on the stony
floor of the cave. It is not too bad. The heat of the spring
keeps the cave at a constant if rather drafty temperature.

I try not to think about how hungry I am getting,
nor that he has been gone longer than he has ever been
gone before. Better to keep busy. I clean the cast-iron
cookwear with hot water and coarse sand from the cave
mouth. I venture out a little farther, to pack the kettle
with clean snow scooped from the jutting rocks just
outside the cave's protective overhang. I am not even
going to sample drinking the sulfur water. I set it in the
cave to melt. And then, although I try not to, I go back
to the cave mouth and look for some sign of his return.

But there is nothing, and nothing for me to do. No
wood for a fire, no food to cook or eat. My clothes are all
still dripping. I'm hungry, chilly, and bored. I think I
should be grateful that today I don't have to face a long
hike, but instead I feel trapped. I go once more to the
cave entrance and look out. Essentially, I've made
myself a prisoner here. I'm certainly not going to cross
that rock face again, not unless I have to. And every day
that my pregnancy grows, the more difficult the crossing
of it will become. So here I am, until my child is born.
His child, I correct myself. And feel a brief flame of
resentment. I try not to think about it.

I decide to remedy the only thing I can. I go back to
the blankets and cuddle into them. My chilled body
gradually warms, and I am actually feeling drowsy when
I hear his hooves on the rocks outside. I scramble up to
meet him, and as he comes into the cave he drops his
burdens and embraces me. His skin is cold to the touch,
hugging him is like hugging winter itself. He steps back

and looks at my naked body gloatingly for a moment, but when he lifts his eyes to mine, I meet his gaze. "My lady," he says, in a voice full of respect and love. I turn aside to keep from blushing, his approving appraisal is that strong. I am suddenly struck by the change in my status, from the Potter family where being Tom's wife and the mother of his child was somewhat akin to being a major appliance, to this cave, where I walk almost as a goddess. A barefoot, pregnant, hungry goddess, perhaps, but worshiped nonetheless.

"I'm sorry I took so long," he tells me. And then, the unnecessary question, "Shall we eat?" He has brought firewood tied in a bundle with a leather strap, and meat, two dead snowshoe hares, almost entirely white. Tied to his back are a number of long, straight sapling trunks.

The long straight poles he sets across two spikes driven into the walls. I busy myself with the fire while he starts skinning and gutting the hares. I notice that this time he uses a knife. He works very competently and quickly, speaking as he works. "I set some snares this morning. Now that we're settled, I'll be able to bring in more food. With a bit of luck, there'll be more by tonight. After we eat, I'll spend some time bringing up firewood for you." He rises and gets the skillet, nods to me that he notices it's been cleaned. He cuts the rabbits into pieces, adds a dribble of snow water, and brings it over to my fire. "There used to be some rocks, ah, yes. Here we go." He arranges three stones in a rough triangle in my fire, sets the skillet atop them. "Now. What's wrong, my love?" he asks gently as he crouches down beside me.

I haven't been aware of it until he asks, and then suddenly I recognize it. "I don't like being this dependent on you," I tell him. "For wood, for food, for everything. It seems I can do nothing for myself up here."

He sets a gentle hand on my belly. "As I depend on you for everything here. As I can do nothing, but take care of you while you do it all. It's the oldest division of labor that exists, my love. Don't demean it. If you do not do one other thing for the next three months, you will still have done what I could not do for myself."

His words do little to assuage the uneasiness I feel. It is too foreign to current thinking, too much Tarzan and Jane, too much "you make baby, I bring food." Not even his total sincerity can change it. He knows that, and gives me a grin that is one part sympathy to one part smart-ass. He knows as well as I do that the only thing I can do is accept the situation. My only real choice is whether or not I'm going to be gracious about it. I decide to be gracious, at least for now, mostly because the simmering meat smells so good that I can't focus my mind on anything else.

While I am poking at the cooking meat, he busies himself with the rabbit skins, scraping every last trace of red meat from them. He leaves them spread out, flesh side up, on the floor. "I'll have to build new stretchers," he comments, as much to himself as me. I can almost feel him remembering another life-style, another life. Another woman? The baby in my belly stirs reassuringly. Not likely.

The rest of the day is spent settling in. He makes several trips to fetch wood, and I build up the fire and manage to dry most of my clothes. When he goes that evening to check his snares, I insist he wear my denim jacket, the only garment I have big enough to contain his shoulders. It looks peculiarly right on him, and I know he is grateful for the warmth it provides, although he would never have asked to use it on his own.

After our evening meal, he settles down to cut the old leather garment from the bottom of the first trunk into long slender strips. These he knots into a rope of sorts, and relaces the old wooden bedstead with it. "Tomorrow," he promises me as he pulls it tight, "I'll bring up young cedar boughs. I think I can make them into a mattress of sorts. Not as soft as a straw tick, but a lot better than the floor."

He rises stiffly from where he has been crouching, and comes to help me tidy things up. There is little to do, really. The pot to wipe out, the fire to bank. Then, attentive as any handmaid, he helps me out of my clothes, clucking over how tight they've become. "Some-how, I'll have to come up with something else for you to wear," he says worriedly. "Something warm and loose."

"It will be fine," I tell him as we walk back toward the pool.

He grins. "You're only saying that because you think I can't contrive it. I'll surprise you yet, my lady."

I have no doubt that he will. We soak together, washing each other companionably. Neither of us speaks of last night's excesses, or makes any move to repeat them. Instead, he towels me off with a T-shirt and escorts me to the blankets. I lie propped on one elbow, watching him sort the things from the second trunk. Some he hangs on pegs on the walls; others he repacks in the trunk. When he comes to the woman's box, he pauses, stirs the trinkets with a long, brown finger. He glances my way, almost apprehensively.

"I don't think I want to know," I tell him, and he smiles a smile that is both wistful and grateful. He carefully fits the lid back on the box, rewraps it in the paper, and sets it back in the trunk.

"The women of my other lives," he tells me as he comes to blow out the lamp and slip into my bed. "One and all, they would have approved of you. One and all." He touches me softly in the darkness, a hand cradling my swollen breast as if he weighed ripe fruit, fingers spreading as he strokes my belly that lies between us. I have to lean far forward over my stomach to kiss him. "You're a wonder," he tells me. "A miracle and a wonder." He pulls me gently over to pillow my head on his shoulder, so my belly rests against him. He places his hand atop the mound of his child possessively. And we sleep.

The days that pass now go like the steady drips of water from the icicles that form at our cave mouth. Each day brings changes as Pan makes every effort to make me comfortable, but the basic routine remains the same. By daylight, he ranges. In the early evening, he brings food and firewood, enough to last until the next evening. There is little variety to the food, mostly meat. He supplements it with nuts stolen from squirrels' caches, frozen berries from thorny tangles, pine nuts, barks for brewing teas. It is adequate, but little more. In the evenings, he kindles the small lamp, and amazes me with the skills of his hands. He makes fresh handles for his tools. He builds a new table, pegging it all together. He builds stretchers for the hides and cures them into leather. From his hands come all manner of small comforts that soften the cave from a shelter to a home. As often as not, he seeks to entertain as much as to be practical. He makes me tops and whistles and jumping jacks, my clothes pegs have faces, the handle of my ladle is as ornate as a carved column. And so pass our evenings.

There are few events to mark one day as different from another. There is the triumphant day he kills a deer, and lugs it, a quarter at a time, up to the cave. It is fat, rich meat, and we feast on it. Some of it he smokes, and some he jerks, and some he simply keeps outside where the glacier now nearly overhangs the cave mouth. The deer hide becomes a part of our bedding, while the rabbit skins become slippers for me. He shows me how to strip the deer sinew into thread. I sew the pelts he takes, mostly rabbit, into a loose sort of gown for myself. Before many days pass, it is almost the only garment I can wear with any comfort. My T-shirts and panties no longer meet over my belly. I wear my rabbit robe fur side in, for the coarse hides otherwise chafe my swollen belly. Socks and rabbit booties complete my outfit. I dare not imagine what I look like. My hair is past my shoulders now, and he revels in combing it for me. I try not to think of what Tom would say if he could see me now, for the thought is oddly painful still. My mind still veers from thoughts of Tom and Teddy. There is healing still to do there, but the time is not yet.

Or so I tell myself, almost every day. When the satyr is gone, the hours are long. There are no books to read, no soaps to watch, no phone to dial, no one to call. I can busy my hands with sewing and woodwork, but my mind still chatters to itself. I play long fantasies of what-if. What-if I had never left Fairbanks, what-if the faun and I had come together this way years ago? What-if

I had never married Tom? Those are the easy ones. But what-if I had stood up to Tom's parents from the very beginning, had never assumed the role they fashioned for me? What-if I had told Tom, well, it was nice visiting, but I've got to get back to my home and job, you just come along when you're ready, dear? These are where they get harder, for in these what-ifs, Teddy does not die. He goes back to Fairbanks with me, and right now we are sitting snug in the cabin together, reading our storybooks, playing Legos, cutting cookies to decorate with raisins and red sugar. These are the what-ifs that can make me pace and weep, and wrap my arms about the unborn child in my belly as if to take some comfort from him.

Only once does Pan catch me so. I will never know what makes him break his routine, but he comes home in early afternoon, comes in soundlessly to stand beside me. I am breathing raggedly, all but cried out, when he puts his arms around me from behind. I do not startle, but turn to his embrace, hide my face on his chest. "I miss him so terribly," I say as he strokes my hair.

"So do I," he says, and that is all. He does not tell me that I will soon have another child to busy me, he does not tell me that Teddy is in heaven with God, he does not attempt to quell my grief in any way. He only holds me and grieves with me. And late that evening, as I am drowsing beneath our blankets, he sets aside the leather he has been softening with tallow, wipes his hands down his hairy thighs, and takes up his pipes.

"If you don't want to hear this, stop me," he says, and lifts them to his lips. His back is to me, and he sits cross-legged before the fire, as I would swear his legs would never bend, but they do. He watches the flames as he plays, and it takes me a while to recognize his song. Then I close my eyes against the sting of tears.

I don't think he can separate the elements. I don't think he perceives them as separate things. So the stream and the saplings, the moss, the frogs, and Teddy are all played as one entity. An image of my child, but filtered through the faun's perceptions. He lingers on the round-calved bare brown legs, on the wet pink toes at first, as if these foreign parts are all important in understanding the boy. I watch Teddy as through a screen of foliage, glimpse him in bits. I hear bits of my own song wind through his, and a deep subdued cadence that briefly echoes Tom before Teddy's song suddenly emerges, distinct and whole. I hear him not as Teddy my child, but as Teddy the satyr's friend. The song is as much Pan's delight in this small human creature as it is Teddy in the forest. Their boats go whirling down the sparkling stream, they pelt each other with oak balls, they doze like lizards in the sun. The pipes stop abruptly. My faun drops them beside him and suddenly leans his face forward into his hands. It is some moments before he speaks, and when he does, his voice is calm with a sort of deadness. "I think that's all I'll play just now," is all he says.

He blows out the light quickly, and comes to me in the dark like a small child fleeing nightmares. He is shivering as he burrows in beside me. I kiss the dampness on his cheek and then set his hands atop my stomach. His son kicks and squirms reassuringly beneath his touch. It is the only comfort I can offer him or myself.

And so the days go. Winter lies white on the valley below. Some days I stand and peer out, learning to mark the passage, white on white, of the rabbits. Occasionally I spot deer on the flanks of other mountains, and once I think I see a cross-country skier. I slip quickly back into the cave, heart pounding, disconcerted at just how alien a figure he appeared in my landscape.

But mostly the days are counted by the turning of the babe within me. He knobs a knee down my rib cage, rattling me like a boy rattles a stick along a picket fence. He butts and squirms and crowds me, and grows larger almost visibly. It distresses me that I cannot guess a due date, that I have no calendar to tell me when the child will emerge from my body and into my arms. Pan is no help, he can only shrug. He keeps no calendar finer than the seasons. "When it's time, he'll be born," is all he can say, and looks perplexed that I would ask. As soon ask what day the river will thaw, or the first leaves unfurl. When the time is right, it will happen.

He seems very calm about it all. Possibly I would be, too, except that his hunting and trapping are taking him farther and farther afield each day. There comes a time when he does not return one afternoon, nor that evening. I lumber up and down the length of the cave and worry, wondering about lynxes and bears, avalanches and broken ice on frozen lakes. I sleep but fitfully, hoping to hear the tap of hoof on stone even as I pray he will not be so foolish as to try to make the climb in the dark. Morning finds me sandy-eyed and weepy, wondering if I am condemned to starve to death in a cave, or risk my life clambering down. I am sure some accident has befallen him. Once more my total dependency on him is brought home with shattering force. I pace and curse my foolishness in ever letting myself be put in such a position. My fears for him turn into a raging anger that he would endanger me and the child so, by putting me where I cannot fend for myself.

But by the time he does return, I have come full circle and can only think of him injured and freezing. He seems shocked at my yelp of greeting, and cannot seem to understand my terrors. I do manage to extract from him a promise that the next time he knows he will be gone overnight, he will let me know.

As the slow, snowy days wear on, the overnight absences become the rule rather than the exception. More and more, I am left on my own, to my own devices. I learn to whittle and carve, to play the pipes he makes for me, to busy myself in all sorts of ways. Our bed has a coverlet of fur patchwork now, and our table a full complement of wooden bowls and utensils. My hands acquire new calluses even as my belly acquires new stretch marks. My pregnancy is immense, and still I do not know when the child will come.

A thick snow is descending on our valley the morning he comes back after a four-day absence. He is wearing an old army surplus backpack that clanks when he sheds it by the entrance. A gallon can of kerosene is cradled in his arms. I know we have been getting low; I suspect this is what he went searching for. Snowflakes cluster thick on his hair and his skin is cold when I embrace him. His eyes are dancing when he steps back from me. "See what I've brought you," he tells me. "While I go soak the cold from my bones."

I drag the pack in by the fire, marveling at its weight. "Where did you get it?" I call back to him.

"Trapper's cabin," he replies.

"Oh," I say, and think how a few months ago I would have thought him a thief. But somehow his attitude to property is contagious, and I now see it as he does, as simple as finding fruit under a tree or eggs under a hen. Taking what you need from the world.

I undo the straps from the pack, tumble its contents on the floor. In it are luxuries beyond measure. Fat cans of evaporated milk, red-and-white labeled cans of vegetable soup. Two towels. A plastic bag of raisins. These I tear open immediately, and chew on a handful as I continue sorting the treasure. A half-full sticky jar of honey. A bag of Oreo cookies. There is more, so much I can hardly comprehend it. All the wonders of white sugar and chemical preservatives. How I have missed them!

I take the bag of raisins with me, and go back to perch on the edge of the sulfur pool and watch him. He is soaking, lying back with only his head out of the water. He looks very tired. "You shouldn't take chances like that," I tell him, even as I munch the raisins.

"I'm careful," he tells me. "And I make sure I create no ill will. I had two fine foxes in my snares, of small use to us. But I left them frozen by his door. The pelts will bring more than ever the food cost him."

The words are hardly out of his mouth when the first spasm hits me. It is so unexpected, I cannot even make a sound. I am grateful that I am sitting down, for this would have felled me. When it passes, all I can do is pant. "Something's wrong!" I manage to call out to him, and then almost immediately another flexing of muscle seizes my body. He is by me instantly, dripping warm water, eyes huge. He starts to put his hands on me, then draws back.

It passes, a lifetime later. "This isn't normal," I wail when I can. "This can't be right. I'm going to lose the baby, this doesn't feel right at all. It's not like the last time."

"No," he agrees, "it's not normal. Not like you were having a child of your own. But I think it is how it is when you bear one of my kind."

The thought is not reassuring. Nor is the fear in his face. "I don't dare move you back to our bed. Lie still. I'll bring blankets and such to you."

He darts away as the third wave hits me. And that is what it is like, a wave of muscle contraction that seizes my whole torso and contorts it. That is all the pain of childbirth is, anyway. The pain of overworked muscles. I prattle to myself reassuringly. Not that bad, I tell myself. Just imagine making a fist. There is no strain to that. But imagine lifting your hand over your head, and making a fist as tight as you can, and holding it for a minute. Do it a hundred times. Imagine your hand doing it even when your mind is telling you that your muscles and nerves can't do it anymore. That's what your stomach feels like during childbirth. Endless muscular effort that you are powerless to stop. That's how I was with Teddy, but I was strong and healthy. I never even screamed until the last three contractions.

But this is more like being run over by a steamroller, and on the next contraction, I wail out my breath like a dying teakettle. Pan is trying to put a cushion of blanket under my head, but I flail at him. "Don't touch me," I gasp when I can. "Don't move me at all."

He retreats, eyes huge and pained. He watches me as I convulse with the muscular effort, and covers his ears when I scream. The sudden onset of this labor has taken me completely by surprise. There is no easing into it, no gradual reduction of the minutes between each contraction, no slow building of the strength of each succeeding contraction. No, this is more like electroshock than any natural bodily process. I am already sweating and shaking, and I do not object when he ventures to cut my loose fur robe free of my body. I barely get my arms out of the sleeves before another tsunami of tightening ripples over my body.

This time, in addition to my belly tightening, I feel

myself start to dilate, an aching, stretching sensation in my groin. It's happening too fast, all of it. The human body is not made to take this. I imagine my flesh tearing, imagine bleeding to death here in this cave, or dying of some childbed infection or fever afterward. Suddenly I long for hospitals and white-gowned doctors and bright lights in my eyes. That was how it was when Teddy was born. Tom had insisted on a hospital. He had wanted to make sure it was done right, as if I were a tricky engine that needed a special type of overhaul. I clearly remember how competently the nurses ran my labor, how coolly they inserted their fingers into me to measure degrees of dilation, how they listened to the baby's heartbeat and took my blood-pressure and offered me sips of ice water. And later, the culmination, on my back on a hard bed, my bare feet up in cold metal stirrups as I stared up into a white light that was supposed to be angled so it wouldn't bother me. As the nurse gently tied my feet to the supports with gauze, she explained how it was so I wouldn't inadvertently kick out at the doctor during a contraction. And as she tied my wrists down to the gripping handles, so I wouldn't flail around, I looked at Tom's white face through the window of the delivery room and wondered. My knees were draped with a white sheet, so I couldn't see a damn thing. Odd sort of modesty, don't let the woman have to look at her own shaved pubis, don't let her see the bloody little skull pushing its way out. Judging from the way Tom's face looked, I wouldn't have wanted to see what was happening. Trussed on a table like a Thanksgiving turkey, with the doctor so earnestly busy between my legs, extracting my baby as if it were a choice morsel of sage-and-onion stuffing. Nurses hovering, pumping up the blood pressure sleeve on my arm, telling me when to breathe and when to hold my breath, when to push and when not to push.

I blink, and I am back in a cave that smells of sulfur, and the only aid I have is a satyr that keeps circling me like a vulture watching a dying cow. "Help me!" I beg him, and see the sudden tears spring to his eyes.

"How?" he asks, and I have no answer. I reach a

hand to him, and he comes to take it, holding it between both of his own. I clutch it as another contraction rages through me.

"Can you see him yet?" I ask desperately, thinking that if it hurts this bad, the baby must be born soon. He moves to where he can look down at me, then raises his eyes to meet mine. He shakes his head slowly.

It is only the beginning. My body battles itself, uterine muscles straining to push a child out through a cervix that is not dilated enough yet. Long after my mind has surrendered, the struggle goes on. I become no more than a tormented observer. There is nothing I can do for myself, and little he can do to ease me. From time to time he brings me sips of cool water. At one point I become aware that he is gently wiping my face with a dampened towel. I shift, I try different positions, on my side, on my back, and once I even try to stand or crouch, as if gravity can help me birth this child. But I don't have the strength for that, my shaking legs give out on me, and I sprawl over onto the blankets he has spread beside me.

Nothing in my life has prepared me for this. I pass into a sort of waking nightmare. In between contractions, I have flashes of memory, vivid as hallucinations. I have long since closed my eyes to the cave and the faun, I am alone in this anyway. There is only me, and the baby struggling inside me. I can feel his movements growing ever feebler, but I cannot find a way to tell Pan this. In truth I do not even think of telling him, it seems to have nothing to do with him. There is only the child and myself, trapped in this body that will no longer hold both of us. Something has to give.

And so the contractions squeeze me, robbing me of breath and thoughts. Screams give way to hoarse cries, and finally to a simple gasping as the muscles drive the air from my body. And in between, the vivid images that have nothing to do with this labor. A memory of yellow birch leaves with delicately serrated edges outlined against an impossibly blue Fairbanks autumn sky. Four blue robin's eggs in a nest. The way Rinky's choke chain felt in winter when he came in, icy cold against my hands in contrast to the ever-warm fur of his throat. Teddy laughing up at the Christmas tree when I plug it in. Tom trying to get the wood stove going with too much newspaper and too little kindling. My mother smiling as she cuts through the cap of a mushroom to show me the white flesh inside. The sudden smell of wisteria blossoms in a long-lost summer.

My water breaks in a gush against my thighs, and I can only think, it's taken this long, and I'm only that far? But the smell of the amniotic fluid is like a catalyst for the satyr. He comes to crouch between my legs. He puts his hands on my raised knees, steadying them without restraining me. "Not much longer," he tries to tell me. We both know he is lying.

But his hands on my knees give me something to buck against, and I start to lift my upper body, curling with each contraction. It seems I struggle against him for hours. He leaves me only once, to go to light the lantern and bring it back. It is my only measure of how much time has passed. He sets it a good distance away from me, for fear we will overturn it, and resumes his post. During the next contraction, he lifts a cautious hand, but does not touch me. "I think I saw something," he whispers. I don't dare believe him.

But on the next contraction, I feel the head moving down the channel, I know it will be soon. He seems so still within me that I know sudden fear, and push as hard as I dare, adding my will to the failing strength of my muscles.

"I do see him!" the satyr yelps, and so his child is born, in the next seven contractions. The head emerges, and turns and Pan reaches to support him, I feel his fingers brush my flesh. Then the shoulders are sliding out, and suddenly I can take no more, and heedless of tearing or pain, I curl my body and push, push violently, even past the contraction, expelling this tiny foreigner from my body. Pan catches him and lifts him down to rest on the blanket between my legs.

"He's born," I gasp.

"Yes," says his father.

And we both listen to the awful silence. It stretches

long, and I am too cowardly to ask. It lasts past the contraction that ejects the placenta in a liverish mass. I see Pan dip his head to sever the cord with his white teeth. I am too exhausted to feel, but the tears sting my eyes. I know without being told, without having to see it for myself. It's all, all of it, been for nothing. But I have to hold him, however briefly.

"Give him to me," I beg him, and the satyr lifts his child, delicate goat legs adangle, and sets him in the crook of my arm.

"He's beautiful," says his father, and the sudden snuffling the baby makes as he scents me is the most beautiful sound I've ever heard. He is beautiful and perfect and alive, so lively. But silent, as so many things born into the wild must be. No lively wailing for this woodland child, to betray his new life to lurking predators. I clutch him to me, slippery yet with my own blood. My hands are shaking, I am so cold suddenly after my long sweaty exertions, but I am grinning, grinning like a fool as I shiver and shake with the child in my arms.

He is incredible. His face is Pan's face, but with a soft unfinished look. There is already a thatch of curls on his head. They do no cover the bony whorls that are the forerunners of his horns. He is already nuzzling and lipping after my breast, and I set him to it. I try to cradle his sleek little legs, but he kicks out fiercely, tiny pink hooves and all. Already he is stretching and limbering those muscles. I end up with him more tucked under one arm than cradled on his back. Already I know that he dislikes being held with his legs folded, and that he is uncomfortable nursing on his back. But we will adapt to each other, we two.

Then Pan is back suddenly, tucking a dry blanket around us both. Belatedly I realize that the one beneath us is soaked through. "Can you move?" he asks me anxiously.

"I don't know," I reply, but I find I can rise. He is right beside me, supporting the baby worriedly with one arm and putting the other around my shoulders. We totter the length of the cave to where the bed is made up with the fur coverlet, and he eases me down under it. I feel no self-consciousness as he folds a towel between my legs to catch the flow of blood before he tucks a blanket around us both. He kisses us both, and then goes to tidy up. The baby has never relinquished the nipple. Now he does, grunting with displeasure that as of yet there is very little milk. I transfer him to the other breast, feel him suckle and then doze off, the nipple still in his mouth.

I listen wearily to the sounds of Pan washing out the blankets and then hanging them on a makeshift line strung across the cave. It will take them at least two days to dry, I think irritably. Then he is back, bringing the lantern and its yellow circle of light. He sets it on the floor by our bed, muting its glow, and crouches beside me. He looks tousled and exhausted, as awful as I feel. He sets a gentle hand on his son's head in a benediction, but removes it when the baby snorts irritably. His eyes are full of wonder and tears. He turns his eyes to mine, and for a long time there is nothing we need to say. I feel sleep creeping up on me. The baby is warm against me, my belly is loose and empty. I am alone in my body again.

I am almost asleep when he says, "I have to know. What was it like, bearing my child?"

I search for a simile, but can find nothing that is both dignified and accurate. I am too tired to edit my thoughts. "Imagine," I say. "Imagine shitting a ten-pound octopus. Head first."

He is still giggling as I spiral down into sleep.

# Twenty-four

And baby makes three.

And total chaos out of what was our orderly lives. His waking and sleeping becomes our only clock. Time is not measured in days or weeks, but in the wonders of each new thing he does.

In odd ways, he is more animal than child, and strangely, this makes him easier to care for. He needs no diapering, for he instinctively does not soil his resting place. His waste is inoffensively pelleted anyway, easy to sweep out of the way and over the lip of the cliff face. He does not cry, nor make much sound of any kind. His skin darkens for the first few days of his life, as if he is a developing photograph, until he is nearly as dark as his father. Camouflage, I realize, as important as his silence. A pink-skinned bawling baby could not lie hidden among leaves and brush. As he stretches his hind legs and practices vigorous kicks, I realize how much longer he is than a human child, and wonder at how he ever folded up to fit inside me. He nurses vigorously and often, looking all the while up into my face with intelligent, wondering eyes. Between feedings, he usually sleeps. At least, so he does for the first week.

Pan assures me this is normal. It does not stop him, however, from waking his son simply to hold him and look down into his face. And when the baby dozes off again, he does not put him down, but continues to hold him, as if he is too great a marvel to set aside. It is good we have smoked and dried meat, for he is reluctant to leave and hunt. We vary the meat with the loot from the trapper's cabin, and it seems like a week-long celebration of the birth, as I taste food long absent from my diet.

But after the first week, things change even more rapidly. Pan has warned me, but I am still unprepared for how quickly this infant masters his body. His neck has never been as weak and wobbly as a human infant's. From the moment of his birth, his back has seemed stronger, his ability to control his own body greater. On the ninth day after his birth, I awaken to find the baby, under his father's watchful eyes, making a concerted effort to stand. His small fists grip his father's fingers as he strives to bring his goat legs under his body, and then to drive his weight up. Pan has put down hides on the hard cave floor, to cushion any falls. I remain in our bed, watching quietly.

His little son looks up into his face so trustingly as he grips each of Pan's forefingers. His eyes are a very deep blue, already starting to darken to brown. He rests most of his weight on his grip, while his goat legs shift restlessly under him. His tiny hooves splay wide, and all his joints seem to give too much as he fights to get his legs under his weight. For an instant he achieves it, and pushes up on his small pink hooves, and staggers a step as he grips his father's fingers. Pan's face breaks from his intent seriousness to a warm smile. The baby opens his mouth in a silent laugh. And then his weight sags again as he oversteps, and has to catch himself, with a bob and a bow, on his grip. Patiently he begins again to maneuver his feet under him.

I have not made a sound, but somehow Pan knows I am awake and watching him. "It won't be long now," he says, speaking softly so as not to startle the child.

I arise, moving carefully, and come to sit on the floor beside them. I am still stretched and saggy, achy and creaky, but surprisingly that seems to be the extent of my complaints. There is much less pain than I suffered when healing from the incision and stitching the doctor did on me when Teddy was born. I feel only overtired, as if I have hiked too far. But it is a good kind of weariness.

Watching Pan with his son, I feel mildly jealous. When Teddy was this small, he was mine entirely. Oh, Tom was a dutiful father, changing diapers and holding his son whenever he was asked. But he never had the possessiveness that Pan has. There is a look on his face whenever he holds his son, a hard shine of triumph. Whatever else he may do in his life, he has accomplished this; his line, his memories, his life, will go on. Another link has been forged in the chain. The intensity with which he looks into the baby's face seems to awaken in those wide eyes an answering fire. I feel excluded when he is with the child like this, as if they are communicating on levels I will never share.

The moment the baby sees me, a different kind of light comes into his eyes. He lets go of his father's fingers and takes two staggering steps, to fall into my arms. Heedless of his tumble, he is already plucking eagerly at the front of my shirt as I arrange him in my lap. He clutches at my swollen breasts through the fabric of my shirt as I struggle with the buttons. I free myself from his pinching grip and bare a breast, only to have him butt against me and then abruptly seize the nipple. He sucks strongly. I feel the aching rush of milk into my breasts and then the relief as he draws it out. My uterus contracts almost in rhythm with his sucking, still shrinking back to normal size. As always, it strikes me as a strange bodily connection. Milk from my other breast leaks freely and runs down my chest. Pan grins sympathetically as he hands me a towel to mop up the flow.

"You know," I say between gritted teeth, "you always think of a mother's breasts as being soft. Mine are rock hard when they're full of milk." Already the baby's eager suckling has taken down the pressure and weight of my left breast. Despite his protests and wriggling, I switch him to the other side, breathe a sigh of relief as he resumes nursing and the pressure on that breast eases also. I look up to find Pan staring admiringly at my breasts. "I don't know why I'm producing so much milk. There's enough here for triplets," I complain embarrassedly. But secretly I am as pleased as he is at how well my body is coping with this child, at the plenty I can provide for him. There is a sense of richness in being all he needs.

Pan moves around behind me, so I can lean back into his arms. I rest in his embrace as his child suckles. The baby's eyes are wide as his gaze wanders from my face to his father's and back again. He has the same disconcerting gaze that Teddy had as an infant, a look that makes me want to turn my head and look behind me, to see what he is staring through me to see. I look deep into his eyes and ask Pan, "How much does he know, right now? I mean, when does he start remembering?"

Pan speaks softly, right by my ear. "Right now? Only about as much as a human child. Oh, he's stronger and has better physical control. But that's what these early days are mostly given to: getting control of his body. In a few more weeks, when he's tripping around here, he'll start remembering the basic things. You know, fire's hot, water is to drink, that sort of thing. But right now, everything is so new that he knows little more than that when he is in your arms, he's warm and safe and has plenty to eat. That's all he knows," Pan croons as he leans past me to run a finger down his son's cheek. "But it's enough for now and for all time."

Surprisingly, the baby smiles, a toothless grin that lets milk trickle freely from the corners of his mouth.

"Are you going to name him?" I ask shyly.

He folds me a little closer in his arms. "He and I are solitary creatures. When he is older, and on his own, he will have no more use for a name than I do. I never had one, you know, until you started calling me Pan. And that sound is like an echo of an echo down the years, a name given to one of us, sometime back then, and shared by all of us since. But"—his breath tickles my ear—"I know you are tired of calling him baby or child. So name him. Give him something now, from you, to carry to the end of his days."

I take a breath, hesitating. He has a name already, the name I have been calling him in my mind, since the first morning I looked down into his face. "Avery," I whisper, looking into his deep gaze. And am rewarded with another toothless smile.

"Of the elves?" Pan asks, slightly perplexed.

"I've always loved the name. But it isn't one you can give to a child that must go to school and endure the teasing of other children. But it's a fine name for a boy who lives in the forest."

"Avery," Pan says, trying it on his tongue. "Avery. There's an echo of you in that. Evelyn Sylvia. Avery. I like it. I have a son named Avery." His finger reaches again, traces his son's features, and then trails up the mound of my breast. "Do you know, this is the most beautiful I have ever seen you? And I think this will be the most perfect moment in my life, no matter how long I live."

His words make a little shiver down my spine.

The season rounds the corner and we do not even notice it, so engrossed are we in Avery. The soft tack, tack, tack of his hooves follows me throughout the cave as he takes a great interest in everything I do. His father's arrival is always greeted with a sudden clattering rush as he scampers to be the first to touch him. He is amazingly spry and surefooted. His round baby belly thrusts out in front of his tiny legs, and it seems it should overbalance him, but his smooth-skinned back is arrow-straight, and his chubby little arms swing a counterbalance.

He is a quiet child, and makes no speech sounds at all. But this does not mean he isn't active. Whatever work is done, his small hands find their way into it. Pan horrifies me one evening by giving an exasperated sigh as Avery's fingers once more grip the piece of wood he is shaping. "Brat!" he tells his son, and rises to go to the chest against the wall. He returns with an extra knife, which he calmly hands to Avery along with a chunk of wood.

"He'll cut himself," I exclaim, but Pan shakes his head.

"No. He just needs to find out that he can't do it quite yet," he tells me. Sure enough, Avery sits down with his block of wood and knife. Chubby little fingers cannot quite close around the handle of the knife, and when he presses it to the wood, the blade has no force behind it. After a few frustrated minutes, he sets it down, to come and lean against me and tug at my shirtfront. I sit down cross-legged and back straight on the floor so he can lean against me like a punk leaning on a lamppost while he nurses. I circle him with my arm. His tail flicks eagerly while he suckles, just like a lamb's, and his hooves shift restlessly. He watches my face with calm intelligent eyes.

"He's already remembering things like how to carve wood?" I ask Pan.

He shrugs, still busy with his task. "Not really. More like the shadow of a shadow. He thinks he knows something about what I'm doing, it's like an itch at the back of his mind, so he has to put his hands on it and try it. He'll be doing a lot of things like that. Sort of fumbling his way along, and then one day, a few years from now, he'll pick up the knife and put it to the wood and remember how it's done. Or how to shape pipes. Or how to talk with words. Or"—he glances up at me and smiles—"just what it is that makes women so dizzyingly wonderful."

Pan is right. As the weeks progress, Avery continues to grow at a prodigious rate. As my milk is his sole food, I find myself eating twice as much as I ordinarily would. His growth and abilities parallel that of a calf or chimp of two months more than that of a human child. Hoof and hand, he is agile. He begins to do things, spontaneously. To feed the fire, to make himself a nest of blankets when he is chilled, to play in the water of the pool and the shallow trickling stream that spills from it. To venture out onto the rocks at the mouth of the cave.

I am terrified the first time I find him there. I pick him up despite his squirming and bring him back inside. I give him bowls and cups and spoons to play with instead. Then I go back to the lip of the cave, to see if there is any way I can barricade it, make it safer. Instead, I find myself looking out over the valley.

Snow still lies heavy down there, but the day is slightly above freezing. The glacier icicles that overhang the cave glisten as they drip steadily. The rock under my feet is wet with more than the slow run of sulfur water. Farther down the mountains, it is spring already, and the river of ice that grips this mountainside is once more beginning its slow running. The snow on the valley, once so smooth, has sunken spots in it at the bases of the trees and bushes, where the darker bark has gathered the paltry warmth of the sun and is melting it. Spring. Back on the farm, the fields will be tilled smooth and fur-rowed. The lawn will need its first cutting. I wonder if Tom has filed for divorce yet, if it will be done in Washington or Alaska. I wonder if the land up in Alaska and the cabin on it belong to me, or if he has followed his lawyer's advice and sold it while I'm not around to contest it. I wonder why I care about any of that.

I hear the clatter of small hooves on the rock behind me and turn to find Avery has ventured out again. I reach to gather him up, but he skips nimbly away. Before I can reach again, he trots over to the cliff's edge, casually leans out and looks over. My heart is in my mouth. The rock there is wet with runoff over a winter's layer of smoothed ice. I cannot imagine a more slippery surface. "Avery," I call softly. He turns to look at me calmly but makes no move to come back. I crouch down to be on his level. "Lovey, come here," I say, opening my arms to him. He gives me a baby smile, then looks back out over the cliff again. I am starting to shiver, and not from cold. "Avery," I call again, and this time when he looks at me, I open my shirt. At the sight of my breasts, his little tail begins flicking happily. He clatters over to me, and is shocked when I snatch him up in my arms and carry him back into the cave. Once there, I release my squirming burden, and sit on the floor to allow him to nurse. We are still there when Pan comes in.

"We've got to do something about the cliff," I blurt

out as soon as he steps inside. "Avery went right out by the edge today. Scared me to death."

"That bold already?" Pan asks consideringly. He sets down the grouse he has brought in, looks at his son appraisingly. "I think it's okay," he judges. "He's about the right age to start exploring. Maybe tomorrow I'll take him with me."

I stare at him incredulously, and then take a new look at the child who stands and leans against me. It suddenly strikes me how physically mature he is. If someone had presented me with this creature a year ago, I would have guessed his human age at almost a year. It is not his size, but his muscular development and coordination. "Are you sure he'll be safe?" I ask anxiously.

It is Pan's turn to look incredulous. "He'll be with me, won't he?" he asks rhetorically, and then adds, in an undertone, "It is time he started to spend more time with me, anyway."

"And less with me?" I ask, swiftly hurt.

"Evelyn." He pauses, gestures helplessly. "I must teach him, must show him the ways, so he can survive. I am taking nothing from you. I am only giving to him what he must have."

I nod slowly. But it takes a direct act of my will for me to set the hurt aside.

That night there is further indication of his rapid growth, when Pan offers him a meaty drumstick from the grouse. Avery accepts it eagerly, and works his gums against the tough meat and bone with a vigor that suggests teeth on the way. After a few minutes of gumming, he discards it in frustration, and comes to lean against me and casually help himself to chunks of softer food from my bowl. The simple sight of him eating solid food elicits an unexpected pang from me. He is no longer solely dependent on me for nourishment. Already my satyr child is growing away from me.

He has always slept between us since he was born. During the first days of his life, I saw him as a link between Pan and me. That night, when we all lie down together, I suddenly feel him as a barrier.

Pan has touched me often since Avery was born, with love and affection and tenderness. He strokes my hair, caresses my shoulder in passing, puts his arms around me and holds me gently while he talks to me. But of his merry lust, there has been no sign. It has been several months at least since the child was born. Of this I am certain, though I have long since abandoned any attempt to keep track of days or months. Surely, it is safe now to "resume a normal marital activity pattern" as the doctor so genteelly put it after Teddy was born. After I have suckled the child to sleep, I lie awake, looking at Pan over his son's head. Firelight plays over his features, touching him brown and gold. He seems to be deeply and comfortably asleep. But I want him suddenly, not out of any physical lust, but simply to reaffirm that other bond between us, the one that is between us two alone and is independent of this child I have borne him.

So I slip my arm clear of the sleeping Avery, and softly say, "Pan?"

He does not move. I reach past the baby to tousle the curls of his head. His eyes open, instantly animal alert. I say nothing, but only look into his face. After a moment he lifts one eyebrow, almost in surprise. Then he slips quietly from his side of our bed. He takes the fur spread from the bed, being careful not to disturb Avery. I climb over the baby carefully, and make sure the blankets are close around him before following Pan deeper into the cave, back near the pool where the rising warmth of the water is greater and the shadows deeper.

He has already spread the fur coverlet on the stones there. I come to him, stepping into his arms. For a moment I feel inexplicably awkward, as if he is a stranger. I lift my mouth to be kissed, hoping it will dispel the sudden shyness I feel. He kisses me, as gently and warmly and deeply as ever. My strangeness starts to melt away and I feel the stirrings of arousal. I run my hands up and down his back, over the familiar ridges and planes of his musculature, and think how good it is to be able to once more stand this close to him with no intervening belly, how good to be able to make love freely and vigorously, unimpeded by pregnancy.

His kiss becomes warmer as he draws me against him, and I feel the jut of his penis against my belly. But I am also aware, too aware, of the hairiness of his legs against mine, of the track of his fingers down my belly, of his other hand in the small of my back, pressing me close. It's all good, and right, and the warmth is building inside me, but something is missing, something is wrong. "What's wrong?" I ask him softly when his mouth leaves mine. For an instant, he stands very still, as if listening. Then he folds me closer in his arms, holds me as if he wants to draw me into his very body.

"Don't worry," he says huskily. "It will be all right. I'll make sure it's all right. Always. Just trust me. Let me touch you."

And I do. His hands move slowly and carefully in intricate patterns, as if he is tattooing my body with his love. His mouth is warm and wet, his tongue sly and knowing. When he gently pushes me down to the furs and mounts me, I am panting with the frenzy of my arousal, I strain him against me and try to drown my knowledge in the sheer sexual sensation of him. But he is unrelenting in his expertise. He plays me as if I were his pipes, sounding note after note of touch upon my body, until I would swear that his lovemaking is something I can hear, that our bodies are moving only to the music he creates from our flesh. He satisfies me and leaves me limp with the totality of my satisfaction.

But I am not fooled.

When all is quiet between us and our bodies have cooled enough that we are once more lying close together, I make so bold as to ask him. "What happened?"

"We had a child," he says. His voice is factual in the darkness, not hard. Perhaps I am only imagining the pang of loss in it. "We fulfilled our purpose."

"I don't understand," I say, and try to keep the tremble out of my voice.

"After the fruit is fertilized, the flower and the nectar are no longer necessary. The tree drops them."

In the darkness his grip on my shoulders tightens briefly, as if to ease his words. My head has been resting on his shoulder. Now I nestle my face into the angle of

his throat and chin. I kiss his neck. I smell only sweat,
taste only salt. He smells good, clean, an honest sweat,
but the spiciness of his musk, the wonderful sweetness of
his skin, is gone. The lure is no longer needed, and his
body has discarded it. He seems to sense my conclusion.

"Is it so bad, my love?"

I don't answer his question, but ask, "When will it
come back? How long does it take?"

He sighs. "It doesn't come back. That part is done
between us. Now we must love as your kind do, staging
our arousals, planning our touches, thinking of our
conclusions. It is a different kind of mating, that which
humans do. But I think we shall still be good together.
Don't you?"

"Why doesn't it come back?" I feel cold as I ask it. I
can sense I am on the trail of something, I am getting
close, I am tugging on the door of what he would just as
soon keep hidden. But I have to know. His silence seems
longer than darkness.

"Because that sweetness is only once," he says
finally. "That headiness is for the making of the child.
Not all human females would welcome the touch of a
beastman like myself. There has to be, for them, a
persuasion, a compulsion."

"Rape by overpowering sensuality," I say into the
dark.

"For some, it might happen that way," he admits
unwillingly. "For some women, that is the only way they
would come into the arms of a faun, lured by bodily
scents and cues, intellect drowning in instincts. But not
you, my love. Never you. Had I been as scentless as
stone, as shy in my lovemaking as a young human, still
you would have come to me. We were always your
decision. You came into my woods, my love, not I into
your garden."

Stillness wraps us both. He is right. Even without
the sweet scent of him, I would have come to him. I
would have borne his child.

"But why?" I have to ask. "Why does it have to go
away?"

"Because it is a lure for the making of a child," he

replies patiently. "And that can only happen once between us."

"Not necessarily. I'm young still, I'm fertile. This wasn't easy, Pan, but it didn't kill me. A year or so, and then . . ."

"Never again." Soft finality.

"But why?"

"Your body would not be tricked so easily again, is what I suspect. I don't really know. I only know my seed will never take root in you again. It's something about our bodies, about the way my kind uses your kind. A biological thing."

I am quiet a long time, thinking. "Like an Rh factor?" I ask finally. "Where the first child may be born okay, but succeeding ones . . ."

"I don't know. It may be something like that. Perhaps an immunity of some sort. All I know is that your body will not be fooled again into nurturing my seed. And my body will not waste energy attempting to lure yours."

His voice is so calm, so matter-of-fact. I think of what has been lost to us and feel newly expelled from Eden. Sex with him had been so easy. I had never been too tired, never not wanted him when he wanted me. I had never wondered if I would reach orgasm, never wondered if he would finish too soon for me, never wondered if he touched me a certain way for his own pleasure or for mine. Never wondered if he was imagining another in my place. Never wondered if he was holding back, waiting like a gentleman for me to finish first. In his wonderful scents, we had mated as simply as animals, free of the courtesies and questions of human matings. Until this moment, I had never realized how much I resented the uncertainty of sex with Tom. He had always made me aware of the mechanics of arousal, always asking me, "Do you like this?" "Do you mind if I do this?" I don't want clever skills and tricky maneuvering of bodies. I want it back the way we had it before, when I never thought about it at all. It had all been perfect, choreographed by nature and chemistry. I feel cheated for it to be gone.

"That's all it was, then," I ask him, trying to sound as calm as he has. "Biology? Pheromones? Chemistry? Instinctive courtship behavior?"

"You know better," he rebukes me.

I am quiet for a minute. I do know better. But I want an excuse to argue and cry. If he were Tom, I think, we would have a fight now. This would turn into an argument, and old hurts would get dragged into it, and we'd both drop off to sleep wounded, and store the pain as ammunition for another day.

But it's not Tom. And if I have learned nothing else from the goatman, I have learned this. I can let a quarrel go, let it die unborn. Because I know he's right, that there is more to us than biological urges and lures. I will miss the biological magic, the simplicity it brought to our love. But I know he is as regretful about it as I am. And because I know I can simply say to him, "It makes me want to weep."

"Weep, then," he tells me, very gently. "I won't love you any less for it."

His words take away the need for tears. Instead, I suddenly want to be back in our bed now, with his baby.

Click.

"It's the way he smells to me, isn't it?" I ask of the darkness. "That's what makes me love him so."

His chuckle is rich and sweet as chocolate. "I thought it was only me. Is he affecting you that way, too?"

I cannot share his humor. "Then I'm being manipulated by his scent as well?"

In the darkness he rolls to face me. "Do you remember that first day, with Teddy by the stream? I stood over him and looked down on him and thought, this is what it is that keeps her away from me. Not the man, but this child. And in that moment, I could have wished him harm. I know you sensed it, the territorial urge of males, kill the intruder's young and take his females. Except for the warm scent that rose from him. The scent of a young thing, an innocent thing, a thing to be protected. The young manipulate us all, my love. Why else do you think there are dogs that raise kittens, pigs that suckle kittens, even wolves that take on human infants? But it isn't his scent that makes you love him. I could roll him in offal, and still you'd hold him. You loved him before he was even born." He pauses. "Now let's both get back to him, for like you, I feel an anxiety when I am away from him too long."

And so we go back, to ease in on either side of Avery. Immediately he wakes up and wants to nurse again. I persuade him to do it lying down. I am drowsing off while he is still tugging at my breast. Sleepily curious, I lean my head down, sniff the top of his curly head at the base of his horn nubs, where his scent should be strongest. He smells of milk and warmth and babyness. The same smell that Teddy had. I cuddle him closer and drop off to sleep.

The next morning, I watch with some trepidation as Pan readies himself and the child to leave. I want to wrap something about his naked baby shoulders, but Pan looks at me in consternation when I mention it. "How will his body ever learn to warm itself in colder weather if you bundle him up?" he asks me. I have no answer for that. "Besides," he adds as he finishes putting an edge on his knife, "you'd better spend the time getting yourself ready if you're going with us."

It is my turn to be shocked. I wonder why I had assumed I had to stay here while they went. In moments I am pulling on jeans that actually snap, albeit a bit snugly, around my middle. I put several pairs of socks on before pulling on my worn sneakers, and put an extra pair in my pocket. I know I will be cold and wet before we return, but the lure of the outside world, so long denied, makes that worry trivial.

I negotiate our rocky cliff porch with amazing ease. The nightmare of my first crossing has haunted me for months. As I follow Pan, who has his small son perched on one of his shoulders, I have little difficulty with the path. His hooves have kept a path clear through the wet ice that coats most of the drop-off, and I stay to this. It was the immensity of my pregnancy, I realize, that made this so difficult to cross. I want to laugh aloud in the suddenness of my freedom.

We reach the flank of the mountain and Pan swings Avery down. He gives him time to touch and sniff the snow, and then we start off. Avery follows him, stepping along confidently. Pan's daily passage has packed a path through the snow, and we all walk in relative ease. Only occasionally does spring betray us, when Pan or I will suddenly break through the crust and find ourselves knee or hip deep in snow. We wallow out and continue.

The farther down the mountain we go, the more plentiful the signs of spring. Even the untracked snow has a soggy, packed feel to it. Sap is running in some of the trees, I can scent it. Tips of willow branches have gone red with it, while the infrequent paper birch has a pinkish flush to its bark. But the most obvious sign is the bundled needles of new growth that tip almost every evergreen branch. I pinch off one, brush the brownish sheath from it, and chew on it as we walk. Sour and pine mix in my mouth.

We walk his trap line. We visit six widely spaced snares, and Pan picks up two hares for his trouble. I notice that at each stop he is taking up his snares and coiling them and putting them into the game sack he carries. There is a curious finality to his actions. Avery is worn out long before we reach the sixth snare. I end up carrying him, marveling at how long his dangling goat legs have become. He dozes off, baby face snugged against my neck, breath warm there.

The sixth snare is set on bared green moss. Nearby, the snow has melted to reveal the green-hearted fronds of a fern. The snow this far down the mountain lies in banks and tongues, interrupted by islands and peninsulas of wet earth. Pan pushes a frosting of crystallized snow from a fallen tree trunk to make a place for me to sit. I no sooner settle than Avery awakens and wants to nurse. But even as he suckles, his attention wavers. He pulls free of me and ignores the milk dribbling in a stream from my nipple. The greenery fascinates him. After a few moments of staring, he goes back to nursing, but his eyes continue to wander. It is not long before he stops suckling and moves out of my encircling arm. Pan settles beside me on the log and we watch Avery explore the fern fronds and mossy patches. Avery takes an experimental mouthful of fern, then spits it out before either of us can say anything. The moss comes in for minute examination, and then the bark of the tree trunk we are sitting on. He pulls loose a handful, then looks under it intently.

"Looking for grubs?" I ask Pan hesitantly.

"Probably," he replies nonchalantly. "Survival skills are among the first memories to waken."

I am relieved when his search is unsuccessful. Pan lets him thoroughly explore the area before announcing, "Time to head back." He hands me the sack and takes Avery back up on his shoulder. We begin the long, steady trudge back up the mountain. When I judge we are about halfway there, I ask curiously, "Aren't we going to reset any of the snares?"

"No," he says, so softly I can barely hear him.

Trepidation fills me. I know what is coming, have known it for weeks, have sensed it as geese sense migration times and fish remember a spawning creek. "Why not?" I ask, hoping to be wrong, knowing I'm not.

"Because it's spring," he says, and his voice goes suddenly husky. But it's on the next words that it breaks. "It's time for me to take you home. Back to your own kind."

# Twenty-five

"I don't want to go."

His fingers are working tallow onto the metal surfaces of his traps. His head is bent over his work. I am lying on the bed, his son curled beside me. Pan is facing the fire, not me, so I see him as a darker form outlined against the flames. I notice that the curls of his hair are down to the nape of his neck now. It softens his silhouette, and makes him appear younger.

"I don't want you to go," he says finally.

"Then why do I have to go? Why can't we just stay here?"

He sighs. "Staying in any one place for very long becomes dangerous. Paths through the snow will melt and fade, but if we continued to stay here through the summer, our comings and goings would soon be plain to read. And some hiker or backpacker would eventually get curious. Besides, this cave is a much less pleasant place in summer. The glacier melts and runs, so you at least get drenched every time you come in or out, and sometimes the flow is enough to make it dangerous, strong enough to nearly wash you away. And there's the noise of it, like living inside a drum. And . . . it's just not very pleasant here, Evelyn. You wouldn't like it." He rewraps the trap in a piece of the hoarded brown paper, sets it atop the others in the chest. Already, it is almost full.

"I don't mean I want to stay here. I mean I want to stay with you."

He is silent for a very long time. I long to go to him, to touch him, but I know it would not be fair. It would make him want to lie. "It wouldn't work," he says finally.

"Why not?"

"It would be too hard on you."

"I don't care!" I cry out, and Avery pops awake with a jerk. His little head swivels as he tries to determine the source of danger. Pan comes to put a comforting hand on him. He sits on the edge of the bed, leans against me. The closeness of him is a body language. He does not want to be parted from me any more than I want to leave him. His words come reluctantly.

"Evelyn. I have to take Avery to a safer place than this. To a wilder place, to a place where humans almost never come. I have to watch over him until I'm sure he can cope on his own. That means living more . . . basically. Not what you would call primitive. What you would call bestial. Like the animals we are. Do you think I always cook the meat I eat? Will you join us when he splits open a rotting log for the grubs inside it? When we huddle under a tree through a winter storm, will you crouch beside us? Run beside us when we chase down a deer? Evelyn, dear heart." His fingers wipe tears from my cheeks.

"I could do it," I say brokenly.

"Perhaps. But neither of us could stand to watch what it would do to you. And so we'd make compromises, dangerous compromises. And when the time comes to let go of Avery, to put him out on his own, to walk away from him, could you do that, too? I don't want to leave you, Evelyn. But I have to, if our child is to survive."

I crawl into his arms, taking Avery with me. For a long time he holds us both. "Please," I whisper. "Please. I can do it."

"We'll see," he says guardedly.

Late the next morning, we are ready to leave. The bed frame is bare, the two chests have once more been pushed back into the darkest corner of the cave. The worn-out bag is packed, as well as a bundle wrapped in the fur coverlet from our bed. The second one contains mostly bedding and smoked meat. Just before we leave, Pan refills his lamp, and hangs it from a spike just inside the cave. "You think you'll come back here, someday?" I ask him as I watch.

"Not me. But someone else might," he says, and I get a glimpse of his strangely hyphenated existence. The I he is today provides for the I that may come tomorrow. Not just Avery, but whoever carries on his memories and may someday need a shelter. Whatever he does for his son, he does for himself, I think. And then I realize that is just as true for humans. We only pretend it isn't so.

We leave. Once more Pan shoulders Avery until we are safely on the flank of the mountain. Then he sets him down and we go single file, Pan, Avery, and finally me. The snow is even softer today, and we break through more often. I am relieved when we work our way down past the snowline and into a part of the forest where the snow has been reduced to patches and islands. Pan sets a steady pace then, and we travel swiftly through the trees, going like I used to imagine Indians going. Without pause or hesitation, weaving through the forest like water flows. I am amazed at how quickly and quietly we go as we thread our way through the shadows. Living so long with him, I have picked up more of his physical habits than I had realized. It is a way of setting one's feet, and in how the path is chosen. We go as the wild creatures go, slipping in and out of the dappling light.

We stop only to let Avery nurse. The second time I feed him, I notice how restive he seems. He suckles, then pulls away and works his mouth, and then nurses again. Running my thumb along his lower gum, I find what I have suspected. Two tiny teeth are breaking through in front. We give him a strip of dried meat to teethe on and Pan carries him for several miles while he gums it down into a slimy mess that he finally devours.

We travel through all of the daylight and most of the twilight before we reach a stopping place. We are on the banks of a stream. The lake it feeds is back the way we have come, but it was covered with ice still. Our camp is minimal. No fire. Only dried meat and cold water. After we have eaten and Avery has nursed, I spread the bedding. I take off my wet sneakers. They are little more than tatters of canvas and sole now. Soon I will have to start wearing the leather slippers I made for the cave. I try not to wonder how they will stand up to steady use.

Avery has been eagerly exploring the bank of the stream. Now, in a sodden tangle of brush, he has found the remains of a paper wasps' nest. He pulls it loose from its attachments and gambols up to his father with it. Pan crouches silently beside him. The boy shows it to him, and searches his face for agreement. Pan evidently concurs, for Avery's small fingers quickly peel away the papery layers of nest to bare sealed compartments of larvae in the comb. I watch as his little fingers worry the larval wasps out of their casing and then into his mouth. He offers one to his father, who accepts it gravely. Pan is sitting, back against a tree, and Avery casually leans against him. As I watch, the boy's eyes droop. In moments he is asleep.

I smile at Pan as his gaze meets mine. I hold out my arms, and wait for him to bring me the child. He closes his forest eyes for a moment, then slowly shakes his head. For a moment I am dumbfounded. It dawns on me that he intends to sleep there like that, with the child beside him. I look at the bare downy shoulders, the little rounded arms curled on his chest. Something like pain divides me. I feel challenged, mocked almost. Slowly I get up from the soft warm blankets. I go barefoot to where they huddle together. I sit down on the other side of Avery, my shoulder just touching his hunched little back. I meet Pan's gaze unwaveringly for a moment. Then I lean my head back against the tree. And try to sleep. I am tired and achy after the long day's walking, but it is hard to even doze. I keep feeling set apart. Rejected by their faunness. The loneliness it wakes in me is too familiar.

Morning comes too early. I am stiff and chilled despite the blanket some traitor has tucked around me. Both Pan and Avery are up already, and involved in some fascinating splashing game by the stream. I struggle out of my blanket and join them, but the water I splash goes on my stiff face. As soon as I have cleared the sleep from my eyes, I confront Pan.

"I didn't need the blanket," I tell him. "I was doing just fine without it."

"I know," he says, refusing the quarrel.

"You think I'm soft," I charge him. "You think I can't take things that you and that baby can."

The trouble with this satyr is that he doesn't know how to have a decent fight. This sort of thing just perplexes him. His brows knit over his eyes for an instant. "My love," he says gently, explaining the obvious. "Avery and I were not uncomfortable. We didn't shiver in the night. You did. So I covered you, against a cold your body could not fight off on its own. That's all."

And that is all, for him. But I have to add, "It hurts my pride when you act like I'm . . ." I trail off in frustration, unsure of what word to use. Weak. Inferior. Helpless.

"Different?" he supplies helpfully. "But, my love, you are. Why do you want me to watch you shiver all night when there are blankets to wrap you in? What purpose does it serve?"

I have no answer for that, and the conversation dies when Avery suddenly deigns to notice me. He charges across the stream in a spray of silver and frolics over to me. And frolics is the only word. He is goat-kicking high as he comes, bounding sideways, pausing to defy gravity with an improbable bound that changes his direction in midair. I am helpless with laughter by the time he reaches me, and even his father is grinning with delight. I stoop down immediately, opening my shirt for him. But he surprises me by flinging his arms around my neck and clinging tightly for an instant. I close my arms around him, and feel how his muscles are developing, how he is already lither than he was when he left the cave. But the embrace lasts only for a second. Then he is tugging at my breast, reminding me that there is more important business to be tended to than hugging. But it is the hug that stays with me through that day's long hike.

That night Avery comes to me to nurse as I curl on the blankets. He stays beside me, drowsy-eyed, but as I am dropping off to sleep, I feel him shift impatiently. He kicks the blankets aside, edges over to where his father is already sound asleep on the moss nearby. Too warm for him, I realize. And all the times Pan slept beside me under the blankets? Sharing his body heat with me, supplementing my poor human system. A biological thing, I tell myself. Different, not inferior.

But in his world, I am undeniably inferior, and every day rubs my nose in it. We are traveling north, following winter's sullen retreat, so the days and nights warm only slightly as we travel. I cannot pretend I do not suffer more from the cold than they do. When the dried meat finally runs out, I am almost relieved, for it means that Pan and Avery hunt fresh meat for us, and that Pan builds a fire for me to cook over. Avery is often too impatient to wait for such niceties, and eats his raw. I try not to cringe when he goes digging through the entrails for the juicy bits. I want him to do well, I want him to survive, I tell myself. The teeth are coming into his mouth like tulips sprouting in a spring garden. There is no denying that every day he takes less milk from me. My supply dwindles proportionately. Soon he is taking no more than a morning and evening nursing, and those more for the comfort of being held than from any hunger.

And Pan? He says very little, but notices all. I sometimes surprise a look of sympathy upon his features when he catches me watching Avery as he sleeps, or forages for grubs or samples independence by bounding ahead of us on the trail. Only once does he speak of it. "It will be hard for me," he says softly, his eyes upon Avery's eagerly wagging tail as it disappears around a very interesting stump, "to let him go when the time comes. Even knowing all I know, it will still be hard."

I do not answer.

There comes a night when Pan awakens me in the darkness. At first I mistake it for a romantic intention.

We have not had sex since we left the cave. Avery is always too wakeful, or I am too weary. I come into his arms, clinging to him, kissing him. He returns my kisses and holds me, but after a moment I sense he is preoccupied. "What is it?" I ask.

"The border," he whispers. He is gathering Avery up, trying not to wake him. "I went to look at it, while you slept. Evidently they are taking things more seriously than they used to. We'd best cross now, in the darkness."

I try to suppress my disappointment as I gather up the little he has left unpacked. The notion of worrying about the border takes me aback. The Canada-Alaska border is ahead. This artificial division of the land into two separate countries seems even more foolish than it used to. I had almost forgotten such things, for Pan has meticulously kept us away from towns and roads. For an instant I glimpse the peculiarity of the human race as he must see us. A border.

I follow him through the woods, trying to move as silently as he does. He carries a sleeping Avery against his shoulder. We come to a break in the trees, a long straight slash down the hill that is a bare stripe in the forest. At the bottom of the hill, I glimpse a road. A dim light that is neither moonshine nor starlight is breaking up the night. He motions for a halt, and comes to stand close beside me. Avery brushes against me as Pan leans to whisper in my ear.

"If we are seen," he begins. "If we are chased . . ." He stops, and waits for me to finish the thought.

I peer in the direction of the vague light that is greying the forest and felling shadows across our path. I imagine border guards with rifles and flashlights down there. Tall, bulky men in stout leather boots. "Carry the child to safety," I tell him. It is the only possible reply.

"On the other side," he whispers, "you'll come to a river. Very swift, very cold. Don't try to cross it alone. Go downstream. We'll wait for you there." He reaches once to touch my cheek. And then we rise and move on.

The border here is a shaved stripe through the forest. There is a minimal tangle of barbed wire down

the middle of it. Far down the hill, there is a black strip
of road, a parking lot, a huddle of cars and small
businesses. Lights illuminate it and other lights, mercury lights, point up the hillside. I see no sign of any
humans. Still, my heart thunders as Pan hands me both
packs. I wait in the shadows as he ventures out. He picks
his way as carefully as a stag, and to me he looks as stately.
Avery sleeps on, his head nestled on his father's shoulder.
As Pan approaches the barbed wire, he closes the last bit of
distance with a few running steps, and then suddenly
springs over it. He doesn't pause on the other side, but
bounds off into the darkness of the sheltering trees. As he
disappears, I let out my breath in a silent sigh.

I count to one hundred, very slowly. Surely by now
they are well back in the trees. Surely now it is safe to
follow. But I take another breath, do another slow count
to one hundred. And another. And another. Then I rise
and follow. Not for me a run and a leap. Instead I creep
like a mouse. I am even too afraid to throw the packs
over, afraid they will make some sound as they land and
rouse some unseen guard. So I step into the wire, let it
catch and bite me, cloth and flesh, and slowly and
deliberately work myself free of it as I move forward. It
takes an eternity, for no sooner am I clear of one set of
prongs before another sets in me. I think I am nearly
free of them, when I hear the unmistakable slam of a car
door. An engine roars to life as headlights flare in the
parking lot below. It galvanizes me, for no sensible
reason, and I pull free, letting barbs tear out of my skin.

I run, in a shambling, crackling rush that carries me
into the woods and the horribly deceptive shadows cast
by the lights from below. I leap over the shadows of
trees, only to stumble over the real fallen logs. I am
sobbing soundlessly before I am a dozen yards into the
woods. I force myself to stop, to breathe, and then to
walk on, picking my way as carefully as I can. I want to
call out, to have Pan come and take my arm and guide
me, but I will not risk betraying them. Instead, I go
stumbling on, for what seems like hours. Only when I
can no longer see anything of the unhealthy grey light do
I pause. For a time I stand perfectly still, listening. I

hope for a crackling footfall, for the whisper of my name. I listen, too, for river sounds. But there is nothing except the normal night sounds of a forest. Eventually I sink down and tug a blanket free of the bundle. I push my way under the low sweep of a spruce's branches, and roll myself up in the blanket. I fall asleep, refusing to wonder if I will ever see them again.

Rain awakens me the next morning. It is not the first time it has rained on me in our journeying. But it is the first time I have awakened alone in the rain, and somehow this seems significant. It is nasty rain, rain with wind that bends the upper branches of the trees and shakes their burden of water down on me at unpredictable moments. As I reroll the blanket and bundle the packs back up, the full significance of my situation comes to me. Here I am, just over the Alaskan border, but with little idea of where over the border. Fairbanks could be three hundred miles away, or six hundred. Rivers to cross? Mountain passes to find? I don't know. I have blankets, and I think there are a few matches left in the pack. No food. No way of obtaining food, other than my bare hands. No compass, other than the night sky. And from the way it is raining, there isn't much hope of using the stars tonight.

I put a brave face on it for myself. The river can't be far, now. I'll be with Pan tonight. And even if I'm not, well, hell, we've been doing this for days, now. No big deal. I can take care of myself. I shoulder my burdens and trudge off through the dripping forest. I try to stay on a straight bearing of the course I have traveled the night before. Not that I'm sure that's helpful. Pan weaves us around in his travels, detouring us past the difficult obstacles. I'm not even sure that he was headed back for the Fairbanks area. My stomach is starting to get quivery again. I realize that if I read about someone in a situation like this, I'd say to myself, the stupid shit deserves whatever happens to her. Imagine going off so ill-prepared! And I'd fold my newspaper and tell myself smugly that I'd be much more self-sufficient than that, much more woods-wise. Silly woman, silly little wailing twit, I'd think to myself. Soaked to the skin, foodless, no compass. What an idiot!

I ignore the wind and the constant rain. I try to move quietly as I go, try to keep my eyes open for possible food. I am not hungry just yet, and I'm hoping to find food before I get hungry. What food, I'm not sure. I doubt I can run down a rabbit with these packs on, and if I discard them to chase a rabbit, will I find my way back to them? About the best I can hope for is early greens.

I have not gone too far before my breasts swell with milk. The discomfort builds as I walk, my breasts growing heavier and tighter, until finally I start leaking milk in sticky blotches that spread on the front of my shirt. I wonder if Avery is hungry, if he misses me. I wonder where they are, and if they are looking for me, waiting impatiently.

It is midday when my ears separate the roar of a river from the soughing of the wind through the tree-tops. In a sort of dull despair, I realize that I must turn sharply to go toward the sound. The rain had masked its smell from me, the wind in the trees concealed the sound of its waters. How long have I been paralleling it? There is no way of knowing.

I set my teeth and work toward the river. The brush seems to grow denser and more prickly as I get closer to it, and finally I resort to a simple bulldozing technique, forcing my way through the bushes to the bank. When I get there, I realize another of my assumptions is wrong. I have pictured myself hiking up a sandy, gravelly riverbank to where I will find Pan and Avery camped on a cute little beach. But it is breakup, thaw time, and the river is jealously rolling down the full width of its bed, eating under the bank I am standing on. There will be no easy hike downstream, but a day spent pushing my way through brush and scrambling down and then up out of the ravines that house the multitude of creeks that feed this river. Nor does the wind and rain ease up.

The day seems to last forever. I try to tell myself that I am making good mileage. Somehow, when I don't know how far I must go, I doubt the value of this. I find a few greens, the still coiled heads of fiddlehead ferns that have a flavor like early asparagus and such, but it is scarcely enough to fill my stomach. Oddly, I do not feel hungry. I am too busy being wet and cold. And worried. Surely I should have seen them by now. Of course they would have waited for me. I refuse to imagine Pan's sure hooves somehow stumbling down that bank, dragging Avery into that hungry river with him. Stupid tricks like that are reserved for me. They are safe, fine, and I am sure they are waiting for me. I try to hurry.

Night comes before I am ready for it. Pan's easy knack of finding a dry tree to camp under has eluded me. When I stop, it is just because it is too dark to go farther, not because of any liking for the spot. There are a few large trees that provide some shelter from the rain. I make myself a nest of blankets and furs at the base of a tree, and strip off my wet clothes before I huddle into it. I don't deceive myself that they will dry by morning, but at least I will sleep warmer this way. Again, I reassure myself that they are probably waiting for me, may even come looking for me. And I doze off quickly, fleeing reality.

In my dream, I stand before the Wild Things and say, "I have come to be Queen of all Wild Things." And the big one with the clawed toes looks down on me with its yellow eyes and says, "You've got to be kidding. You're not a wild thing. You're a big fake."

It is light when I wake up, but I don't move. I stay in my huddle of blankets. I draw my knees up to my chest and lean my arms on them and stare out through the grey-misted forest. I really see it now. The wildness. Thousands of acres of it. Uncut by roads, untamed, unwalked by men. And I wonder when I started doing it. Was it when I was ten or twelve, ranging over probably no more than eighty acres and pretending to myself it was the great wild world? Eighty acres crosshatched with survey cuts and bordered by roads. Overgrown dirt roads, true, but roads on at least three sides. I suddenly see the immensity of those woods from an adult's perspective. A playpen. A large playpen, with moose and a few lynx, a porcupine and some rabbits thrown in.

But a playpen compared to this wilderness I am in now. And had I believed myself a wild thing? Sure. A wild thing with a pocket full of matches, or a rifle, a pocket-knife, and half a dozen candy bars. A wild thing that went home to sleep in a bed at night, to feed from a full refrigerator. My self-sufficiency, my woodsiness, has all been an elaborate charade. For my family, for Tom, for Tom's family. But most of all, for myself.

I haven't fooled Pan for one minute.

He has fed me and sheltered me, I have been his little forest princess. I chew my lower lip as I think on these things. What had I told him back at the cave? I can do it, I can take it? Do what, take what? Continue to do what he told me, continue to take the food he provided, and to pretend to myself that I was tough and self-sufficient. Because I can sleep outside all night, and eat food cooked over a fire.

I pull the blankets up higher around my shoulders, huddle deeper. How hard is it for him to keep things to a pace I can manage, avoid obstacles that are too difficult for me, hunt enough to feed him and the child and me?

What was he really asking me, back there at the cave?

I have too many emotions, I cannot sort them all out. Bewilderment, at how stupid I have been. Shame. Hurt. Angry that he never came out and told me. Relief that he didn't. Abashed, that I never realized all he was doing for me. And shame again. Because it seems my first thoughts were never truly for him, never truly for the child.

I don't cry. Crying seems childish to me now, and I have been childish long enough. Time to try to be what I've been pretending to be. Self-sufficient. Because I suspect the truth is that I am lost. That perhaps I have intersected with the river below the point where Pan is waiting for me, perhaps every step I take downstream takes me away from him. I realize I have no way of knowing. Nor does he. When he decides to go looking for me, he will look upstream. But I am downstream. Maybe. Or maybe not.

If you are lost in the woods, the common sense

goes, stay where you are. So the searchers can find you.
All I have to do is crouch here on this riverbank, and
sooner or later Pan will come to find me. He'll bring me
food, he'll hug me, he'll protect and guide me.

Regardless of the cost to himself.

And the cost to Avery?

I repack the gear, being ruthless. What do I really
need? Discard anything extra, get it down to one pack. It
isn't as hard as I would have thought yesterday. I
bundle the rest and leave it under the tree for squirrels
to make nests of. And I set off. My plan is simple, and
realistic. Follow the river downstream. Not because I
am looking for Pan. But because rivers attract fishermen
and boaters and home builders. And those things mean
roads. Roads means cars, and I can hitchhike. I fabricate
a hard-luck story about my boyfriend dumping me out of
the car after we quarreled. Get to a town. Wing it from
there.

Go back to where I'm not a burden to those who
love me.

When I come to a clear stream, in midafternoon, I
pause, not just to drink, but also to pull myself together.
Wash my face, hands, and arms. Comb my hair out into
a semblance of order. Straighten my clothes as best I
can. When I come to a road, I'll put on my cleanest shirt.
Drink more, lots, to try to convince my stomach it's full.
The cold water numbs the hunger pangs. My breasts are
leaking again. There is much less pressure. Another day
of not nursing, and my milk will probably dry up
entirely. Last link with Avery dried up and gone.

I cross the stream, continue downriver. The rain
lessens, and hiking is relatively easy through this
stretch. I push myself, resolving to cover as much
ground as I can today. Tomorrow I'm going to be very
hungry. Already I'm noticing that it's harder for my body
to keep itself warm.

The third time I trip over a snag I didn't see, I
deduce it's time to stop for the night. I make my nest
again, and debate starting a fire. But an inventory has
shown I have only three feeble paper matches left. Best
save them in case I get a really cold night.

It is harder to fall asleep tonight, perhaps because I am hungry, perhaps because I have so much to kick myself for. Oh, love, I silently mourn. Why didn't you just tell me? I feel ashamed, not to have known. The fourth time I get up to shift around and try to find a more comfortable way to lie, I see the light through the trees. It's quite a ways away, but it's white light, not yellow. Not a campfire, but someone's window, shining through the dark.

I stand, staring at it. I hadn't considered this scenario. Okay, I'm a stupid statesider who went hiking with her boyfriend, quarreled, ran away from him, and got lost. Where are we hiking to? I don't know, he was in charge of that. Where did we start out from? Oh, the road by the bridge. There's bound to be a road with a bridge somewhere around here. Okay, go now, before you lose your courage, before you stop to think how full of holes your story is. Even if they don't believe me, they'll have to let me in, they'll have to point me toward the road tomorrow. How bad can they be? Rapists and murderers? I lie to myself, tell myself I'll be able to tell if they're good people by how their cabin looks. And I pack up my blankets and head for the light.

After an hour of bumping into trees and scrabbling in and out of two ravines, I come to the cabin. It looks promising. The light is obviously the blue-white glare of a Coleman lantern. I stand and look across a rabbit-fenced garden. Not planted yet nor even tilled, it's still too early for that. But I smell a compost heap. Back to the earthers. Anyone who believes in compost can't be all bad. Even as I debate circling to find a front door, a dog starts barking. Chained dog, some kind of baying hound. The cabin people lose points in my estimate for chaining their dog, and for owning something with floppy ears. I wait silently, trusting that someone will turn out to see what's spooking the dog. Let's see how they sound before I step clear of the trees.

A door opens and shuts. I am unprepared for what happens next. A voice from the trees behind me hisses, "Evelyn!" while a halogen spotlight hits me. I am blinded, stunned by the light, and I freeze. Stupidly I

wonder if they can see me clearly, if perhaps I can stand
so still that they will be uncertain of what they see. The
weeds are high by the fence, my clothing is muted in
color. "Who's there?" a woman's voice demands.

"Evelyn!" someone gasps behind me, and a hard
hand grips my wrist. He pulls at me, and I start to move,
to tell them I don't know what. "Who's there!" the voice
demands again, and this time it shakes. Something in the
tone, I don't know what, I know the danger, I pant out,
"Run!" And the shotgun explodes the world.

I can't separate the noise from the white light, and
the hot buzz that rips past my ear. All sound is gone for
an instant, and then there is screaming and yelling from
the cabin and the dog is baying and jerking on its chain.
I turn, and in a horrifying instant I see that Pan is
holding Avery. "Run!" I shriek, and I am the one
dragging at his hand, charging back into the shadows and
safety of the forest with Pan in tow. He stumbles and I
smell the hot sick smell of blood. My heart jumps
sideways and almost stops, but something else takes over
me, and I keep my grip on his hand, even manage to
guide him around most of the larger obstacles. The
shouting and the baying of the dog fade behind us.

On and still on. Dry throat, hammering heart, but
go on. Splash into a stream, and it's easier to run
upstream than to clamber out the other side. On, and
there is an unevenness to his gait, I pray it's only Avery's
weight. When I realize I am no longer running, but only
jerking along at little more than a walk, I come to a halt.
I am shaking violently. Pan has not made a sound, not in
all this time. I scrabble up the bank of the stream, right
into some kind of thickety bushes. Cover is how I see it,
and I push my way into it. We sink down and huddle
together, clutching at one another. Avery hiccups suddenly and comes clambering and clinging into my arms.
I hold him tight, as tightly as he clutches me. After what
seems like a very long time, I stop shaking. Pan is
leaning heavily against me.

"Are you all right?" I whisper to the darkness.

"I'm okay," he hedges, and I hear the pain in his
voice. I am too great a coward to touch him, to try to feel

for damage. Instead I scrabble in the darkness, drag out and untangle a blanket and wrap us all in it. Avery has recovered enough to dig at my shirt. I open it, and he nurses what milk is there, but I sense it is more for comfort than hunger. He can't be hurt, I tell myself. He wouldn't be interested in nursing if he were hurt. Except that Teddy always wanted to nurse if he were uncomfortable or sick. I bend to kiss the top of his curly head. I manage to free an arm and draw Pan closer beside me. "It's going to be all right," I promise him.

He shifts in my arms. "You were going back to them," he says bewilderedly.

"Hush," I tell him, and rock them both until sleep claims us all.

# Twenty-six

My cabin looks different from the ridge. Foreign and abandoned, a newsreel scene from a faraway land. Looks like the snow-load took out one corner of the porch roof. The garden is completely overgrown with dead weeds from last summer. The pickup sits unevenly on one flat front tire.

"Are you sure?" he asks me again. I wish he wouldn't.

I picked seven pieces of shot from his shoulder and the side of his neck that morning. But the one that we dug out of Avery's soft little arm hurt us both the most. I watched Pan lick and suck at the little red hole until he was sure there was nothing else in there. Then I nursed Avery again until he fell asleep, and we coddled him into a nest of blankets and both sighed and looked at each other. Sadly. Wearily.

After a while I took the one remaining blanket and spread it for us and drew the satyr down beside me. Halfway into our lovemaking, I reached and stilled his hands on my body. "You're doing this for me, aren't you?" I asked him.

He didn't answer for a long time. Then. "I don't mind," he told me.

"But you don't understand," I pressed him.

He pulled a fraction of an inch away from me. "There is no child to be made," he admitted. "Nothing can come of this. Except the pleasure. The same sort of

358

pleasure that comes from eating good food even when one is not hungry. Humans do that, too."

"Yes," I agreed. "We do." He moved a hand, but I put mine over it, stilling it again. Thinking. I asked, "Will you ever reach for me again? To want to touch me, this way, without my touching you first?"

He didn't exactly answer the question. "I understand the hunger to have a child," he finally told me. "That passion I know."

"This is the hunger of the heart," I told him. "Such as humans always suffer from. And I ask you, one last time, to soothe it for me."

And he did. I rested under him, feeling him touch me not for his own lust, but for the love he had for me. Letting him make love to me, solely for me, accepting what he willingly offered. And I didn't feel guilty or inferior or patronized. I felt loved. And then I had told him, "Now you can take me home."

Days ago, miles ago. And now we are here, and his simple question makes it hard all over again. "I'm sure," I finally say. I turn and stoop and Avery comes into my arms. For the last two days, he has refused to be carried. He is too big for that now. I look into his huge brown eyes, kiss and smell the curly hair. I kiss the palms of each of his hands, and his belly button, and bury my face in the softness of his neck for one last minute. Then I stand. I dare not hug Pan, nor kiss him. I only look at him and say, "Take care of him. Teach him all he needs to know."

"I will," he promises.

I stand a moment longer, looking at him. He doesn't need me anymore. Neither does Avery. But they love me. Love without need. It can be done. I am trying to do it now. But some perverse devil in me says to the satyr, "Come back to me. If you ever feel the hunger of the heart. I'll be here. You know the way."

Then I turn and walk down the hill. I try not to look back. But when I get to my doorstep, I cannot stand it any longer. I look back up the ridge. They're gone. I knew they'd be gone. I knew it, I tell my shaking heart. I told them to go.

The door is locked. Someone has been here, somebody tidying up loose ends. I walk slowly through the house. Tom's things are gone, and so are most of Teddy's. Just as well.

Big Brown envelope on the table. Divorce papers. Certified check for five hundred. I wonder whose idea that was. Deed to the land and Tom's quit claim clipped to it. Keys to the house and truck. Quit claim to the truck. And one battered copy of Maurice Sendak's *Where the Wild Things Are*.

I set down the papers and the book and look around the cabin. "He loved me, at least a little," I tell the walls. "For a while." Then I look around, at the shrew droppings on the counters and the dust on the table. "Time to clean house," I say aloud. And I do. I haul water and I make the fire and I clean the cupboards. I can do all this myself, for myself. I think of the tops I will carve, of the jumping jacks I will give merry faces to, and of taking them to Annie's shop, I'll be okay. I eat canned Dinty Moore stew, and try to believe in tomorrow.

I make up the bed with homespun blankets that still smell of satyr. That night, when I go to sleep, I am exhausted. But I dream of an old woman, a toy maker who wakes up in the night and goes to the window and looks out over her garden. Peas and pansies, carrots and roses. She leans her forehead against the cold window glass and looks out. Because she hears piping in the moonlight. And she isn't afraid to run out in her white nightgown with her greying hair loose on her shoulders. To where the wild things are.

A Special Preview
of the new novel by
Megan Lindholm

Widely praised for her insightful fantasy, Megan
Lindholm turns her talent to her first science
fiction novel. In the following scene, deep-space
mariner Connie makes a port of call on her home
planet.

Orange door. C-72. And there was the wrought-metal grille over it. She reached through the metal to pull the chime lever, then stood waiting to be let in. She let her fingers idly trace the wrought work, trying to enjoy the abstract design, only to be surprised by the sturdiness of the metal. This was no decoration. Forgetting herself for a moment, she took hold of the grille and tried to rattle it. It wouldn't budge. It was cold and rough and real under her hands, and the most anti-social thing she'd ever encountered. If a pre-pube or a pube had put up such a barrier, they'd have been taken away for Adjustment before the day was out.

But a post-pube could get away with almost anything. And usually did. Adjustment for post-pubes was just not cost effective. That was the most often cited reason. The other one, quoted in undertones, was that Adjustment didn't work after a certain age; the personality just gave way and withdrew under the pressures. And when that happened, a humane and timely termination was the only possible prescription left. What else could they expect?

Connie pushed the thought out of her mind and began to bargain with herself. I will wait twenty more seconds, and then I will leave and tell Tug that I tried, but no one was home. She reached and yanked the door chimes hastily, as a gesture to prove to herself that she had really tried, that she wasn't running away. But the door jerked back from her fingers, the chime handle rapping her knuckles as it moved away. Without thinking, she raised the injured fingers to her mouth, and there she stood, sucking at her fingers like an infant with the old man staring out at her.

"Well?" he demanded.

She snatched her hand down from her mouth, tried to find an answer to what wasn't a question. "Tug," she blurted stupidly. The grating still stood between her and the old man. Beyond him she could glimpse a very dim and untidy room. He kept staring at her. His eyes had been brown, but the colors seemed to have leaked out into the whites, giving his eyes a smeary look. "Tug sent me to get some recordings from you," she finally managed.

"Idiot," the old man hissed at her. "Do shut up, now." He did something on his side of the door, and the grate suddenly swung out toward her. "Come inside, and quickly now. Quickly!" the old man barked when she hesitated.

And she obeyed, stepping inside into the untidiness, feeling her bowels churn as first the grate and then the door shut behind her. It was suddenly darker, and an odor of closeness and spilled food swelled up around her. She stepped forward, stumbled on something and stood still again. The old man ignored her hesitation and moved deeper into the shadows of the room. "Move something and sit down," he advised her testily. "I'll be right back with his things." And then he was gone, vanished into some darker alcove, leaving her to bumble in the dimness.

The only light came from a single wall strip, probably set on minimum. It also seemed to be behind the couch or some long, low piece of furniture. She saw the shape of a chair, moved toward it. Something was on it, hard little blocks, many of them.

"Just put them on the floor, or anywhere."

The voice so close behind her startled her, and she jumped, sending whatever-they-were cascading to the floor.

"Dammit, not like that!" the old man hissed, as if she had done it deliberately.

Her nervousness at the whole situation suddenly blossomed into anger. "I didn't mean to knock them down. If there were a little more light in here, I could see what I was doing."

"If there were a little more light in here," the old man retorted sarcastically, "there wouldn't be much left to move around. All the stuff in this generation was made photo-sensitive. Light is all it takes to start triggering the breakdown. Remind Tug of that when you give them to him. He'd better plan on using them in the dark, or on re-recording them immediately. Because they're right on the cusp. Put them in light, and they aren't going to last long."

The old man was acting as he spoke. Connie couldn't see clearly what he was doing, but there was the click of little plastic boxes being stacked against one another. She leaned closer; he was packing box after box into a woven carry-sack. He started to fold the cover flap, then paused a moment. Connie could feel him looking at her in the dark.

"Now, he's going to find there's more here than he asked for," the old man declared suddenly. As if the statement marked a decision he had just reached, he knelt stiffly down and reached under the couch. He grunted, struggling with something, and then Connie heard a light thud as something dropped to the floor beneath the couch. The old man dragged out a heavy box, letting it scrape across the flooring. When he pried open the lid, Connie heard a sudden hiss and smelt the tell-tale sour of preservegas. Illegal for private citizens to have that. She swallowed.

The old man sat down on the floor by the box, his knees popping protestingly as he did so. He took out something wrapped tightly in white film and held it close to his eyes. He grunted in satisfaction and pushed it down deep in the carry sack, talking as he did so. "I know the kind of stuff he told me to watch for. Old literature in non-standard languages, poetry, damn mystery novels. Well, he got what he paid for. But here's a little bonus. Maybe the biggest mystery of all. Ever hear of Epsilon station, kid?"

"Epsilon is a myth," Connie replied automatically. Everyone had heard of Epsilon, at least everyone old enough to be allowed unsupervised time. Connie thought of her generation sibs clustered in little groups on their rest mats, sharing deliciously scary stories of Epsilon station. Epsilon station humans had mutated, or mutinied, or just opened their own vents one day and spaced themselves away. Epsilon station had created a plague that killed them all and nearly spread to the rest of the Human population, except that one courageous woman had vented the station to space. Epsiloners had stopped taking growth inhibitors and they grew too big for the station and it just burst open under the pressure. Epsiloners had had their own babies, from their own bodies, and made too, too many people, so they killed one another in the corridors and rioted over food and all lived together in the same dwellings, regardless of age.

Connie thought of the story of the shuttle that went way off course and landed on Epsilon and barely escaped from the plague-ridden survivors there. Later, the crew found a mutant tentacled hand, dead and gripping the air-lock wheel. Epsilon was still out there, looping in an exaggerated orbit, and Beastships that ventured too close had been fired upon. She'd heard that last one at the Merchant Marine Academy, from a student old enough to know better. But the story would still be repeated and passed on. Everyone had heard of Epsilon.

"Bullshit!" the old man hissed. Connie recognized it as an ancient oath. "Epsilon wasn't a myth. It's a lesson, and one we shouldn't forget. The Conservancy vented Epsilon, twelve hundred years ago. Because Epsiloners dared to live as their ancestors had, dared to believe their right to a natural life was as important as a plant's. So the Conservancy vented them, before their attitude could spread. It's all here, right here. And I want Tug to have it. See, here, it's called, 'A Brief History of the Abomination of Epsilon.' Conservancy made it, so they masked the truth with their philosophies and lies, but it's all there, for anyone with one ear and half an eye. Then a few decades later, they got scared some of us might get smart to them, so they hushed it up. Destroyed all copies and references to Epsilon. You tell Tug to study this one. It's a real mystery all right. If Epsilon was just a myth to scare little children, why'd they make this record? And then why did they destroy every single copy and everything that referred to this record? You answer me that, kid. Answer me that."

He crawled over the floor to Connie, and she instinctively backed away. Questions, again. Why did they always ask her questions? The man was crazy. Not just unadjusted, but mentally unbalanced. Dangerous. She backed toward the door. But he only started gathering up the boxes Connie had spilled. "He can have all this shit, too. Can't sell it. No one's smart enough to buy it. Some of it's pretty esoteric, and some of it's weird, and some of it is just plain useless. So I can't sell the damn things. Fools don't know what they're buying anymore, all they talk about is whether or not it's a collector's item. They only want the fancy stuff with the pretty pictures. But these are knowledge, damn it all, and it should be saved by someone, somewhere. Even if it's some 'throp alien.'"

The shock of hearing Tug referred to as 'throp', let alone an alien kept her silent. Alien? She had grown up knowing that the only aliens on Castor and Pollux were humans. Everything else had a perfect right to be there. She swallowed, but kept her silence. Besides, what was she going to say? Perhaps 'Are these recordings contraband? Are these illegally salvaged tapes that I'm going to be carrying back though Delta station?' Sure. Some small sane part of her mind was advising her to get out now, to refuse to take them, so she wouldn't be involved, so they couldn't take her for Adjustment again. But a sadder, wiser part of herself already knew the truth, had known it since her last Adjustment. She was marginal. Anything like this, any merest brush with illegality and they'd adjust her. Again and again, until they got it right. Or until nothing was left of her. Funny, how sometimes thoughts like that, the ones that should have terrified her the most, calmed her down and made her feel some measure of control over her life.

The old man was still talking, but something in his voice had gone dead. "Just have him do the credit transfer, like before. And tell him goodbye for me. He's been a good customer. Better than John. John quit coming when he found out Tug knew about me. John's such a prick sometimes. Who cares, anyway? I'll be long gone before Evangeline puts in here again. Everytime I go in for my heart, they shake their heads more, and do less for me. 'Is this quality of life really worth living?' they ask me. 'Do you feel you're still an asset to society?' Like I ever was. Hell." The old man paused and cleared his throat with a disgusting wet cough.

"You tell Tug that if I find someone who's interested in the business, I'll put him in place, and Tug will be able to reach him, same old way, same codes. But I don't think I will. Every year there's less and less to save. Of the old stuff, I mean. So much already gone, and some of the tapes I get now are irretrievable. Too far decayed when I get them. So you tell Tug he's got as good a collection as anyone has of the Old Earth stuff. He should be able to trade duplicates with other collectors, if he wants. But if he makes too many copies and trades them, his own collection will lose value. Not to mention that sooner or later, he'll get caught."

The carry bag was bulging. The old man tottered upright, suddenly wheezing with the effort. He caught the back of the chair and sat down on the place he had just cleared. Connie stood silent, watching him. Her eyes had adjusted to the dim light. She could see the bony structure of his face, holding up under the sagging flesh. He might have been handsome, a very long time ago. Now she could almost see his body biodegrading, could imagine the rot working through him, breaking down his muscles and bones . . . She felt a wave of panic, wanted to leave. But his knotted old hand still gripped the strap of the carry sack. "Now I told you about light, didn't I?" the old man queried himself.

"You told me," Connie replied softly.

The old man stared at her suddenly, as if he had just noticed she were here. "You're not like the others," he accused her. "You're no paid courier. What's in this for you, boy?"

"Girl," Connie corrected him quietly, taking no offense. It was a common error. Her big boned structure made her look masculine, she knew that. Maybe puberty would change that, but she doubted it. "Doing it as a friend for Tug. I work on his ship," and she stopped talking, wondering if she had said too much.

"You do, huh? Huh. How about that. That used to be my job, I was Talbot, the crewman.

Until that prick fired me. Well, you watch these tapes, too, then. Learn a little about your roots, about what you really are. What we were." He didn't hand the pack to her. His old hand just let go of the straps, so they fell limply on the floor. He leaned his head back on the chair, sighed heavily. "Door'll lock behind you," he told her, and sat still, breathing.

Connie accepted the dismissal, and stooped to take the straps of the carry sack. It was heavy, too heavy for her to carry comfortably in station gravity. Weighed like old generation plastic, the stuff that was illegal to possess in any form. She looped the woven straps over her arm and blundered her way out. After the metal grille swung shut behind her, she realized she had not said good-bye. It didn't matter; he wouldn't have noticed.

She trudged off down the corridor, trying to walk as if she were used to both station gravity and the load she was carrying. Paranoia, she told herself, was making her imagine that all the old people loitering and chatting in the courtyard turned to watch her go, and that their eyes lingered on her sack and their withered pink mouths worked more busily after she had passed.

She glanced down once at her burden and was dismayed at how the carry sack gaped open. The tumble of illicit plastic recordings were visible for anyone curious enough to glance. She tucked it uncomfortably under her arm, hoping her arm and sleeve covered most of it. She got back onto Main Corridor G and found a commercial sector. Here her bulging bag didn't look so out of place.

She entered the first garment shop she came

to and attempted some hasty shopping. Up until this moment, she hadn't intended to buy anything on this shore leave. The bright new colors and the gauziness of the new generation of fabrics almost overwhelmed her with indecision. She reminded herself that all she wanted was something to stuff in the top of the carry sack to conceal the plastic. Finally she selected a fluffy shawl, and then, in a sudden burst of impulsiveness, one of the new brightly-colored long skirts and tunics so many of the women seemed to be wearing. She handed the bored clerk her consumer chit and then her credit card. He keyed in her purchases without looking at her, then ran her consumer chit to make sure she wasn't over her allotment for clothing commodities. He considered his screen for a moment, leaned closer as if he couldn't believe his eyes, and then looked up at her.

"As near as I can read this," he said carefully, "You have about fifty years of commodity allotment waiting to be used."

Connie smiled embarassedly, wishing only that the transaction were over and that her purchases were in her bag covering her guilty cargo. "Mariner," she explained, gesturing at her orange coveralls. "I'm out in deep space a lot. No time to use up my allotments when I'm in port."

"Oh, yeah?" A faint stirring of interest in the clerk's brown eyes. "You sure you want to buy this skirt then? The degradable on it is only three years. Probably just rot away in your locker while you're in Waitsleep. Unless you preservegas it. I hear you guys are allowed to do that."

"I'll gas it," Connie promised him, and tried to

gather up her purchases. He let her get the shawl—tunic and skirt billowed into her carry bag—but stood holding her cards.

"You got a lot of back clothing allotment on here," he told her, as if it were something she hadn't understood.

"I know." She held out her hand for the cards.

He ignored the gesture, but put an elbow on the counter and leaned across it to say quietly. "I know people who would be interested in that back allotment."

"What?" Connie asked stupidly, instinctively drawing back from him.

"No, really. Everybody does it, anymore. You don't need it, so pass on the allotment to someone who does. Gotta be your size, of course, but the customer tells us what she wants, she pays, but you rack it up against your allotment, and she puts a generous credit to your account. Of course, you're not exactly the most common size, but there's still a market for all that unused allotment."

Connie tightened her grip on the carry bag. Had he seen the plastic? She didn't think so. So why was he approaching her with something so monstrously illegal? "I'm a good citizen," she informed him faintly.

Something in his face changed. It wasn't what she had expected. Instead of recoiling, his eyes widening as he realized he'd approached an honest citizen with his criminal plan, he just sighed and rolled his eyes, as if he'd told her a joke and she'd asked him to explain it. With a condescending sneer, he flipped her cards onto the counter so that they nearly slid off. She almost dropped her bag catching them. "Of course you're an honest citizen," he said sarcastically. "We all are. Aren't we? Aren't we all just perfectly adjusted and totally happy being good little citizens? Besides," he leaned across the counter toward her, and lowered his voice to a nasty register. "I didn't offer to do anything illegal. I was just telling you that such a market existed. The very fact that you thought I was making you an illegal offer probably means that you are Maladjusted, with illegal longings just lurking all through your brain. So think on that, good citizen."

He pushed himself back abruptly and stalked off across the shop, muttering to himself about 'good citizens.' Connie stared mutely after him, then stuffed her cards into her carry bag with her new garments and the illegal plastic recordings. She hurried out of the store and down Main Corridor G, feeling obscurely shamed and guilty. But hadn't she done what was right? Shouldn't she feel virtuous and pleased with herself? The goal of the consumer allotment chit system was to prevent excess consumption of goods, a behavior that always resulted in needless harvest of raw materials and future waste. By refusing to sell her own excess allotment, she had worked within the system to prevent waste and discourage foolish greed for consumer commodities. She had taken the correct action. So why did she feel foolish and embarassed? Why was she hurrying away as fast as she could go with the heavy bag, desperately afraid that mocking laughter would follow her?

She was halfway back to the Dock before she realized she had hours still of leave to spend.

Forget it. Forget everything except getting back to Evangeline and a world where the rules were hard and fast. She shifted her carry bag, set her face, and walked on.

*Since the publication of her first fantasy novel, Megan Lindholm has been praised for her graceful writing, captivating worlds, and characters of depth. Now she brings these talents to her first science fiction story. Here is the engrossing tale of Connie and John, two human deep-space mariners on a mission to discover if Earth is truly dead. What they learn about themselves and the aliens who rescued humanity from a dying Earth makes for fascinating reading.*

*(On Sale June 1992)*

## The Masterworks of
## Elizabeth Ann Scarborough

### Nothing Sacred

Shot down over the Tibetan Himalayas during a war
that neither side can win, Viveka Jeng Vanachek is a
prisoner lost in the no-man's land between battle-
fields. Captured, she survives cruel treatment only
to arrive at a hidden prisoner-of-war camp where she
is faced not only with torture but with ancient ruins,
weirdly beautiful dreams, and mysteries that only
the heat of nuclear fire can burn away.
"A powerful story."
—Minneapolis Star-Tribune

### The Healer's War
#### *Winner of the Nebula Award*

Kitty McCulley's hopes as an Army nurse in Vietnam
were dashed by the realities of war. In a warzone,
there's little time for real compassion or true healing.
It all changes, however, when Kitty is given a
magical amulet by one of her patients, a dying
Vietnamese holy man. Now she sees things no one
else around her perceives, and can heal even the
near-dead. The question is, when faced with the
ultimate threat to her own survival, can she use
these powers to save herself?
"Scarborough writes powerfully and
convincingly of the war."
—Kirkus

Look for the works of Elizabeth Ann
Scarborough on sale now wherever
Bantam Spectra Books are sold.

AN 372 12/91

**AN227 -- 12/91**